THE
BLUE WALL

Also by Kenneth Abel
in Large Print:

Bait

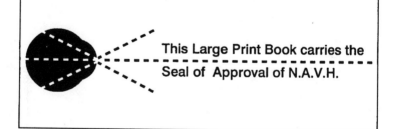

This Large Print Book carries the
Seal of Approval of N.A.V.H.

THE
BLUE WALL

Kenneth Abel

Thorndike Press • Thorndike, Maine

Published in 1996 by arrangement with Delacorte Press, an imprint of Dell Publishing, a division of Bantam Doubleday Dell Publishing Group, Inc.

Thorndike Large Print ® Basic Series.

The tree indicium is a trademark of Thorndike Press.

The text of this Large Print edition is unabridged.
Other aspects of the book may vary from the original edition.

Set in 16 pt. Bookman Old Style.

Printed in the United States on permanent paper.

Library of Congress Cataloging in Publication Data

Abel, Kenneth.
    The blue wall / by Kenneth Abel.
      p.   cm.
    ISBN 0-7862-0823-6 (lg. print : hc)
    1. Large type books. 2. Police — New York (State) — New York — Fiction. I. Title.
    [PS3551.B336B57 1996b]
    813'.54—dc20
                                96-24153

For my wife and daughter

We die with the dying:
See, they depart, and
  we go with them
We are born with the dead:
See, they return, and bring
  us with them.

        T.S. Eliot, *Four Quartets*

Chapter 1

On Thursday, July 20, twelve hours after his open-mike debut at the Last Laugh Comedy Club in Garden City, Long Island, Joey ("the Wiseguy") Tangliero entered federal protective custody. He was still wearing his double-breasted silk suit with a pale gray tie, diamond clasp, gold link bracelet, and pinkie ring, but he'd lost his Gucci loafers. There were holes in both heels of his nylon Gold Toes.

"Sons'a bitches put me in the trunk of Tony Giardella's Lincoln," he said, peeling off the remnants of his socks. "I'm in there with the fuckin' spare tires. Oil filters, stuff like that. They took my shoes so I couldn't kick my way out."

He was seated in a conference room down the hall from the office of Merrill Conte, Assistant U.S. Attorney for the Eastern District of New York, wincing as he dabbed at the cuts on his feet with a moist paper towel from the men's room. He had grease smudges on his bald spot, and several buttons were missing from his shirt, so that it spread open across his broad stomach when he leaned forward.

"You see the show?" he asked Deputy Federal Marshal Claire Locke. She glanced up from the pad in her lap. A telephone was tucked between her ear and shoulder. On the other end of the line, violins were playing "Penny Lane." Every few seconds a voice came on to tell her that all operators were busy, but if she'd hold on, a customer service agent would be happy to take her reservation.

"Yeah, I saw it."

"Tell me the truth. Was it that bad?"

Claire shrugged. "I'm not really the one to ask."

"You laugh?"

"No."

He sighed, gazed down at his feet. "I died up there, huh?"

Claire remembered how he looked when, acting on a tip, they'd pulled the Lincoln over on the Cross Bronx, opened the trunk. When he heard the key in the lock, he'd wet his pants. The smell hit them as soon as they got the trunk open, Tony Giardella backing

8

away in disgust.

"Jesus, Joey! My car!"

And there he'd been, curled up like a frightened child, his feet gashed and bloody from kicking at the hood latch, peering up at the cluster of federal agents and state police in the glare of the headlights. Only when he saw the traffic whizzing past on the expressway, not some empty stretch of dirt road in the Jersey swamps, could he be coaxed out of the trunk. Even at that moment, his hands still trembling as they helped him out of the trunk, he couldn't resist tugging at his cuffs, giving his tie a quick tug like Henny Youngman, saying —

"Hey, fuck 'em, they can't take a joke."

Now, watching him heave a sigh, then dejectedly crumple the blood-soaked paper towel and drop it into the trash can beside him, Claire felt sorry for him.

"The Gotti bit was kinda funny."

He looked up, his eyes brightening.

"You liked that? It's a good bit, right? Just needs a little refining. The timing's off, but it's good material." He leaned toward her. "Which part did you like best?"

"Well, uh . . ." She searched her mem-

9

ory. "The thing with the snake, I guess. In the plate of tagliatelle."

He pointed a finger at her. "True story! I heard it from one'a the guys carried the casket at the funeral."

"Yeah?" She glanced at him, made a note on her pad. "And the guy really ate it?"

"Hey, Gotti says eat the snake, you gonna be the one tells him no? Trust me, you ever find yourself in this situation, you tell 'em, pass the parmesan, 'cause you're gonna have yourself a little snack." He gave a surprised look, slapped his forehead. 'Ah, shit. How come I couldn't think of that last night, huh? That's the punch line. "A little *snake* snack.' I'm gonna use that next time."

He placed both feet gingerly on the carpet, groaned as he raised up a few inches off the chair. "Look't this. I really fucked up my feet."

Claire hung up the phone. "All right, we got you set up in a suite at the York. We'll keep you there for a few days, until Mr. Conte's satisfied with your testimony. After that, we can talk about the future. Okay?"

Tangliero shrugged. "How's the food there?"

"It's not the Ritz, but you won't starve."

He nodded, watched her cross to the door, call one of the secretaries over. He gave a sigh, wondering if there was a law that said cops had to dress like they sold auto parts. Navy sport coat, black pants, a little bulge at the hip where they carried the gun. A nice-looking woman, really. Small, her figure hidden under the cop clothes, mostly, but everything where you'd expect it to be. Her dark hair cut short, but soft-looking. She brushed it back off her face, making her blue eyes come at you like searchlights. Still, Joey thinking, not a bad deal, you gotta kill a few hours with a cop.

When she'd introduced herself as a deputy federal marshal, he'd thought of Wyatt Earp, riding into Tombstone on a black horse, shooting it out with the gunslingers. Her partner looked the part, a big guy with shoulders like he pumped iron, a little mustache that he kept neatly trimmed. Put a cowboy hat on him, Tangliero thought, stick a horse between his legs, that's a federal marshal. But he'd paused just long enough to grip Tangliero's hand, introduced himself in a southern drawl as "McCann," then vanished into the adjoining office. Joey, glancing over at the slim, dark-haired woman who remained, thought, *This is my protection?*

"How long you been a deputy?"

Claire took some papers from a briefcase, laid them out on the conference table. "Two years in January."

"Yeah? What'd you do before this?"

"I was in law school."

Okay, he thought. *I'm dead.*

While they waited for lunch, Joey Tangliero told her how he'd grown up in Queens, running errands for the local bookies.

"My ma, she used to *walk* me to the school. I mean, I was *fifteen.* Right up the steps, so the brothers could see me. They used to wear those, what'ya call 'em, surpluses? You know, those black robes, with the white collar goes halfway down their chest? Brother Marcus, he weighed like three hundred pounds, looked like one of those garbage cans with the swinging lid. He used to stand in the door, wait for me. Grab my ear, drag me away. My mom's watchin' this, she's on *his* side. I'd wait like half an hour, till he was writing something on the board, sneak out the room. Crawl out, on my hands and knees. There was a window in the boiler room, you could climb right out onto the street. Three years, they never figured out how I did it. The guys I worked for, they hung out in a diner a couple blocks away on Rockland. Most'a those guys, they're out every night, sleep till noon. So I'd get to the diner first, grab a booth, start takin' bets from the cabdrivers. Ten-year-old kid, I'm writin' up bets. One'a my friends, his dad drove a cab. Used to come in every morning, lay bets with me."

He paused, lit a cigar. Closing his eyes, like he was trying to swallow a telephone pole.

"My ma, she keeps yellin', what's she gonna tell the brothers, I don't go? What I'm thinking, she can't say. Anyway, time I dropped out, I was hanging out over at the Azores Coffee Shop in the garment district, workin' for Tony G. Makin' three hundred a day, cash. This was a while back, too. I used to walk all over the neighborhood, stop at the Chinese sweatshops, the trucking companies, the suppliers, every kind'a place. I had this little briefcase, made me look like I worked for Met Life. Lunchtime, I'd head back to the Azores, go upstairs, dump a pile of cash on Tony's desk. That's a nice feeling, let me tell you."

Claire, nodding, tried to imagine what he'd looked like as a teenager. Little fat kid in a silk suit, nylon socks? But then she decided, no, he'd have been skinny back then, like the Italian boys who worked behind the deli counter at the IGA back in Alabama. Handsome guys, until you put them next to their dads, see where it's all headed.

"After lunch," Joey went on, "I'd drive uptown, hit the precinct houses. Drive by a patrol car parked in an alley, toss an envelope on the backseat. The big money, I used to pass that across counter over at Holy Donuts, down the block from Midtown North? Wear an apron, hand 'em a cup'a coffee at the same time, like I'm makin' change."

For a decade, he told her, he'd walked the same route, until the day a pair of junkies tried to grab the valise from him right outside the Azores. Joey Tangliero hung on to the valise's handle, screaming, while they kicked him in the face, then laid the bag on the ground and stomped on his hand, breaking three of his fingers. By the time the junkies had wrenched the bag free, they looked up to find themselves in a tight circle of six of Tony Giardella's boys, who'd watched the whole thing from the window of the coffee shop. They relieved the junkies of the valise, escorted them into the building and down the stairs into the basement, where Joey got to shake his broken fingers in their faces before Tony Giardella shot them both in the head.

"The cops, they're findin' pieces'a those guys in garbage cans all over midtown for weeks. Fingers, toes. I remember they found a nose once. Tony, he kept their balls in a jar on his desk. Some garment district guy'd start causin' him grief, he'd just lean across the desk, pick up the jar, give it a shake. Look up at the guy, say —

" 'You got some balls to sit there and tell me that.'

"Then he'd set the jar back on the desk, lean back in his chair, tell 'em —

15

" 'I got some, too.' "

Claire watched him grin, shake his head. She thought about telling him that she'd heard the story before, in a briefing by some lawyers from the U.S. Attorney's office, then decided, why spoil his fun?

Six lawyers, not one of them over twenty-eight, crowded around a conference table, briefing the team from the Marshal's Service. All of them sneaking looks at her while one guy told the story, waiting to see how she reacted. The same way, she thought, that Joey was looking at her now. . . .

"So, anyway, Tony's up in his office, showing these guys the value in, ah, playing ball, you might say? Me, I spend six weeks sittin' in the coffee shop, reading the papers, one hand stuck in an ice bucket. Silver one, Tony got it from Fortunoff. Nice gesture, but I gotta tell ya, I'm goin' out of my mind down there. What's there to do? This one waitress, her name's Estelle, she's like sixty years old, she keeps comin' over to refill the bucket, like she's sweet on me, right? So one day I take this piece of ice from the bucket, grab her hand, and put it on the back of her ring finger.

Tell her how she gives me chills. The whole place cracks up, I mean, on the floor."

He paused, looked at her.

"With the ice, right? Like a diamond?" He sighed, shook his head. "See, they used to call me the iceman, 'cause I was the guy used to ice the cops. Pay 'em off? And here I was, on ice." He chewed on his cigar for a moment, thoughtful. "What'ya call that? You know, like an irony?"

Claire looked up at him. "Poetic justice."

"Nah, it's another word." Joey looked down at the table, frowned, then waved it away. "Anyway, Tony, he's having a great time. He's got the junkies in a freezer behind the Azores. Every few days, he cuts a couple pieces off, we take a walk around the neighborhood, leaving Junkie McNuggets in all the trash cans. Like a warning.

"Couple months, I can't take it anymore. I go up to Tony's office, knock on the door, tell him, 'Hey, c'mon, I'm goin' crazy down there. You don't give me something to do, I'm gonna end up like one'a those guys down in Port Authority, spit runnin' down my chin. How

17

would that look to the customers, huh?' "

" 'How's your fingers,' Tony says."

"Hey, I got frostbite already." Joey made a gun with his hand. "Anyway, it's only one finger counts. Am I right?"

Claire looked at him, expressionless. "I'll bet you say that to all the girls."

The next day, Joey had gone back to work, making the rounds. But this time, his only stops were police precincts, from the 34th in upper Harlem all the way down to the Battery.

"I'd walk down a row of patrol cars at the shift change, flipping envelopes in the rear windows. Cop sittin' there, all of a sudden, he's got some paperwork that needs his attention. Then I go inside, stroll through the squad rooms. Nothin' to it. Every few desks, I make a deposit. After a couple weeks, I got an idea. I started stopping at ATM machines on my way home, grabbing their whole supply of deposit envelopes."

" 'See, it's a courtesy,' I told Tony. 'Somebody sees it on a guy's desk, he just says, 'Oh, yeah. I forgot to make that deposit for my wife. College fund.' You watch, they'll appreciate it."

"So Tony, he just shrugs, tosses 'em back across his desk. 'It's your deal,' he tells me. 'They want it in subway tokens, that's fine with me. Just keep 'em happy.'"

Joey was silent for a moment, his face thoughtful.

"See, the man trusted me," he said, looking over at Claire. "Like a brother."

She nodded, watched as he gave a sigh, raised his cigar. It had gone out. He dug in his pocket, found his lighter, got it going again.

"Anyway, I drove that route every day for six years. The cops, they started calling me "Joe College," showed me pictures of their kids graduating from NYU, Rutgers, Yale. I tell 'em, 'Hey, I got a commitment to higher education. You have three more, we'll send 'em too.'"

He enjoyed the work, he told her. The way cops greeted him on the street, stopped to laugh at his jokes, slap him on the shoulder. He'd pull up in front of a precinct, leave the car next to a hydrant, make his rounds. After a shooting incident at the Three-Two, he bought a janitor's uniform and ID from a maintenance guy, used it to get

19

through the new security.

"I walked around with that badge on for two weeks, never even looked at it. Turned out, it was a picture of a black guy, looked like Don King on a bad hair day. I heard later some of the cops started calling me 'Ice T.' "

One of the secretaries came in with lunch from a Chinese place down the block. They ate out of the boxes with chopsticks. Beyond the window, Tangliero could see office workers on their way back to work, glancing up at the sky briefly before they disappeared into the office buildings. Claire watched his eyes on the window, wondering how long it would take him to make a run for it. At the Academy, the instructors had told her mob guys were notorious for ditching their guards, heading back to the neighborhood. They went crazy sitting in hotel rooms, waiting to testify. After a while they started missing their old buddies, thinking maybe it was all a mistake, if they just talked to the right people . . .

"Is there anything they haven't called you?"

Tangliero grinned at her. "Hey, call me what you want. Just call me, right?"

He kept looking at her gun, every time she leaned forward to take a bite of Kung Pao Shrimp. It was a little .38, silver with a black grip. She kept it in a leather holster clipped to her belt.

"Tell me something," he said. He waved his chopsticks at the gun. "You know how to use that thing?"

She looked at him across the table. "At this distance?" She shrugged, took a bite of shrimp. "How many shots do I get?"

He chewed slowly, watching her reach for the box with the rice. "You're kidding me, right?"

"It makes such a loud noise." She wiped her mouth on a paper napkin. "But don't worry. I'm a great typist."

He stared at her, caught her sneaking a glance at him, checking out his response. He sighed, shook his head.

"Everybody's a comedian."

The cowboy joined them for the ride uptown. Claire sat in the backseat of the gray government Ford with Tangliero, her eyes on the passing traffic. Her gun lay in her lap, one hand resting lightly on the grip.

"You expecting trouble?"

She glanced over at Tangliero. "Depends."

"On what?"

Joey could see the cowboy watching them in the rearview, a little smile on his face.

"Could be they figure you can't hurt 'em," Claire told him. "I mean, it's not like you're Sammy the Bull, right?"

She looked away, but not before she saw his eyes widen, his head jerk back like she'd slapped him.

"You think I'm not worth a hit?"

She shrugged. "I can't say. These guys know you. If they think you can give us the real skinny, we could have trouble."

In the rearview, Claire saw McCann wince. *The real skinny?* For a moment she pictured her mother, sitting around with the other women at the country club in Greenwood, Alabama. All of them smiling away at some doctor's wife across the room, giving her that little wave like Miss Apple Blossom, 1962 — *Hi there!* — dishing her the whole time in delicate whispers, giving it to each other through their smiles, *the real skinny.*

But Tangliero didn't seem to notice.

22

He slumped back in his seat, shook his head.

"Did I miss something here? Look't me! I got blood all over my feet, my suit's a fuckin' mess. They had me in the trunk, for Christ's sake. What was that, a joke?"

Claire bit her lip, but couldn't hold it back. "Hey, don't ask me. I saw your act."

He stared at her for a moment, sighed. "Terrific. I ask for protection, I get Siskel and Ebert." Tangliero looked out the window, watched a midtown bus pull away from the curb, packed to the windows with guys in suits, all of 'em reaching up to grab the bar as the bus lurched into traffic. "You wanna hear the thing? What kills me 'bout this? I'm standing there on the side of the Cross Bronx, watchin' you put the cuffs on Tony, all he's gotta do is call his lawyer, he'll be out'a jail in, what? Five hours? Me, I'm in for life."

Claire glanced away. According to the local cops, Giardella's lawyer had walked into the precinct with a bench order two hours after he'd been arrested. Twenty minutes later, they'd walked out to a waiting car.

"Those guys," Joey went on, "they were my buddies. I tell those stories over drinks, they're on the floor. 'Joey, you're killin' me here. You should be a comedian.' Okay, so now I'm a comedian. I get up there last night, same stories. Only I look out in the audience, they're not laughing. Not one of 'em. I'm thinking, it's a joke, right? They're bustin' my balls, like always." He shook his head, sadly. "I come out in the parking lot after, I'm like, 'Hey guys, thanks for coming. You like the show?' I figure, okay, maybe I stunk. But these guys are my friends, right? The minute I'm out the door, they grab me, stuff me in the fuckin' trunk."

He stared at the street beyond the window. Then, as if somebody had flicked a switch, he turned to Claire, grinned. "Hey, I should open the act with that. Like, 'Hey, if *you* guys think I'm bad . . .' I could make it a whole routine. 'They'll *kill* me for telling you this, but . . .' Like I can't help myself, you know? Or if they're not laughing, I could say, 'Oh man, I'm dying up here.' But like I'm really gonna *die* for these jokes. You get it?"

He could see the cowboy watching

him in the rearview.

"Mr. Tangliero," McCann said. "You're entering protective custody. It's not like we're gonna book you into Vegas."

Joey looked up at him, then over at Claire, as if he was seeing them for the first time. Then he sat back, looked out the window, his eyes following the edge of a skyscraper toward the evening sky.

"Yeah, okay. But a guy's gotta dream," he said. "Without dreams, you're dead. You're walkin' around, maybe. But inside, you're a dead man."

Claire looked at him, felt a twinge of guilt. *Terrific.* Her first wiseguy, she's gotta draw one with *feelings.*

Chapter 2

"Try it."

Dave Moser leaned in the window of his ancient Chevy, turned the key. There was a click, then a grinding sound. When he released the key, it stopped. Vinny Delario stuck his head out from under the hood, said —

"Again."

Moser hit the key. The car coughed once, then nothing. Vinny looked up at him, shook his head.

"Not good, Dave."

Moser glanced at his watch. The car was parked in the driveway of Moser's house in Hempstead, when he should have been edging off the Whitestone Bridge to pick up the Cross Bronx Expressway, halfway to upper Manhattan by this time. The sun was heating up the pavement already, and he was sweating under his sport jacket, his skin itching where the .38 tugged his belt tight. The city was gonna be brutal.

Delario came around the front of the

car, wiping his hands on a rag. He had an oil-stained BudMan sweat shirt pulled over his dress shirt and tie. His thick black hair was pulled back into a ponytail. Just like half the guys Moser hung out with growing up, only they were easing up toward forty now, getting thick around the middle, little streaks of gray in their long hair. Vinny still had that look, the one told you he was only hanging around until he made the big score. No hurry, just a matter of time. Twenty-two, living with his parents two houses down since getting out of Rikers. The last two fingers were missing from his left hand, where the black powder charge in the steering wheel of a 1989 Honda Accord parked in the Roosevelt Hospital staff lot had denotated while he was removing the air bag. Two patrol cops had found his fingers in the backseat, followed the trail of blood down the block to the emergency room, where the attending surgeon had accepted the plastic Baggie containing the severed fingers, listened to their report, then asked —

"What color did you say the car was?"

Vinny, when he noticed Moser looking at his hand, grinned, shook his head.

"Some luck, huh? Guy comes back into the room, tosses the bag in my lap, says 'Don't fuck with people's cars.' "

"What'd you do with the fingers?"

"Gave 'em to my mom." He nodded at the house. "She's got 'em in the freezer. Takes 'em out when she yells at me, shakes 'em in my face, remind me how I fucked up." He glanced down at his hand, shrugged. "Could'a been worse."

"Yeah?"

"Guy I know lost his whole hand." He grinned at Moser. "And, hey, I ever get married, no wedding ring, right? Wear it on a chain around my neck, maybe. Tuck it in my shirt, I get frisky."

Lately, he worked for his uncle at an electronics store in Levittown, selling stereo gear and sixty-four-inch televisions to newlyweds, no payments till January. Every year in May, the store hired some off-duty cops to ride around the apartment complexes, standing around while Vinny and a Jamaican kid from the warehouse hauled all that fancy gear out of the tiny apartments, loaded it back in the truck. Moser had done it once or twice over the years, but gave it up when he got his detective's shield. It was easy work, and Vinny's uncle paid cash, but Moser found it depressing, watching some girl just out of high school burst into tears as they cleaned out the living room.

Welcome to real life.

Moser walked around the front of the car, leaned under the hood, watched Vinny reach across to the back, tug at a few wires. When he drew his hand back, there was a faint crease in his fingertip. Moser looked at it for a moment, then reached in, ran his finger across the same wire, held it up in the light.

"You know what I love?"

Vinny straightened, leaned on the edge of the car with the palms of both hands, keeping the grease off the paint. He watched Moser glance down at his finger, smile. "What?"

"You ever take a girl out to the beach, when she gets out of your car, she's got this little line across the backs of her thighs from the seat. But she doesn't know it's there, right? It's a thing just for you, like from the gods."

Vinny rubbed at his jaw with the back of his hand, shrugged. This guy, you never knew what he'd come out with. Not like most of the cops you run into, all badge and bad attitude. More like a kid, he's got a turtle in a bucket, poking at it to see if it'll climb up on a rock.

Vinny waited until he glanced up, told him, "Your starter's fucked, but that's the least of your problems." He took a rag from his back pocket, wiped his hands.

Moser looked down at the engine, sighed. "How much?"

Vinny spread his thumb and forefinger a quarter of an inch. "Like this."

"I got any choice, here?"

Vinny shrugged. "You can walk."

He was good with cars, liked working on them. And if a cop needed a favor these days, hey, no problem. He'd kept the Chevy running through most of the summer, making no promises. Even Moser knew the car was on its last legs; on the highway, it pulled to the right, as if drawn to any stretch of shoulder, looking for a quiet place to die.

Vinny walked past Moser, tossed the rag into the trunk, stripped off the sweat shirt. He had a plastic badge pinned to his shirt over the breast pocket — *Mad Mike's Stereo.*

"I can get the part, I'll try to fix it this weekend."

"Get it legal, okay?"

Vinny shrugged. "Cost you more."

"I'm a cop, Vinny."

Vinny looked up at Moser's house, pursed his lips. "Just saying you could save a few bucks, is all."

Moser followed his gaze, said nothing. Three weeks had passed since Janine moved out, stripping the rooms of their furniture, rugs, mirrors, the set of "Masters of Impressionism" prints that she'd bought for two hundred dollars down at Frame-Up during the first month of their marriage. She'd given him no warning. One morning, she finished her breakfast, packed her clothes into a few suitcases, tossed them into the trunk of her Celica, then sat in the kitchen drinking coffee until the guy from the finance company came to get the living room suite. She hired two boys from the local high school to move the rest of the furniture into a self-storage unit in Maspeth, "until we get it settled." Moser came home from work that evening to find the place empty except for his clothes, an ancient green Hide-a-Bed in the den, and a card table leaning against the refrigerator in the kitchen. He walked through the house, slowly, looking at the marks on the bare walls where the pictures had hung, looking at the way the color had faded from the wall around them.

Funny what you notice.

He'd dug through some old boxes in the basement, come up with a tiny black-and-white TV, a clock radio, and three boxes of old kitchen junk. He slept that night on the Hide-a-Bed, while the silent TV filled the room with gray light.

A week later, he'd received a letter from an attorney in Rockville Centre, notifying him that Janine intended to file for divorce. He laid the letter on the kitchen counter, picked up the phone, and dialed her sister in Queens.

"Anne, it's Dave. Put Janine on the phone."

"She doesn't want to talk to you."

"Either she talks to me now, or I'm getting in the car to come out there. Jimmy's not gonna like that. Bad for business."

Janine's sister was married to a former bond trader named Jimmy Tedesco, who lost his license in an SEC crackdown on insider trades. After that, he'd used his family connections to set up a lucrative business fencing swag for a crew of wiseguys who fed off the trucking companies down in the Forties, west of Tenth Avenue. At family holidays, he would draw Moser into a corner, pull up the sleeve on his left arm, show off his new Rolex.

"Nice, huh? You want me to get you one?"

Now, Moser heard Anne hesitate. "Hang on."

She put the phone down, and Moser heard voices in the background. Then Janine came to the phone.

"What do you want, Dave?"

"I want to know why you left. I never hit you. I never cheated on you. Maybe I yelled some, we had a fight, but so did you. I didn't do drugs or gamble. I thought we had a life. So you tell me, why?" He was silent for a moment, waiting. "I'm not mad, I just think you owe me an answer."

She said nothing for a long time, then he heard her sigh. "I'm tired, Dave. That's all. I just can't do it anymore. You understand?"

"No."

"Then I'm sorry. You'll have to take my word for it." There was a long pause, then she said, "Let's just start over, okay? Sell the house, meet new people, all that. I quit my job yesterday, and I'm thinking about going back to school. Maybe become a teacher. I want a future I can't predict."

He was silent for a moment, listening to her breathing.

"You're a cop, Dave. That's what you'll always be. I can't live that way."

"You need money?"

"From you?" She laughed. "You been holding out on me, Dave? You live on a cop's salary. What could you give me? I'll take my share of the house, use it for school. You want to help, you can get the place fixed up, raise the selling price."

When he hung up, he stood there for a long time, his hand on the phone, wondering if he should feel angry. He looked around at the kitchen, trying to see it as she had. A prison cell, maybe. A grave.

To him, it looked like a kitchen.

Now, watching Vinny Delario glance up at the house, seeing the pity in his eyes, he thought, *Fuck it.* What was he hiding, anyway?

"Vinny, you want to save me some

money, get me a deal on interior latex."

"What color?"

Moser looked up at the house, shrugged. "Nothing too bright. It's for the bedroom."

"You planning to sell?"

"That's how it looks."

Vinny nodded. "Okay, I'll ask a guy I know." He crumpled the sweat shirt into a tight ball, tossed it into the backseat of the car. "You need a ride into the city?"

Moser glanced across the street. His neighbor, Marty Stoll, was a patrolman working out of the 30th Precinct in upper Manhattan. Some weeks, when their duty rosters matched, they shared a ride into the city. "I'll ask Marty. If he can't, maybe you could drop me at the train."

"Suit yourself." He walked back toward his parents' house a few steps, turned. "Hey, tell Marty I got those speakers he ordered. They're up at the store."

Marty Stoll was having breakfast, coffee and a bowl of frosted flakes. He had a napkin tucked into his collar to protect his uniform. He waved Moser into the kitchen, pushed a chair away from the table with his foot.

"You remember when we were kids, your parents took you out to eat, they'd make you sit there while they finished their coffee?" He spooned some sugar onto his cereal. "Twenty minutes, nobody saying a word, while my dad took these little sips."

He nodded toward the dishes piled in the sink.

"Now, I'm lucky if my kids take two minutes for a piece of toast. Down the stairs, out the door, they still got toothpaste stuck to their chins. I gotta lock the door to get 'em to eat something."

Moser slid into the chair, stretched his feet under the table. "They eat at the mall. McDonald's is packed with kids every morning. You can't get a cup of coffee without climbing over 'em."

Stoll shook his head. "That's great. I spend two hundred dollars on groceries every week, my kids are eating breakfast burritos out of a paper sack. I mean, who thought of that? Breakfast *burritos*?"

"People eat 'em."

"Yeah, well, they'll eat linoleum, you price it right." Stoll glanced at his watch. "You're running late."

"Chevy's dead."

Stoll picked up his coffee, looked at Moser over the rim. "You got some luck lately."

"Pile it up high enough, you get a view."

Marty Stoll drove a Cadillac Seville he leased through his brother's carpet-cleaning business. Whenever Moser asked for a lift into the city, he had to wait as Stoll got in, flipped the master lock on his door, then leaned across the passenger seat to run his hand over the upholstery.

"Fine Corinthian leather."

And Moser would nod, smile, remembering the party Janine threw when he'd passed the detective's exam, Stoll taking him aside to ask him, gently, if he really knew what he was doing.

"It's the uniform that brings in the bucks," he whispered, squeezing Moser's shoulder. They were standing together in a corner of the den, and Moser could see Janine passing a plate of little egg rolls with mustard dip in the living room. Stoll leaned in closer, his face serious. "Look't me. I'm fourteen years on the street. I got a boat, a nice car. Every year, I take Rita to the Bahamas. She loses fifteen pounds before we go, buys herself a new bathing suit, and we fuck like monkeys. A couple years, I'll send my kids to college. Tell me, why should I give all that up for a gold shield?"

He drove with the tips of two fingers resting on the steering wheel, his other hand making constant adjustments to the air-conditioning, the rearview, the radio. He wove through the heavy traffic on the Cross Bronx, his foot barely touching the brake. He kept the radio tuned to a morning shock jock, whose voice sounded like a chainsaw cutting through sheet metal.

"This guy kills me. I listen to him every morning on the way in. Some Jewish kid from Long Island, he gets on the radio, sounds like Mussolini on speed. You imagine how much coffee this guy puts away every morning, screamin' like that?"

Moser smiled, feeling his forehead start to tighten like somebody was twisting the screws down hard. He nodded at Stoll's badge, the thin strip of black ribbon stretched across it. "You working off-the-books today?"

Stoll glanced down at it, then hit the brake hard as the traffic slowed to a stop just ahead. "Shit." He reached up, slipped the ribbon off, shoved it in his pocket. "I put in some hours last night. They're shooting some kind of TV thing up by the bridge." He laid on the horn. "Come on, ya fuck!" They inched forward a few feet, and Stoll reached for the air-conditioning, turned it up high. "They hired a bunch of us to work security. Mostly standing around, keeping the locals from stealing their equipment."

Moser stared out the window. The guy on the radio belched loudly, getting a laugh from the woman who fed him straight lines. He did a few minutes on how he hated people who cover their mouths when they belch. Like you'd put your hand on your ass when you fart? In the background, one of the clowns in the "morning zoo" laughed so hard, he snorted.

Stoll looked over at Moser, grinned. "I'm tellin' ya, this stuff keeps me going. I listen to enough of this shit on my way into the city, by the time I get out on patrol, I hate *everybody*." He leaned on the horn, swerved hard around a Chevette that had strayed into his lane. Then he waved a hand at the Manhattan skyline beyond the bridge. "It's all animals out there, Dave. You got your hunters and your hunted. Trials of life. The whole place is just a fuckin' watering hole, we get to watch all the pigs come out for a drink. They should build a wall around it, charge admission."

"They did," Moser said. He nodded at Stoll's uniform. "It's blue."

Chapter 3

The girl drifted in the delicate light, her long black hair spread out behind her. She was new to the water, and it bore her, rocked her gently. The waves drifted across her face like a veil; the current tugged at her body, turning her in a lazy arc as the fishing line tightened slowly around her ankle. She seemed to stretch one foot toward the bridge column, as if straining toward it, her last contact with the city. The river spread from her outstretched fingers. Far above her, in a distant world, cars whined across the bridge.

Dave Moser, hands shoved into his pockets, watched from the south bank as the police boat churned the water beside her, fighting the current. On the far shore, a few people lingered on apartment balconies, watching. An officer leaned over the side with a boat hook, snagged the girl's waist and pulled her closer. Her body tipped in the water slightly, and Moser could see she was naked. Eighteen, he thought. Maybe twenty. Another man hung over the stern with a long pole, a curved blade at the tip. Moser watched him skim the water behind her feet, until the blade snagged the line, pulled it taut from the water, then sliced through.

The girl started to drift, her arms and legs folding into the current as the hook pinned her to the side of the boat. Two men caught her by the arms and heaved her shoulders out of the water, her head rolling forward so her dark hair trailed in the water. They braced her on the side of the boat while the man with the boat hook slid it down her hip to catch her at the knee. They paused for a moment, breathing hard, then dragged her up onto the side, the boat tipping. With a quick step back, they rolled her onto the deck.

Moser scratched at his neck. Before nine, and the heat was brutal already. His shirt was plastered to his back under his sport coat from the ride uptown. He'd been hoping for a breeze off the river, anything. But the air was thick and heavy, the fumes from the traffic up on the Henry Hudson Bridge settling on the riverbank. He turned and angled up the embankment to the road, where his partner, Ray Fielding, leaned against the car.

"You see?"

Fielding shrugged. "Looked fresh." He had a tiny scar above one eye, like a pale half-moon against his black skin. Moser watched it vanish into the corner of his eye as he squinted against the sun.

Moser glanced back down at the boat, drifting slowly with the current now. A heavy man squatted, hands braced on his massive thighs, beside the body. He tugged a pair of latex gloves onto his hands, poked at the body.

"Ruben," Fielding said, his voice caustic. "He's the guy screwed up the cause of death on that Academy Homes kid last month. Two-year-old wanders outta his mother's apartment, falls down a flight of stairs." He shook his head. "Ruben takes one look at the body, declares it accidental death. Two weeks later, the tox reports come in, show the kid ate his mother's stash. Acute cocaine poisoning. Cops talk to the mother, she breaks down, admits she left it out on the coffee table. The kid crawls out of his crib in the morning, thinks it's sugar. But fucking Ruben won't change the ME's report. Accidental death, massive head trauma. The mother walks."

Moser watched the fat man lift an arm, probe at the muscle near the shoulder, checking for rigor. Taut and stiff, he thought, like a piece of fresh beef. For a moment he pictured a lover's hand moving lightly over the woman's skin, reaching for her breast. He took a deep breath, shook the thought away.

The Metroliner clattered over the railroad bridge a few hundred yards to the west. Moser's eyes followed it past the railway yard, up the curving shoreline. He was tired, his neck stiff. He rubbed at it, watched Ruben sort through the girl's tangled hair, carefully separating the debris into evidence bags. Her face stared up at the sky.

"Come up to me, love, out of the river," Moser murmured. "Or I will come down to you."

Fielding looked at him. "What?"

"It's from a poem."

"Yeah?"

"Some guy in the hospital, having his lungs drained. Tells you how it feels

when they stick a knife in his chest."
Moser smiled, thinly. "Janine left it on
the kitchen counter when she moved
out. One of her books from college. She
marked the page for me."

Fielding nodded, looked down at the
river. "Cute."

"She thought so."

The boat moved back toward the
bridge stanchion, and one of the men
fished around in the water with a pole.
The water drifting over her, Moser
thought. *Light shimmering through it.*

He felt Fielding's eyes on him.

"You okay, Dave?"

"I'm fine. Tired."

"You still sleeping on the foldout? I
told you, get a real bed, you're gonna
stay there." Fielding shook his head.
"We get back to the squad room, talk
to Lou. He's got a cousin deals whole-
sale, get you a good price."

Moser shrugged. "Couch is fine for
now."

He stared down at the boat. After a
moment, he felt Fielding look away.
Ruben rolled the girl's body onto one
side, the black hair falling across her
face.

"Floaters." Moser shook his head.

"Three years of this shit, still creeps me out. First time I caught one, this guy from the ME's office calls me over to the autopsy table, shows me where the crabs were chewing on the guy's face. Skin all scraped off his forehead where his face was dragging the bottom."

Fielding smiled. "They do that to new guys. Rite of passage."

"They do it to you?"

"I caught a sailor, jumped off an oil tanker out in the harbor after it caught fire. Took four weeks for him to float. Guy in the ME's office was thrilled. Had a real special one to show me, burned *and* drowned."

Moser winced. "That's cold."

"It was the burns got me. Floaters I can handle."

"Yeah?" Moser glanced over at him, grinned. "You can have this one, Ray, you want it."

"Pass."

Moser laughed. He looked down at his watch, then up at the sky. The sky was draped over the tops of the buildings like a sheet of plastic.

"I tell you how I almost drowned when I was a kid?"

Fielding looked over at him. "Last

summer. We caught that kid fell in the public pool up in the Heights."

"Yeah?" Moser watched the uniforms on the boat roll the girl onto her belly, Ruben leaning over her to examine her back. He shook his head. "I'm gettin' old."

Fielding rubbed at the scar on his forehead with the edge of his thumb, glanced over at him.

"You put the house on the market?"

"Guy's coming out one night this week, to do the paperwork."

"Janine have to sign?"

Moser shrugged. "The lawyers handle it. It all goes into escrow until the divorce is final."

"Better that way."

"I guess."

Ray drew a handkerchief from an inner pocket of his jacket and touched the edge to his forehead. Silk, Moser thought. Gets 'em at Brooks Brothers when he picks up his suits. Three years working Homicide together, and he'd never seen Fielding sweat.

"I always heard black absorbs heat."

Fielding smiled, shook his head.

"You gotta think cool." He tucked the handkerchief into his jacket. "Anyway, you sweat enough for both of us."

Hundred degrees, ninety-eight-per-cent humidity, the sun beating down on an alley in Washington Heights, they're standing next to some hapless junkie, his face blown off by a shotgun blast, and there's Fielding, pressed and righteous, at peace with the world. His wife was a features reporter with CBS. Moser watched her many nights on the News at Five, wondering where they kept all the clothes. She'd be reporting on the garbage strike, standing in front of an overflowing Dumpster, rotting food spilling out behind her, and she'd look like she just strolled out of a fash-ion spread. They owned a brownstone over in Park Slope, where they'd con-verted a guest room into closet space. Ask Fielding, he'd just shrug.

"Man's gotta dress to his level." He'd swing the coat open, showing the silk lining. "Let 'em know who you are, right?"

And Moser, wearing the same blue sport coat and red tie he'd worn for the past five weeks, had to agree. Fielding was working on a law degree at CUNY. Two years, Moser figured, he'd be in the DA's office. Couple more, he'd be running for office.

Send me a Christmas card, Moser thought. *"Greetings! from the land of the living."*

Moser reached into the car, took a can of soda from under the seat, the cold metal beaded with moisture, and rubbed it across the back of his neck. He let the cool metal of the can slide across his jaw, feeling the tiredness settle in behind his eyes. Too many nights with Letterman. Sitting there in the flicker of the television, the hours passing.

Like drowning.

He popped the can, took a long swig, looked down at the scene on the boat. The uniforms were spreading a black body bag on the deck. Ruben knelt beside the girl's left hand, uncurled it, examining the tips of her fingers closely. Satisfied, he bagged it, got up, crossed to her right hand.

"So she went in last night."

Fielding shrugged. "How it looks."

"Midnight swim."

"You know anyone swims in the Harlem River?"

"Not by choice."

"They say who found her?"

"Couple rowers from Columbia. They practice up here at dawn, got a boathouse over at 215th."

Fielding looked down at the sun burning on the water. "That's not what they call them."

"Who?"

"You don't say rowers. It's something else."

"Yeah?" Moser smiled. "This like a sensitivity thing? What're we supposed to call 'em, Aquatic-Americans?"

Fielding looked at him. "Sculls."

"That's the boats."

Ruben knelt beside the girl's right hand. He pressed the hand open, examined each of the fingertips briefly, slipped a bag over the hand. Then he got up, slowly, peeling the latex gloves from his hands.

The cops bent over the girl, rolled her into the body bag. One of them knelt beside it, tugged at the zipper. Ruben found a seat as the pilot brought the boat around, punched the throttle. The bow lifted off the water as they headed downstream, a thick plume of spray rising behind them.

"End of story." Moser drained the can, crumpled it and tossed it into the weeds at the base of the embankment. He nodded at the train station on the opposite bank. "I tell you I had a girlfriend lived up in Yonkers?"

Fielding shrugged, got into the car, digging in his pocket for the keys. Moser got in beside him, rubbed the sweat from his neck.

"This is before I met Janine. I used to take the train up on Friday nights, the six-fourteen out of Grand Central, runs along those tracks down there. The conductor'd come through the car, yelling out the stops. We got up here, he'd call out, '*Spike* . . . and Duyvil.' Same thing, every night. '*Spike* . . . and Duyvil!' One night, there's this guy sitting next to me, he's pretty corked. Carried a drink onto the train, probably had a few before he left. The conductor comes through, calls it out, same as always, '*Spike* . . . and Duyvil.' This guy next to me, he gives a big sigh, throws his hands up, his drink going all over the place. Like he's just had it, right? Grabs the conductor's arm, says, 'It's *Spuyten! Spuyten* Duyvil, you jerk, like this . . .' And he takes this big slurp from his drink, spits it all over the guy." Moser looked down at the river, shook his head. "Spitting devil."

Fielding started the car. "So what'd you do?"

Moser laughed.

"Me? I got off at my stop."

On the table, she looked young. No bloating, and the crabs hadn't found her yet. Not bad as floaters go. She'd been pretty, Moser thought. High cheekbones, pale skin, good teeth. A thin gold ring on the third finger of her right hand, and a dark band of bruises high on her throat. Both eyes were missing. Wickert, the Medical Examiner, spread his hands under her chin.

"Tracheal bruising's inconsistent with a hand spread," he said. "Too wide. And the pressure's even. Most people squeeze harder with the first two fingers, so the top of the bruise is darker." He drew back, studied her for a moment. "More like what you get with arm pressure." He laid his forearm across her throat, pressing down lightly. "You see it sometimes with erotic asphyxia. Couple gets to playing rough, something goes wrong."

Moser had his notebook on the table, scribbling. Wickert flipped through his papers, peering over the top of his glasses at them.

"Who's chain-of-evidence today?"

Moser raised his hand, and Wickert passed him the Police Identification form. Moser glanced at it, checked to be sure the First Officer, who had the initial responsibility for preserving the evidentiary chain, had signed the form, identifying the body when it was turned over to the Medical Examiner's office.

Fielding walked slowly around the table, studying the body. He kept the back of one finger pressed against his nose, Moser noticed, as if he was thinking. He kept a can of breath spray in his coat pocket, sprayed it on his finger outside the autopsy room. Moser smiled. Spearmint. When he thinks nobody's looking.

Fielding stopped at the head of the table, looking down at the girl's face. "And the eyes?"

"Defacement, maybe. The killer attaches some symbolic importance to the eyes, directs his violence at them. Trying to depersonalize the victim." Wickert shrugged. "Or maybe she saw something she shouldn't. You get this on witness killings sometimes. A drug gang sending a message."

Moser looked up at him.

"So you're saying maybe it's not erotic asphyxia."

"I'm saying it's unclear."

Wickert moved down the table, lifted her left foot, pointed to the narrow band around her ankle where the fishing line had flayed the skin away.

"This is where she got tangled up, but if you look at the other ankle, you can see some chafing there, too. It's faint, but it's there. Same with the wrists."

"Then she was tied," Fielding said.

"Not tight, and nothing that would burn the skin like rope." Wickert took off his glasses and rubbed his eyes. "Scarves are popular."

"A bondage thing."

Wickert spread his hands.

"Too early to say. She's got bruising on her upper thighs and breasts, which might support that thesis." He picked up one of her hands. "Look at the nails. She took care of herself. Got some fancy bridgework in her mouth, cosmetic caps. This girl came from money."

Moser flipped his notebook closed,

tucked it into the inner pocket of his coat.

"So how'd she end up in the river?"

"The eternal question." Wickert pulled a surgeon's tray over to the table, selected a scalpel. "One way to find out."

He made a Y-shaped incision at the breastbone, sliced quickly down to the pubis.

Fielding gave a cough, glanced at his watch. "Who wants coffee?"

Chapter 4

Growing up down South, Claire had always pictured New York the way she saw it on *The Big Movie*, WKCB television, Birmingham, Saturday afternoons. The mornings crisp in black-and-white, Audrey Hepburn stepping into a taxi in hat and gloves, or Kim Novak, maybe, in *Bell, Book and Candle*, stroking her cat in a store-front window, some tiny street down in the Village, her face thoughtful. Later, when she was in high school, it was streets strewn with garbage, Charles Bronson on the subway, gun in his pocket, waiting as a gang of black kids came down the car, getting ready to mug him. Al Pacino, sticking a needle in his arm. Watching it in Greenwood, Alabama, she always wondered, there's . . . what? Seven million people living in New York? All those people, they couldn't figure out this is a stupid place to live?

Telling him with that southern accent,

Joey thought, making him think of sweet whiskey in short glasses, heat shimmering on water. But then she'd shift in her chair, so he got a quick glimpse of the gun. An edge in her voice when she's doing her job, lets you know she doesn't take any shit. No way round that accent, though. Like being run over by a truck full of flowers.

When she got her assignment, she told him, three weeks out of training at the Academy down in Glynco, Georgia, the guys in her class let her know it was 'cause she was a woman. Most of them heading for Portland, Denver, Sacramento, house in the suburbs, home by six. But Claire, looking at her name typed next to the words *New York Field Office* on the assignment draw sheet, could only think —

On my salary?

"Hey," Joey told her, "you wanna play with the big boys, you gotta bring something to the table."

She stared at him, thinking, *Huh?*

"Anyway," she told him, "I found a place up on Ninety-sixth, between West End and Broadway. It's like two closets and a kitchen, but I can almost afford it." She shrugged, the way she always did when she talked about her apartment, even on the phone to her mother. Catching herself, the New York in her voice, her mother coming back at her, saying, *What'ya mean, 'almost'? Can you afford it, or not?* What could she tell her? That she paid $1,300 a month for a place to sleep, hang her work clothes, grind coffee on Sunday morning? Nobody she knew in New York really *lived* in their apartments, not like down South. In six months, she'd bought a bed, a futon couch, one bookcase, an old kitchen table from a resale shop on Lexington, and a set of refrigerator magnets shaped like food, to go with the one her mother had sent from Biloxi, shaped like a cop, pointing an enormous finger at you, saying *Stick to your diet!* She dreaded the day her mother came to visit, looked in her refrigerator. Ketchup, salad dressing, a jar of black olives, and three packages of frozen Chicken Tikka for the microwave. She couldn't remember the last time she'd used the oven.

"The woman before me?" she told Joey. "She papered every room in these light pastels, hung a mirror on the living room wall. Like they tell you in

Cosmo to make rooms look bigger."

"It work?"

She shrugged. "I spend a lot of time fixing my hair."

Joey looked at her, wondering what there was to fix. She wore it cut short, like a man's, almost. For a while he'd wondered if she was a dyke, then decided, *Nah.* Lots'a women like that around now, like they all suddenly realized, hey, fifty bucks for a haircut? Let's try the *scissors.*

Claire glanced over at him, saw him get that look again, like he'd just surprised himself. Digging in his pocket for a scrap of paper now, scribbling a note.

"Hey," he glanced up at her. "You ever wonder how come white guys got no names? I mean, all the other groups, they got a name only *they* can use, right? Dyke, spic, nigger. You say it, that's discrimination, you're violating their rights. For them, it's like a pride thing. But white guys, we got no names." He paused, shrugged. Well, 'honky.' But, what's *that* about?"

He watched her face. Smiling at her, hands spread. All he needed was a microphone, curtain behind him.

"Is this a routine, Joey?"

"Depends. You like it?"

"Not much."

"I'm thinking, go for the harder-edge kind of material. Offend people."

"Isn't that what got you here?"

That stopped him. He looked down at the scrap of paper in his hand. Then he crumpled it up, tossed it away. "Yeah, you're right. Just what I need, huh? More people pissed at me."

He shook his head, settled back on the couch.

"Anyway," she told him, "I know what honky means."

"Yeah?"

She nodded. "It's from down South. Rich white guys used to go over to the colored part of town, try to pick up women. Only they were scared to get out of their cars, so they'd sit out there in the street, honk until the woman came out."

Joey looked at her, smiled.

"That's what they told you down in Alabama, huh?"

Later, when Joey got up to go to the bathroom, Claire leaned over, picked up the scrap of paper from the floor, unfolded it.

Dyke hair, it said. *'Try the scissors.'*

She heard the toilet flush, tossed the paper back under the coffee table. Joey came out of the bathroom, reaching down to tug at his zipper.

"I used to work in a law office," Claire told him. "When I was in school? They gave me this desk opposite the men's room. All day, I'm sitting there, typing away. Every time I look up, some guy is coming out of the bathroom. You know, not once did a man come out of there, he didn't reach down, check his zipper?"

Joey looked up at her, taking his time. "You don't say."

"What I want to know is, why do you wait until you're out the door to check? Isn't that too late?"

Joey hitched his belt up a few inches under his belly, gave his crotch a pat. "You find a guy doesn't do that, I wanna know about it."

She laughed. "I find a guy who's got the sense to do that while he's still *inside* the bathroom, I'll probably marry him."

Joey shook his head. "Nah. Trust me, you don't wanna do that. Guy like that, he's got nothing to hide, you know what I mean."

"Now there's a guy thing."

"What?"

Claire smiled, shook her head.

He turned, walked over to the window, looked out. After a while, he said — "You know, I spent my whole life in this city."

"Step back from the window, please."

He glanced back at her, surprised. "Oh, yeah." He eased back a few steps until she nodded.

"Forty-two years old, I never been west of Jersey. Couple trips to Atlantic City, Miami, that's it." He waved a hand at the window, the row of buildings across the street. "My whole life, it's right here."

Claire shrugged. "Now's your chance."

"I guess." He turned to look at her. "I'm just sayin', this is all I *know*. Can you picture me, some little asswipe town, middle of Nebraska?"

"Joey, I knew people back home, they've never left Morgan County."

He nodded, gazing out at the skyline. "Could be worse, huh?"

"Sure," she told him. "Look at you."

Chapter 5

Moser leaned on one elbow, staring at the blank spaces on a form in the typewriter. *Okay, now what?*

At the next desk, Fielding rubbed at a scuff mark on the side of one loafer with his thumb, phone pressed to his ear. Two desks away, Lou Nicolaides leaned way back in his chair, twisting a rubber band between his fingers. He was listening with a bored expression as a painfully thin woman in a yellow miniskirt and bedroom slippers described a shooting outside a crackhouse on upper Lexington. The woman's eyes darted around the room. She scratched at the edge of Nicolaides's desk with one fingernail, peeling away a long strip of green paint.

"Like I *tole* you before, I didn't see nothing," she was saying, her voice high and scratchy, "on account'a I'm legally blind, you know?"

Nicolaides nodded, yawning behind his fist.

Moser looked down at the Investigative Summary in his typewriter. No witnesses, no identification, no evidence except the body. The kind of case that lies on your desk for six weeks, until you can't stand to look at it anymore, so you get up, stroll over to the green metal filing cabinet beside the lieutenant's door, stuff it in among the other sixty files for that year in the drawer marked *Open, Inactive.*

He rubbed at his forehead, glanced at the coffee cup beside him. Empty.

Fielding put a hand over the phone. "You see what Hewitt caught last night?"

Moser shook his head. Fielding took an incident report from a stack on the corner of his desk, leaned over and handed it to Moser.

"Guy stabs his wife six times, breaks a window and tells the responding officer some story about an intruder. He's got this little cut on his arm. Says the guy attacked him first, he passed out from the pain, woke up to find his wife dead. Hewitt goes over to the window, there's no glass on the floor. He looks at the guy, where's the glass? I cleaned it up, the guy says, after I called you.

Didn't want anyone to get cut. Hewitt goes outside in the back alley, there's glass all over the place. The guy breaks the window from *inside,* figures nobody's gonna notice."

Moser sighed, looked down at the blank form in his typewriter.

"Dunker."

"Booked him this morning." Fielding took the report, tossed it back on the pile.

Moser heaved himself out of his chair, walked over to the coffeepot. He poured a cup of black sludge, dumped in some sugar, and stood looking up at the duty board. On the last line of the board, in red ink, were the words *Jane Doe, H93425, Moser.*

From nothing to nobody, three easy steps.

On the duty board, every open case looked like an accusation. It was a white display board, like you find in hotel conference rooms. Each detective, returning from a crime scene, wrote his or her new case at the bottom in red ink: victim's name, primary detective, case number, status, comments. When a case went down, the ink changed from red to black. A black board meant success — cases closed, charges filed. Red was failure — random shootings, missed connections, evidence trampled into the mud by a crowd, witnesses who glared at you, stone-faced, refused to talk. One bad night, and the board was like a virulent rash. Three lines up, Fielding's last case was still red. A bad one, from two nights before: no witnesses, a back-alley crime scene washed clean by a steady downpour. The victim, a homeless man, had been beaten to death with an empty bottle. Another shit case.

This one, Moser thought, heading back to his desk, had all the signs of a hooker killing. Nothing special, some guy having fun on a hot summer night. Pick up some pitiful whore, drive her to a deserted spot, make her die.

Problem was, the girl looked wrong. He settled into his chair, sipped at his coffee. The typewriter hummed at his elbow. No needle tracks, no old scars. None of the starved pallor you see with crackheads. This girl looked healthy, clean. She was somebody's daughter, a girl whose dreams went beyond a needle or a pipe.

Moser eyed the blank spaces on the

incident report. Every guy in the squad had one of these cases: a walk-around. Two, three days of aggravation, chasing leads that go nowhere, then pitch it. Dead whore, no case. Drop it in the file cabinet on your way out the door. If he was lucky, the summer would bring a rush of new files to bury it. The girl would drift through the system, un-identified, until the swift tide of violence that swept through the city's emergency rooms, its morgues, its homicide squad rooms, would bear her away.

Fielding hung up the phone, got up from behind his desk, slipped his jacket off the back of the chair.

"Your lucky day, Dave," he said. "We got something on the floater."

Fielding swung the car into traffic, headed east. He drove with one hand, holding a styrofoam cup of coffee from New China Takeout in the other.

"Quinlan got a message during the divisional meeting," he said. "Some guy called his daughter in missing an hour ago. Quinlan wants us to go see him."

"He just called it in? How'd it get to us?"

"Park Avenue address." Fielding

pulled up in a bus zone at a red light, then swung out in front of the line of traffic when it turned green. "This guy didn't dial 911."

The building took up half a block in the Seventies. Twenty stories of red brick, topped by glass spire. It had an arched entryway, an iron gate decorated with tiny fleurs-de-lis. Beyond, a canopy led through a shaded terrace to the entrance. A doorman in a gray uniform, gold braid hanging from the shoulder boards, looked like he'd just wandered off a ship's bridge. He stood in front of the glass door, hands clasped before him, smiling coolly at the world.

"Good morning, gentlemen. May I help you?"

Moser let Fielding come up from behind him, slip his badge from an inside pocket, flip it open like on the cop shows. Ray loved that part, watching their eyes shift from the badge to his face, then down to his suit, taking in the whole effect. Some black cops got angry after a while, taking the look as a challenge. But Ray used it, let them look him over, smiled, then gave them his softest, most cultured voice. MoMA talk, he called it. You could smell the chardonnay.

"Detectives Fielding and Moser, to see Mr. Cruz."

The doorman gave a slight smile, swung the door open. Sunday morning, Moser thought. You run out for a paper, maybe some bagels, you gotta get all dressed up for the doorman. Checking out your shoes when he opens the door.

The lobby was polished marble and black lamps, plants in the corners so lush they had to be shipped in from the rain forest. The elevator was paneled in mahogany. No buttons, just a brass lever for the operator, who stood at parade rest, one hand at his back. The elevator rose so smoothly, Moser glanced up at the numbers over the door, surprised. Beside him, Fielding smiled, enjoying it.

The fourteenth floor had a small lobby with a baby palm and one door. A security camera was mounted near the ceiling.

"Smile," Fielding said, and rang the bell.

Adalberto Cruz was a small man, his silver hair combed straight back and shining. He looked them both over in silence, examined their badges. His eyes met Fielding's, held them for a long moment. Then he turned to Moser.

"You may come in."

He spoke with an accent, each word distinct, perfect. He led them into a broad living room, windows from floor to ceiling, a view of the city spread below them. The room was white, a few pieces of furniture placed with obvious care, as if he wanted you to know he gave thought to such things. *Decorator,* Moser thought.

A thickset man sat in an armchair beside the door, smoking. He watched them come in, motionless except for his eyes and the thin curl of smoke rising from his hand. The smoke had a sweet smell. Moser glanced at the cigarette in the man's hand. As he watched, the man raised it to his mouth, took a long pull, let it out his nose, slowly. Cloves, maybe.

A white piano stood by the window, with two framed photographs and a manila envelope on it. Cruz crossed to it, picked up one of the photographs, handed it to Moser.

"My daughter, Eva."

Moser glanced at the picture, passed it to Fielding. The girl was slim and beautiful, with long black hair and a tentative smile. She posed in ski clothes, on a stone balcony before mountains. Her right hand rested at the base of her throat. Shy, Moser thought. Like she's just finished waving the camera away. She wore a small gold band on her third finger. Fielding glanced at him, raised an eyebrow. Moser shrugged. Maybe, maybe not.

"This was taken last December," Cruz said. He took the picture back, placed it back on the piano. Beside it stood a picture of Cruz in a military uniform, his chest thrust out. Cruz stepped back, waved them toward the couch. Moser noticed that his hands were trembling. Cruz caught his glance, frowned. He shoved his hands in his pockets.

"Eva did not come home last night," he said. "This is not her way."

Moser took his place on the couch, glanced around the room slowly. He and Fielding had an arrangement — Fielding handled the politics, distraught relatives, divisional brass. Moser listened and let his eyes wander. When the time came, he asked questions. His eyes came to rest on the man sitting silently beside the door.

"Mr. Cruz," Fielding began, leaning forward. "The fact is, we can't file a missing persons report until twenty-four hours have elapsed. I appreciate your concern, but at this point . . ." He looked at Cruz, shrugged. "She may be staying with a friend, sleeping late."

Cruz was silent for a moment. He turned to gaze out the window.

"You speak like a policeman," he said. "Not like a father."

"I have two children," Fielding said. "I understand how you feel. That doesn't change the situation."

Cruz drew one hand from his pocket, rubbed his jaw.

"This morning, when I learned that my Eva had not come home, I called on the phone an associate of mine, who called for me your Commissioner Corman. Perhaps I shall make this call again."

Fielding sat back, folded his hands.

"Mr. Cruz, we understand that you have important friends. If you didn't, we wouldn't be here now. What I'm trying to tell you is that it's too soon to worry. Chances are your daughter will show up later today. In the meantime, if you have a photograph you can give us, and any information that might help us find your daughter, we'll look into it."

Cruz went over to the piano, picked up the manila envelope, and tossed it onto the couch between them.

"I was a policeman as well. You will find there her passport photograph, medical and dental records, and a copy of her records from New York University."

Moser glanced at Fielding, picked up the envelope.

"Who was she out with last night?"

"She had no plans. I returned from a dinner engagement, and she was not here. She was not allowed to go out alone."

"Who were her friends?"

Cruz turned back to the window. Million-dollar view, Moser thought, you might as well use it.

"She did not have friends here. A few classmates, perhaps. I do not remember their names."

Moser opened the envelope, glanced at the papers.

"So who'd she go out with," he asked,

"she wants to see a movie?"

Cruz nodded at the silent man. "Eduardo accompanied her everywhere." He paused. "I am from Guatemala. I must take precautions. Eva knew this. In my country, there are people who would enjoy to cause me pain."

Fielding looked over, met Moser's eyes. They glanced over at Eduardo, who remained still, the smoke drifting before his eyes.

"You're telling us this could be political," Fielding said.

Cruz was silent for a moment.

"I am telling you what you must know."

"Where was Eduardo last night?"

"He was with me."

Eduardo lifted the cigarette to his lips, slowly. He watched them through the cloud of smoke.

"Does he speak English?" Moser asked. He passed the envelope to Fielding.

"Yes."

Fielding flipped through the papers, paused.

"The girl's mother?"

"She's dead."

"Boyfriends?"

Cruz shook his head. "I do not permit it."

Moser glanced at Fielding, fought back a smile. Fielding shoved the papers back into the envelope, stood up. Moser got up, walked over to the window, looked down. A girl was sunbathing on the roof of a building across the street. *Tar beach,* he thought. Even the rich girls do it.

"We'll look into it," Fielding said. "My advice is to stay by the phone. I wouldn't be surprised if you hear from your daughter this afternoon. She got a wild hair, went shopping, met a class-mate and slept over. Something like that."

Fielding extended his hand. Cruz looked down at it, then up at his face.

"Not my Eva," he said. He turned and walked out of the room.

Fielding's eyes went hard. His hand came up to his tie, adjusted the knot.

"You ready, Dave?"

On the sidewalk, Moser lit a cigarette, ignoring Fielding's look.

"I thought you quit," Ray said, getting into the car.

"I did. It made me crazy, so I started

again last week. Three a day." He picked a speck off his lip, examined it. Then he frowned, flicked the cigarette into the street. "Thing is, I don't even like it anymore. My body wants it, I don't."

Fielding dropped the envelope on the seat beside him.

"It's filthy, and you're gonna die."

"Like being a cop."

Moser picked up the envelope, pulled out the dental records as Fielding fought the traffic heading downtown.

"Wickert's gonna love this." He dug out the picture, studied it. "You think it's her?"

"Could be. Hard to tell now."

"Feels too easy."

Fielding shrugged. "So you get an easy one. Don't argue."

"Yeah, I guess." Moser looked at the picture closely. He felt Fielding's eyes on him, slid it back into the envelope. "But that's not how it goes, Ray. First, we gotta ride all over the city, checking out missing persons reports. Talk to a bunch of sobbing mothers, most of them don't speak English. Get shit from the ME's of-fice to go on. You watch, we'll end up putting her down as just another kid off the bus, met the wrong guy at the Port Authority."

Moser glanced out at the buildings going past, each with its doorman meeting cabs, opening the door for some rich guy's wife coming home with her packages from Bergdorf or Saks.

"Tell me the truth," he said. "You think one of these girls goes for a swim up in the Bronx, the whole city's not gonna know about it the next day?"

Fielding hit the brakes as a delivery truck cut them off, pulled up at the curb. Fielding cut hard to the left, glared at the driver as they went past. "Gotta find her first."

Moser opened the envelope, looked at the picture, thinking about the one on the piano. Shy, waving the camera away. Like girls at the beach, smiling. Or his mother, shoving his father away on family vacations, flirting over the camera. The kids groaning, embarrassed. He thought of the girls you'd see in gangs on the boardwalk, posing like models, laughing at themselves. Not a bit shy.

Who took the picture, Moser wondered. Daddy, or Eduardo?

"You know your problem, Dave?"

Fielding nodded at the buildings along Park, the doctors' offices with their discreet entrances, the black nannies pushing white children in expensive Swedish strollers. "Your problem is you believe this shit. You think rich kids don't end up in the river?"

"Not often."

"All right, maybe not. But why do you think we just spent an hour out of our jurisdiction, taking an MP statement a rookie could've handled?"

Money, connections. Whatever Cruz had, he'd reached down through the chain of command to pull two homicide detectives off an investigation with just a phone call. Enough pull to make Bill Wilder, the Chief of Detectives, actually sit down at the computer, pull up the file on an unidentified floater, then drag Lieutenant Martin Quinlan, the shift commander, out of a divisional command meeting to send them across town chasing a missing girl. Moser sighed. He closed his eyes, leaned his head against the window. That's a lot of juice.

"If this isn't the girl," he said, "who gets the MP complaint?"

"We give it back to Quinlan, he dumps

it off on someone else."

Moser glanced down at the picture again. Pretty girl. With any luck, she'd met a guy. They'd send Daddy a card from Chicago in a week or two. His mind flashed on Eduardo, the smoke curling before his eyes. Maybe they'd skip the card.

"And if it is the girl?" He shoved the picture back in the envelope.

Fielding cut over behind a cab, picked up car lengths before getting stuck behind a bus. He looked over at Moser, smiled.

"Then this guy Cruz'll have your balls in a vise."

Wickert clipped the dental chart to the rim of a drafting table in his office, arranged a series of Polaroids of teeth below it — molars across the top, front teeth and incisors in a shorter row below them. He peered at them for a long moment, nodded. Perching a pair of half-glasses on his nose, he flipped through the medical records, pausing to consult his notes. When he started humming quietly, Moser knew they had a match.

"No fingerprints in the file," Wickert

said, straightening. He turned to face them, tucking the glasses into the breast pocket of his lab coat. "But that's your girl."

Fielding got up, pointed to the phone. Wickert nodded, turned back to his work. Moser watched Fielding dial the squad room, speak to Quinlan, arranging a notification. A patrol car would pick up Cruz, bring him down to the morgue to identify the girl. By late afternoon, a squad of evidence technicians would be swarming over Cruz's apartment. Uniformed officers from the local precinct would canvass the building, talking to residents, their eyes moving over the expensive furniture. For a moment, Moser imagined Eduardo, motionless in his chair, smoke rising from his hands, as the technicians dusted his shoes for prints.

He got up, went over to the drafting table, tapped Wickert's notes with one finger.

"What's the preliminary?"

Wickert shrugged. "Death by asphyxiation, violent compression of the trachea with a blunt object, possibly a forearm. Abrasion damage in the eye sockets, suggesting a dull implement with a serrated edge. Car keys, maybe. She wasn't in the water long, but there's not much in the way of fibers or prints. She'd been drinking, but the toxicology will take a while."

"So nothing on drugs."

"Be a couple weeks."

"Why'd she float?"

"Her lungs were inflated when the trachea was crushed. Like she was breathing hard. The tracheal block traps the air, and with a strong surface current, you'd see her float for a few hours." He shrugged. "Rare, but it happens."

"The heavy breathing," Moser said. "It's consistent with the rough sex theory?"

"Could be. Or maybe she was just scared, trying to get away."

"Any evidence of sexual activity?"

Wickert nodded, shuffled his notes. "Seminal fluid, also traces of a possible contraceptive cream."

Fielding, on hold, looked up from the phone.

"Recent?"

"Can't tell at this point," Wickert said. "Have to wait on serology."

Moser shook his head, flicked his notebook closed.

"Whatever happened to slow-dancing?"

Chapter 6

Miiko Reyes hated the heat. He only stole Japanese cars, because he considered the air-conditioning superior. The '95 Acuras, with the instant-cool feature, won his highest rating. He wished he could write the company, let 'em know he approved.

"Check it out," he told Eduardo, flicking the dial. "It's, what? Ninety-two, plus the humidity? Three minutes, it'll be like a refrigerator in here."

Eduardo said nothing, just stared out the window, flicking ashes from his cigarette onto the floor mats. Miiko wished he wouldn't smoke. Weird smell, sweet. It ruined the air quality in the passenger compartment, but every time he glanced over at Eduardo, sitting there like he's carved out of stone, he couldn't bring himself to ask him to put it out. Anyway, he'd read in the manual somewhere that this new air circulation system had some kind of special filter, so you could drive down the

Garden State, past all the chemical plants, and breathe air so fresh you'd think you were in the Swiss Alps. He cranked it up another notch. Give it a test.

And here it came, the burst of cold air, just as he swung onto the FDR Drive, heading up past Roosevelt Island.

"Ah, man, that's nice. Cools it right down." He laid the seat back a notch, steering with the tips of his fingers. "New York in the summer, man. Worse than Guatemala." He glanced over at Eduardo. "My dad, he took us down to Guatemala once, me and my mom. She was from Finland, a stewardess on Finnair, you know? Met my daddy out at La Guardia. He was a mechanic, worked on the jets. That's why I'm so pale." He laughed, glanced over at Eduardo, who was watching the tram dangling above the East River, moving slowly across toward the island. "I mean on account'a she was from Finland, not 'cause he worked on planes. I'm like her that way. Got her skin, my daddy's hair. Put me in the sun, twenty minutes, I'm cooked on both sides."

Eduardo hit a button, and the window

descended. He flicked his cigarette out in a flare of sparks, reached into his coat pocket for the pack.

"Anyway, my dad, he wanted us to see his village, meet the family. First day, they set up this huge feast on a table outside the house. The men put out this local tequila, start making toasts to my dad, to me, to my mom's blond hair. Took an hour to get through all the toasts. By the time they brought the food out, I was sunburned so bad they had to wrap me up in wet sheets to get the heat outta my skin. My mom, she put us on a plane home the next day." He laughed, reached over to turn the fan down a notch. "They were something, those guys. All those toasts." He looked over at Eduardo. "Were you really some kind'a cop down there?"

Eduardo shook a cigarette out of the pack, slipped it back into his pocket. He took out a pack of matches, folded one over, and struck it with one finger. He raised the whole pack to his face, cupped in both hands. The flame lit his face, making his eyes glow yellow.

Miiko watched, fascinated. The car started to drift, and a horn sounded behind them. He lowered his window, flipped the guy the finger as he shot past. "You asking to get burned, doing that."

Eduardo looked over, his eyes expressionless. He let the smoke out of his nose, pressed the match out between his thumb and forefinger. He licked the tip of his finger, wet the match with it, folded it back into line. Then he slipped the pack back into his pocket. Miiko laughed, shook his head.

"You ever have one'a those go up on you? When you got it up to your face like that?" He looked over, grinned. Eduardo rolled the cigarette between his fingers, tapping the ash onto the floor. "Be something, huh?"

He got off at 125th Street, cut over to St. Nicholas, followed it up into Washington Heights. He turned onto 174th, edging past a garbage can lying in the intersection. Near the end of the block, in a row of stores with security grates pulled down and padlocked, was a bricked-up storefront, its heavy metal door unmarked. A few men leaned against parked cars, smoking. Miiko slowed, and the men eyed them as they cruised past. He could hear the thump of drums, the faint wail of horns.

"No windows in the whole place, you can hear the music out here. Jano, man, he like his music *loud!*"

He took a right at the corner, found a space in front of a hydrant. Eduardo was out of the car before he could get the wires separated, tucked back under the dash. Miiko slipped his old .38 from under the driver's seat, tucked it into his boot, pulled the leg of his pants down over it. He caught up with Eduardo at the corner. As they turned onto the avenue, two men pushed up off a car, stepped onto the sidewalk, blocking their way. Miiko got in front of Eduardo, raised both hands, smiling.

"Hey, we come to see Jano. You tell 'im it's Miiko Reyes. He know me."

The men looked at each other, one of them nodded, crossed to the steel door, knocked once. It opened a crack, then just enough for him to slip through. For a moment, the music was deafening, then the door swung closed. The other man, wearing a white suit cut tight around the waist, red silk shirt buttoned up to the neck, and alligator shoes that made Miiko wince, they looked so soft, he waved them over toward the wall, swung his coat open

87

slightly with both hands.

Miiko smiled, shook his head. "Jano have to trust us, my man. 'Less he wanna see us walk back 'round the corner, drive on home."

The man cocked his head at Miiko, considering. Then he smiled, shoved Miiko toward the wall. His hand brushed Eduardo's arm slightly, and suddenly he was on his knees on the sidewalk, his hand clutched between his thighs. His breath made a whistling sound between his clenched teeth. The other two men came off the car, reaching under their coats. Then they seemed to hesitate, came out slow, letting the guns hang loose next to their legs. Miiko glanced over at Eduardo. He held a Tech-9 automatic in his left hand, pointed at the sidewalk between the two men's feet. In his right hand, he held his cigarette. He flicked the ash onto the sidewalk with his thumb.

Miiko sighed, looked down at the man kneeling on the sidewalk. "Eduardo, he don't like to be touched." He nodded toward the car, smiled. "Put 'em on the car, behind you. We all calm down a little, all right?"

They looked at each other, then at

Eduardo. One of them stepped back to the car, laid his gun gently on the hood. Then he leaned against the car, folded his arms. The other man gave it some thought. Then he shrugged, laid his gun on the car, made himself comfortable. Miiko looked over at Eduardo. The Tech-9 had vanished. Eduardo raised the cigarette to his mouth, squinting through the smoke.

The man kneeling on the sidewalk seemed to catch his breath. He got to his feet slowly, looked down at his hand. The thumb was pointed back at the wrist.

"Oh, man." Miiko shuddered. "I *know* that hurts."

The metal door swung open in a blast of music. The man who had gone inside slipped out, holding the door with one hand. He waved them over, stepped back, held the door open.

Jano Benitez stood at the end of the long bar, laughing, his arms draped across the shoulders of two girls. The room was dark, illuminated only by a red light that ran the length of the bar. Miiko could see Jano's eyes on them in the mirror over the bar, but he made a point of turning his back as they approached, leaning in to whisper to one of the girls, making her glance over at them, throw her head back in laughter. And then he turned, opened his arms, gave them a broad smile, shouting over the music.

"Hey, Blanquito!" He clapped Miiko on both shoulders, gave him a shake. Miiko grinned, his hands coming up to grip Jano's forearms. Jano's coat was open, and he could see the double shoulder holster, a .45 tucked under each arm. Jano Benitez was a traditionalist; when the ghetto kids started carrying Glocks, seventeen rounds in the magazine, he went out, got himself another .45. Doubled his firepower, didn't have to profile a new gun. Hey, got two arms, right? What're they for, you don't put a gun under 'em?

The music switched from salsa to Latin disco. Miiko could see a DJ spinning records in the corner, a black kid, his face lit by the red glow of his equipment. The tiny dance floor was crowded. Several women were dancing together, while their boyfriends drank at the bar. Jano tapped his ear, shrugged, pointed toward a door at the back of the room. Two men got up off their barstools nearby, but he waved them back.

Beyond the door was a narrow stairway, lit by a single bulb. Jano led them down the steps, through a dark basement, chairs stacked against the wall. There was a stove in one corner, a pile of folding tables, a dozen mattresses in clear plastic bags leaning against a pillar. At the far end, partly hidden behind liquor cartons and a broken refrigerator, Miiko glimpsed a freight elevator, the kind that rises up through the sidewalk. It came up in an alley behind the building. Miiko had taken a walk around the building earlier that morning, about the time Jano's guys were crawling into their beds. He caught Eduardo's eye, nodded toward the elevator. Eduardo looked, his face expressionless.

Jano paused before a door, dug a ring of keys from his pocket, unlocked it. He flicked the light on, waved them in. The office was small, most of it taken up by a huge desk and a metal cabinet, a padlock on the door. There were no chairs in front of the desk, just a leather couch against one wall. Miiko glanced around at the pictures on the paneled walls — Escuintla, Puerto de San José, the Castillo de San Felipe, with a view out over Lago de Izabal. He'd never been any of those places, but every Guatemalan he knew had the same pictures on his walls. They like it so much, he thought, why'd they leave? Come up to Washington Heights, sit around staring at pictures of home. Irish were the same way. Go into one of those bars in the West Forties, they got those Aer Lingus posters on the walls, gives 'em something to cry over when they get drunk. He grinned, thinking how when this whole thing was over, maybe he'd find himself some little village on the Pacific coast down there, open a bar, hang a picture of Bay Ridge next to the door.

Jano moved behind the desk, lowered himself into a leather chair. He leaned on the desk, spread his hands.

"So?"

He looked over at Eduardo. Eduardo settled onto the couch, took out his cigarettes, shook one from the pack. Jano watched, fascinated, as he raised the pack of matches to his face, lit it, folded the burned match back into the pack. Jano grinned, shook his head. He looked over at Miiko.

"So I guess you're doin' the talking, huh?"

Miiko glanced over at Eduardo, cleared his throat. "Mr. Cruz, he's *unhappy,* you know? Way he sees it, you had *understanding,* now it's broken."

Jano Benitez looked weary. He sat back in his big leather chair, crossed his arms. "You ever learn Spanish, Blanquito?"

Miiko shrugged. "I'm getting by."

He nodded, rubbed at his chin with one finger. Then he rubbed the bridge of his nose, between his eyes. Finally, he looked over at them, one finger tapping the leather arm of his chair.

"See, this is too bad," he said at last. "You and me, we could go upstairs, have a few drinks, maybe I could introduce you to some nice ladies. But now we got a problem, we're all tense."

Miiko crossed his legs, flicked a speck off his white jeans.

"I'm okay. Eduardo don't get tense."

"Hey, I'm glad to hear that. 'Cause what I *anticipated* here was a gesture of mutual respect, you know?"

"I guess that's 'tween you and Mr. Cruz."

Jano thought about that for a moment. Then he rolled his shoulders, jerked his head to both sides like Jose Canseco before a pitch. He leaned forward, folded his hands on the desk blotter.

"I like you, Blanquito," he said. "You're a good kid. Got no respect for your heritage, but that's how it is for *mestizo*, huh? You out there floating 'round on the ocean, got no place to land. Am I right?"

Miiko shrugged. Beside him, Eduardo raised his hand, examined his cigarette carefully. It was almost down to the filter. He let his hand dangle over the side of the couch, flicked ashes onto the floor. Jano frowned, his jaw tightened, but his eyes came back to Miiko.

"You tell Cruz I'm not who I was." He threw his head back, laughed. "It's a joke, you know? Tell Cruz, when he's ready to do this right, I be glad to talk with you again." He raised one finger. "Just you. No muscle."

Miiko glanced over at Eduardo. He had the stub of his cigarette to his lips, taking a last few puffs. Overhead, the music boomed. Miiko looked back at Jano, sighed.

"That's it?"

Jano leaned the chair back, put his boots up on the desk, crossed his arms.

"That's it."

Eduardo dropped his cigarette to the floor, crushed it out with his shoe. He got up, drew the Tech-9 from under his coat, and fired the whole clip into Jano Benitez. Thirty-two rounds, the chair shaking, skittering back to the wall, Jano's arms dancing in the air beside him, his face showing surprise until it vanished into a red mist that drifted back across the desk at them. Miiko winced, tried to wave it away. It took only a few seconds, and when it stopped, Miiko heard the music thumping over their heads. He sat for a moment without moving, then he leaned forward, threw up onto the floor between his shoes.

Eduardo popped the empty clip out of the gun, dropped it into his coat pocket. He reached under his coat, took out a new clip, slapped it into the gun. He tucked the gun away, dug in his other coat pocket, came out with a sheet of paper. He walked around the desk, dropped it on Jano's chest. The blood soaked into it. He dug in his coat pocket, came out with a switchblade and a Ziploc sandwich bag. Then he bent over Jano's outstretched hand, sliced off the thumb. He dropped it into the bag, sealed it closed on the edge of the desk.

Seals freshness in, Miiko thought.

Eduardo folded the bag twice, the plastic streaked with red. He tucked it into his pocket, slid a desk drawer open, took out a ring of keys. He came back around the desk, went over to the metal cabinet, tried several keys until he found one that opened the padlock. He tossed the lock aside, swung the door open. Inside, Miiko saw a food scale, two boxes of powdered sugar, several plastic jugs of chemicals, and a small briefcase. Eduardo snapped the case open, glanced inside. He took out a small packet of white powder, held it up to the light. Then he returned it to the briefcase, snapped it shut. Without a glance at Miiko, he crossed to the office door and went out.

Miiko took a deep breath, wiped his mouth on the sleeve of his coat. He got up off the couch, followed. Eduardo was moving liquor cartons from in front of the freight elevator. Miiko joined him, and they cleared a path wide enough to squeeze through. There was no light at that end of the basement. Eduardo struck a match, held it over the control panel so Miiko could see.

"Okay, got it," Miiko said as the match burned out. He'd used one before, emptying out a fur storage warehouse on the Lower East Side one night a few years back. Just a lever, you push it forward, the elevator goes up, pull it back it goes down. A metal bar up over your head pushes the metal doors open as you come through the sidewalk.

Like in those old movies on TV, Miiko thought. *Big dance number around a swimming pool, some girl comes floating up outta the water, fountains shooting up everywhere.*

He pushed the lever. The elevator didn't move.

"Shit." He pulled it back, jerked it back and forth. Nothing. Eduardo struck another match, looked closely at the control panel. He ran his hand down a thick cable from the bottom of the control box to where it ended just above the floor. He held up the frayed end in the light of the match, turned it slowly. His eyes met Miiko's. He smiled.

He blew out the match, stepped down

off the elevator platform, headed for the stairs. His hand disappeared into his coat, came out with the Tech-9.

"Ah, man." Miiko dug in his boot, drew out the .38. "I can tell I'm not gonna like this."

He jumped down, ran after Eduardo.

Chapter 7

The doorman was on his lunch break, sitting in a tiny office at the rear of the lobby, where the rumble of the elevators shook the framed pictures of English cities he'd hung on the walls. He was working on a shrimp salad from the Au Bon Pain on the next block. He kept the dressing in its plastic cup, dipping each bite before eating it. A copy of the *Post* on his desk showed a picture of the after-hours club on 174th, where two gunmen had walked through the room, shooting as they went. A banner headline read: BLOODY HELL!

Moser picked up the paper, glanced at the story. The doorman chewed slowly, watching his eyes move down the page.

"Busy day for you gentlemen."

Moser folded the paper, dropped it on the desk. *Busy day.* They'd left a squad room swamped with autopsy reports, witness interviews, and evidence summaries. The gunmen had scattered eleven bodies across the floor of the club, three more on the sidewalk out front, then vanished into the night. The first officers on the scene found the music still blaring, bloody footprints on the sidewalk where patrons had fled the scene. Only after several hours did anyone think to check the basement, finding one final victim, shot gangland style in a tiny office at the rear of the building. A cabinet next to the body stood open, filled with supplies used for the distribution of cocaine. Stuck to his chest was a blood-soaked paper. When the Medical Examiner peeled it off, he saw that it was an immigration application in the name of Joaquin Yano Benitez. A box on the form had been checked: DENIED.

Fielding examined a photograph of a medieval abbey, surrounded by trees and a row of stone houses on the hillside above it. "Homesick?"

"A bit. More humane pace, you know." Without his cap, the doorman looked to be in his early thirties, with thinning blond hair and a weak chin. He told them — with a faint smile — that his name was John Dowell, and he came from a town called Kenton on the south coast of England.

"What brought you over here?"

He gave an ironic smile, poked at his salad. "That's the eternal question, isn't it. I am — or should I say, I *was* — an actor. America's the golden goose for a Brit. At least, that's what I heard." He gestured at the photograph with his fork. "That's Bath."

Fielding looked at him. "I know."

Moser took out his pad. "I wonder if you could clarify some things for me. You told the interviewing officer that you didn't see Miss Cruz leave the building on the night she disappeared."

Dowell shrugged. "Doesn't mean much. She might've gone out through the garage."

Garage, Moser thought. Rhymes with marriage.

"According to her father, she didn't drive."

The doorman considered this for a moment, fork poised before his mouth. At last, he slipped it in, chewing slowly. "She might have slipped out the front. I often have to step into the street to hail a cab. If she left on foot, you know, it's out the door, down the sidewalk, gone before I know it."

"How well did you know Miss Cruz?"

He smiled. "Ah. The question."

"Did she talk to you?"

"With the Shadow of the Pampas always at her back?"

Moser looked at him. Dowell ran his tongue across the front of his teeth carefully as he dipped a tomato slice in the dressing.

"I take it you mean the bodyguard." Moser glanced down at his notebook. "Eduardo Sosa."

"Mmm. Like something from a Borges story, isn't he? The silent gaucho. Knives and tangos."

"I believe he's from Central America."

"Yes, well." The doorman stabbed at a shrimp. "That's different, isn't it."

"So you never saw Miss Cruz out alone."

"Perish the thought."

"Any boyfriends?"

"Only the knife artist."

Moser frowned, glanced over at Fielding.

"Eduardo? You see anything to suggest they . . ."

The doorman sighed, raised one hand. "Forgive me. I was being ironic."

Fielding watched Moser's eyebrows rise very slowly, thought, *Uh oh.* "What about the father?" he asked quickly. "He have people in?"

Dowell sighed, nodded. "Frequently."

"Care to tell us about them?"

The doorman hesitated. "Let's just say he has an interesting collection of friends."

Moser seated himself on the edge of his desk. "Let's say a bit more than that, okay?"

Fielding fought back a smile. "Interesting how?"

"Diverse. From all points on the social spectrum."

"Can you be more specific?"

The doorman fixed his gaze on a photograph of the coast of Cornwall, rocks and crashing waves.

"How to put it? If you needed a political favor, or a stolen car stereo, for that matter, I'm quite sure Mr. Cruz would have access to the appropriate channels."

"He had these people coming here?"

"I gather Mr. Cruz conducts his business from his home."

Moser frowned.

"Cruz told us he was retired."

The doorman looked up at him, amused.

"Did he?" He considered this for a moment, smiled. "Then I must be mistaken."

"What made you think he was conducting business?"

He shrugged. "His visitors tend to arrive at regular hours. One man comes every morning at nine, carrying an athletic bag. Like they carry at the health clubs. He stays . . . oh, twenty minutes, perhaps. Then he comes back out with the bag, leaves on foot."

Moser and Fielding glanced at each other. Moser turned the page of his notebook, slipped a pen from his pocket.

"I take it this was unusual in this building?"

The doorman was silent for a moment, then he dabbed at the corners of his mouth with a napkin, rose from behind the desk and brushed a few crumbs off the front of his uniform. He turned to consider himself in a small mirror mounted on the wall behind his desk. His expression was formal now. Playing a scene, Moser thought.

"Most of our tenants keep to more

traditional business hours," Dowell said, adjusting the knot in his tie. "At the office by eight usually, then home by six or seven. There's quite a parade of limousines along this block every morning."

"How would you describe this guy?"

The doorman glanced at Fielding in the mirror.

"He's an Italian gentleman. Small, heavyset. Wears expensive suits, like in the movies."

"What do you mean?"

Dowell smiled. "Oh, you know." His face shifted into a tough-guy expression, his voice into a thick Queens accent. "Hey, don't *worry* 'bout it. He sleeps wit da fishes."

Moser smiled, rubbed at his jaw. *Actors.*

"He come by this morning?" Fielding asked.

Dowell cocked his head. "No, you're right. He didn't come today. That's unusual. He's come every morning since I've worked here. Like clockwork."

What is it about that phrase, Moser thought, makes people want to use it to cops? Pick up some junkie strung out in an alley, ask him did he see the

105

woman get stabbed behind the Dumpster thirty feet away, and he'd give you that shivery look, say, *No way, man.* Did he notice the guy from the restaurant pitch the sack of garbage out the back door, the one they'd found strewn across the body? *Hey, sorry.* Did he know the old wino who came through digging for empties and found the body? And to that one he'll agree, adding in his thin, raspy voice, *That old guy, he's through here like clockwork.* Moser shook his head. Find a set of bones in the desert, been there thirty years, there'll be somebody who figures a way to use that line.

"Can you describe any of the others?"

"As I've said, an assortment. Rich man, poor man, beggar man." He smiled. "Thief. Perhaps if you showed me the pictures, like on television. What do you call them here?"

"Mug shots."

"Exactly."

"Anyone come by on the day Ms. Cruz disappeared?"

"Only the nine o'clock delivery."

Moser slipped a card from his coat pocket, dropped it on the desk. "If you think of anything else . . ."

"Of course. It would be my pleasure." Dowell gave them the briefest of smiles, put on his cap, taking a moment before the mirror to get it at the right angle. When he turned to face them, slipping on his white gloves, the cool smile was back, and he seemed to vanish into the background. He escorted them into the lobby, swung the door open.

"Good day, gentlemen. Come again."

Chapter 8

For Joey Tangliero, the smell of fish, any fish, was enough to make him gag. One whiff and he'd feel his throat seizing up, like somebody had a grip on his neck, trying to reach inside to grab his tonsils, yank him inside out. So when the deputy marshal, Claire Locke, ordered tuna on rye for lunch, easy on the mayo, he screwed up his face in disgust, went around the hotel suite, jerking the windows open. Then he lit a cigar.

"I don't get it. How can you eat that stuff?" He watched her put the cover from the room service plate aside, pick the sandwich up with the tips of her fingers, look up at him wearily. "I mean, what's a fish, huh? It's not an animal, it's not a snake. Like a cockroach, only wet. Am I right?"

Claire took a bite, chewed slowly. He shuddered. "You know what they put in the water now? The East River's a fuckin' toilet, gets flushed right out in the ocean. And the fish, they swim around in it, scarf it up."

Claire looked down at her sandwich, swallowed hard. "You mind? I'm eating."

"Hey, I'm doing you a favor." He pointed at her plate. "You call that a tuna sandwich, I call it mayo on a turd."

"Oh, for Christ's sake!" Claire dropped the sandwich on her plate, shoved it aside. "You hear me complaining about your food? Look what you eat."

Tangliero glanced down at the pile of fried chicken wings on his plate, french fries in gravy in a little dish on the side. "What's wrong with my food?"

"What's *wrong* with it?" She shook her head. "Hey, just call up your buddies, tell 'em where to come get you. Get it over quick."

He frowned at his plate. "Forty-two years I'm eating like this. Do I look sick?"

"You want the truth?" Claire wiped her hands on a napkin, her eyes shifting from his plate to his broad belly, then back to his plate. "I should take your picture, just like that. Sell it to Mount Sinai, they could use you as a poster child for coronary thrombosis."

Tangliero grinned. "Stop it, you're scarin' me." He picked up a chicken wing, bit into it.

Claire watched him, shook her head. "I'm serious. You keep eating like that, we can forget the whole thing. Those mob guys, they got nothing to worry about."

He waved the chicken wing at her, chewing. "Lemme tell you something, honey. My line of work, you don't worry about cholesterol." He picked at a molar with his fingernail. "You got clogged arteries? No problem. Some guy comes along, cleans 'em out with an ice pick."

Claire smiled. "Preventive medicine, like."

"Hey, what are friends for?"

He stripped the last few bites of meat from the chicken wing, laid the bone on the edge of the room service tray.

"I don't know," Claire said. "You ask me, I'd rather eat a few carrots, maybe get some exercise."

Tangliero looked up at her. "Like what? Those guys you see jogging every morning over in Riverside Park? You ever look at those guys? They got this expression on their faces, like every muscle in their body just turned to barbed wire." He picked up another chicken wing, shook his head. "Do me a favor. Just shoot me now."

In the afternoon, Assistant U.S. Attorney Merrill Conte arrived with three assistants, two FBI agents, and an NYPD detective who introduced himself as Tom Richter, from Internal Affairs. Conte's assistants were young guys, with expensive haircuts and tailored suits. They had broad shoulders, narrow at the waist, like they spent a lot of time at the health club. Two of them snuck glances at Claire as they came in, curious. The third kept his eyes on Conte, watching his face. Gay, Claire thought. Or ambitious.

The detective, Richter, nodded at her, handed over his revolver, and settled into an armchair near the window. He was in his early forties, sandy-haired, built lean and hard. His face had laugh lines, but there was a toughness around the eyes. He fixed his eyes on the window, as if the whole business left him cold.

The assistants set up a pair of tape recorders on the table next to the sofa. One of the FBI men took a third from his briefcase, placed it next to them, not taking any chances. Then Conte pulled up a chair, slipped his jacket off, draped it over the back of the chair. He took a cigar from the inside pocket of his jacket, offered it solemnly to Tangliero. Claire could picture him in a courtroom, smiling at the sound of his own voice on the tape.

Conte settled into his seat, glanced at the tape recorders to make sure they were turning. He nodded, tugged at his cuffs.

"Let's begin, then, shall we?"

Claire sat in the corner, watching Tangliero puff at his cigar as Conte led him through the basics. Name, aliases, known associates, which he asked Tangliero to confirm audibly for the tape. Tangliero sat with one arm stretched along the back of the couch, his legs stretched out before him, rolling the cigar between his thumb and forefinger.

He loves it, Claire thought, watching him. *Mob guys, they live for this.*

"And from 1978 to the present," Conte was saying, glancing down at a paper one of his assistants handed to him, "you were affiliated with Anthony Giardella, a resident of Staten Island.

On Mr. Giardella's instructions, you made a series of payoffs to active duty officers of the New York Police Department to protect various illegal activities by the Luccario crime family within Manhattan. Is that right, Mr. Tangliero?"

"Yeah, that's right," Joey said. He smiled, waved the cigar at Conte. "Tony G."

Conte glanced over at one of his assistants, licked his lips carefully. "Mr. Tangliero has confirmed his association with Mr. Giardella."

Watching him, Claire felt a pang of sympathy for Tangliero. Poor guy figured he'd dodged a bullet, landed in clover. But this guy, Conte, sitting there in his Brooks Brothers suit, he looked as tough as any wiseguy. He figured on having Joey Tangliero for an early afternoon snack, saving his appetite for the big fish.

Still, Tangliero had his cigar, an audience, and plenty of time to spare. He reached down, popped the top button on his pants to give his stomach some room, raised his cigar slowly to admire the curl of smoke rising from its tip. One of the FBI men started to ask a question, but Conte shot him a withering look.

"Let's talk about the payoffs," he said to Tangliero.

Joey tipped his head slightly. "Okay."

Conte passed the paper back to his assistant, smiled at Tangliero. "Now, I'd like you to describe your procedures for us. Just walk us through it, okay?"

Joey raised his cigar to his mouth, squinted at Conte through the smoke. "Well," he said at last, "the *procedure* we generally followed was, Tony G. gives me the money, his cousin Bobby's mother, lady named Esme, she does the count. We started puttin' the money in deposit envelopes a couple years back, and I kept 'em in bunches, dependin' on the amount, see?" He patted the pockets on his jacket. "Before I go into the building, I load up, put all the different amounts in separate pockets, so I don't get confused. That way, I just walk through the precinct, don't have to stop and figure the amounts. It's like a system I figured out."

"How much did you disburse, on a weekly basis?"

"Average?" Joey took a pull from his cigar, thought about it. "Two-eighty, maybe two-ninety. Esme could tell you for sure."

One of the assistants gasped audibly. Joey looked at him, grinned.

"That's only for Manhattan, though. You gotta figure the other boroughs separate. Queens is more, 'cause they got the airport. But that's outta my jurisdiction."

Conte wet his lips. "That's a *weekly* average?"

"Yeah, it's down this year some on account'a the Mollen Commission thing. But it's coming back. Then you got Christmas, which pushes it up. Two-ninety, that's my guess."

One of the assistants took out a tiny pocket calculator, keyed it with the tip of his thumb. He glanced at the total, then passed it to Conte.

"So we're talking about over sixteen million in a year."

Joey frowned. "That sounds low." He thought for a moment, doing the math, then he shrugged. "Yeah, I guess that makes sense. Figure an extra week at Christmas, that puts you up closer to sixteen five."

Conte leaned forward, aimed the corner of his glasses at Tangliero. "You're telling me that Tony Giardella spent over sixteen million last year, just on payoffs to cops?"

Joey laughed. "You should see what he brings in."

"Can you tell us?"

"Gross?" He shrugged. "Million a week, maybe. But he's gotta split that with his partners, pay off the guys work with him. You wanna know what he nets, you gotta ask Tony."

Conte sat back, slowly. One of the FBI men was scribbling hurriedly on a legal pad. Conte's assistant, the ambitious one, leaned over and checked the tape recorder.

Tangliero shifted his weight, gestured with his cigar. "See, this kind of business, you don't have equipment, depreciation, all that stuff. Paying off the cops is just overhead. Tony likes to keep it under ten percent of gross, but he's also collecting from all the other guys." He paused to puff at his cigar. "What Tony figured out, back in the eighties, is you gotta centralize the payout, or you're looking at all kinds'a duplication. Say you got three guys working numbers up in East Harlem. They're all affiliated, but each one of 'em makes his own deal with the cops. What for? Tony figured, get one guy in charge of all the money going out, like in a company. 'Cause you're paying out all at once, the cops take less. That's three less guys they gotta shake down, right? 'Course they still go after the drug guys, street dealers, all that. But our people, they leave 'em alone. It comes to them."

Conte's mouth twitched slightly. He raised his glasses, laid them against his chin. "And Giardella's the paymaster?"

"It was his idea, so he's the guy. His cousin Bobby Amondano runs the show up here, but he don't like to get too involved, since the RICO thing. Tony, he's the day-to-day guy. All the other guys in the family, they split with him at . . . I don't know, twelve percent of gross, maybe. Ten percent for the pay-off, plus two for Tony. Except for special deals, like when Bobby wanted a guy hit up in Washington Heights, we paid off some cops to spot the guy for the hitters. But that kind of thing's extra. Mostly, it's just business, you know? Spend a little to make a lot. Some of these cops, they're taking home like sixteen hundred a month from the city.

Who can live on that? With us, they can make two, three times that. They work the dealers too, they can pull down another couple thousand. End of the year, everybody's happy." He grinned at Conte, flicked the ash off his cigar onto the carpet. "Except you, I guess."

Conte leaned over to his assistant. Claire could hear him whisper, "Call Jean. Have her clear my schedule for the rest of the day."

Richter, the Internal Affairs guy, moved his eyes off the windows for the first time. He sat forward, looked Joey over slowly. "How many cops are we talking about here?"

"On my route? A hundred fifty-two."

For a moment the room was silent. Richter rubbed at his forehead.

"You got names on these cops?"

"Like a list?" Tangliero shook his head. "Nah, we try to keep on an informal basis, you know what I mean?" Then he leaned forward, tapped his forehead with one finger, smiled. "But I got something just as good. I got *mnemonics*."

Chapter 9

The daily surveillance transcripts from the Organized Crime Task Force arrived on Merrill Conte's desk at 6:30 each evening. It was his habit to glance through them briefly before leaving for the day. If anything caught his interest, he would toss the packets into his briefcase, take them home to Greenwich to examine more carefully while lying on the couch in his den after dinner. This evening the only transcript pertinent to matters at hand was a short page near the end of the packet, identified as a telephone conversation between Anthony Giardella and an unknown subject recorded at 11:23 A.M. from a pay phone two blocks east of the Azores Coffee Shop, known to be used by Giardella for business purposes.

What Conte read was:

SUBJECT #1
　Hello?

GIARDELLA

Put him on.

SUBJECT #1

Who's calling, please?

GIARDELLA

Never mind, ya fuck! Get him on the phone, now!

SUBJECT #1

One moment.

SUBJECT #2

Yes?

GIARDELLA

You know who this is, asshole?

SUBJECT #2

Yes.

GIARDELLA

So where's the fuckin' money? I gotta come over there, cut your heart out? I want the money, now! (DIAL TONE) Ah, shit!

END OF CONVERSATION

Conte sighed, laid the packet aside. As a scholarship student at St. Boniface, he'd read Cicero in the original Latin. At Georgetown, he'd majored in Classics, even toyed with the idea of an academic career. Instead, he'd chosen the law, joined the Suffolk County DA's office as an assistant prosecutor, worked his way up to Assistant U.S. Attorney, Criminal Division. Yet, on occasion, late in the evening, he would take his battered copy of the *Orations* down from its shelf, page through it until he came to the Prosecution of Verres, savoring its eloquence in the people's cause. Now, he thought, it was he who rose to speak against corruption, violence, and conspiracy, matching his own voice against —

He looked down at the transcript on the desk before him. A high school dropout, screaming *Where's the fuckin' money* into a public phone.

Moser stopped at the coffee machine, carried a styrofoam cup back to his desk, stirring as he walked. Fielding had his feet up on the edge of his desk, a file open on his lap. He nodded at a message slip next to Moser's phone.

"You just had a call, guy from the Hundred-fifth."

Moser settled into his chair, put the coffee on his desk, and picked up the message slip. "That's Queens, right? By the airport?"

Fielding looked up. "It's the long one, runs along the Belt Parkway."

Moser picked up the phone, dialed. He got the main precinct switchboard, asked for Frank Lukowitz. The operator put him on hold, transferred the call up to the squad room. Moser sipped his coffee, waited.

"Lukowitz."

"This is Dave Moser, up at the Three-Four. You left a message for me?"

"Oh, yeah. Thanks for calling back." Moser could hear him chewing. He swallowed, cleared his throat. "We picked up a kid in a rental car lot over by JFK last night, he was stripping parts off a Chevrolet Caprice. Said he was working for you."

Shit. Moser closed his eyes, took a deep breath. "Yeah, he works on my car."

"Uh huh." Lukowitz shuffled some papers around. "This puts me in kind of a position, you know? Kid's on probation."

Moser was silent, figuring he'd get around to it.

"You want me to lose the paper on this?"

Moser hesitated.

"I can't ask you to do that."

Lukowitz laughed. "No, I guess you can't."

Moser heard him chewing, swallow.

"Okay, listen. I'm looking on my desk here, and I don't see the sheet on this thing. My desk, it's a surprise I can find anything."

"Thanks. I owe you one."

"Damn right. You can start by keeping this kid outta my jurisdiction, okay? These car rental guys do a lot of business out here. Fact is, they make it worth our time to keep an eye on things. Your kid needs a part, tell him to try La Guardia."

"I'll send him over to NAPA."

Lukowitz took a bite of something, laughed. "Hey, don't get crazy now."

Moser hung up, saw Fielding watching him.

"Everything okay?"

"I've been on the job, what? Twelve years?" He shook his head. "I think I just figured out why they call us cops."

Chapter 10

In the evening, Adalberto Cruz sent Eduardo out to the Sav-More for bananas, bread, and toothpaste. He made a list. Then he took the phone off the hook, made himself comfortable on the couch with a glass of single malt Scotch to consider his options.

He closed his eyes, let his head sink back against the cool white leather of the cushions, thought of a beach spread out at his feet, a warm breeze, the sun setting into an ocean the color of blood. It was an image that always steadied him, a place he had left behind, forever.

Now, his mind calm, he allowed himself to think, briefly, of Eva. Dead. Floating, naked, in a filthy river. Her eyes gouged out.

He took a deep breath, felt it catch in his throat. His heart felt as if somebody had reached in, grabbed it, squeezing it in his fist, hard. Tears rose to his eyes.

Enough.

He forced his mind back to the beach — aware, now, of voices behind him. Shovels biting into dirt, men laughing. The air smelled of cigarette smoke, freshly turned earth. Feeling the muscles in his neck ache. His eyes were glad for the sunset, let it take him away.

He reached for the Scotch on the table next to him, took a small sip. The room had grown darker. He switched on a lamp.

A man must be disciplined, meticulous, even in his own mind. Especially there. You must allow yourself the emotion, but in small doses only. The mind must stay clear, like the sun dipping into the water. The ocean changes, blue to red to more profound blue, as if it has swallowed the sun. But then, as the minutes pass, the light fades, the water turns to black. Black sky, black sea. All vanished, all one.

So it is, he thought, with emotion. There is a time for such things, a moment when everything becomes clear. Until then, a man must stay quiet. Let the mind focus on more immediate concerns.

What mattered, now, was the money.

And so, as the light faded in the room,

he thought about the money. The way it moved, like water. Tiny streams flowing together, moving faster. Where it pooled, even for a moment, more streams poured in, as if drawn to it by a common gravity, an urge to grow larger. One simply had to guide it, shape its course with your hands. And if you could slow it, briefly, as it flowed past, it would grow deep enough to dip your cup, drink from it.

Cruz smiled. That was what Tony Giardella, with his threats, his crude accusations, had never been able to comprehend. A simple lesson, but too difficult for those without imagination to perceive: *A man does not need to steal, as long as there are other men who do.*

"Do the numbers," Tony Giardella had told him when they started. "You get six percent, cut your people in at one percent, that's a nice deal."

Sitting there in Lindy's, one o'clock in the afternoon, the place full of tourists, eating a bowl of lime Jell-O, a glass of Coca-Cola. Every few bites, Cruz watched him reach over, tip the glass into the bowl.

Cruz watched him dip his spoon into the bowl, take a little green, a little brown. When he was satisfied, he raised it to his mouth, parted his lips slightly, and sucked it noisily off the side of the spoon.

Like a child, Cruz thought.

"So what I'm sayin' here, just so we understand each other, is that I view this as a *mutual* relationship. We get along, I can't see why you won't do very nicely." He looked up at Cruz, the spoon hovering in front of his mouth. "But I'll tell you this just once, you steal from me, I'll cut your fuckin' head off and piss down your throat."

Cruz, meeting his gaze, thought: *This is a very stupid man.*

Still, he had smiled, and for the next six years, kept his accounts to the penny. Every morning, he took delivery of a gym bag full of cash, made the man wait as he counted it, recorded the amount twice, once on a computer disk that required his own password to access, the second time with the decimal point moved two spaces to the left, on a pad of sales receipts from Liquid Assets, a liquor distributor on Roosevelt Avenue in Queens. He gave the receipt to the delivery man, who glanced at it, tucked it into his pocket. Then Cruz refilled the gym bag with stacks of clean bills from a briefcase on his desk, gave it back to the delivery man. The man zipped it closed, got up off the sofa, and left, carrying the gym bag.

Later, Cruz would deduct five percent of the pile on his desk, set it aside. Then he'd wrap the rest in bundles of a thousand dollars each, snap a rubber band around a stack of ten bundles, load them into his briefcase. In the evening, Eduardo would bring the car around, and they'd drive out to Roosevelt Avenue, where Cruz would pay far too much for a case of Cordon Negro, delivery included.

The next morning, a truck would make stops at Spallone Liquors, a chain of twelve stores in Queens, Brooklyn, and upper Manhattan. Daily receipts were entered into the distributor's accounts, less one percent. Profit shares were paid at the end of each week by electronic transfer into three corporate accounts, which then divided the money among a group of seven corporate shareholders, all employees of Liquid Assets, Inc. Each of those employees — recent Guatemalan immigrants, who spoke little English — had signed documents granting power of attorney to an investment advisor, Adalberto Cruz. By a second signature, they authorized the electronic transfer of all profit shares into a limited investment partnership that held one stock only: InterAmerican Development Corporation. According to its glossy brochure, InterAmerican developed "investment properties in the vibrant heart of the Americas!" Photographs showed three miles of white sand beach, set against the green hills of coastal Guatemala. The brochure showed an architect's designs — roads, luxury villas, restaurants, an eighteen-hole golf course, tennis courts. The property's owner of record was Adalberto Cruz.

Funds from InterAmerican's project accounts were wired to a bank in Guatemala City every Monday. On Wednesday, a call from New York would order a varying percentage wired to a second bank on the island of Anguilla, where it was divided among several accounts for transfer to Bogotá, Nassau, Palermo, and Menderisio, Switzerland. The balance, however, was paid out to Lento Construction, Inc., which wired the money back to its corporate accounts in New York.

Tony Giardella, staring down at the diagram Cruz had drawn up, had pushed it aside, shaking his head.

"I'll take your word for it." He lit a cigar, blew the smoke at Cruz. "Just make sure it comes back."

And Cruz had sighed, slipped the diagram back into his briefcase. He'd been proud of the arrangements, their complexity, their grace — like a mountain stream, flowing over rocks. Three cut-outs, all within a week. If the IRS tried to trace the cash flow, they'd get as far as the shareholders, or at worst the investment fund. Once the money left the country, there was no way they could trace it back to Giardella. Maximum security, minimum risk. That was a principle he'd learned the hard way, watching other men give orders from behind mahogany desks in spacious offices, while his own hands got dirty.

Never again.

For six years, he'd watched over his creation, tuning it, keeping the employees prosperous and frightened. But in recent years, Cruz had become concerned. Two delivery trucks had been held up by crackheads in a six-month period. The drivers carried no cash, but the thieves had made off with the trucks and thirty-seven cases of assorted whiskeys, covered in dust from being wheeled in and out of the same storerooms day after day for six years. Cruz swallowed the loss, wrote it off as an expense one had to expect, doing business in New York. But it got him thinking.

Were the deliveries necessary? One could simplify matters, put the shareholders directly to work making cash deposits into their own accounts. Seven accounts, two deposits a day, five days a week. Keep the deposits under $10,000, so no IRS forms. Use branch banks across the city, to avoid curious tellers.

And if one did become interested? The money could be traced to the shareholders, but how much farther? He had brooded on the question for several days, then decided that he should avoid making the cash delivery to Roosevelt Avenue. A few weeks later, Liquid Assets, Inc., through its corporate attorneys, negotiated the purchase of Vallardi News on Madison, near 78th. Every evening, Cruz would walk four blocks, accompanied by Eduardo, for his copy of *The Wall Street Journal.* He would greet the clerk, set his brown leather briefcase down next to the counter as he paid. A few hours later, the clerk — a longtime employee of Liquid Assets, Inc. — would close up the store and, carrying a brown leather briefcase, board a bus for Grand Central, where he would catch the Flushing Local out to Queens. He would get off at 103rd Street, walk up the block to Spallone Liquors for a bottle of Dos Equis before going into his building.

Better, Cruz thought. *Not perfect, but clean.*

The idea of the clerk riding the subway every day, almost $200,000 in his briefcase, troubled him at first. But he'd picked a squat *mestizo,* his face pocked from a bad case of acne. He wore the same leather jacket every day, a blue work shirt in the summer, with *Jaime* stitched over the pocket. He sat with the briefcase between his feet, eyes half closed, scowling. In seven months, they'd never lost a penny.

Until now.

Cruz sighed, reached for his whiskey. The glass had left a wet ring on the table, and he swept it away with the edge of his hand.

The system had worked, the cash moving steadily into the bank accounts, no problem. Then the transfers, the part Cruz liked best. He'd watched it done the first time, leaning over the desk as the bank's corporate services agent tapped a few keys on his computer terminal, leaned back, said — "Okay, done."

Amazing. Like watching a squirrel jump from one tree to the next. A little flurry of leaves, then gone.

This, Cruz had thought, is a beautiful thing.

A quick call to Guatemala City confirmed that the money had arrived. By careful manipulation of the dates of deposit and withdrawal, Cruz had maintained an average balance of $2.4 million. On the last day of the quarter — the day that Adalberto Cruz had purchased the strip of coastal property in Barrita Vieja, Guatemala, signing the documents in his New York apartment, then feeding them into the fax machine — the account had stood at $3,450,700. Enough money to send the bankers of Guatemala City scurrying to approve his credit, to change him, in the course of a few hours, from a police captain, who might be asked to wait in the hall, to a major landowner. The cash, as it flowed through the accounts of InterAmerican Development Corporation, drew more money to it, like a rock tumbling down a hill. Soon, he would commence construction on Costa de Oro, a luxury resort at Barrita Vieja. After that, he had his eye on some commercial properties in Guatemala City. Within five years, if all went as he planned, he would no longer need Giardella's money. His own wealth would fill the banks of Guatemala City. He would return, a man reborn. His enemies, the wealthy men who had betrayed him, would turn to greet him as he entered their clubs . . .

Cruz took a sip of his whiskey, sighed. He reached over, picked up a sheet of paper on the table. A list of twenty-three names, typed, single-spaced, nothing else. It had emerged from his fax machine six days ago, the paper warm against his fingers. He recognized the sender's number, printed at the top of the page — an office in the Ministry of Justice, Guatemala City. He'd taken a pair of scissors, cut off the top of the page, burned the narrow strip in an ashtray. Then he'd folded the list of names once, carefully, tucked it into his pocket.

Now, two of the names had a small check beside them in pencil. He laid the paper aside, closed his eyes.

So close, he thought.

But then, the dead had awakened.

Chapter 11

Claire watched Merrill Conte glance down at his notes, frown. He had his tie loosened, his reading glasses perched on his nose. The three assistants had shed their jackets, tugged at their ties and collar buttons until they got the look just right: Brooks Brothers, worn as if it came easily. Each had a legal pad balanced on his lap, a styrofoam cup of cold coffee at his feet. They sat with pens poised, ready to scrawl hurried notes whenever Conte glanced their way. Like Conte, they wore expressions of strained patience.

Tangliero was stretched out on the couch, eyes closed. He held an unlit cigar between the middle fingers of one hand, resting it on his chest like a dying Roman clutching a spear. When he spoke, he flicked at the cigar with his thumb, as if to scatter ashes across the carpet.

George Burns, Claire thought. *Alan King, maybe.*

"Me," he said. "I'm a joke guy. None'a this *observational* humor, like that guy on TV, what's his name?"

One of Conte's assistants glanced up from his legal pad. "Seinfeld."

Conte shot him a look, and he ducked his head quickly, scribbling something on his pad.

"Yeah, that's the guy." *Flick, flick.* Joey spread his hands, eyes wide. " 'Did'ya ever wonder why they make stoplights red?' " He shook his head, disgusted. "I hate that stuff."

Conte gave a tight smile. For three hours he'd sat patiently as Tangliero identified a list of corrupt cops as "Frankie the Nose, up in the Two-Five ("on account'a his big nose, see?"), or ".45 Jack." At one point, he leaned over to glance at the legal pad on which Conte's assistant scribbled the names down, divided into columns by precinct. He shook his head, pointed at the page.

"No, look't, 'Stash,' he's over at the One-Seven. And you gotta put 'Fat Sam' downtown at the Fifth, 'cause he just got transferred on this parking deal." He ran his finger down the page, nodded. "The rest looks okay."

And now, he was telling jokes. In his

hand, Conte held a sheet listing Manhattan precinct commanders, a dollar sign scribbled beside two of the names. There was a blank for the figure to be filled in. He tried hard not to look at it.

Joey Tangliero stretched, opened his eyes, pointed his cigar at Conte. "Now Frankie Luccario, he likes toilet jokes. The guy's worth forty million, easy, he runs the most powerful family in the country, he's got me down there tellin' him ca-ca jokes." He shook his head. "Go figure, right? He sits down there in Miami Beach, got a suite at the Fontainebleau with a pool right there in the living room, does all his business by pay phone. He's got these guys, all they do is drive around Miami, dropping quarters in phones so Frankie can keep in touch. Frankie never picks up a phone, he's scared to death of wiretaps. You hear from him, it's some guy standing on the corner of Collins and Sixty-first, he's gotta stop every couple minutes to put money in."

Conte glanced at one of his assistants, who made a note.

"Anyway, one day, I'm sitting in Tony's office, we're talking. The phone rings, it's for *me.* This, let me tell you, never happens. Tony, he's lookin' at me, I can see he's not happy 'bout it, but he passes me the phone. It's one'a Frankie's guys, callin' from a pay phone, I can hear the traffic. You wanna know what the guy asks me? Who's my favorite comic." He shook his head, grinned. "Frankie, he owns like ten comedy clubs, hotels, up and down the East Coast, he's got no idea who works there. It's just an investment to him. Three years, I been askin' him to let me take over one'a those places, run it right. He can't be bothered, too much trouble, movin' people around. Now this guy tells me Frankie's havin' a big party, wants to make sure everybody has a good time, so he's gonna bring in any guy I name, one night, to do his routine, right there in his apartment. Command performance, like. I don't even have to think about it. I tell the guy, 'Benny Leonard, no question.' He's like, 'Benny who?' You believe that? This guy never heard of Benny Leonard. He opened for Sinatra, Martin, used to be on Joey Bishop once a month, at least. Man's a genius, it's that simple. So Tony and me, we go down there a couple months back

139

with the books, so Frankie can check the accounts, and —"

"Wait a minute," Conte sat forward, holding up one hand. "You kept *books?*"

Joey shrugged. "Well, they weren't, like, *books.* They were, you know, like a . . . what'ya call that, on the computer?"

Conte stared at him.

"It's like a chart," Joey said. "You know, so you read it sideways, like." He reached out, took a legal pad from one of the assistants, turned it sideways on the table. "Like that."

"A spreadsheet?"

"That's it. Tony, he had some accountant over in Jersey set it up. Guy did two years in Lewisburg on a tax rap, he figured out how to put the whole thing on the computer so it looks like the coffee shop accounts. He knocks two digits off every number, gives every precinct a code name, like a supplier. So Midtown North, he calls it Maxwell House Coffee. That way, Frankie can look at the figures, decide if the profit margin's big enough on coffee, or maybe we should cut back. We're sittin' around the pool, he's saying things like, 'Pastrami's not pullin' its weight.' Tony, he knows he's gotta get more action outta pastrami." Joey held up his cigar. "Could I get a light for this thing, maybe?"

Conte gestured to his assistant. "Give him a light."

Tangliero puffed, squinting at Conte through the smoke. For a brief moment, Claire saw shrewdness in his eyes. Then he lay back on the couch.

"What was I saying?" He frowned, raised a hand, tapped his head at the temple. "Oh, right, Benny Leonard. So, like I said, Tony and I go down there, we get finished with our business, I ask Frankie, how'd you like Benny Leonard? You know what he said?" Joey stuck his lower lip out, lowered his voice into a growl. " 'That fuckin' kike, he didn't know shit about funny.' I'm sittin' there, you could'a knocked me over with a feather, I'm that surprised. I ask him, 'Frankie, what happened?' But now he's pissed off, just remembering it, he won't say another word. Later, I talk to one of his people, turns out Benny was doin' his routine, real classic stuff, all of a sudden, Frankie interrupts him, asks him does he know any jokes aren't about Jews. Benny, he's thrown by this. You can imagine. But he says, 'Yeah, sure, whatever you want.' He starts doing, you know, some other material, still classic stuff. Few minutes go by, Frankie interrupts him again, tells him this stuff ain't funny. Benny, he can see everybody in the room, they're on the floor. But he knows Frankie's the man, right? So he asks, real polite, 'What kind of thing did you have in mind?' Frankie, he gets up, takes him over in the corner, starts telling him all his favorite poo-poo jokes, wants him to tell 'em *back* to him. Benny's like, 'Hey, you *know* these jokes, what's the point?' You know what Frankie tells him? 'I like these jokes. They're funny.' So Benny has to get back up there, tell these toilet jokes like it's his material. Frankie, he's laughin' his head off. Everybody else is acting like they think it's funny." Joey sighed, shook his head. He puffed at his cigar for a moment, said — "He's playin' the Taj down in Atlantic City this week. I was figurin' on going down, before all this other stuff came up."

Conte watched him for a moment, waiting. When Tangliero glanced over at him, Conte leaned forward, said quietly —

"Perhaps you could tell me more about this accountant."

"The accountant, yeah." Joey examined the red tip of his cigar, wet one finger and moistened one side to slow the burn. "Little guy, glasses. No sense of humor. Cut off his dick, you'd have a lawyer."

Joey took a long draw on his cigar, glanced over at Conte. The Assistant U.S. Attorney for the Eastern District of New York sat very still, his face intent. For a moment, Claire wondered if he'd heard what Tangliero had said. When he spoke, his lips barely moved.

"It would help if you could give us his name."

Joey smiled. "Nah, I doubt it." He puffed at the cigar. "Tony had him waxed a few months back. Caught him squeezing the fruit. Figures, right? Once a crook, always a crook."

"Do you have information on who carried out this murder?"

Joey shook his head. "That's not how it works. One day, he's there, the next he's just gone. No more accountant. You do the math."

Conte thought for a moment. "And the books?"

"We burned 'em. Out on Frankie's terrace, in the hibachi."

"And the computer?"

Joey spread both hands. "Hey, you're asking the wrong guy. What I know from computers is, sometimes they *'go down.'* " He flicked two fingers on each hand, making little quotation marks. "I heard that, I thought, 'They can make a *machine* do that?' So how come, six years, I couldn't get my wife to do it once?"

Conte glanced at one of his assistants. "Look into it."

"We'll need a name."

Conte glanced at Tangliero, who shrugged.

"Jimmy the Jew. That's what we called him." He flicked the ash from his cigar. "Anyway, you don't need the computer. That whole thing with the charts, it was just for Frankie. He likes that stuff. You want the numbers?" He tapped his forehead with one finger. "They're all up here."

Conte slid the list of precinct captains off the table, uncapped his pen. "Then let's begin."

"Okay, sure." Joey sat up, rubbed at his face with both hands. Then he looked up at them, grinned. "Hey, you hear the one about the accountant, the lawyer, and the skunk? They all go into this bar. The bartender takes one look, says . . ."

Chapter 12

Tony Giardella caught the waitress's eye, waved her over to order another bowl of nuts and a Campari, up. Then he sat back, watched one of the lawyers at the next table catch her arm as she went past. He leaned back, smiling at her, said something Tony couldn't make out. She dug a check out of the pocket of her apron, laid it on the table, said —

"Give it a rest. Okay, Larry?"

The guy's partner laughed, and she walked away. The lawyer grinned, shook his head. Tony watched them reach for their wallets, take out a twenty each, straighten them on the edge of the table.

The first lawyer said, "Two fours."

"Three eights."

"Call."

His buddy sighed, tossed the twenty on the table. They got up: blue suits, wingtips, leather briefcases. Neither one of 'em out of their twenties, Tony guessed, but they were both losing hair on top.

Weenies, Tony thought. *They go back up to the West Side, people call 'em hot dogs.*

He glanced around the bar, all the tables full of guys like that. This kind of place killed him — dark wood, brass rails on the bar, those mirrors with the stained glass in the corners. You go out for a beer, think you're on a ship. He looked at the main bar, raised a few feet in the middle of the room, with a row of stools and a brass rail, wondered if guys ever had too much, leaned over the rail . . .

But now the cop was coming toward him, picking his way between the tables. Out of uniform now, wearing a brown sport coat, gray slacks. Like a guy who sells carpet. Tony watched him walk past without glancing at him, making a slow tour of the room. He paused at the bar, ordered a beer, and stood for a moment with his back to the bar, his eyes moving across the faces at the tables. When the bartender came back with his beer, the cop dropped a few dollars on the bar, picked up his beer, and came over to the table. He sat down, glanced at the empty bowl on the table.

"You eat all the nuts?"

"I got the waitress comin' with more." Tony leaned across the table, asked, "So? You find him?"

Marty Stoll leaned back, sipped at his beer. "Yeah, we found him."

"Where?"

Stoll smiled. "You're not gonna believe it."

"Try me."

"He's right across the street. The York. Room 907. They got the rooms on both sides, too. Room service brings the food, the guy in the next room signs the check. They don't open the door until the waiter's gone."

Tony caught himself glancing up at the entrance, like he could see Joey sitting in his room over there, watching TV, stuffing his face. "You're sure it's him?"

"I was just over there. Showed the desk clerk a picture, from when they took you guys in on the loan-sharking rap a few years back? The guy takes one look at it, says, 'Yeah, that's the guy.' They brought him in two days ago, stopped at the desk for the key, the guy was on duty." Stoll grinned. "You know what your boy asked him?"

"What?"

"He's standing there at the desk, two U.S. marshals getting him checked in, he looks at the guy behind the desk, says, 'Hey, you got magic fingers?' "

Tony sighed. "Yeah, that's Joey."

The waitress came over with more nuts, the glass of Campari on a little tray. She put it down in front of Tony, glanced over at Stoll. "You okay?"

Stoll looked at his glass, maybe two sips gone. "Take you what? Five minutes to get me another?"

The waitress gave a slight smile. "Think you can wait that long?"

Stoll grinned. "Nah, you better bring me two."

She shrugged, walked away. Stoll turned in his seat, watched her go.

"Cute kid."

"Uh huh." Tony took a sip of his Campari, glanced at his watch. "Listen, there's something else I need you to take care of for me."

Stoll came back around to look at him, his eyes hard. "We got another problem, I don't know about?"

Like that, *we* got a problem? The cop

letting him know that he saw this as a personal matter, his ass on the line, too. The guy taking close to twenty thousand bucks off him in the last couple years, bringing his cop buddies to the tit, until it seemed like half the force was feeding off them. Buying boats, fancy cars. Marty Stoll driving around in his Cadillac like the King of New York. Every cop's buddy, most popular guy on the force. Got 'em all feeding at the trough, so Tony felt like he was shoveling money out with both hands. And for what? *Not* busting his balls? Now listen to him. *We got a problem here?* Like the guy who takes your toll at the tunnel suddenly jumps in your car, says, "So, where we going?"

Fine, Tony thought. *So let him help clean it up.*

The problem being Cruz sitting on more than $3 million in some bank Tony had never heard of, down in Central America. Not taking his calls. And then, like he didn't have enough problems, he sits down to do the figures, finds out there's another million five he didn't even *know* about, went into the system and never came out. Like socks, in the fuckin' laundry.

"It's the same deal," he said, leaning in close to Stoll. "I want you to have a talk with Cruz."

Stoll sat back, looked at him. "Why tell me? You got people do that stuff, right?"

"He's got the money. We've been using him to wash it, before we paid you guys."

"And that's *my* problem?" Stoll shook his head. "Hey, what you do with the money before it gets to me, that's your business. You ask me to help on this thing with the U.S. Attorney, I figure, okay, nobody wants to see this guy in front of a grand jury, right? But this other deal? Hey, you pay me. I don't give a fuck where you wash the money. You can wash it in the toilet, wipe it on your pants. That's *your* problem, understand?"

Tony sighed, shook his head sadly. "I don't think you get the picture."

"I get the picture." Stoll leaned forward, jabbed a finger at him. "Pay me! That's the fuckin' picture."

Tony raised both hands, palms up. "I hear you, but I'm telling you, I got nothing to pay you *with*. The money, this guy's got it all tied up. I can't get at it."

"Don't give me that shit. Every hooker in my neighborhood pays off to somebody. You're tellin' me you guys can't come up with some cash, stick it in an envelope?" He shook his head. "Bullshit. Get it from Miami."

Tony leaned forward, his voice just above a whisper. "Marty, listen to me. I don't get this money back, Miami's gonna shut me down. So maybe you don't give a shit about what happens to me. I can live with that. But they close me down, that's it. You guys are back to jackin' up guys on the street. You want that?"

Stoll looked at him for a moment, then raised his beer, drained it off. "You got an address, this guy?"

Giardella took a pen from his pocket, wrote the address on a napkin, slid it across the table. Stoll picked it up, glanced at it, then looked over at him.

"This is where he *lives?*"

Giardella nodded.

Stoll shook his head, tucking the napkin in his pocket. "So how come you never figured out he was stealing from you?"

He shoved his chair in with his foot, walked away. Giardella watched him pass the waitress coming down the steps from the bar. She turned, watched him go out the door, then glanced over at the table. She came over, carrying a tray full of drinks.

"Your friend take off?"

Giardella drained his Campari, stood up, reaching for his wallet. "Yeah."

She took two beer mugs off her tray, set them on the table, smiled.

"Looks like he stiffed you on the beers."

Bobby Amondano sat in his Lincoln on East 56th Street, his eyes on the hotel entrance at the corner. As he watched, Tony Giardella came out of the bar across the street, crossed the street between two delivery trucks. He came down the sidewalk at a trot, breathing hard, looking like his stomach was running at its own pace, out of step with the rest of him. *Cut it loose,* Bobby thought, *he could dribble it inside for the score.*

He leaned across the front seat, popped the lock on the passenger door, and Tony climbed in. He put one hand on the dash, raised the other toward Bobby, trying to catch his breath. He fumbled a handkerchief out of his pocket, swiped at his forehead.

"Okay, he's in there," he gasped. He swallowed, took a few deep breaths. "Jesus, I'm outta shape."

"You been sittin' on your ass too long."

He gave a weak grin. "Only way I know how."

Bobby gave him a look. "You're a comedian now? You and Joey, the two'a you could work as a team." He took a cigar from his coat pocket, punched the dashboard lighter. "Ratso and Fatass."

Tony gave his brow a final wipe, tucked the handkerchief away. He unfolded a small scrap of paper, showed Bobby a room number scribbled on it. "I talked to the cop. They want him as bad as we do. They got a secretary down at the federal building to check the room requisitions yesterday. Last two days, they've been in half the hotels in Manhattan. I told 'em, check room service. You're looking for a guy orders cheeseburgers and Coca-Cola for breakfast."

Bobby stared at him. "They find him, or what?"

"They got him in a suite up on the ninth floor. Marshal outside the door, another one inside. Three teams, so they change every eight hours. There's a whole crew from the U.S. Attorney's office up there now, been in there with him all day."

"Little fuck's got a lot to say." The lighter popped out, and Bobby reached over and snatched it from the dashboard, puffed at his cigar until the tip glowed bright red. Then he jabbed the lighter back into the dash, blew a cloud of smoke at the hotel. He waved at it with his cigar. "I don't care how you do it, but I want that son of a bitch gone."

Tony nodded. "No problem. He's dead."

"Hey, ~~fuck~~ dead. I want him *more* than dead. You finish with him, I don't even wanna know he existed. I want him blown away so good, I come back here, all I see is a little spot of grease on the sidewalk. Shove a stick of dynamite up his ass, *then* shoot him. You get me?"

"You got my word. It's done."

Bobby looked over at him. "I got your *word?* That's supposed to make me feel better?" He jabbed a finger at the hotel.

"That little punk up there, I had his word, too, and now every word he says is tellin' me to bend over, 'cause he's gonna ride my ass right into Lewisburg. Only thing that's gonna make me happy is you blow this rat fuck into so many pieces, they'll need a mop to clean it up. *Then* I'm happy."

"You got it."

"Damn right, I got it. And I ain't gonna give it up 'cause this *stronzo* told a few jokes."

Tony held up both hands, nodding. "Go light a candle, 'cause he's dead."

"All right." Bobby reached down, started the Lincoln. "So let's go eat."

Bobby waited until he had his fork in his hand, just starting to dig into his pesce spada alla sarde, to ask him —

"You talk to Cruz yet?"

Tony, looking down at his plate, felt his appetite vanish. He sighed, laid his fork down, said —

"Nah, he won't talk to me."

"The fuck you mean, he won't talk to you?" Bobby leaned across the table, pointed his fork at him. "You got a big problem here, Tony. Only reason Frankie hasn't pasted your ass already is he's scared shitless 'bout this Tangliero thing."

Yeah, Tony thought. *I know.*

But what he said was —

"Hey, Bobby, don't worry about it. I got it under control."

"Like how?"

"I got his people workin' for me, now. All those *huckaleros* he had moving the money around. I drove over to Queens, told 'em, 'Nothing changes, 'cept you work for me now.' Turns out, they hated his guts. They were so happy, I thought they were gonna kiss me. Anyway, I know a guy works at First Union in Brooklyn, he owes some money around. I sat him down, told him, 'Listen, I'll clean up your debts, all you gotta do is set up some accounts won't trace back to me.' No problem. First of the week, we get 'em to sign some papers, they can start sticking the money in there, until we can figure out some way to wash it."

"None'a this, you gotta send it to some guy in Bolivia."

"Nah, that's done. We'll work out something in town."

Bobby stabbed at a piece of swordfish, pushed it around in the sauce. "Okay,

157

what about the other money?"

"That's a problem."

Bobby looked at him. "Are we talkin' a problem here, or a *problem?*"

"Without Cruz, we can't get at the money."

"Shit."

Tony took a breadstick from the basket on the table, bit off an end. "See, they had some kind'a civil war down there. This is like ten years back, before Cruz came up here. Anyway, now they got this human rights commission that's runnin' around, diggin' up all the bodies. You know, see if somebody violated their human rights when they shot 'em?"

"Yeah, so?"

"Cruz had the whole thing set up as a real estate deal. Bought a piece of land on the coast, like we're gonna build a resort. The money comes back to us through a construction company, labor contracts, that kind'a stuff. Worked great for three years. Only, 'bout three weeks ago, these human rights guys show up, start diggin' up bodies on the land. Cruz, you know, he used to be in the National Police down there . . ."

Bobby looked up from his swordfish, stared at him. "You gave our money to a cop?"

"We work with lots'a cops. Anyway, he told me the army down there had these death squads, cops too. You get busted, it's not like here, they got to read you your rights, you can pay some lawyer to get you off. Down there, they don't like you, they just grab you off the street, take you out in the countryside, put a bullet in you."

"These're cops?"

"Yeah, you believe it?" Tony shook his head. "Only Cruz said it was mostly political. Communists, labor guys, like that. The thing is, they gotta find places to dump the bodies, some farmer's not gonna come along, dig 'em up by accident."

"Tell me 'bout it." Bobby grinned. "You ever see that movie, guy spends all night burying a body out in a field? Some guy, he's not even dead. He's tossing dirt in there, it's landing on the guy's face. He gets it all done, the sun comes up, he sees he's like fifty feet from somebody's house. Some luck, huh?"

Tony laughed, spread his hands.

"What're ya gonna do?"

"Not dig him up, that's for damn sure!"

The waiter came over, asked if everything was satisfactory. Tony, looking down at his plate, realized he hadn't touched it yet, the guy probably worried they were gonna make him take it back. He picked up his fork, got some of the pasta, a chunk of sardine in fennel sauce, raised it to his mouth as Bobby glared at the waiter, told him —

"Hey, we're fine, okay? Now leave us the fuck alone."

The waiter looked surprised, glanced over at Tony, then turned, walked quickly away.

"Why do they do that, huh?" Bobby tucked his napkin into his collar, picked up his fork. "I hate that. You get the food, five minutes later, they're comin' over, they want to hear you tell 'em how it's the best thing you ever ate." He took a bite of swordfish, looked up at Tony. "Okay, so they buried these guys, what's that got to do with us?"

"They found some of 'em on our land."

"So?"

Tony dipped the breadstick in the fennel sauce, swirled it around. "This human rights commission? The first thing they do, they find a body, is find out who owns the land, freeze their assets."

"What? Just 'cause they found some stiffs?"

Tony shrugged. "They claim some of these big landowners were helpin' the guys on the death squads, letting 'em dump bodies on their property." He leaned over his plate, bit into the breadstick, then sat back, chewing. "I think maybe it's a shakedown. They find a body on some rich guy's land, they bring in these forensics guys with toothbrushes, dig it up one bone at a time. Meanwhile, they got the assets frozen until the case is 'resolved.' You make a donation, they'll bring in a backhoe."

"So pay 'em."

"It ain't that simple."

"Why?"

"Ask Cruz. He won't talk to me."

Bobby put his fork down, let his eyes travel slowly around the restaurant. "That ain't good enough, Tony."

"What can I do? The money's in fuckin' Guatemala."

Bobby watched him reach over, take another breadstick, dip it in the sauce.

"We're talking about three million dollars, plus. You think Frankie's gonna care?"

Tony looked at him. "I was hoping you could talk to him. Straighten it out."

"You know what he's gonna say? 'Fuck you, pay me.' " Bobby shook his head, sadly. "You gotta get this thing straightened out, Tony. It wasn't for this Joey thing, he wouldn't sit still for this. He'd send some guys up from Miami, you'd have two days to come up with the money, that's it. Joey talks to the grand jury, we're all fucked. They'll find us both out in Jersey, stuffed in the trunk of a Buick, like matched luggage." He stared at Tony, who was just sitting there, no expression, the breadstick in his hand. Bobby could see his tongue moving around in one cheek. "You hear what I'm sayin' to you?"

"Uh huh." Tony put one finger in his mouth, feeling around. He winced. "Shit."

"Now what's the matter?"

"I think I cracked a tooth."

Chapter 13

Marty Stoll, heading south on Broadway, under the George Washington Bridge, asked Moser, "Listen, you in a hurry?"

Moser shook his head. "For what? Go home to an empty house?"

"Yeah, I figured." Stoll took a quick right on 178th. "You mind if I head down to Ninety-sixth? I want to talk to a guy. Just take a minute."

He got on the Henry Hudson Parkway, going south, took it four exits to 96th Street, swung right off the exit ramp into a parking area. Almost a dozen cars were pulled up at the south end of the lot, their headlights shining on the narrow strip of grass that sloped down toward the water. Moser could see a group of men leaning against the cars, drinking beer. There were more stretched out on the grass, two of them standing up now to pitch their cans into the river, laughing. A boom box on the hood of a car played Motown. The men

— mostly white guys in their forties — sang along, moving with it. Down at the other end of the parking lot, a small group of black teenagers stood around their own cars. They had their music turned low. Every few minutes, one of them would glance over, warily.

"I love this," Stoll said, grinning. He pulled the Seville to the curb at the end of the row of cars, switched off the lights. "Most nights, you turn in here, those kids would have your car stripped before you stopped rolling. But every couple nights, you come by, there's like twenty cops drinking beer after shift change. They pull in, half the kids jump in their cars, take off. You put a unit over by the on-ramp, you could serve half a dozen bench warrants, those first five minutes."

He took the keys out of the ignition, got out. "I'll just be a couple minutes. You want a beer?"

"Nah. I'll wait here."

Stoll shrugged. "Hey, up to you." He swung the door closed, and Moser watched him walk over to the group standing by the cars. They shook hands. One of them put an arm around Stoll's neck, said something Moser couldn't make out, and they all laughed. Then Moser saw a guy he recognized from the Two-Five, Jimmy Lucas, ease off the hood of his car, reach in through the window and come out with three cans of Coors in a plastic six-pack. He held the six-pack by the empty rings, walked away down the row of cars with Stoll, toward the end of the lot. Two of the cops on the grass got up, followed them.

Moser leaned his head against the back of the seat, closed his eyes.

"You want a beer?"

"You're *asking* me?"

Jimmy Lucas peeled one of the cans out of the six-pack, handed it to Stoll. He watched Stoll open it, drain half the can off, then wipe his mouth on his sleeve.

"So how you guys doin'?"

Lucas grinned, looked over at the other cops. "Hey, how we doin'?"

The cops laughed. Behind them, the moonlight glittered on the river. From down the row of cars, the radio started playing "My Girl," and half the cops on the grass set their beers aside, sang it up at the night.

"Hey, Walt," Lucas said to one of the cops. "Show the man your bruise."

The cop set his beer down on the curb, pulled his shirt up to show a purple welt spreading between his shoulder blades. Stoll winced.

"Ah, man. That's gotta hurt. What happened?"

"Some kid pegged me with a golf ball from a roof up on 147th. Hurt like a son of a bitch. For a minute there, I thought the asshole shot me."

"Jesus. You catch him?"

The cop bent over, picked up his beer. "Nah. I went up on the roof, but he was gone. So I tore out all their cable connections."

Stoll laughed. "Get 'em where it hurts."

Lucas watched him drain the rest of the beer, pitch the can into the weeds. "So, Marty. You wired?"

Stoll glanced up, surprised. "What?"

"You wearing a wire?"

Stoll stared at him. "You're kidding, right?"

The other cops were sipping at their beers, watching. "We gotta be sure, Marty."

"Hey, fuck you! How long you guys known me?"

Lucas shook his head, sadly. "That don't mean nothing. You know that."

Stoll stood there for a moment, his mouth open. "I can't fuckin' believe this. I was the one set you guys up."

"Uh huh. That's what we're worried about."

Stoll shook his head. "No way. Fuck you."

Lucas glanced around at the other cops, sighed. Then he looked back at Stoll, his eyes calm.

"You're not leaving here till we check you."

"Or what? You gonna shoot me?"

Stoll saw Lucas stiffen. He looked around at the other cops, none of 'em saying anything, staring at him. He felt his throat tighten, swallowed. There's some things you don't say, no matter how pissed off you are. It's easy to take out a cop, you want to. Everybody knows it. Set up a drug buy, let the guy chase some kid into a dark alley. Thirty seconds, that's all it takes. You play it right, the kid goes down too. Plant the gun on him, you're a hero.

Stoll spread his hands. "Listen, I'm

sorry." He held out his arms. "You want to check me, go ahead."

Lucas nodded at a cop from the Two-Five named Ray Janes. He stepped in close, ran his hands over Stoll carefully. Then he stepped back, said —

"Open your pants."

Stoll sighed, unzipped his pants, pulled out the waistband of his under-wear so Janes could glance in. Janes nodded to Lucas, picked up his beer off the pavement, looked off at the river.

"Sorry, Marty." Lucas pulled another beer out of the six-pack, handed it to Stoll. "It's just, we're hearing bad stuff. You understand?"

"Okay. No problem." Stoll shoved his shirt into his pants, zipped them up. He picked up his beer, rubbed the cold can across the back of his neck, feeling the tightness in his muscles. "Every-body's tense. That's how it is right now."

Lucas nodded. "Look, here's the deal. We gotta start busting some of these guys. Show that we're doing the job, you know?"

Stoll took the can away from his neck, slowly. "That's a real bad idea, Jimmy."

"Yeah? So's goin' to jail."

"Look, these guys pay us, it's an in-

168

vestment. You're saying we take their money, then we go bust up their operations? Trust me, they're not gonna like that."

Ray Janes said, "Hey, who gives a fuck if they like it? They're wiseguys. We been bustin' these guys' balls their whole lives. So get used to it, already."

Stoll shook his head, raised both hands to slow them down. "Look, we all got expenses. Am I right? Me, I can put 'em off for a couple weeks, things blow over, but at some point, hey, I come up with the money or they take my car. You guys ready to go back to livin' on your paycheck now? 'Cause you start bustin' these guys, that's what you're lookin' at. You start that shit, the money's gone, man."

"What fuckin' money?" Lucas looked around at the other cops. "You guys seen any money lately?"

Stoll popped the beer open, took a sip, looking out at the river. "That's what this is about, huh?"

"Hey, it's not *my* fault their guy gets his ass in a crack," Lucas said. "They want us to take the heat, yeah, I expect to get paid for that. The money stops coming, I'm gonna cover my ass."

Stoll watched the lights flicker on the water. Like there was a whole other city in the river — the same buildings, the same cars flashing past on the road — only shifting in front of your eyes, moving with the waves. Not as clear, maybe, but cleaner, the way it had looked when he was a kid, lying on the backseat of his dad's Buick on the ride home from Jersey, watching the lights flicker across the roof of the car, like snow blowing across a road.

All gone, now.

Car note. Mortgage. Sixty-five hundred on the boat. Toss a couple thousand on top of that, betting on the fucking Mets this year. And that's not counting food, electricity, insurance, all that shit. These guys, they didn't get it. You get used to the money, you *count* on it, it's part of your life. Take it away, it's like somebody cut off your arm, tossed it on the garbage. Go learn how to live without it.

He drained the beer, pitched the can away. "I make sure you get paid, you'll shut the fuck up?"

Lucas shrugged. "Hey, none of us wants this. We liked it how it was, same as you. All we're sayin' is, they're not gonna pay us, we gotta do our jobs. If that means some'a their guys get busted, that's how it is."

Stoll glared at him. "Yeah? That's how it *is*, Jimmy?"

"It's what I'm sayin'."

Stoll looked down at the pavement. Bits of glass from broken wine bottles shining in the darkness. "Just don't do nothing till you hear from me, okay?"

Lucas reached over, draped an arm over Stoll's shoulders. "Marty, you *know* we trust you, right? It's just, I'm talking for a lotta guys here. You say we should wait, fine, I'm with you. But if the shit comes down, it's them or us. You see how that is?"

Stoll shrugged. "I got no problem with that."

Lucas grinned, squeezed his shoulders. "Hey, that's all I needed to hear."

An hour later, Moser watched Marty Stoll back the Seville across the empty street into his own driveway. It vanished into the shadow of the nineteen-foot Bayliner Sportsman that Stoll kept on a trailer next to his garage. The garage door went up, a brief shimmer of light across the boat's canvas cover, then it was gone. Moser turned, went up the front walk. On the front stoop, he found six gallons of frost-blue semigloss latex, the lid of each can stamped *Property of New York State Department of Corrections*. Moser sighed, nudged at one of the cans with his toe. He wondered if it was worth trying to explain the problem to Vinny. He could picture it, Vinny looking down at the cans, scratching at his neck.

"What, you need more time? I can talk to the guy, you want."

"It's not the money, Vinny."

"You don't like the color?"

"The color's fine."

"So what's the problem?"

"Vinny, I'm a cop. This stuff fell off a truck."

And Vinny, hands shoved in his pockets, saying, "You can't think of it as surplus?"

Moser shook his head, carried the cans into his house, lined them up along the bedroom wall. He went into the kitchen, got a beer from the refrigerator door, wandered back into the living room, stood there, drinking it. He glanced around at the bare walls, trying to remember how the room had looked before Janine moved the furniture out, the shape of his life these last few years. There was a faded rectangle on the wall where a picture had hung. He stared at it, trying to remember which picture it had been. The water lilies, maybe? Or those Matisse goldfish, the ones that always looked to him like Gladys Knight and the Pips doing "Midnight Train to Georgia" in a pitcher of water.

He stood there for a while, thinking about it. Then he gave up, took his beer into the bedroom.

When he'd met Janine, Moser had told her, "See, the thing that made me a cop is, I've got a photographic memory."

They were standing together in the kitchen of a friend's apartment, watching New Year's Eve spiral down toward midnight, Janine touching a button on his shirt, saying —

"We've met before." Her tone flirtatious, testing him to see if he'd remember.

"Yeah?"

"Six weeks ago." She bit her lip, smiled at him. "You and your partner came to my sister's house, arrested her husband for possession of stolen property."

He glanced down at her hand, pressed flat on his chest now. He remembered the bust — Jimmy Tedesco, a fence who fronted for the wiseguys, selling appliances, stereo equipment, and ladies' apparel that had fallen off trucks to discount stores over in Jersey. The guy asking them, as they snapped the cuffs on, if they needed anything for the house. Looking over his shoulder at them, grinning. Little something for the wife?

"And you want to ask me a favor, right?"

Janine smiled, shook her head. "Nah, fuck him. He's got it coming. Got a whole garage full of car stereos, my sister can't get him to buy her a new refrigerator."

"But he asked you to talk to me."

She leaned back on the counter, reached for her beer. "Sure."

"So?"

"I'm talking to you, aren't I?" Looking at him as she raised the bottle, her eyes laughing.

When midnight rolled around, they were both a little drunk, both wonder-

ing if they'd kiss without embarrass-
ment when the big moment came.
Moser, leaning on the edge of the stove,
had told her it was the details he never
forgot, little stuff. He pulled out his
wallet, handed her a dollar bill.

"Ask me the serial number."

"You memorized it before, right?"

He laughed. "Hey, go trust a cop."

He liked her smile, the way she
glanced at him from the corner of her
eye, turning slowly. He liked her faded
jeans, too — not the fashion kind, tight
across the ass, like all the other girls
at the party, but plain Levi's jeans.
Soft-looking, from lots of washing, so
you knew they felt good to the touch.

"Still, it's true about the memory,"
Moser told her, tucking the bill back
into his wallet.

Later, she tested him. Stepping out of
her jeans, even before he got the door
to his apartment locked, she touched
him, lightly, on the forehead, said —

"What's my name?"

"Why? You forget?" He bent, caught
her behind the knee, lifted her into his
arms, and headed for the bedroom. "I
have that effect on you?"

She smiled, bit his ear.

Later, as she slept, he slipped out of the bedroom, found her pants in the entryway. She kept her driver's license in a plastic holder clipped to her keys. He flicked the light on, glanced at it.

Janine.

But some things stayed with him, effortlessly, like leaves, crumpled, whipped around by the wind, still clinging to the trees in February. Tonight, wandering through the empty house, he kept thinking about Eva's room the day they'd gone to see Cruz, her things left just so, the faint scent of her perfume, like a promise in the still air. But as he thought about it, the image that kept coming into his mind was Janine, standing in the middle of their bedroom, glancing around at the empty room the way she always did before she left a place, as if she was checking to make sure she hadn't forgotten something. Her eyes taking it all in, he remembered, so you knew that what she was afraid of losing was the place itself, how it felt to be there.

He went back to the dark living room, stood there for a moment without moving. What was it, making him put that with Eva Cruz? His mind working on a problem, telling him something he couldn't make out yet.

He glanced around the room, bare except for the foldout, TV sitting on a folding chair against the wall.

Two women, he thought, *who weren't coming back.*

Chapter 14

"Okay," Conte said, passing a typed sheet to his assistant. "Let's turn to another matter."

Claire could feel his frustration growing. Seven hours last night, another four today, with a short break for lunch. The assistants looked tired, while Conte still wore that same tight-lipped expression, like the world had pissed in his coffee. He'd dressed for the occasion: a blue power-suit, double-breasted, with a pale rose tie. He had a tiny American flag pin on his lapel, which Claire guessed he wore in court, reminding the grand jury that he wasn't just a lawyer, he was the law.

She was starting to enjoy this, listening to Tangliero tell his stupid jokes, one after another, never quite finding his way back to the stuff Conte wanted to hear. She glanced over at Richter, caught him looking at her. He didn't smile, just held her gaze for a moment, then shifted his eyes over to look at

Tangliero. *Watching him,* she thought. *Deciding.* Joey seemed to avoid looking at him, just sneaking a look every now and then, like the thought of an NYPD detective hearing all this made him nervous. He kept his eyes on Conte, measuring his response, how far he could go before he had to ease off, drop some hints about payoffs, an unsolved murder, money laundering, just enough to keep the lawyer interested.

"Now, if I remember correctly," Conte was saying, sorting through a small pile of papers until he found the one he wanted, "you drew a distinction last night between what we might call 'regular' payments to law enforcement officers and special payments for services that these officers performed at Mr. Giardella's request."

"Okay, sure." Joey sipped at a cup of coffee. "Beyond-the-line-of-duty kind of thing."

Conte looked up at him. "You mentioned an incident involving a murder in Washington Heights commissioned by Mr. Amondano. According to your testimony, several officers received payments for their participation in this killing."

"Yeah, that's right. Ten thousand, split three ways. We paid some guys up at the Three-Oh, couple guys who worked a patrol car and a desk sergeant."

Claire saw Richter shift in his seat. He kept his eyes on the window, but she could tell he was listening closely. Tangliero put his feet up on the coffee table, scratched at his belly.

"We gave 'em the guy's address, his girlfriend's, couple places he stashed his rock. Few days later, Tony gets a call from the sergeant, they picked him up outside a Chinese-Cuban place on 151st, just finished his black beans and fried bananas. The cops drive him around for half an hour, then hand him over to Bobby's guys up at Fort Tryon. They shoot him in the head, dump him under the bridge, so it's outta the cops' jurisdiction. Nice paycheck for them, one less homeboy on the streets. Public service, like."

"Can you identify these officers?"

Tangliero shrugged. "I know 'em."

Conte watched Joey sip at his coffee, his eyes moving to the window.

"Does this present a problem?"

Tangliero thought about it for a moment. "Well, I don't know. These guys, I got no grudge against them. Fact is, they always treated me right. I wasn't just some wiseguy comin' 'round to pay them off. I liked 'em." He hesitated, looked up at Conte. "Look, I got no problem with talking about Tony G., 'cause I figure he's got it coming. I mean, trying to kill a guy always trusted you, way I see it, he can go fuck himself. But you gotta bear with me on this other thing, 'cause this don't come easy to me. I was brought up, a guy treats you with respect, you don't rat him out. Period. End of story. That's like a law. Without it, nothing makes sense."

Conte glanced down at the papers in his lap, frowned. "Mr. Tangliero, let me remind you that you've signed a cooperation agreement with the U.S. Attorney's office. Your participation in the federal witness protection program, and any immunity from prosecution that you may expect on these matters, is contingent upon your disclosure of all information in your possession."

Tangliero shrugged. "That's the deal, I guess. Still, everybody's got their limits."

From the corner of her eye, Claire saw

Richter get up, walk over to him. He crouched down so he was looking Tangliero in the eye. Tangliero drew back, surprised.

"You're talking about cops," Richter said softly. "That means you're in my territory. Now you can give me the names, or I'll drag your rat ass down the stairs and toss you out into the street." He gave a faint smile. "You want to take a guess how long you last out there?"

For a moment, nobody spoke. Then Tangliero wet his lips, grinned. "The sergeant's name is Jimmy Lucas. But he wasn't the guy I dealt with. The main guy was a patrolman, Marty Stoll. Lives out on the Island someplace, got a line to the Delario brothers through one of their cousins lives in the neighborhood. I forget his partner's name. Some kid, always looks the other way when the money changes hands."

He shrugged.

"Call me a survivor."

Chapter 15

The technician spun a large dial with the palm of his hand, put the videotape on fast forward. Lines scrolled down the screen, blurred the picture. Not much to see anyway, Moser thought. An elevator, a door, a potted plant.

"It's just like a bank camera," the technician told him. "Gives you date and time in the upper left. That's the numbers you see over here."

He pointed to the corner of the screen, where a series of numbers flashed past. The technician was a young black kid. He had a lightning bolt shaved into his hair above each ear.

"You guys got lucky. These security cameras are on a forty-eight-hour loop. That's the most they can hold, even with digital compression. Your partner hadn't called me yesterday, it would've taped right over the stuff you want."

They watched the screen in silence for a moment.

"We're in the morning here," the kid

said, glancing over at him. "Got a ways to go."

"Just let it roll. See what we get."

After a few moments, there was a flicker of movement in the lobby.

"Roll it back," Moser said. "Slow."

The technician spun the dial, and the tape stopped, began to rewind. He ran it back a few seconds, then let the tape run. The time display said 9:19:42. The elevator doors opened, and a man crossed the small lobby to the apartment door. He rang the buzzer, waited for a moment, then the door opened, and he stepped inside.

"Let's look at that again."

The technician spun the dial, ran it again. The man was in his mid-forties, running to fat. He wore an expensive suit, carried a gym bag. As he waited at the door, he ran a hand over his bald spot.

"Okay," said Moser. "Let's see when he comes out."

"You want a still shot?"

Moser looked at the technician. "You can do that?"

"My man, you're looking at a master of the video arts."

The kid rolled the tape back until he

got the man standing at the door, then ran it forward frame by frame until he got an image he liked. He punched a button on the keyboard with the base of his hand. The screen dimmed for a moment, the machine hummed, and a grainy print emerged from a slot under the screen. The kid peeled it off, handed it to Moser.

"Can't do much for the quality."

It was a profile shot. Moser could see where the man's nose had been broken.

"This is fine."

The kid spun the dial, ran it forward until the man came out. The timer read 9:34:23. The man crossed to the elevator, hit the button, looked down at his feet as he waited. The doors opened, and he got on.

"Not much there." The kid ran the tape until 10:13:19, when Eva Cruz emerged, followed by Eduardo. She was wearing jeans and a white shirt, carrying a backpack. Moser leaned forward, curious to see her in life. They waited for the elevator, Eduardo standing behind Eva, to one side. She looked at the floor. He looked at her. The elevator came, they got on.

"Print that," Moser said.

The kid spun the dial, ran it back slowly, got a shot of them both looking up as the doors opened. He peeled it off, handed it to Moser.

At 15:37:04, they returned. Eva waited as Eduardo produced a ring of keys, opened the door. He stood back, let her pass through, then followed her into the apartment. At 16:07:52, Cruz emerged. He was dressed in a white suit, dark shirt. Eduardo followed a moment later, carrying a briefcase. Without asking, the kid slowed the tape, found a good still, printed it. At 16:40:12, a black man got off the elevator, rang the bell.

"Whoa," Moser said, sitting up. "What's this?"

The man stood with his back to the camera, looking back at the elevator.

"Hey, I'm just guessing," the technician said. "But looks to me like a *black* man." He shook his head. *What's this?*

Moser looked at him. "You wanna back it up, run it nice and slow for me?"

"You're the detective."

Moser leaned into the screen, watching, frame by frame, as the man stepped out of the elevator, rang the bell, stood looking at the potted plant in the corner.

"What's he got in his hands?"

The door opened, and the man turned to face it. He held out a flower in a small glass vial, a card attached with a ribbon. A woman's hand appeared, took it. The door closed, and the man rang for the elevator. It came, and he got on.

"Interesting," Moser said. "Run it back."

He watched it three times, his eye on the card as the flower changed hands. Then he waved the technician on, sat back, thoughtful, as the lines scanned across the screen. At 17:12:37, Eva Cruz came out of the apartment, the flower in her hands. Moser sat forward abruptly, watched with fascination as Eva locked the door, turned not toward the elevator, but toward the *camera*. Her head filled the screen as she came toward it. Then she vanished.

"Where the fuck'd she go?"

The technician ran it back. They sat in silence, watching her disappear.

The kid looked over at him, shrugged. "I guess there's a door there."

Moser settled back into his chair, frowned.

"I guess you're right." He motioned for the kid to run it back, rested his chin on one hand, watched as Eva Cruz emerged from the apartment, turned toward the camera, moved out of sight. "Makes sense, they'd have a set of fire stairs, door on each floor. They must hide the door, paper over it. You don't know it's there, you wouldn't see it."

"Nobody told you?"

Moser was silent, staring at the empty lobby. "Run it forward."

But nothing happened. The lobby remained empty, silent, until 00:07:19, just after midnight, when Adalberto Cruz stepped off the elevator. He waited for Eduardo to unlock the apartment door, went past him into the apartment. The clock ticked off the hours, until 11:32:56 the following morning, when Eduardo went out, returned at 12:17:02 with a sack of groceries.

"Business as usual," Moser murmured. "She never came home."

At 14:43:39, Moser saw Ray Fielding step off the elevator, glance around, one eyebrow rising. He saw himself come into the picture, take the same look around, one hand rising to scratch at the back of his neck. Fielding nodded at the camera, turned to say something to him. *Smile.* Then he rang the bell.

The kid looked over at him.

"You always wear that tie?"

Back at his desk, Moser spread out the prints the kid had made for him. In the center, he put Eva Cruz, holding the flower in her left hand, slipping the keys into her jeans with her right as she turned toward the camera. *No pocketbook,* Moser thought. *She didn't plan to be gone for long.*

He opened a drawer, took out the Manhattan Yellow Pages. He flipped to the pages for florists, ran his finger down the column, checking street listings. He hit it on the first call, Flowers by George, right there on the block.

"Sure, that's Tomas. He does my deliveries," the owner told him when he passed the print across the counter. He dug through a drawer under the register, came out with a sales slip. "Here it is. One white lily. Delivered up to the fourteenth floor. Guy came in, paid extra for delivery. We have a minimum, but this guy paid the balance." The florist was a young guy, looked like he could work construction. Shaved head, T-shirt, rolled sleeves, jeans, Doc Martens. Moser took the sales slip, watched him consult a pad, then pull a length of blue tissue paper from a roll, tear it off against an edge. He laid it on the counter, selected a dozen roses from the refrigerator case behind him, clipped a half inch from the stem with a pruner that hung on a chain next to the counter.

"Can you describe this guy?"

"Hispanic, but light-skinned." He laid the roses at an angle across the middle of the paper, took some baby's breath from a vase on the counter, tucked it in among the roses. Then he folded the paper over, stapled it. "Looked like he might have some kind of skin condition. You know, has to stay out of the sun? Dark hair, but *real* pale."

"He wasn't a regular customer?"

"No, I'd remember." He leaned across the counter, tapped the photograph. "This is from a security camera, right?"

Moser nodded. The florist smiled, turned to point at a statue of Cupid holding a bow, mounted on a high shelf over the counter. He was leaning on a pink heart, naked, hand over his crotch, smiling. One foot rested on the other, casual. A video camera was mounted between his thighs.

"I got one, too."

Moser dropped the florist's security tape and the sales receipt, sealed in a plastic evidence bag, with the video technician. He went downstairs for two cups of coffee. When he got back, the kid shoved a grainy print across the desk at him.

"Register marked the time on the sales slip," he told Moser, peeling the lid off his coffee. "Took me, like, thirty seconds to find it."

Moser picked up the photograph, an overhead shot of a man passing cash across the counter, the florist reaching out to take it. The angle made it hard to figure out what the guy looked like, except that he had curly hair, cut short, and very light skin, his hand the color of paper next to the florist's Fire Island tan.

"This the best shot you could find?"

The technician looked at him over the cup. "Oh, you want a *good* one? Man, why didn't you say so?" He shook his head, went back to looking at a mail-order catalog spread out on the desk, color shots of video gear, each machine in a spotlight, like it was taking a bow. The kid flipping a page now, telling a high-end dubbing board —

"Can't fool this man. He's a de*tec*tive."

Chapter 16

Tom Richter tapped at the office door, waited until the man behind the desk spun his chair from the window, waved him in. Captain Richard DeStefano, the commanding officer of the NYPD's Internal Affairs Division, was on the phone, talking to his girlfriend.

"So what'd he say?"

DeStefano motioned Richter toward a chair, put his feet up on his desk, stared at the ceiling.

"He called *you* to say that? What's the matter, he can't talk to his father?"

He picked at a molar with the nail of one pinkie, examined the results. Then he sighed, lifted his feet off the desk, and leaned forward, rubbing at his forehead.

"Uh-huh. Look, he's got a problem at work, that's too bad. Tell him to call me, I'll see what I can do. But I don't like this trying to go through you. What's he think, I'm not gonna listen to him? He's gotta get you to yank my dick before I'll call?"

He winced, rolled his eyes at Richter.

"Honey . . . Listen, honey? It's an expression. I'm a cop, all right? We talk like that."

He listened for a moment, then nodded wearily. "Okay. Yeah, okay. I'll call him. Right. Me too. Bye."

He leaned across the desk slowly, let the receiver drop into its cradle. He looked up at Richter, shook his head.

"Unbelievable. My kid? First he wants to be a cop, so I get him on the force. Couple years go by, he decides he's sick'a being a cop, wants an office job. I say okay, pull a few strings, get him a civil service job, over at the INS. Tell me, how can you screw that up? You're working for Uncle Sam, got a nice warm office, all you gotta do is shuffle immigration papers, try not to let Fidel Castro get a green card without asking nice. How hard is that? So now he's calling up my girlfriend, for Christ's sake, telling *her* how he's in some kind of jam. Like I don't have to hear it enough from his mother." He leaned way back in his chair, sighed. "Do yourself a favor, don't have kids."

Richter smiled. He had two. DeStefano shoved some papers around on his desk, found his appointment book, made a note.

"So what's on your mind?"

"You asked me to keep you posted on the Tangliero interview."

DeStefano nodded. "So? He got anything real for us?"

Richter hesitated, looked down at the pad in his lap, wet his lips.

"Hard to say how *real* it is, yet. But he's talking about a system of payoffs involving over a hundred and fifty cops, spread out over every precinct in Manhattan." He paused, looked up at DeStefano. "Sounds like he knows what he's talking about."

DeStefano took a deep breath, let it out slow. He leaned back in his chair, gripped the arms. He twisted the chair until he could look at the window. The glass was filthy, making the afternoon sky look like concrete.

"Okay," he said, wearily. "Hit me."

The first time Dave Moser saw Rat City, he was just out of the academy, working patrol out of the 7th Precinct. His partner, Harry Bruno, an old-line street cop, had driven him across the

Brooklyn Bridge, down Henry Street, and past the old 84th Precinct house on Poplar in Brooklyn. He slowed, leaned across the front seat to nod at the entrance.

"See that?" He pointed to the iron bars covering the windows. "Everybody hates these guys. They got those bars to keep the real cops out of there, 'cause they're scared of us."

He nudged Moser, showed his yellowed teeth.

"Rat City," he said. "IAD. They bust cops. You don't have nothing to do with that place, right?"

And Moser had nodded, turning as they drove away for a last look at the building where cops spent their days destroying men like Harry Bruno, old cops who took a few bucks under the table from a gambler every couple weeks, just to look the other way when a few guys wanted to shake the dice.

"So what's the crime," Bruno would ask, tucking the envelope into his pocket. "These guys, they work hard. Their wives got the kids, they got what? Couple friends, maybe one Friday night a month they can get out, have some fun? Guy like that, he gambles 'cause he needs hope. Dice could fall his way, he gets a new transmission for his car. That seem wrong to you?"

Moser shrugged, watched the traffic. Riding patrol with Bruno was an education. Moser learned the streets, from the Mafia guys who left their Cadillacs idling as they made their collections, windows down, keys in the ignition, daring any punk to have the balls to jump in, to the ten-dollar whores who worked the corners along Canal. Bruno had a simple method for keeping the whores in line: every night, he'd make a slow pass along the line of hookers, his eyes moving over them. At some point, he'd let the car drift over to the curb, lean out the window, and wave one of the whores over. She'd climb in the back, and Bruno would pull into traffic, turning into a narrow alley behind a Korean grocer's, park the car, and open his door. For the next few minutes, Moser would lean against the rear fender, smoking, while Bruno sat in the door, murmuring quietly into the girl's ear, stroking her hair gently, reminding her to be a good girl, not to make trouble that required old Harry Bruno to come by and knock some sense into her. The girl's head bobbed up and down in his lap. The first few times, when the girls finished, they'd walk around to the back of the car, kneel down beside Moser, and calmly reach for his zipper. When he stopped them, they'd look up at him, curious. A few laughed, and soon the whores along Canal began waving to him as they drove past, calling out, "Officer Cherry, honey, look what I got!" And they'd flip their skirts up, roaring with laughter as Moser blushed, looked away.

He'd been a young cop, fresh out of the army, both fascinated and disgusted by his partner's easy style. When the cops at the precinct house picked up on it, hung a bunch of cherries on his locker, Moser saw he'd have a rough time unless he could figure out a way to win Bruno's respect. His chance came in the form of a summons from Rat City.

When Lieutenant Tom Richter first approached Moser, in a Greek diner on the Upper West Side, he'd simply stopped by Moser's table, stuck out his hand, and said —

"Hey, you're Moser, right? They got a

name for you down at the Eight-Four, don't they? Officer Cherry."

Moser, shaking his hand, had felt his heart sink. "Jesus. It's all over, huh?"

"Like shit." Richter slid into the booth, waved the waitress over with coffee. "I'm Tom Richter. From IAD."

Moser examined his coffee, then looked up at Richter, squinting through the smoke from his cigarette. Moser shook his head.

"I got nothing to say to you people."

Richter shrugged. "I hear that a lot." He waited while the waitress poured his coffee, gave her a smile.

"Fact is," he said, reaching for the cream, "you could get a name just for having coffee with me."

Moser drained his cup. "I was just leaving."

"Suit yourself." Richter lifted his cup so the steam rose before his eyes. He watched Moser reach for his check. "But if you're smart, you'll stick around, hear what I have to say."

Something in his tone made Moser pause, a weariness, as if Richter had seen too many cops walk away, missing the one chance that would be offered them. Moser left the check on the table.

"I'm listening."

"You're a rookie," Richter said. "Word is, you're still cherry." He smiled. "That must take some doing, teamed up with Harry Bruno."

Moser shook his head. "I'm not gonna talk about my partner."

"Oh?" Richter frowned. "That's funny, 'cause he's talking about you."

For a moment, Moser didn't move. He stared at Richter, watching his eyes glance down at his coffee, avoiding Moser's gaze. Even at that moment, Moser had to admire his technique. Move in, then back away. Don't let the suspect feel threatened, even as he feels the noose drawing tight.

"Go on," Moser said.

Now Richter's eyes came up, examined him closely. Then he nodded slightly, gave a thin smile.

"One of the funny things 'bout being a cop," he said, lifting his coffee, "you learn nothing is what it seems. Guy works on Wall Street, drives a fancy car, wears a nice suit, turns out he's a crackhead. You meet a nice girl in a bar, schoolteacher, kind of girl you want to take home to meet your dad. By the end of the night, you gotta bust her for trying to sell you a half kilo she's got in the closet, next to the shoes. Mirror land. We're through the looking glass here." He reached in his pocket, drew out a pack of cigarettes, shook one out of the pack. He stuffed it in his mouth, reached for the matches, then hesitated. He frowned, took the cigarette between his fingers, looked at it. With a sigh, he shook his head, slid it back in the pack. "I'm trying to quit. My wife, she hates it."

"You always do what she says?"

Richter grinned. "Hey, I'm IAD. We're the Boy Scouts, right?"

Moser caught the waitress's eye, gestured to his empty cup. "What is it you're trying to sell me?"

"Harry Bruno is one of our field associates."

"Bullshit."

Richter shrugged. "Think what you want. One of the things he does for us is check out rookies. Every couple months, we see he gets a new partner, fresh out of the Academy. Harry's job is to act like a shit, which happens to be one of Harry's real talents. A couple weeks with him, and the kid's learned all the ways to get dirty on the job. If the kid seems interested, we move him on, try to make sure he gets a real hardass for a couple years. A clean marine type, busts his balls for every free cup of coffee." Richter smiled, reached across the table, picked up Moser's check. "Lemme get this."

Moser let his eyes wander around the restaurant. "Fine with me."

Richter gave a laugh, slipped the check under his coffee cup. "Every now and then, we find a guy like you. Officer Cherry. Maybe he's just a guy with a strong sense of personal hygiene, doesn't care to have his pole waxed by some hooker every couple nights, but he'll take cash from the pimp. We let Harry try him out. Bruno pockets a few envelopes, the kid starts getting hungry, too. Only he doesn't know Harry's passing those envelopes off to us every night. Got a conscience as clear as Gandhi's piss."

Moser stubbed out his cigarette. "Except for the occasional blow job down on Canal."

Richter raised both hands. "Hey, he's got a role to play. Happens he's a method actor."

"You don't get complaints about him?"

"We got a file for that kind'a stuff."

Moser thought about that for a minute. Richter watched him slowly tear a napkin into long strips. Finally, he looked up. "What's this got to do with me?"

Richter sat back, smiled. "According to Harry, you're the real thing. An honest cop. Harry comes across one like you, it rings the bells over on Poplar Street."

"Rat City."

"That's what they call it. I've heard worse."

Moser nodded, rubbed at the sore spot on his neck, just above the collarbone, where a drag queen on a three-day drunk had sunk a fingernail into his flesh as they shoved her into the squad car the night before.

"You asking me to work for IAD?"

Richter nodded. "That's the general direction of this conversation, yeah."

"I can't bust cops."

"Hey, I know how you feel. I been there." Richter picked up his spoon, rubbed at it lightly with two fingers. "You're up against the blue wall, don't want to lose all your friends." He scowled, his voice taking on Harry

Bruno's gravelly rasp. "In this life, kid, all you got is friends. Man's got friends, he knows who he is. You keep to the program, don't look too close at what ain't your business, you'll be okay. Let go'a that, you're out. And it's crazy out there, kid. Nothing makes sense." He grinned. "Harry give you that routine yet?"

Moser smiled. "Last week."

Richter spread his hands. "There you go. So let me ask you a question. Did you know we exonerate on eighty percent of our cases? It's true. We get about two thousand reports a year, maybe twenty percent go to administrative hearing. Most cops don't know that. They hear IAD, they think we're there just to bust their balls. It's not an easy life, I can tell you that from experience."

"You're breakin' my heart."

Richter looked up at him, smiled slowly. "Tough, huh?" He peeled a match off the book, stuck it between his teeth. Moser watched the tip jump around when he talked. "You gotta work on that, Dave. The hard-guy bit. It doesn't match your face."

"Gimme time."

"That's exactly what I'm trying to do."

Moser thought about that for a moment. He wondered what Richter saw when he looked at him. Rookie cop, early twenties. Kind of cop who still gets excited when the lights go on, his hands gripping the dashboard as the traffic parts before them. A kid, likes the way girls look at him in a bar when he tells 'em he's a cop, the surprise in their eyes. Figuring him for a teacher maybe, or a lawyer. Who takes a guy named Moser for a cop?

Now, looking across the table at Richter, Moser tried to imagine what the cops saw. What's a kid like that — a college boy, a Jew — got to lose by turning rat? Not like he was going to join the Sons of Eire, play the pipes at PBA picnics. The most he could expect from the beat cops was acceptance; he wants friends, he's gonna have to look somewhere else, among the outcasts, maybe, where your name meant less than what they saw in your heart.

"You guys got a profile," he said to Richter. "Must fit me like a glove."

Richter shrugged. "You ever had a pair of gloves that fit? Me, I always feel like if I can't pick my change up off the bar, I'm wearing the wrong pair. So, I don't wear 'em."

"You know what I mean."

"Sure. And, if you want the truth, we do have a profile. Looks a lot like you."

Moser looked out the window. Across the street, a woman in a business suit and sneakers was trying to flag down a cab. Behind her, two guys from the pizza joint were leaning in the doorway, checking out her legs.

"What happens if I say no?"

Richter took the match from between his teeth, tossed it into an ashtray. "You go back in the rotation. We get you a new partner. Harry goes to work on someone else."

"How do you know I won't spread the word on Harry?"

Richter laughed. "Harry Bruno, working for IAD? Who'd believe you? The guy's so dirty, he's a legend. He invented some of the scams. Anyway, we'd know where it came from. Anything happens to Harry, I'd come down to the station myself and kick your ass into the street."

"Just wondered."

Richter leaned forward, aimed a finger across the table at Moser. "Fact is, you're with us. Doesn't matter if you agree or not. Any cop who doesn't take, he's on our side. Maybe he looks the other way, says all the right things in the locker room about guys like me, but that doesn't mean a thing. There's clean and there's dirty. You pick your side of the wall."

Moser kept his eyes on the window. "I got other plans. I want to work homicide."

Richter smiled, drained his coffee cup. "You like the movies, huh? Tough cop getting out of his car at the murder scene, flashing his badge. Kojak." He glanced at the check, tossed a few bucks on the table. "Way I see it, you keep the cops clean, the whole city runs better. But, hey, I can respect your position. You got ambitions, they don't include rat work. Keep your nose clean, we'll have a chat in a few years."

Richter slid out of the booth, looked down at him. "It's tough out there, Dave."

"I can handle it."

"I hope so." He slipped a card out of his wallet, tossed it on the table. "You get in too deep, gimme a call."

Moser watched him walk away, raising a hand to the waitress on his way out the door. That night, when Moser showed up for duty, Harry Bruno was perched on the edge of a desk in the squad room, telling a young cop how he'd learned to tell a hooker from a drag queen, *the hard way.* In the car, he laughed about the kid's expression, his face sick with disgust, like he'd just grabbed a power line with both hands, *tzzzz,* when he got to the part where . . .

Moser listened, smiling, while Harry made his rounds, stuffing the envelopes into his pocket in the car. Within a week, Moser was transferred to Midtown North.

Now, sitting in a coffee shop on upper Broadway, watching steam curl up off his cup, it all seemed so distant, another life. Or like the way you imagine night on a bright afternoon, the world seeming to hold its shadows like a secret it could tell you. Just wait awhile, and it all comes back.

One phone call. Moser, at his desk, a cup of stale squad room coffee in front of him, had picked up the phone, heard a voice say —

"Dave Moser?"

"Yeah. Who's this?"

"Tom Richter. You remember me?"

It took a minute, but then Moser said, cautious, "Yeah, I remember you."

He heard Richter laugh, the sound of traffic in the background. "Listen, what do you say we grab a cup of coffee, have a talk?"

"I got a choice?"

A bus roared past, and Richter waited a moment, then said, "Not really."

Moser glanced down at the paperwork on his desk, sighed. "Okay, where?"

"I'll meet you at the Greek place."

"Which Greek place? We're talking ten or fifteen, this neighborhood alone."

"You remember the place we met, a few years back?"

"Athena. Over on Broadway, Eighty-eighth."

"That's the one."

"They went out. They got a new place in there now. Tuscany. They serve roasted pears on everything. Order a burger at lunch, they put roasted pears on it. They got tables out front, under an awning."

"On Broadway?"

"Go figure."

"You pay extra for the bus fumes?"

"Yeah, but the pigeon shit's free. Me,

I want to eat outside, I'll go down to Battery Park, get a knish off a cart."

"So name a place."

"Three blocks up, on Ninety-first, there's a coffee shop. I forget the name."

"An hour?"

"Fine."

"Tell me something. How'd the Greeks ever get into this business, huh? Coffee shops. You ever had good coffee, one of these places? I mean, who drinks Greek coffee. Okay, if you're on Corfu, maybe. But these guys?" He shook his head. "It's the Colombians should have coffee shops, right? Or the French. They got coffee."

Richter sipped at his coffee, grimaced, shoved it aside. "And this menu? It's like the Brooklyn phone book, for Christ's sake. I mean, look at this." He flipped through the pages, the plastic scraping the edge of the table. "Italian food, Jewish food, seafood. Look't, they even got enchiladas. I want enchiladas, I'm gonna go to a *Greek* restaurant?"

The waiter came over, flipped Moser's cup over on the saucer, filled it with coffee. They ordered — scrambled eggs, toast, fried potatoes. The waiter scribbled it on a pad, dropped it in a pocket on his apron. He took their menus, slid them into a slot on the edge of the booth. Moser took a sip of his coffee, looked up at Richter.

"So?"

Richter sat back, lit a cigarette. "You live across the street from Marty Stoll, right?"

Ah, shit.

"I'm not gonna talk to you about Marty."

Richter nodded, slowly. "Okay. How about I talk to you?"

Moser was silent for a moment, then he shrugged. "Do what you want."

"We got Stoll's name from an informant," Richter said, picking up his coffee. "He's been implicated in a series of payoffs from some OCFs in midtown, including a contract hit."

"Some what?"

Richter smiled. "Organized crime figures. You hang around with the feds, you start talking like 'em."

Moser sipped at his coffee. "So why tell me?"

"You live across the street from him. Last couple weeks, you been riding in

211

to work together. Maybe he talks to you."

"About contract hits?"

"Hey, you'd be surprised. We busted a guy in narco a couple years back for ripping off dealers. Turned out he told his poker buddies all about it." Richter smiled. "One of 'em was a Transit cop, got sick of the guy braggin' about how much he'd stolen."

"Marty plays the radio."

Richter raised both hands, palms out. "Okay, I won't push." He took a card out of his shirt pocket, slid it across the table, facedown. "But you hear anything, give me a call."

Moser looked down at the card lying in front of him, then up at Richter. He got up, dropped his napkin on the card.

"Yeah, right."

When he left the coffee shop, Moser stopped at a pay phone, called in for messages. He waited while Fielding checked his desk, heard his chair squeak when he settled in, picked up the phone.

"Dave? Some guy named Vinny called. Says he's got a price on the part, but wants to know if he should try to find it cheaper. That make sense?"

"Yeah." Moser closed his eyes, let his head rest against the cool glass of the phone booth. "He calls back, tell him I said to go ahead."

"And do what? Buy it, or look around?"

Moser opened his eyes, looked out at the traffic rushing past. Someone had scratched the word *RICK* into the glass; someone else had changed it to *PRICK* with a ballpoint pen.

"Buy it." Moser rubbed at the ink with his thumb, smearing it. "Anything else?"

"Marty Stoll. Call him if you need a ride home."

Moser stared out at the traffic. "That's it?"

"What can I say? You're a popular guy."

Chapter 17

"Check this guy out."

Moser glanced up from the coffee cups he was bracing between his feet, peered through the windshield. Fielding pointed across the intersection. At the corner of Broadway and 168th Street, an elderly black man stepped into the early morning traffic, brandishing a shovel. His hair was white, falling in tight curls below his shoulders, and his silver beard hung in braids down his chest. He was wearing a green bathrobe.

"Oh, for Christ's sake." Moser laughed, shook his head. "Looks like Jeremiah in the wilderness."

"You gotta respect a beard like that."

The old man raised the shovel over his head, traffic screeching to a halt around him. He stood, motionless, as the drivers leaned on their horns. A truck driver leaned out his window, gesturing at him, shouting over the noise. A crowd began to form on the sidewalk. A very fat woman stepped into the street, waving him back to the sidewalk, but the old man gave the shovel a threatening shake and she backed away.

Moser started to get out. Fielding caught his arm.

"Let the uniforms handle it."

The old guy threw his head back, swung his shovel at the sky. He swayed back and forth, slowly. Over the crackle of the radio, Moser could hear him singing. Then he arched his back, brought the shovel down against the pavement, sparks flying.

"So, what's your guess," Moser said. "Social commentary or buried treasure?"

Fielding smiled. "Better be buried deep, in this neighborhood."

"Could be after the IRT. Stake a claim to the Broadway local."

"Let him have it."

In the distance, a siren wailed. The old man bent down, caught the shovel near the blade, and swung it up over his shoulders again, brought it crashing down against the street again. He put one bare foot on the blade, trying to wedge up the pavement. Fielding started the car.

"Tear it up, buddy. Root and branch."

He got one tire up on the sidewalk and edged past the stopped traffic, made a right. At the end of the block, he made a left, headed uptown. Near the east end of Dyckman, at the edge of Fort Tryon Park, two uniformed cops were standing near the bushes, smoking.

Fielding got out, walked over to the cops. Moser ducked under the crime scene tape, parted the bushes, looked in. A girl was curled up on her side like a child, her eyes open. She was young, maybe fifteen. She looked Hispanic, long black hair, olive skin. She was dressed in a tiny skirt, a shirt tied beneath her breasts, high heels. Her neck was twisted at an odd angle, and one of her front teeth was broken off at the root. She had blood on her lip.

He heard Fielding come up behind him, stepped back. Fielding glanced in. "Jogger found her, 'bout six-thirty this morning."

"You see the way her legs are bent?"

"On her knees."

Moser nodded. "Your basic grab-and-twist."

A van from the Medical Examiner's office pulled up. Ruben got out, carrying his medical bag. He ducked under the tape, came down the slight incline from the road.

"Detectives." He looked at Moser, nodded. "What's the story?"

"Girl in the bushes." Moser took a couple steps back. "We'll want a throat swab."

Ruben looked in, shrugged. "Hooker. You won't get anything admissible. Too many samples. She could'a done five guys last night."

Fielding looked at Moser, cleared his throat. "Just get us the swab."

Ruben tugged on a pair of latex gloves, grabbed a branch, dropped to his knees. "Fine. But it's pretty pointless."

Moser squatted beside him, holding the branch back. "Larry, we'd like to know if this guy came before or after he killed her. If it's the killing he gets off on, you'll find it on her clothes, the bush, maybe. Think you can check that for us?"

Ruben glanced up at him. "Sure, Dave." He reached down, felt the girl's neck. "How's everything?"

"Okay. You?"

"Can't complain." He looked up at Moser, the girl's head rolling slightly with the motion of his hands.

Moser let the branch fall back, got up. "I'm gonna look around. Let me know when you're ready to turn her, okay?"

"Sure thing."

Moser walked over to where Fielding was pushing the grass aside with his foot, bending over to pick up a cigarette butt. He took an evidence bag out of his pocket, tossed it in. "Fuckin' Ruben."

"I explained it to him."

"Terrific."

"He's all right, Ray."

"I'm glad you think so." Ray bent, picked up a cap from a beer bottle, examined it, then tossed it under the tape. " 'Cause I'm gonna let you deal with him from now on. I'm about ready to get in his face."

"Fine. I'll handle it."

Ray kicked at the grass. "You see that girl? She's a baby."

"That's how it is in the big city, Ray."

"Tell me." He shook his head. "I don't know, sometimes this job . . ." He bent down, picked up a crushed beer can, looked at it, then bagged it. "I see a girl like that, makes me think about Darnell."

"You can't do that, Ray."

"She's twelve, Dave. The other day, I heard her on the phone, talkin' to one of her girlfriends about boys. Blew my mind. Couple years, she'll be going out." He glanced over at the girl's body, Ruben hunched over it. He had the scalpel out, making a cut in her side, just above the hip. He took out a thermometer, attached it to a long probe, slid it into her. Fielding shook his head. "I've seen too many of these girls, you know? Scares the shit outta me."

"This girl was a whore."

"Still somebody's kid." He looked up at the sky, took a deep breath. "I ever tell you about the bird feeder?"

"No."

"When we bought the house, the old owner left this bird feeder hanging in the tree at the corner of the yard. You know the one."

Moser nodded.

"Darnell was about three, then. So I figured we'd put some seed in the feeder, she could watch the birds. One Saturday, I take her down to the pet store, and we got some seed. Special

219

kind, for wild birds. I get the ladder out of the basement, put it up against the tree, climb on up there with this bag of seed. Darnell, she's standing down at the bottom, all excited, 'cause we said this was gonna be her thing, she should watch and let me know when it needed filling. Anyway, I get up there, it's this wooden bird feeder, the roof lifts off to put the seed in. So I lift the lid, and I see there's some kinda crud wedged down in there. I figure, okay, I gotta take it down, we'll hose it out. But when I start to lift this thing off the branch, man, all these bugs started pouring out. Like thousands of 'em, ugly motherfuckers. Crawling up my hand, jumping down on the ladder. I'm like, *shit!* I drop the bird feeder, it lands maybe two inches from Darnell, all these bugs spilling out. Turns out there's a dead bird in there, real bug banquet. Darnell, she goes screaming into the house, can't sleep for a week. She keeps crying out during the night, scared the bugs are gonna get her. Felicia decides I should sit down and explain to her about the bugs, the dead bird, tell her, honestly, what it's all about. I'm thinking, no *fuckin'* way I'm telling my daughter about death at three years old, right? So I make up some stupid shit about how this is like a bug cleaning service, and they've come to get the place ready for the birds. You know, one of those Dad stories."

"She buy it?"

"Not a chance. She looks up at me, these big eyes, asks me, 'Daddy, are the bugs gonna get me?' I'm like, 'No, baby. No way.' But the whole time, I'm thinking about all these fucking bodies we see out here, maggots and shit crawling out of 'em, and in the back of my head, there's this voice, it's saying, *Yeah, baby. Someday, they gonna get you too.*" He looked away. "This job, man, it'll steal your soul."

Moser let his eyes wander up toward the little crowd of spectators gathering along the tape on Dyckman. "How 'bout I take this one, Ray?"

Fielding shook his head. "I'm fine. Just too many dead people, you know? After a while, it's like there's no room left in your heart." He glanced down at where the girl lay. "So you know what I say, Dave?"

"What?"

"I say fuck 'em. Fuck 'em for dying on my shift. Fuck 'em, they're so careless that I gotta come out here, eight o'clock in the morning, clean up after their ass. You hear me?"

Moser laughed. "Yeah, I hear ya, Ray. Fuck 'em."

Fielding turned back to the stretch of weeds, swinging his foot. "Gotta carry them outta here like so much garbage, spend my morning digging through these *fucking* weeds, so I can send some other asshole upstate for, what? Ten years on a dead whore? Fuck 'em both."

"Okay, Ray."

Ray stopped kicking the weeds, squatted down to examine something on the ground. "Well, what have we here?"

Moser used his foot to shove a clump of weeds aside, saw a small plastic Baggie, rolled tight, with a rubber band around it. Inside, he could see traces of white powder.

Ray smiled. "You know what that is, Dave?"

"I can guess."

Ray shook his head. "Nah, you're wrong." He took out his handkerchief, picked it up, held it up for Moser to see.

"That's an answer. Something you can tell yourself, keep the bugs away." He smiled. "Meantime, I'm gonna put it in this evidence bag, take it back to the squad room, do the two hours of paperwork it takes to convince a judge it means something. How's that sound?"

"You feeling better, Ray?"

Fielding shrugged. "Just need an angle. Like with Darnell. If Daddy can explain it, she don't need to worry 'bout it." He walked up the hill to the car, popped the trunk, took out a cardboard box and a black marker. He scribbled over the date on the side of the box, wrote in a new one. Then he dropped the evidence bag in the box, carried it back down the hill to Moser. He nodded at the bush, where Ruben worked on the girl's body. "One piece of evidence, that stops being a dead whore. You know what she is now?"

"Bug banquet?"

Fielding gave him a look. "She's a victim, Dave. One piece of evidence. That's all it takes."

Ruben looked up from the body, waved them over. "Gentlemen? You'll wanna see this."

They went over, pushed the branches

back. Ruben had the girl's shirt unbuttoned. He lifted the left side, exposing her small breast. She had a tattoo just below the collar bone: a heart with a crack, a tiny drop of blood clinging to the edge, ready to drop. In neat script below the heart was written, *Corazón.*

"Looks like someone broke this girl's heart."

Chapter 18

"Go get the car."

Miiko was sitting in the entry hall room of Cruz's apartment, leafing through a copy of *Forbes.* He glanced up, saw Eduardo walk past from the kitchen, a glass of Scotch in his hand, carrying it to Cruz's study. He closed the door behind him.

Miiko stared after him. "What?"

For a moment, he wondered if he'd imagined it. Six weeks, riding around with the guy, he never says a word. Miiko'd begun to wonder if he *could* talk, maybe'd got his tongue pulled out, one'a those things they do to each other in wars down there. But then one night they'd stopped at a Chinese-Cuban place up on Amsterdam, ordered black beans and rice, and he'd watched Eduardo raising the fork to his mouth, caught a glimpse of his tongue in there. No scars on his throat, like they'd cut out his larynx. Nothing wrong with his head, as far as Miiko could see, once you get past the fact he likes to kill people.

Now, just like that, he tells him, *Go get the car.* Not even that much of an accent. Like he'd lived here all his life.

Miiko sighed, tossed the magazine on the entry table, where Cruz kept his mail. He got up from the chair, went out to call the elevator. Nodded at the operator as he got on, the guy shifting his eyes away. *Okay, fuck you, too, buddy.* The guy into his job, always shining up the brass in the elevator, checkin' his uniform in the mirrors. The guy thinking he looked like a marine in that uniform, all that gold braid. Miiko expected to come in one day, find him wearing a sword.

Miiko leaned against the back wall of the elevator, whistling, hands on the shiny brass railing as they descended to the lobby, give the guy something to clean. When the door opened, he brushed past the operator, said —

"At ease, Sarge."

He went out the front door, turned right, walked up three blocks to 77th, headed east two blocks to the parking garage. For the last few days he'd been driving a gray Acura Integra he'd picked

226

up out by the airport, switching the plates in the garage every day before he drove it out. He liked the car, enjoyed driving it all over the city, feeling how it handled on different kinds of road. All week, Cruz'd had them running out to Queens, then back to midtown, up to the Bronx, all over. Miiko getting sick of it, except for the car. Shit, so take off, *keep* the fuckin' car. But still, he was curious. Wondering where they expected a payoff, this kind of job.

There had to be a payoff. It only made sense, right? You gotta have a *reason*, go 'round killing people like that. Eduardo kept a list of names folded in his shirt pocket. Spanish names, every one of 'em had accents, little squiggles over the letters, like heat rising off 'em.

Miiko, sneaking a look over Eduardo's shoulder, had counted twenty-three names. Seven of 'em had a single line drawn through them, the letters *L.A.* written neatly in the margin. Two more had been checked off. *Joaquin Yano Benitez.* And two names below, *Eva Solana Cruz.*

Just like that, Miiko thought, smiling.

But then, between those last two names, right there in Cruz's neat handwriting, Miiko saw the name *Adalberto Cruz*. For a moment, he wanted to turn to Eduardo, ask, *Hey, why'd he put himself on the list?* Then he pictured Eduardo looking over at him, those blank eyes, and he bit his tongue. Better to wait and see.

He'd been waiting for six weeks, ever since Cruz spotted him out at Liquid Assets, loading flats of beer onto a truck. He'd been talking with Jaime, another Guatemalan guy, never said a word. Tellin' him how his parole officer liked to play it real hard-ass, made him piss in a cup every time he went in, right up to the end of his probation. He'd looked up, saw him standing in the door to the warehouse, watching him. Adalberto Cruz, the *man.*

Cruz walked over, said something to Jaime in Spanish that made him put down his beer flat, walk away. Miiko let the hand truck stacked with beer down slowly, turned to lean an elbow on it.

"You are Reyes," Cruz said, his face expressionless.

"Uh huh." Miiko stripped off his work gloves, tucked them into his jacket pocket, thinking — *Here it comes.*

"You have served time in prison?"

Miiko rubbed at his jaw. "Eighteen months. I finished my probation last month."

"What were you arrested for?"

Miiko hesitated, then shrugged. "Possession with intent."

"You sell drugs?"

"Used to. But I'm clean now. I load trucks, that's it."

Cruz looked at him for a moment, silent. Then he nodded once, turned away. Two days later, Miiko was called into the manager's office. Cruz was seated behind the desk, signing checks. Javes, the manager, stood nearby, hands in his pockets.

"You wanted to see me?"

Cruz closed the checkbook, stood up. "You will come with me. I have other work for you."

Now, walking into the garage, taking the stairs up to the fourth floor, he thought, *Six weeks of this shit. So what's the payoff?*

He walked up the row of cars, past the Integra, found a blue Camry backed into a spot near the end of the aisle. *Not a bad car, you were in a hurry.* He walked around the back, squatted down in front of the plate, took a Swiss army knife from his pocket, folded out the screwdriver blade. The plate had a crease in it, as if the car's driver had bent it against a curb, then tried to fold it straight. Miiko hesitated a moment, then shrugged. What did he care, it was bent. Cops wouldn't stop you for that, long as they can see you got a valid plate, doesn't come up on their computers.

He reached in with the knife, twisted the screws loose. The lower ones were rusted, and he had to lean his shoulder against the car's hood, get some elbow into it, before they came free. *Jesus! Stop at a hardware store, pick up some oil,* he thought, *you're gonna change the plates every day.*

He took the plate off, lined the screws up on the bumper, walked back over to the Acura. He'd backed it in the night before, next to a pillar, thought he'd left enough room to crouch down in there. But now, coming around behind the car, he realized he'd have to pull it forward a few inches. He leaned the plate against the pillar, walked around to the driver's side, got in, the radio coming on, loud, when he started the car. Miiko grinned, reaching over to shut it off. The only time he could use the fancy Blaupunkt sound system, after he'd dropped Eduardo off at Cruz's place, taking the car six blocks, all the one-way streets in this neighborhood, to park it. He put the car in gear, let it roll forward a few feet, shut it off. Then he grabbed the screwdriver off the dash, got out, went around back. Crouched down, got the old plate off, carried it back over to the Toyota, put it on. Leaving the screws one twist from tight, like they told you. Shaking his head as he walked back to the Acura. *Guy should read his manual sometime.*

He walked around behind the Acura, stopped, looking at the base of the pillar. The plate wasn't there. He glanced under the car, walked up to look in the passenger window, thinking maybe he took it in with him when he moved the car. Nope. He glanced back over at the Toyota. He couldn't be *that* stupid, right?

Nah, no way. He'd walked over there, the old plate in his left hand, the screwdriver in his right, flipping it up into his palm, the belt ring on his finger.

So what the fuck?

He looked down at the Acura, thinking, *Okay, go get another one.* Except he wouldn't have one to trade for it, so the guy'd notice pretty quick, report his plate stolen. The cops put the number on the computer, you could get pulled over. Unless he switched a couple, so if the guy who ends up without a plate calls it in, they pull over some other guy, not you. Or, even better, switch three. That way, if they stop the second guy . . .

He was standing there thinking about it, so he didn't hear Marty Stoll coming up behind him, almost jumped out of his skin when he said —

"Hey, you lose something?"

"Jesus!" Miiko leaned against the car, one hand coming up to his chest. "You scared the fuck outta me."

Coming up on him, the way cops like to do, so you know they've got you, taking their time, enjoying it, watching you try to squirm out of it. Stoll grinned, reached over, laid the license plate on the trunk.

"Cruz'll be pissed, you don't get back with the car."

Miiko straightened, picked up the license plate. "Fuck him." He squatted down behind the car, took one of the screws off the bumper, and used the knife blade to twist it tight. "I'm gettin' real sick'a this deal, I can tell you that."

Stoll frowned. "Yeah? You find the money?"

Miiko paused, looked up at him. Hair starting to go thin on top — a thing, Miiko had learned, always made a cop mean, they catch some young guy havin' a good time. Cheap brown sport coat, a bulge at the hip where his gun rode. Like getting busted wasn't bad enough, they had to make you think about living in Jersey.

"Did I *say* I found the money?"

"So what're we talkin' about here?"

Miiko turned back to the license plate, tightened the last two screws. "Cruz told the Italians there's nothing he can do. The money's stuck in a bank down in Guatemala. They froze the assets, some legal thing."

"You believe that?"

He shrugged. "Your boy Tony don't. He keeps calling up, threatening him."

Stoll stared at him. "He thinks the guy's stealing from him, he calls him on the *telephone?*" He laughed, shook his head. "Jesus. Some fuckin' mob-ster."

"What's he gonna do? Cruz stays in that apartment all day, no way to get at him. Anyway, it's a corporate ac-count, and Cruz signed the papers. They go whack him, that money's fuckin' gone, man."

"Don't worry 'bout what's in the ac-count," Stoll said. "That's their problem. You find out who was moving the money on this end. Giardella just raised his outstanding balance to four and a half. That means there's some serious money still in the system. We find that, I'm happy."

Miiko stood up, folded the knife closed, dropped it into his pocket. "Like old times, huh?"

"How you figure?"

Miiko grinned. "You remember how we set up those guys from 148th Street? Man, they saw you pull up in that squad car, I thought they'd run half-way back to Santo Domingo. I tell 'em I can fix the problem, they wanted to kiss me. Six hundred a week to buy a cop? Hey, they spend that on sneakers. Next thing they know, they got six more cops on the payroll. Now they're working for *you*. First time they miss a payment, you come in, bust 'em, grab all the cash, hand 'em over to the INS. Two days later, they're back on the street in Santo Domingo, tryin' to explain to the guys who run the gang what happened to all the money. We split the cash, start lookin' for the next crew to bust." He shook his head. "Man, that was a sweet deal."

Stoll looked across the row of cars toward the stairs. *Yeah, right.* A sweet deal, until one of the dealers they'd busted got angry, told his lawyer to fuck the plea bargain, get on the phone to IAD. A few days later, Miiko was sitting in a cell over in Riker's, playing it stupid while a pair of IAD guys threw questions at him about payoffs to patrol officers. But they'd screwed up, arrested Miiko on the expectation that he'd turn for them, give 'em the cops in exchange for a suspended sentence. Instead, Miiko sat tight, did eighteen months on the drug charge, came out expecting to be paid for his time. By then, Stoll had become bored by his arrangement with Tony Giardella, his interest shifting to the man working the cash flow behind the scenes. Adalberto Cruz.

He'd done some research, found an employee with a liquor distributor called Liquid Assets, Inc., with two recent priors for cocaine possession, spent three Friday nights following as he made the rounds of Hispanic bars out in Queens before he caught him making a buy. He chased him down, put him in the backseat of his Seville, had a long talk with him about his future if Cruz became aware of his personal habits. The man's face went pale at Cruz's name, and he broke down in tears. Stoll reaching across the front seat to pat his shoulder, telling him, quietly, not to worry, he only wanted a small favor.

When Miiko got out of jail, he told his parole officer that a cousin he'd never met had arranged a job for him, working in the warehouse of a liquor distributor out in Queens. The guy nodded, bored, wrote it down on a form, *Liquid Assets.*

Now, Stoll could sense the IAD boys sniffing around once more. Nothing he could put his finger on yet, just a feeling he got that somebody was watching him. He'd had it ever since Tony Giardella met him in a donut shop across the river in Brooklyn, told him how the feds had grabbed Tangliero. Since then, he'd started paying for his lunch when he stopped at a diner, checking the rearview carefully before he set up a meeting. Any money that changed hands would have to get passed through somebody else. Vinny, maybe. So far, he hadn't spotted any surveillance, but he could sense that time was running out. A couple days, to clean up the mess. Then get ready to duck, 'cause the shit was gonna fly.

Stoll hitched up his pants under his belly. "Just find the money. We get our hands on that, we can clear out. Let Giardella take care of Cruz."

Miiko shrugged. "Might go the other way."

"Whatever. Long as we're clear."

Miiko flipped his keys against the palm of his hand, one finger through the ring. He watched Stoll hitch his pants up one more time, walk away toward the stairs. Miiko frowned. When's the last time you saw a cop wear pants that aren't too small for him?

Miiko got into the Acura, started it up.

The guy losing weight. Like he was worried.

Chapter 19

Bobby Amondano felt like an idiot. Out for a walk on South Beach, with all the muscle guys, girls in G-strings, he's wearing a double-breasted Brooks Brothers, the pants rolled up. He was carrying his new Ferragamo loafers, the socks wadded up and stuffed inside. He gritted his teeth, feeling the sand between his toes. No way he was gonna get it all out, they got back to the boardwalk.

Frankie Luccario, *capo di capi,* wore a tiny blue Speedo, his belly hanging way down over it so, you didn't look close, you'd think he was naked. *All that fat hanging off the front,* Bobby thought, *and no ass. Like somebody took a knife, sliced it off.* He wore a pair of black Ray Bans, carried a styofoam cup of Mocha Supremo from The Beanery! up on the boardwalk, sipping at it through a straw. Bobby glanced up at the hotel windows along Collins, wondered if the FBI surveillance guys were snapping pictures of this. Fat Frankie waddling along, sucking on a straw like a five-year-old. *Probably hang this shot on the office wall,* Bobby thought. *Cut a headline from the paper* — WHALE BEACHES ON SOUTH COAST.

Cesare, a guy Frankie had brought down from New Orleans a few years back to handle the wet stuff, trailed along behind them, looking at the girls. Bobby watched them looking back, checking him out. He'd run one hand over his chest, proud of his body, not pumped like the muscle guys, but lean like a model in his bathing suit. Dark hair, quick eyes. Smiling at them with the corner of his mouth, like he was telling 'em, *Yeah, I see you. Catch you later, maybe.* He kept a toothpick in his mouth, playing with it with his tongue so the tip flicked back and forth. He glanced over, caught Bobby looking. He met Bobby's eyes for a moment, held them, the toothpick coming around to point right at him.

Bobby looked out at the water, thought, *Jesus. Frankie trusts this guy?*

"You listening to me?" Frankie stopped, sand creeping up around his pink toes. He shoved his Ray Bans up, stared at Bobby from under them. Little eyes, squinting against the sun.

"Yeah, I heard you."

" 'Cause I ain't gonna say it more than once, okay?"

Bobby saw Cesare grin at him, the toothpick making a slow tour of his mouth, coming back to him, like a batter taking a practice swing.

"Okay, Frank."

Frankie shook his head, stabbed at the cup with his straw.

"I get these calls, my lawyer's 'bout to go out the window, he's so scared. You come down here, tell me the whole thing's gone to shit up there. You know what I say? *Handle* it. That's what I fuckin' pay you for, right?"

Bobby raised a hand. "Frank, it's not that simple."

"The fuck you mean it's not simple? I pay you, you handle it. That's as simple as it gets." Frankie raised the cup, sucked at the straw, moving it around to get the last few drops from the bottom. Then he handed the cup to Cesare, belched. "You *don't* handle it, I gotta reconsider my investment."

"Sure, I understand that. And you got nothing to worry about. I'm gonna handle it. But it's gonna take a while, is all I'm saying."

"How long?"

Bobby shrugged. "Couple days on Joey. We got some guys workin' on it. The money, that's gonna take longer."

"I'm askin' you, how long?"

"Tony figures a couple weeks, till he can get this thing cleared up with Cruz."

Frankie looked down at the sand, wiggled his toes. "Don't even talk to me about fuckin' Tony. Way I see it, I got him to thank for this whole thing." He spat into the sand, nudged at it with his foot. "With his fancy ideas."

Bobby kept his mouth shut, watched a muscle guy talking up a pair of girls down by the water, the guy trying to look relaxed, but his thighs kept twitching, like somebody'd snuck up behind him, nudged him with an electric prod. Frankie turned, pointed a finger at Bobby.

"You know your problem? You got an ineffective management style."

Bobby looked at him. *Huh?*

"You let Tony think you're his friend. He comes to you, tells you it's gonna be a couple weeks till he comes up with the money, there's no *fear* there." He

241

glanced over at Cesare. "Am I right?"

Cesare flicked that toothpick around, shrugged. "You're right."

Frankie grinned, spread his hands. "See?" He reached down, tugged at his bathing suit, shifting things around. "Trust me on this, Bobby. What we need here is a *neutral party.*"

Shit, Bobby thought.

"Somebody can drop in on Tony, motivate him a little."

"We need him," Bobby said. "His name's on the papers. He's gone, we can't get at the money."

"Did I say we didn't need him?" Frankie shook his head. "I'm not sayin' we take him out. Just make him see the *gravity* of the situation." He looked over at Cesare. "You think you can handle that?"

Cesare kept his eyes on Bobby, smiled. "Sure, no problem."

Flicking that toothpick around, slowly, so it looked like he was sighting down a barrel.

Chapter 20

In the afternoon, Moser fought the traffic downtown, left the car in a bus zone near Washington Square. He crossed the street against the traffic, ducked into the NYU library to get out of the heat. He checked his copy of Eva Cruz's course registration form, consulted a campus map he got from a wall display in the lobby, and managed to work out that her Intro Psychology course had just let out, and she would have been hurrying across campus to the art studios, where she took figure drawing from one to two-thirty.

Rich girl classes, he thought, as he headed out into the heat. Adult babysitting.

Walking across the campus, eyeing the college girls in their tiny skirts, stripped down for summer, he counted the girls who met his gaze, feeling his age. *The invisible man.* They probably figured he was there to see his kid, bringing the tuition payment. Just another walking checkbook.

He cut across a plaza, found the art building. By the time he found the right studio, the class had started. He slipped into the back of the room, watched as a dozen students made preliminary sketches of a nude model. The model sat in a straight-backed chair on a riser, elbows on her knees, head tipped to one side at an odd angle, looking at the floor. She had a book open between her feet. She was thin, with small breasts and narrow hips. Her long black hair was pulled into a braid, hanging off one shoulder. Moser decided she was beautiful. The students studied her as an interesting problem, sketching the line of her shoulders, the way her hands hung limp in front of her knees. The instructor moved among them, giving advice. He was in his late thirties, thin, with a gaunt face and a closely trimmed black beard. He was dressed in a wrinkled sweat shirt and pants that tied at the ankle. His black hair was pulled back into a ponytail. As Moser watched he paused beside one girl, resting his hand lightly on her shoulder.

"Interrogate your image," he said.

"Don't let it hide from you."

As he turned away he saw Moser watching from the back of the room. He frowned, walked over toward him.

"I'm sorry," he called out, gave a little wave of his hand. "I don't allow observers."

Moser glanced at his copy of the course schedule.

"Are you Professor Paley?"

He stopped before Moser, looked down at the paper then up at Moser's face.

"I am. Can I help you?"

Moser shielded him. "Detective Moser. I'm with Manhattan Homicide."

Paley glanced at the badge, gave a laugh.

"No kidding?"

"Nope."

He smiled, shook his head.

"I'll bet you love saying that." His voice dropped a few registers. "Detective Moser, Homicide. Like in the movies."

"Not much, no." Moser slipped the badge back onto his belt. "We don't do car chases, I've never slept with a beautiful suspect, and the butler almost never did it." He took out his notebook.

"I would like to ask you some questions, though."

"Me?" He smiled. "I wouldn't kill anyone, I'm tenured."

"It's about a student. Eva Cruz."

"Don't know her."

Moser tapped the course schedule in his hand.

"Says here she's registered in this class."

Paley shrugged, swung a hand to indicate the students. "I got ten students. There's, what, fourteen on that list? The summer semester just started Wednesday. A lot of kids sign up, then drop. Takes about a week for the list to catch up with reality."

"So you don't know her?"

"She might have been here the first day. I couldn't tell you. I'm not good with faces."

Moser glanced over at the naked model, slumped on her chair.

"That why her head's down?"

Paley smiled, raised one finger to his lips. "Let's keep that quiet, shall we? These kids look up to me."

Moser nodded toward the students.

"You mind if I ask around?"

"During class?" Paley shook his head.

"You want to come back at the end, I'll quit a few minutes early. How's that?"

Moser looked at his watch. "That's, what? An hour?"

"We go ninety minutes, so you come back in an hour, you can have 'em for the last twenty." He grinned. "Hell, you can keep 'em as long as you want. Give 'em milk and cookies. After this class, I'm headed out to Montauk."

An hour later, Moser stuck his head in the door. Paley was seated at a desk in the corner, waved him in. At the front of the room, the model was slipping into a pair of black jeans. She looked up, caught Moser looking at her. She had a long, narrow nose, a broad mouth, pale blue eyes. He could see a birthmark just above her left breast. She held Moser's gaze for a moment, her face expressionless. Then she turned, reached for her shirt.

The students were packing up their pads. Paley stuffed some papers into a gym bag, got up, rapped a knuckle on a metal storage locker behind his desk.

"Listen up. This is Detective Moser, Homicide." He smiled. "He wants to ask you some questions. I want him in pencil on Monday."

The students groaned, started taking out their pads again. Paley picked up his bag, passed Moser on his way out the door. "All yours, detective."

Moser walked over to the front of the room. The model sat in a chair against the wall, lacing up a pair of Doc Martens. She looked up at him, her face serious. Then she dug around in a backpack, came out with a sketch pad and pencil. She flipped to a clean page, started drawing.

Moser glanced around the room. The students were staring at him, their eyes darting down to their pads.

"Thanks for your time," Moser said. "I'm looking for information about a girl named Eva Cruz. She was registered for this class. Anyone know her?"

The students were intent on their drawing, the only sound the scratching of pencils. A boy stole a glance at him, frowned. Then he reversed his pencil, erasing furiously.

Moser dug in his coat pocket, took out the photograph of Eva Cruz. He held it up, turning it slowly so they could all get a look at it.

"About five eight," he said. "Dark hair, thin."

A girl smiled at him, shook her head. A few others gave the picture a quick glance, then went back to their sketches. Moser sighed, slipped the photograph back into his pocket. He took a few copies of his card from his breast pocket, dug out a pen. He wrote *Eva Cruz* on the back of each card, handed them around.

"Any of your friends know her, my number's on there."

From the corner of his eye, he saw the model flip her sketch pad closed, tuck it into her backpack. As she got up, he handed her a card. She glanced at it, then up at his face. She tucked his card into the back pocket of her jeans, draped the backpack over her shoulder.

"I know her."

Chapter 21

Eden Howe, Moser wrote in his notebook.

"Don't laugh," she said, smiling. They were sitting on a wall in the plaza. The sun made her black hair shine. "My parents missed Woodstock. I'm lucky they didn't call me Stardust."

"I like it."

He scribbled more notes as she talked — *Age–20. Parents in Englewood, NJ. Shares apt. on Bleecker, near 7th Ave.*

"I have my own room," she told him. "You need the number?"

She knew Eva Cruz, had been in two classes with her over the last year — Intro to Classical Archeology in the fall semester and Modern Novel in the spring. They used to nod at each other in the hall, then in March, Eva's backpack had been stolen during her dance class, and she'd lost her notes. She approached Eden in the hall before class one day, introduced herself, explained the problem and asked if she could copy her notes. They went to a copy shop over on Broadway, then got sandwiches in a Syrian place down the block.

"Just the two of you?"

"There was a guy who followed her around. Her father was some kind of big shot in Central America. Very creepy. But he kept out of the way, waited on the sidewalk."

"So what'd you talk about?"

"Classes, stuff like that. I'm a double major, theater and film studies. She thought that was cool. It's all right, I guess. Mostly I just do tech work on other people's films. A little acting. I'm taking a directing class next term."

"She talk about herself?"

"Not much. She didn't have a major yet. I got the impression she was just taking classes. Nothing directed."

"Anything outside of classes?"

Eden sipped at her iced tea, shook her head.

"She seemed pretty sheltered. The bodyguard and all. That would make me crazy. I asked her if she ever did any acting. You know, since she was so pretty. She laughed. Her father wouldn't let her."

"So he was pretty strict."

"Yeah. Made me wonder if the bodyguard was to keep her safe or to keep her from doing what she wanted." She looked at him. "Guess it didn't work, huh?"

"What do you mean?"

"Keeping her safe. You're a homicide cop."

He closed his notebook, slipped it into his pocket. "How long have you been posing naked?"

She smiled. "Paley asks for volunteers. He wants us to see what it feels like, sensitize us. A subject-object thing, you know? The looker and the look."

"I figured he just wants to see you naked."

"He's got a boyfriend." She sipped her drink. "It's exciting for about two minutes. Then you get stiff."

Moser smiled. He liked her voice. It was deep, like the women in old movies.

"What's it feel like? The look."

"Weird. All those eyes. And then you realize they're just trying to get the shading. Like you're a plate with apples."

She glanced at her watch. "Class."

She finished her tea, tipping her head back to drain the bottle. There were beads of sweat at the base of her neck. She put the cap back on the bottle, stuffed it into her backpack. Then she stood up, slung the backpack over her shoulder. "I could draw you sometime. Let you see how it feels."

He smiled at her. "I don't think so."

Her eyes held him for a moment, then she smiled.

"Okay." She tapped the pad in his coat pocket. "But I guess you've got my number."

Chapter 22

Marty Stoll stood in a doorway behind a gay bar near the corner of Amsterdam and 132nd. From the street, the place looked like a construction site, all the windows covered with unfinished wood planks, a sign mounted on a pair of horns over the door, RAWHIDE. Stoll wondered if they ever got a real cowboy, up from Texas for the rodeo at the Garden, maybe, feeling homesick.

He grinned, imagining it.

Leather boys on the dance floor, disco lights flashing away. Some guy telling him, "Try the back room, you like a little bareback riding."

A car pulled to the curb by the corner, gray Acura. Stoll walked over, got in. Miiko grinned at him.

"Hey, you ever been in that place?"

Stoll shot him a look. "I was in there on a call, once. Some of the local boys tried to bust the place up. Big mistake. We get there, there's a bunch of guys standin' around, look like Rambo, all the muscles. They had one of the guys locked in a storeroom. He tried to cut his way out a window with a knife, slit his finger down to the bone. Had to take him to the emergency room."

Miiko shook his head. "Not me, man. No way."

He put the car in gear, pulled out into traffic. On Amsterdam, he took a right, heading north.

"So what's the story?" Stoll reached over, turned the air conditioning down.

Miiko took a piece of paper from his pocket, passed it over to Stoll. He unfolded it, read:

Valeria de Guzman
2417 Fort Washington Ave.,
Apt. 6D

He glanced up at Miiko. "What the fuck's this?"

"Cruz's got some kind of operation uptown. Never lets me get near it. This afternoon, I hear him talking to Eduardo. He says they got to talk to Valeria about *el dinero* like they think I can't understand, they talk in Spanish. Hey, even I can understand that. So I wait till Cruz is in the bathroom, sneak a look at his desk, he's got a copy of Eduardo's list lying right there, little mark by her name. I got the address from his Rolodex."

Stoll said, "You think she's got the money?"

"Could be." Miiko accelerated to beat a red light, grinned at the chorus of horns from cars that had to stop short. "I'm thinking maybe we should pay her a visit."

Chapter 23

When Moser got back to his desk, he found a yellow Post-it note stuck to the back of his chair. It said: *Dinner, 6:00 P.M., Ray.* He smiled, crumpled it up, tossed it into the trash basket between their desks. Felicia worked the News at Five, the early show, where they did interviews to follow up the features. Reporter on the scene, making happy talk with the anchors back at the station. Dinner at six meant Ray grilling salmon steaks in the backyard. Dark beer, salad, his mama's cole slaw with the touch of hot sauce in it. That was fine with Moser, who preferred this kind of invitation to the Sunday dinners Felicia had felt compelled to include him in after his marriage broke up. On those evenings, he and Ray would sit at the table, joking with the kids, trying hard not to catch each other's eye as Felicia brought out her best efforts. They'd praise her warmly, then sneak out for barbecue while she put the kids to bed.

As a cook, Felicia made a terrific reporter.

Moser left work, caught the subway over to Brooklyn. He stopped for a six-pack of Guinness on the way up the hill, paused at a bench to peel the price stickers off each bottle. *A little taste of Eire,* he thought. Must be tough to miss the old country like that, at a buck ninety-five a bottle.

Ray opened the door, waved him in. "Felicia's not home yet. She was interviewing some girl who won a math contest out on the Island, and traffic's tied up on the expressway."

Moser handed over the beer, went into the kitchen, where the kids were arguing over whose night it was to set the table. Darnell, the oldest, was twelve. Lately, she'd begun to plague her father with probing questions about his work, his politics, his minor vices, until he backed away, rolling his eyes, hands raised in surrender. He called her "the Judge," claimed he was saving money for law school already. Her brother, Jarrod, was ten, but already affecting the gangsta look — hooded sweat shirt, baggy pants, unlaced high-tops, street-wise scowl. It worried Ray, Moser knew, but the kid had a way of bursting into a brilliant smile at the slightest provocation, like his mother's TV voice, with its formal tones.

"Daddy," he'd shout from the family room, one finger pointing at the screen. "Come see! It's that lady again, Mom's evil twin!"

Moser had seen Jarrod stand, rapt, before the window of a Japanese florist on Fourth Avenue, fascinated by the colors. The gangsta thing, Moser figured, was no different than his own career as a leather-jacketed biker, roaring down Highway 61 on his midnight-blue Schwinn, a pair of playing cards clipped against the spokes for sound effects. He'd caught one glimpse of Marlon Brando in *The Wild One* when he was seven, then terrified his parents with his biker dreams for the next three years, until he saw Gary Cooper in *High Noon* on TV and decided to become a laconic Texan. It made no difference in the end; none of it prepared him for what he'd become, for what he'd lived.

The kids made him do his card tricks while their father made dinner. He showed them how to deal from the bottom of the deck, from the middle, how to cut four aces from the pack, to shuffle one-handed. Fielding watched from the counter, where his fish was marinating, shook his head.

"Man, you're nothing but a thief with a badge. I ain't *never* playing cards with you again."

Moser shrugged. Fielding had a regular poker game with some detectives from the squad room. When they'd become partners, Ray had invited him to sit in one night. When his turn came to deal, he'd reached for a beer, shuffling the deck with his other hand, then firing cards across the table with a quick flick of his thumb. By the end of the night, he was up close to two hundred bucks. It was the last time Ray invited him to play.

When they heard the front door, the kids ran off to greet their mother. Ray looked over from the scallions he was chopping, watched Moser pack up the cards.

"Where'd you learn that shit?"

"In the 'Nam."

"Yeah?" Fielding shook his head. "They never taught me none of that. Just the basics, shootin' and dying."

Moser closed the box, dropped the

cards in a drawer full of kitchen junk. "Guy taught me in a medevac. He had the bed next to me, used to be a dealer in Vegas. Lost both legs to a mine up by the DMZ, so he'd sit there all day, shuffling the cards, dealing 'em out on the bed. He said the one good thing about losing his legs was it gave him a nice smooth playing surface."

"So you decided to become a card-shark."

"He gave me his deck before he shipped out. I took 'em with me when they sent me back up-country. Gave me something to do with my hands."

Fielding smiled. "Most guys I knew kept their hands pretty busy. This one kid, I swear he used to jerk off ten times a day. You're on patrol, sergeant calls a break, this kid wanders off into the bushes for some recreation. One time, he came back, the whole squad was gone. Just forgot about him. We hear him comin' along the trail behind us, like 'Hey, guys! Wait up!' "

"They didn't cut him a Section Eight?"

"Nah. He was a terrific sniper. Real quiet hands, you know? No tremor."

Moser laughed. "Makes sense."

Felicia came in with the kids. "Uh oh,

guy stories." She steered the kids toward the stairs, calling over her shoulder, "Don't you believe none of those war stories, Dave. Best I can tell, Ray spent the war chasing girls in Saigon."

Darnell gave a wince of disgust, jerked out from under her mother's hand. "Mom, that's disgusting."

They went on up the stairs, Felicia telling Darnell, "Just 'cause he's your daddy, honey, don't mean he's got good sense."

Ray sighed, gestured after them. "My family."

Moser sat with Ray in the backyard while the grill heated up. He'd put up a redwood deck back there a few years back, with comfortable lounge chairs and cafe umbrellas. Moser felt like he was on a cruise ship.

"How you doing on the Cruz thing?"

Moser sighed. "Don't ask."

"That bad, huh?"

"I got a victim with no friends, no bad habits. She goes to school, comes home, that's it. I went down to NYU today, talked to a couple of her classmates. Nobody can remember anything except that she seemed quiet, and that Eduardo followed her around all day.

Her father won't let her talk to boys. She goes out, it's with a *bodyguard.* So one night, she gets a flower some guy sent up from a shop right off Park Avenue. She sneaks out, next thing anybody knows, we're dragging her out of the river."

"You got anything on the guy?"

"A picture. The florist had a security camera." Moser shrugged. "He could be anyone."

Fielding nodded. "That's how it feels. Until you catch 'em."

"You know what I think? This girl, she's never been out with a guy. Somebody sends her a flower, note on it telling her where to meet him. There's nobody home, so she figures why not? Turns out to be the wrong guy."

Fielding sipped at his beer, watched the charcoal briquettes turning gray at the edges. "You ever see those pictures of coal miners, back in the thirties?"

"Sure."

"Some days, I feel like one of those guys. Like the city's this dark pit I descend into, you know? Little light on my head. Only it's backwards. Our job is to dig out all the dirt and filth, leave that little vein of stuff that's worth

263

something where it is. And it's just a matter of time until the whole thing comes down on our heads, buries us."

Moser looked at him. "This connected to what I said, or just a random thought?"

Fielding picked up a barbecue fork, leaned forward, poked at the charcoal. "These look ready."

"You want me to get the fish?"

"Nah, I'll grab 'em."

He got up, went into the kitchen. Moser could see him through the kitchen window, standing over the sink, washing the fork. As he watched, Felicia came over, put a hand on the back of his neck. She smiled, said something. Moser looked away.

Fielding came back out with the salmon steaks, put them on the grill. They had a tangy smell as the flame hit them, from the Thai paste he'd spread on them earlier.

"Man, I love that smell," he said, settling into his chair. "You ever watch 'em grill fish over in 'Nam? The villagers, they'd toss the whole fish right on the coals, let it cook through, then just peel the skin back. The meat gets seared, so it just flakes off on the knife. Incredible."

He passed Moser another Guinness. "Wickert give you anything on the hooker?"

Moser shrugged. "Grab-and-twist. Like we thought."

"I ran her prints. She's an illegal, from down in Central America somewhere. Lived over in the Bronx."

"So what's she doing in Fort Tryon Park?"

Fielding poked at the fish. "Hooking, looks like."

"You're saying she comes down from the Bronx, hooks in Washington Heights? What do they got, an exchange program now?"

Fielding got the fork under the fish, flipped them over. "This is New York, Dave. Nothing makes sense."

Chapter 24

Vinny Delario pulled into the Amoco station on Yonkers Avenue, just off the Cross County, swung around back of the garage to where they parked cars that were in for service. Like you'd trust a guy who pumps gas all day to work on your car. Vinny had a '78 Dodge Charger, sweet car, that he'd bought off a guy up in Rikers who was heading for ten to fifteen upstate. Bright yellow, with black stripes up over the hood, so the carb intakes looked like a pair of black nostrils, flaring. He'd jacked the suspension up a few inches in back, so now it looked like some kind of big cat, ready to charge. He liked to pull up at lights next to some guy in a station wagon, put the clutch in, punch the gas, make it growl. The guy glancing over, feeling old.

But now he saw the gold Seville pulled up at the end of a row of cars, Marty Stoll behind the wheel, the only guy Vinny knew who took better care of his car than he did. He swung the Charger over, pulled up next to the Seville, rolled his window down.

"Hey, Marty. What'ya got?"

Stoll slid across the front seat, passed a paper bag through the window. "Some rock, also a pair of thirty-eights, two-inch barrels. Don't take less than two-fifty."

Vinny opened the bag, looked in. "That's high."

"Fuck 'em. Your guys don't want it, find somebody else."

Vinny shrugged. "Okay." He leaned over, stuffed the bag under the front seat.

"Will you fuckin' listen? I'm not done." Stoll reached into his jacket pocket, pulled out a manila envelope, folded twice. "I need you to go up to Hunan Village on Broadway at 168th, two o'clock tomorrow. Get a booth." He held up the manila envelope. "There's envelopes in here. Some guys are gonna come in, you give 'em each an envelope. Under the table, okay?"

Vinny looked at the envelope, then up at Stoll. "These are cops?"

"What the fuck do you care?"

Vinny thought about it, shrugged.

"Okay, I don't."

"You get done with this, they'll love you. Invite you out to the PBA picnic, play softball."

"What's that on your shirt?"

Stoll glanced down at the front of his shirt, saw that it was splattered with dark spots, like somebody'd swung a paint brush at him. He looked up, saw Vinny watching him.

"Don't worry 'bout it." Stoll slid back across the front seat, behind the wheel. He reached down and started the car. "Just don't fuck up, okay?"

A half-block away, in the parking lot of an Odd Lots store, Tom Richter watched the Cadillac pull out of the service station, turn south. He lowered his camera, laid it on the seat next to him, the telephoto lens taking up half the seat. Richter picked up the cellular phone on his lap, punched the speed-dial with his thumb. It rang once, then a voice said —

"Murella."

"Stoll's coming out," Richter said. "Heading south."

"They make the pass?"

"Brown paper bag and a manila envelope." Richter paused for a moment, squinting through the windshield at the Amoco station down the block. The yellow Charger started up, headlights coming on, then pulled out to the edge of the street, waiting for a break in traffic. "Okay, here comes the kid. Stay with him."

A moment passed as the Charger turned into traffic, then Murella said, "Got him."

Richter punched the button to disconnect the phone, tossed it on the seat next to the camera. He reached down, started the car, pulled out into traffic, going north.

You want to bust cops, he thought. *Follow the money.*

Chapter 25

Ray drove Moser home after eleven. Five hours later, Moser lay awake in the darkness. His head ached from the beer. An idea shimmered at the fading edge of his dreams, just out of reach. He lay there for a few minutes, trying to get it back, but all he got was an image of the girl, Eva Cruz, watching him from behind a wall of blue tiles that shimmered like waves in the sunlight. He glanced at the alarm clock beside the couch: 4:48. He sighed, tossed the sheets back, went into the kitchen to make coffee.

The house smelled like paint. He'd spent three hours on the ladder the night before, using a roller to spread frost-blue semigloss over the bedroom walls. When he was done, he climbed down off the ladder, glanced around. *Shit.* The room looked like a prison cell. Or an aquarium, the way the fish see it. Anyone who slept in there, he thought, would dream of drowning.

Still, the room was newly painted, and you couldn't see where he'd patched flaws in the plaster with spackle. No more scuffs where Janine's carved headboard had scraped against the wall. No smudge near the window where she'd left a candle burning to make the room smell like a secluded cabin one Valentine's Day. The faded spot where their wedding picture had hung was gone, as well as the hole in the plaster where she'd flung a shoe at him one night when he'd come home late, forgetting that her parents were coming for dinner.

He went into the bathroom, glanced up at where the ceiling had begun to blister over the shower, like some poison was trying to work its way out. Janine had complained about it for months, but he'd never gotten around to fixing it. He pulled the ladder in from the bedroom, set to work. Within forty minutes, the ceiling looked like a cloudless sky. He thought about stripping the old wallpaper, but decided to put if off until another day.

Another day. It sounds so promising as you climb into bed, but when it comes . . .

He rubbed at his eyes, glanced up at the kitchen window. The darkness was still thick in the eastern sky. He could see a light in Marty Stoll's basement across the street, a small patch of his lawn lit by the glow from a window set into the foundation. Moser took a filter from the cabinet, spooned some coffee out of the can, thinking that he'd have to remind Marty to shut it off before they left for the city. He carried the pot over to the sink, ran some water into it. As it filled, he watched the first headlights of the morning rush moving on the parkway a few blocks south. He started to look away, but something caught his eye. A man was moving in the shadows beside Marty's boat.

He set the pot down on the counter, watched. The man moved slowly around the front of the boat, running his hand along the hull. He stepped over the front edge of the trailer, resting one hand on the winch, then disappeared into the darkness beyond. A moment later, Moser saw the canvas cover thrown back at one corner, caught a brief glimpse of Stoll's face in the glow of the streetlight as he climbed in. He watched Marty toss the cover aside, come forward to sit behind the wheel. He was wearing his pajamas and a gunbelt. A plastic six-pack with two cans left dangled from his left hand.

Moser went into the bedroom, pulled on his pants, a pair of running shoes. He came back to the kitchen, poured a cup of coffee, carried it across the street. Stoll had one of the beers open, sipping from it. He was sighting his .38 on the streetlight at the end of his driveway.

"You gotta get a special permit for streetlights?"

Stoll lowered his gun, looked down at him. "Hey, Dave."

Moser sipped at his coffee, nodded at the beer.

"Little early for that?"

He looked at the can in his hand, then tipped his wrist to glance at his watch, spilling beer onto his leg. "Nah, it's late."

Moser nodded, his eyes on the gun resting against the wheel, thinking, *Okay, how do I get to work today?*

"Permission to come aboard?"

Stoll gestured toward the stern. "Ladder's on the right."

Moser walked around the back, set his coffee on a ledge next to the ladder, climbed up. He picked up his coffee, squeezed between the seats to sit in the forward passenger seat. Stoll bent over, hooked the six-pack with one finger, offered him the last beer. Moser shook his head, held up his coffee. Stoll put the can on the floor between them.

"You ever wonder," Stoll said, tapping the wheel with the barrel of his gun, "why they make boats with the steering wheel on the right?"

Moser shrugged. "Beats me."

Stoll gave a sigh. "I got a boat, I should know this."

"It wasn't on the test?"

"What test?"

"For the license. You need a license for this, right?"

Stoll thought about it for a moment, nodded. "Must'a been on the test."

Moser sipped his coffee. "They make all boats like that?"

Stoll frowned. "They made this one like that. You think I got a defective boat?"

"Maybe it's English."

"Nah, I only buy American. Guy at the dealership, he told me they make 'em in Missouri." He drained his beer, tossed the can into the back of the boat.

"That make sense to you? Make boats in fuckin' *Missouri?*"

"Makes as much sense as anything."

"Like that ice cream, the one with the Swedish name? They make that shit in New Jersey, some advertising guy made up the name, figured it sounded classy."

Moser nodded. "I heard that."

Stoll reached down for the last beer. "Sure you don't want this?"

"Yeah, I'm good."

He pulled it out of the plastic ring, popped it open, took a long swig. Then he wiped his mouth on his sleeve.

"Breakfast of champions."

"What's up, Marty?"

Stoll was silent for a moment. He rubbed at a stain on the dashboard with his thumb.

"You know what I paid for this boat?"

"Not a clue."

"Too much." He took a pull at his beer. The gun was easy in his hand, moving idly between two spokes on the wheel. He rested the beer in his lap for a moment, then raised it to point one finger at Moser. "But, you know what? I earned it."

Moser nodded.

"I'm proud of what I've done here. My kids, they got things I never had. Comes time for college, they're not gonna have to worry." He leaned his head against the wheel, and Moser saw his shoulders sag. "Anything I done, it was for them. You understand that, Dave?"

"Sure, Marty." Moser set his coffee down on the edge of the boat, reached out. "What'ya say I hang on to the gun, okay?"

Stoll looked up at him, smiled. "I got you worried? You scared I'm gonna blow my brains out?" He sat up abruptly, put the barrel of the gun in his mouth. "You wanna watch?"

"Marty!"

Stoll laughed, let the gun fall into his lap. "Nah, I got too much invested now." He shook his head. "Might as well stick around for the payoff, huh?"

Moser took a deep breath, let it out. "Just give me the gun, all right?"

"Sure, Dave." He flicked his wrist, flipped the cylinder open, passed it across. Moser looked down at it. Six hollow-point rounds, snug in their chambers. He shook the bullets out into his palm, pocketed them. Then he laid the gun gently on the dashboard, picked up his coffee. Stoll leaned back, rested his head on the back of the seat. The sun was flirting with the horizon, making the sky look like a bruise.

"What's going on, Marty?"

"Nothing I can't handle."

"You sure?"

"Hey, I got this far, right? Few years, we'll both be fat and ugly, sitting on a porch, some cheap apartments down in Florida. Cop heaven." He closed his eyes, his breathing growing steady. Moser leaned over, took the beer can out of his hands, poured it out on the grass. Stoll opened his eyes slightly, watched him. "Fuckin' waste." His eyes closed again.

"Wake me when it's time to leave, okay?"

Chapter 26

According to her neighbors, Valeria de Guzman came home to her Washington Heights apartment shortly before 7:00 P.M., let the cat out onto the fire escape outside her kitchen window, as usual, then began to prepare dinner. Her downstairs neighbor, Hernando Achoa, recalled hearing her footsteps moving around the kitchen, the sound of her radio, tuned to a Spanish-language station that offered a World Cup summary each evening during July, including scoring highlights, with the announcer's voice rising to an ecstatic moan, *"Gooool!"* Irritated by this nightly assault, Achoa had prepared a clever counterstroke, popping the third act of his new Deutsche Grammophon *Wozzeck* into the CD player, then tipping the thirty-six-inch Harman-Kardon speakers on their backs so that when he raised the volume, the ceiling tiles trembled.

Lou Nicolaides and Harry Dietrich,

the first detectives on the scene the next morning, determined that Valeria de Guzman had fled her killers, leaving a trail of blood that led from her bedroom door down the narrow hall, across the living room, ending where her body finally came to its rest near the apartment's front door. A second body, an unidentified Hispanic male, was found in the bathroom, his head shoved in the toilet, blood still dripping from a slash wound across the base of his throat.

Asked if he heard her screams, Hernando Achoa went pale, stammered a protest about the beating of a timpani and the crescendo of the death scene. When Nicolaides and Dietrich glanced at each other, their eyes agreeing that, yes, this was exactly the kind of squirrel who'd stab a woman seven times, then tell the police he'd heard the heavenly chorus raising their voices in praise, Achoa rushed to the CD player, put on the final scenes of Berg's opera, loud. As the chorus screamed its accusation — "Murder! Murder!" — Nicolaides reached for his cuffs, congratulating himself on having gotten lucky on this one while it was still possible to get home in time to catch the last innings of the Mets game.

But even as he launched into his Miranda two-step, he caught a glimpse of an officer in the blue jumpsuit of the forensics unit descending the steps to tap at the hall door, a large file box in his hand, and Nicolaides, like Isringhausen on the mound out at Shea, watching a two-run homer sail off Tony Gwynn's bat at that very moment, felt it begin to slip away.

"Got a second set of shoe prints upstairs," the forensics guy was saying. "On the landing. It's faint, like he tried to step over the blood on the way out, maybe got in the other guy's trail."

"So two killers?"

"That's how it looks." The technician set the box on the table, opened it. "Also, we found this stuff."

He reached inside, took out a pair of money-counting machines, a box of rubber bands, a thick stack of deposit slips, two cellular phones, and a box of Hefty garbage bags.

"Looks like somebody's been handling a lot of cash."

Nicolaides sighed, clipped the cuffs back onto his belt. He put a hand on Achoa's shoulder, shoved him down into a kitchen chair. "Your lucky day, son."

An hour later, Nicolaides sat at a desk in the squad room and watched Ray Fielding open the file box, shake his head.

"Oh, man. Look't this stuff." He grinned. "I hope you ain't countin' on closing this one, Lou."

Nicolaides looked up at him. "I used to tell my kid, 'Son, there's only one thing you can count on in this life.' But, Ray, last few years? It's been letting me down, too."

Fielding winced, raised both hands. "Hey, I don't wanna hear nothing about that."

"Just warning you, Ray."

"Terrific." Ray looked down at the evidence box, reached in and picked out a stack of crime scene photographs. He flipped through them, shook his head. "These some bad boys, did this." He tossed the pictures back in the box. "You watch. A couple days, we're gonna find 'em in a Dumpster, no hands."

"Maybe."

"That's what happens, you steal from a stash house."

Nicolaides shrugged, tossed the paperwork across the desk at him. "So file it. Save me some work."

"Yeah, right." Fielding picked up the investigative summary, glanced at the evidence log. "IRS guys call you yet?"

Nicolaides picked up a pink message slip from his desk, held it up. "Before I got back. I got their full support. Oh, and would I mind copying 'em on the daily summaries?"

Fielding grinned, shook his head. "You bring the K-Y?"

"I try to stay greased."

"Spoken like a veteran." Fielding passed the paperwork back to Nicolaides. "You can't catch all the breaks, Lou."

"Why not?" Nicolaides got up, took the forms over to the photocopier, started to run the first of many sets.

Fielding leaned over to the evidence box on the desk, dug through it. He glanced at the crime scene photos, tossed them aside. He found an address book, took it out of its bag, flipped through it.

"No way it's the neighbor, like you thought?"

Nicolaides looked up from the copier,

shrugged. "Still looks like a suspect to me. But I checked out his shoes. His foot's too big for the prints."

"Too bad."

"Yeah. If you could've heard that record. All these people screaming 'Murder! Murder!' in German, the music all skittery and ugly, like. I'd'a booked him just for listening to it."

"Berg," Fielding said, glancing through the address book. "He studied with Schoenberg, the guy who started all that atonal stuff. I guess that's how he figured a murder should sound."

"Yeah, maybe." Nicolaides turned back to the copier. "Most murders I work, they don't sound like nothing, 'less it's that Snoopy Dog shit on a boom box."

Fielding glanced over at him. "Snoop Doggy Dogg."

"Yeah, him." Nicolaides laughed. " 'Couple years, he'll be down to one name, like Elvis. Or Madonna. 'Ladies and Gentlemen, please welcome . . . Snoop.' "

"Or Dog. Like Sinatra."

"See? Even you can't take this guy serious, and it's your music."

"*My* music?" Fielding shook his head.

"I'm strictly Coltrane and Bird."

Nicolaides looked over at him. "Bird?"

"Charlie Parker."

"How's that turn into *Bird*?"

Fielding started to reply, then sighed. "It's a black thing, all right, Lou? You wouldn't understand."

He looked down at the address book. Two of its pages were stuck together. Fielding used his thumbnail to part them, peel one back. At the center of the page, there was a tiny pearl of blood, partly dried.

"Oh my."

Nicolaides looked over. "What?"

"Looks like someone left us a clue."

"Yeah?" Nicolaides came over. "Let's see. I always wondered what a *clue* looked like." He took the address book by an edge, looked at the page. "Yup. That's a clue." He handed it back. "Cops get those in the movies."

Fielding leaned forward, laid the book on the desk. "Lou," he said. "You think maybe we could get the forensics boys up here, dust this for prints?"

Chapter 27

Richter paused at the door, glanced through the small window in the inter-rogation room door, saw Vinny Delario slumped at the table, his head resting on his arms. His hair was still covered with gravel dust, where they'd had to take him down in the parking lot — Jimmy Kendrick, the IAD detective who'd made the buy, sitting on his head while Richter cuffed him. Now, he looked like he was sleeping.

Richter opened the door, went over to the table, and slammed his hand down on it, *WHAM!* Vinny jumped, his chair tipping back against the wall behind him.

"Jesus! What the fuck's wrong with you?"

Richter stared at him, tossed the ma-nila envelope in his hands on the table. "Sit down."

Vinny stood there for a moment, look-ing at him. Then he reached back, slowly, straightened the chair, sat down. Richter pulled out the chair opposite him, nodded at the envelope on the table.

"That's a nice stack of money you were carrying."

Vinny rubbed at his lower lip with one finger, smiled. "I was over at Aqueduct, caught that last couple races. I did okay."

Richter sat back, folded his arms. "That where you got the crack and the guns, too?"

Vinny raised both hands. "Hey, I don't know where that shit came from. I found it under the seat of my car. I gave a guy a ride last week, maybe he put it there."

Richter sighed. "That's the best you can do?"

"It's the truth, man. I swear it."

"So you find this stuff in your car, figured you'd sell it."

"What? You see a way to make a couple hundred bucks, tell me you wouldn't take it."

Richter was silent for a moment, staring at him. "You really that stupid, Vinny?"

Vinny met his gaze for a moment, then looked away, shook his head.

"Okay, so I fucked up."

Richter nodded at the manila envelope on the table. "Open it."

Vinny hesitated. "What?"

"Go ahead. Open it."

Vinny shrugged, picked the envelope up, tore it open. Richter looked at his left hand, holding the envelope; the last two fingers were missing. As he watched, Vinny looked inside, then turned it over, spilled a pile of white envelopes onto the table. A photograph came out with them, landed upside down on the edge of the table. Richter reached over, slid it over toward Vinny with the tip of one finger. Vinny glanced at it, but didn't touch it.

"What's that?"

"Turn it over, have a look."

Vinny flipped it over, looked at the photograph of the Cadillac parked next to his Charger in the gas station lot, Marty Stoll leaning out the passenger window to pass the envelope across to him. The photograph had a weird look to it, their faces looking green against the darkness, like when they catch some guy breaking into a house at night on TV, show it to you on the news, the announcer saying, "Caught on tape!"

"I got another one," Richter said, "shows him handing you the bag."

Vinny tossed the photograph on the table. "That don't prove nothing. So he's giving me something, so what? It's my lunch, 'cause I forgot it. He lives by me, so my mom asked him to bring it." He nodded at the envelope in the picture. "She sent my mail too."

Richter smiled, pushed his chair back to stretch his legs out, scratching at his thigh. "That's fine," he said. "We got enough with the buy, anyway. I figure you'll pull ten to twenty upstate just on that, and that's if you get an easy judge."

Vinny looked at the floor. He could see the cop's shoes sticking out from under the table. Sneakers. He wore the laces double-knotted.

"But maybe not, if I give you Marty," he said.

Richter smiled.

"I guess you're not so stupid after all."

Chapter 28

His second day in the hotel, Joey Tangliero had sent Claire down to Macy's, made her buy him two pairs of silk pajamas, red, six pairs of boxer shorts ("Calvins are okay, if they don't carry the good stuff"), six pairs of nylon Gold Toes, black, and a three-pack of cotton handkerchiefs. Standing on line at the register, Claire had tried to figure out the rotation: two days on each handkerchief, three on the pajamas.

A pair of off-duty patrolmen from the 106th Precinct drove out to pick up his clothes at his apartment in Ozone Park. They found the closets empty, his suits slashed to ribbons, dumped in a pile on the floor, stinking of urine.

"Hey, no problem," Joey said. "My tailor keeps all my measurements. You call up, the suits are ready in a couple days." He grinned at McCann. "Maybe I'll get one of those western ties, like you wear. Cowboy hat. Be all set for my new life in Dipshit, Arizona."

"You'll fit right in."

And so, Claire found herself back in the checkout line, carrying three pairs of men's slacks, with matching shirts ("For the casual man"), two pairs of Bostonian loafers.

"We're not buying you a new wardrobe, here," McCann told Joey when he protested. "This is just for while you testify. You want Guccis, buy 'em on your own time."

Tangliero sighed, looking at himself in the hotel mirror. "I look like a cop."

When the tailor called, Claire had to ride out to Queens, pick up the suits: one gray, two blue. The guy behind the counter gave her a funny look.

"You're a cop?"

"Deputy federal marshal."

"Yeah?" He frowned, shoved the suits across the counter. "Tell Joey I don't want his business no more."

Coming out of the store, the suits draped over her arm, she paused on the corner of Atlantic Avenue, waiting for the light, when she felt a hand on her elbow. Turning, she saw a man smiling at her, another man watching them from a few paces back.

"Miss Locke?" The man nodded at the suits. "I guess you're in a hurry to deliver those, but Mr. Giardella would like to speak with you."

And he reached in quick, slipped the .38 from its holster on her hip, dropped it into his pocket. The hand tightened on her elbow.

"Joey can wait. He ain't goin' nowhere."

"You drive a *Toyota?*"

Claire felt a hand on her back, pushing her into the car. Tony Giardella slid across the backseat to make room. He looked the way Joey Tangliero described him, heavy, with a squinty look and a hairpiece like he'd trained a rat to squat on his head.

"What? You think it's like the movies?"

She slid onto the seat, felt the door shut behind her.

"You wanna know, they impounded my Lincoln on the kidnapping charge. My lawyer, he gets me out on bail in, what? Two hours? But they keep the car. You believe that? No respect for private property." He shrugged. "I got a deal on this, long-term lease. Thought it might be a good idea to lower my profile, you know?"

The man who had approached her climbed into the front seat, folded the suits across his lap. The other man walked around to the driver's side, got behind the wheel. Claire watched him pull out into traffic.

"Am I gonna get my gun back?"

"No problem," Tony G. told her. "After we talk, we'll drop you back at your car. Ten minutes, tops."

They drove her out Atlantic, taking it slow in the morning traffic. Tony G. dug a paper out of the inside pocket of his jacket, smoothed it on his knee.

"Lemme show you something, here."

He passed her the paper, an account summary from Chase Manhattan, showing a savings account in the name of *Claire G. Locke,* with a balance of $637.38. Claire looked up at Giardella, her eyes angry.

"How'd you get this?"

"What's it matter?" He took the paper out of her hand, dug a pen out of his pocket. "Now watch."

He leaned forward, pressed the paper against the back of the front seat, wrote in two zeros after the balance. Then he passed the paper back to her.

"How's that look?"

Chapter 29

Moser caught the train into the city, rode the Broadway local uptown. Two hours, twenty-three minutes, door to door. He dropped his jacket on his desk chair, tapped at the glass door to Marty Quinlan's office. Quinlan waved him in. Moser shut the door behind him, pulled a chair over, waited while he got off the phone.

"Unbelievable," he said, hanging up the phone. "You wanna hear something? My daughter, Elaine? She comes home last night at three o'clock. The kid's sixteen, she's got an eleven o'clock curfew, she comes waltzing in at three, gets mad at us 'cause we waited up. Like we're spying on her. I ask you, Dave. Is it too much to ask, she should listen?"

"*Waltzing in,* Lieutenant?"

He threw up his hands. "All right. So I'm getting old. My father, he used to say *parading,* but that was a lotta years ago."

"You get my summary?"

Quinlan sighed, looked down at his cluttered desk. "Yeah, it's here somewhere." He shuffled some papers aside, pulled one out. "Here it is." He took a pair of reading glasses out of his shirt pocket, sat back, settling the glasses on his nose.

Quinlan flipped the page on the Investigative Summary, then slipped his glasses off, rubbed at his eyes with the back of his hand. "What this looks like to me, Dave, is you got squat."

Moser shrugged. "That about sums it up."

"You want to shuck it?"

"Not yet. There's a couple things I can chase down."

"The flower guy."

"For one. Also, according to the doorman, Cruz was taking deliveries. Guy with a gym bag, every morning at nine. But Cruz told us he's retired." Moser smiled. "I thought I might stop by, ask him to clarify the matter."

Quinlan rubbed at his eyes. "And you want me to cover your ass, he gets on the phone to Corman."

"That would help, yeah."

Quinlan sighed. "Okay, Dave. But do

me a favor, huh? Try not to piss him off too much."

"Hey, you know me."

Quinlan looked at him, shook his head. "I'm serious, Dave. Go easy, or this guy's gonna bury you in shit."

"Hey, all this shit, there must be a pony somewhere."

Quinlan glanced up at him. "What?"

"It's an old joke."

Quinlan raised his eyebrows. "Yeah?" He looked back down at the summary, then reached across his desk, pulled a file marked *Active* from a metal organizer on the edge of his desk. He dug through it, pulled out a sheaf of papers, stapled together.

"Take a look at this, tell me what you think."

Moser reached over, took the papers. On top was an Investigative Summary, filed that morning. The victims were identified as Valeria de Guzman and an unidentified Hispanic male, mid-forties, identified on the form as *Juan Doe.*

Moser looked up. "This Lou's case?"

"Yeah. Why?"

"Looks like his handwriting." Moser flipped the page, glanced at the evidence log. "Gang hit?"

"Maybe." Quinlan sat back in his chair, folded his hands. "If they were washing cash for one of the drug operations, got caught with their hand in the till."

Moser thought about it, shrugged. "You whack the people handling your money, it's cause they're stealing. But why leave all the equipment lying around, get the cops asking about your business?"

"You want to make an example."

"You do that by killing 'em. Anybody who's in that line of work, they're gonna get the message."

Quinlan nodded. "Okay, it's not a hit. So what is it?"

"Somebody jacked 'em."

"Don't see that much. Not on money laundries."

Moser smiled. "That's 'cause you gotta be crazy to try it. The drug guys won't stop till they find you, and when they do, they don't leave much for the funeral."

"Cheaper that way."

"Sure, the families save on the casket." Moser passed the papers back across the desk. "You didn't need me to tell you this."

Quinlan smiled, tucked the papers back into his file. "No."

"So what's the point?"

"Valeria de Guzman was a resident alien. You happen to notice her country of origin?"

Moser shook his head.

"Guatemala."

They were silent for a moment, both of them looking down at Quinlan's desk. A half-eaten bagel rested on a paper napkin, next to a jar of Smucker's grape jelly. There was a stain on his desk calendar, the last week of the month, where he'd spilled his coffee.

Moser said, "You realize there were so many Guatemalans in this city?"

Quinlan grinned. "Dave, until a couple days ago, I didn't know where Guatemala was. I had to look it up."

"You find it?"

"You hit Texas, take a left." Quinlan picked up his coffee cup, took a sip. He grimaced, put it down. "Every morning, I come in, get a cup of coffee. An hour later I end up drinking it cold. Never fails."

Moser smiled. "I always end up drinking the one from yesterday. Got that layer of scum on top?"

"Get a life, Dave."

"I had one. It didn't work out." He nodded at the file on Quinlan's desk. "You ever heard anything about Guatemalan gangs?"

"No." Quinlan shrugged. "Doesn't mean they don't exist."

"Gang war?"

"It occurred to me." Quinlan picked up the file, flipped it open. "When was the last time we had *one* dead Guatemalan?"

"Would we know, we got one? This neighborhood, most of the victims are from down there somewhere."

"You don't pull the immigration record?"

"Some guy gets shot in a liquor store holdup?" Moser shook his head. "We got enough to worry 'bout, where they died."

Quinlan thought about it, nodded. "I could get Records to do a search."

"You don't mind waiting six months."

"I'm startin' to worry we could be looking at something we got no idea about here." Quinlan reached over to a stack of files, dug through it until he found another folder. "You hear what came in on the after-hours shooting?"

Moser shook his head.

Quinlan opened the file, pulled out a sheet of paper, passed it across the desk.

"Our dead guy, Jano Benitez? Lou ran an immigration check on him, sent his name into the computer down in Washington. Turns out he was some kind of professor down there. Guatemala, again. Economics professor, I think. Got into the country as a political refugee back in the eighties."

"You sure it's the same guy?"

Quinlan raised a hand to stop him. "Wait, you haven't heard the best part. We figured, okay, it's a mixup on the name. So we run it again, Joaquin Yano Benitez. 'Ee-ano,' I guess they pronounce it. How many can there be, right? Guy down at INS calls us back, says he can't figure it out. According to the computer, this guy was granted political asylum in eighty-seven, submitted an immigration application last month. Denied. He figures, okay, it's a political thing, so he calls up a guy he knows over at the Guatemalan consulate, gets him to check with the National Police down there, see if we can confirm his identity."

Moser looked up. "You think we could get 'em to check out Eva Cruz, they're at it?"

Quinlan shrugged. "This point, why not?" He made a note on a yellow Post-it, stuck it to his phone. "They turn up anything, I'll have 'em send it to you."

"They get anything on Benitez?"

Quinlan sat back, smiled. "He gets a message the next day, it turns out the guy's *dead.*"

"So you're back where you started."

Quinlan shook his head. "No, you don't get it. He's *been* dead for a couple years now. Got killed during the war down there."

Moser stared at him. "That's a new one."

"You gotta love this job, huh? Seems the guy was some kind of leftist, disappeared back in 1984. His family went to the police, but got nowhere. That's how it works, the death squads they got down there. Then a few weeks back, this construction crew digs up a burial ground behind a church in some little coastal town . . ." He glanced at the paper. "Barrita Vieja. They're building a fancy resort down there. Tourist thing. So the district police chief calls up his boss in Guatemala City, says he's got twenty-three bodies, all of 'em showing gunshot wounds. The government stops the project, turns it all over to this new human rights commission they set up, and they send in a team of forensic anthropologists, who start matching dental records. Guess whose name comes up."

"Jano Benitez."

"Except he's Joaquin Yano Benitez, the professor." Quinlan sighed, put the paper aside. "So now, not only don't we have a suspect, we've got a victim who comes back from the dead just to get blown away in my jurisdiction."

Moser smiled. "You remember that joke about the bug on the windshield?"

Quinlan looked at him, shook his head.

"I'll bet he don't have the guts to try that again."

Ray Fielding sat over the sheaf of photocopies he'd made of the address book before he turned it over to the crime lab, studying the names. Six names, with addresses and phone numbers: Angel Cardoza, Juliana Carter, Ana Calderon, Dr. Richard

Clauson, Abraham Cowley & Sons, and Ernesto Cardoza. An arrow led down the margin from Angel to Ernesto Cardoza, whose address Fielding recognized as a retirement home out in Queens. The father, probably.

He got up, walked across the squad room to the computer terminal, keyed in the names, and sat back to study the copies in his hand while the machine searched through the NYSIIS system. A few moments later, the screen shifted. He glanced over. No hits. He tried a few alternate spellings, but still came up empty. None of the people listed had a criminal record or known aliases.

He went back to his desk, put his feet up on the edge, pulled the telephone over to him. He dialed the first number, got an answering machine, and left a message for Angel Cardoza to call him. Juliana Carter was eager to talk. She used to work with Valeria at the Red Apple grocery on outer Rockaway, a few years back.

"We were cashiers," she said. "Valeria, she was a pistol. You should have seen her when this guy tried to snatch her purse last year? She chased him right down the street, screaming at the top of her lungs. Finally, he just dropped it and took off. Too much trouble." She gave a sigh. "And now she's dead."

"She ever talk about having trouble with anyone?"

"Valeria? Honey, that girl got along with everybody. She could talk the spots off a leopard, you know? 'Course, this was a couple years ago, before Valeria took the job over at the liquor place? After that, she changed."

"Changed how?"

"She got quiet. Didn't come 'round much, even when Claudia had her baby. Like she had things on her mind."

He got no answer at Ana Calderon's number. Dr. Richard Clauson was a therapist down on West End Avenue, but his receptionist declined to answer his questions about Valeria de Guzman, citing patient confidentiality. Fielding put a star beside Clauson's name.

Abraham Cowley & Sons was a funeral home up in the Bronx. The owner, Alfred Cowley ("one of the sons"), drew a blank on Valeria de Guzman.

"But that's not unusual," he told Fielding. "She could be a relative of one of our clients."

Clients? Fielding wondered if he should try that out on Moser. Pull up at a crime scene, walk up to some guy with half his face blown off, say, *Let's have a look at the client.*

Finally, a receptionist at the nursing home listed under Ernesto Cardoza regretted to inform him that, according to their records, Mr. Cardoza had passed on last year.

"Became a client, huh?"

"I'm sorry?"

"Thanks for your help."

He still had to hear from Angel Cardoza, and the doctor might offer an interesting angle, but so far, he was striking out. He flipped through the pages, sighed. There were several dozen names in the book. Just running them through the computer could take days.

Nicolaides came in, stopped at the coffee machine. Fielding glanced up at him as he came over to his desk.

"What's up, Ray. You still workin' my cases?"

"Somebody's got to."

Nicolaides sighed. "You bored, Ray? Got nothing to do?"

"No." Ray sat back, nodded at the photocopied pages of the address book.

"There's something here bothers me."

"Yeah?"

"Think about it. You put in your Investigative Summary that the victim was dead at the front door, the killers had to step over her on their way out. But the forensics team found the address book next to the phone in the kitchen. So how would blood get into the book?"

Nicolaides sipped at his coffee, shrugged.

"I mean, was she holding it when they grabbed her? Maybe, except you say the blood trail led from the bedroom to the front door, away from the kitchen. If she had it in her hand when they stabbed her, how would it get back to the telephone?"

"One of 'em moved it."

Fielding nodded. "Or it was in the kitchen the whole time. Either way, the killers stopped to look at it after they killed her."

Nicolaides looked down at the pages in his hand. "Interesting."

"They thought so."

Across the empty squad room, a phone rang. Nicolaides looked over at it, then glanced at the duty board.

Fielding sighed, laid the list of names on the desk. He got up, walked across the squad room to pick up the phone. "Homicide, Fielding."

Nicolaides watched him pull a pad over, feel in his pockets for a pen. He looked on the desk, tried the drawer, which was locked.

"Just a second." He looked up at Nicolaides, mimed writing on his palm. Nicolaides dug a pen out of his drawer, tossed it across to him. Fielding caught it just before it hit the ground.

"Okay, shoot."

He scribbled the address, then straightened slowly, looking over at Nicolaides. Gently, he tucked the pen into his pocket. "Ten minutes," he said, and hung up.

Nicolaides watched Fielding look down at the slip of paper in his hand, shake his head. "Jesus."

"What's up, Ray?"

Fielding turned, walked over to the desk, laid the paper down next to the photocopies. Nicolaides leaned over, looked at it — *2387 Nagle, Apt. 601.*

He looked up at Fielding. "Yeah, so?"

Fielding bent over the photocopies, ran a finger down the page until it came to rest at an address: *2387 Nagle Ave., Apt. 601.*

Then he straightened, took his coat from the back of the chair, slipped it on.

"Angel Cardoza."

"You ever see an angel looked like that?"

"An-*hel*," Fielding said, stepping over a pool of blood to squat beside the body.

"So? Means the same thing, right?"

Angel Cardoza was short and fat, with a face scarred by boils. His throat had been cut so deeply that his head was barely attached to his body. He lay tilted back in a recliner, a book in his lap. His shirt, the book, and the floor behind the recliner were covered with blood.

"I guess," said Fielding. "Anyway, he's with the angels now."

Fielding took a pencil from his pocket, used the tip to lift the pages of the book so he could get a look at the title. *La Cabeza de la hidra,* by Carlos Fuentes. "This mean anything to you?"

Nicolaides shook his head. Fielding let the page fall. He glanced up at the crime scene technicians, who were dusting for prints, taking blood samples, photographing the body from different angles. "Weird," Fielding said.

A uniformed cop came in, waved them over.

"We got a witness," he said. "Old lady who lives downstairs. She was sitting by the window, watching the street. Saw the victim come home from work a couple hours ago, then two guys drive up in an Acura, park it by the fire hydrant across the street. She watched them get out, come across toward the building. Got a good look at them. She heard them ringing doorbells, at random, like. Somebody must've buzzed them in, 'cause she hears them going up the stairs. About fifteen minutes later, they come out, get in the car, drive away."

"Can she ID them?"

The cop grinned. "Oh, yeah. She recognized one of them. He's a guy used to hang out up here, sold a little crack up in Fort Tryon Park a few years back. Hispanic, but very pale. She said they used to call him 'Blanquito.' "

"Terrific." Nicolaides flipped his notebook closed. "Even with an eyewitness, we draw a blank."

* * *

Miiko Reyes, the computer told them. Fielding sat back, smiled as the screen listed a conviction on a "criminal sale of controlled substance" charge back in 1993, his release date from Rikers, and the name of his parole officer. He printed the sheet, carried it over to Nicolaides.

"You remember that ad on TV, the cats used to do that little cha-cha dance?"

Nicolaides looked up at him. "Huh?"

"Man, that's what I feel like doing, we catch one of these guys through the computer. Makes me happy."

Nicolaides took the sheet from his hand, looked at it. "You need some time off."

"You know how you say 'hit the mark' in Spanish?"

"How?"

"*Hacer blanco.* You hit the white, like in a bull's-eye." Fielding tapped the paper in his hand. "There it is."

"Maybe," Nicolaides said. "We got anything current on this Miiko Reyes?"

"Last known address in Bay Ridge, back in 1991. The old lady made it sound like he hasn't been uptown in a

310

while. So maybe he's been working closer to home."

"Yeah." Nicolaides studied the paper, frowning. "This guy, you'd think we'd remember him, huh?"

Chapter 30

Watching Cruz, Miiko couldn't help wondering how the guy hadn't ended up in the coronary ward, Mount Sinai, the way he carried on. Screaming, waving his arms around, until the muscles in his neck were twisted tight, his face getting red, until it reminded Miiko of those licorice sticks he'd steal out of jars on the counter of a candy store when he was a kid. Take 'em out to the beach, feel the sand crunching between your teeth.

What ever happened to those, anyway? Miiko wondered. Cruz screaming at Eduardo how he was going to cut their throats, these *güilas* who knocked over his money works. *Did they even have candy stores anymore, or just a rack of Milky Ways behind the counter of a liquor store, next to the* Penthouse Forum?

He'd been listening to Cruz curse for two days, pacing around his apartment, furious.

"They do this, an insult to me!" Waving a finger at Eduardo, like he was going to walk over, poke him in the eye. "A threat!"

Not mad 'cause his people were dead, Miiko thought. Just pissed because he figured Giardella beat him to it. Couple days, he'd have killed 'em himself. Eduardo checking their names off his list with that little pencil stub, like guys use out at the track. No, what had Cruz spitting blood was that somebody else did it, walked off with the cash.

Not like it was so much, Miiko thought.

A hundred sixty-four thousand, and some change. By the time they split it, he was looking at, what? Enough to fly down to Miami, buy some product, get set up in a nice business. Enough to get your ass out of this fuckin' apartment, the guy screaming all the time, but not enough to get off the street.

"Hang in there," Stoll told him. "Keep your ears open. You hear them talk about Tangliero, you listen good."

Stoll standing in a switching shed at the north end of the subway yard just below 215th Street, washing blood off the blade of his buck knife in a filthy sink. Miiko grinned at the memory,

313

shook his head. Jesus, the guy was changing his image of cops for good. He was as bad as Eduardo, you get him started. Whipping that knife out, that crazy music screeching away in the background. Two minutes, it was done.

The cop telling him how this guy Tangliero walked off with a million five, his buddies at the coffee shop going crazy trying to find him. Now *that's* some serious money. For that, he'd stick around, put up with Cruz's screaming, ride around with Eduardo smoking those fuckin' cigarettes all the time, stinkin' up the car, in case the guy turns up. Stoll told him he'd put the word out with his cop buddies, keep an eye out for the guy, even sent his picture to all the station houses, so the cops would recognize him. Telling 'em how the guy was in business with Cruz, some deal to grab the money, take off.

That much made sense. Cruz, he was gettin' ready to run. Making lists of people he wanted gone, shutting it all down. Spending hours on the phone with some guy down in Central America, talking about what island he'd go live on. Staying long enough to clean up the mess, shut down the money operation, leave no traces.

And the guy, Tangliero, was mixed up in it somehow. Little fat guy, used to show up every morning, wait in the hall while Cruz counted packs of bills out of his gym bag, then refilled it with the clean money withdrawn from the bank accounts. Then, suddenly, he'd stopped coming. Miiko'd waited to see if Cruz would mention him, put his name on the list. If they were in it together, that's how it would end. But then, why would the delivery guy need to split with any-one? Grab the money and walk, what's so hard about that? But Stoll had said the Italians figured Cruz was in it, put the guy up to it, maybe, when the money got frozen in Guatemala.

Miiko smiled. Like *anything* could freeze down there.

So what could it hurt to stick around, find out? Keep your eyes open, see what happens.

Miiko, watching Eduardo glance over at him, expressionless, thought —

Long as your name don't get on that list.

Claire draped the suits across the back of a chair, switched off the television. Tangliero came out of the bathroom, wearing only his pajama bottoms. His stomach was covered with a thick mat of dark hair. He had shaving lather on his face, except for a patch on his chin where he'd scraped it away.

"I was watchin' that."

"While you're shaving?"

"I keep the door open, I can see it in the mirror." He walked over, switched the set back on. "This guy, Regis, cracks me up. I got an aunt up in the Bronx, he talks just like her. You ever see when they show the audience? All these women, they love him. It's like he's having 'em all over for coffee, the husbands leave for work. They chat."

Claire glanced at her watch. "You better get dressed. They'll be here at ten."

He went back into the bathroom, left the door open. "I'll bet you watch a lot of TV, huh? Sitting around hotel rooms all the time?"

She didn't answer, thinking about Tony Giardella tossing the bank statement into her lap. Telling her how they'd arrange it so she just had to turn her back for a few seconds, getting the car door open, say. That's all it takes, a few seconds, right there in the parking garage. Couple weeks later, she'd get a key in the mail, a safe-deposit box down at Dime Savings. She could leave the money there, clean it out, Tony shrugged, it's up to her.

"What happens if I say no?"

Tony spread his hands. "Nick here gives you back your gun, we drop you at your car. None of this ever happened. Only problem for you is, when the time comes, how do you know when to duck?"

Tangliero came out of the bathroom, rubbing his face with a towel. He draped the towel over his shoulder, picked up one of the suits.

"Look't this." He rubbed the edge of the fabric between his thumb and forefinger. "You ever see work like this? Beautiful."

Claire looked at him, feeling the anger swell within her.

"Enjoy it. He doesn't want your business anymore."

Joey let the suit down, slowly. "He said that?"

"I guess your friends spread the word. He wouldn't take any money."

His face crumbled. For a moment, she thought he might cry. *Oh, Christ.* She regretted telling him now, but saw no way out of it. "Look, just get dressed, okay? You can't use this guy, anyway. When they get you set up, you'll find a new tailor."

He shook his head, sadly.

"What? In Idaho? Probably get my clothes at Leisure Suit City. Work in a fuckin' bowling alley, eat at Kentucky Fried."

"KFC."

"What?"

"They changed the name. It's KFC, now."

Tangliero stared at her. "This, she knows. So what do they call it in Kentucky?"

"How should I know?"

"Where you from?"

"Alabama."

"Eufaula?"

"Greenwood."

He threw up his hands. "Listen to you. You don't know a straight line when you hear one? That joke's so old, it's got rigor: I say, 'Eufaula?' And then you say, 'No, I lead.' "

"Get dressed, Joey."

He held up a finger. "You ever watch those commercials? KFC? Bunch'a black kids, rappin' about the chicken. So you tell me, maybe it's KFC up here in New York, you really think they're gonna call it that in Idaho?"

He raised his eyebrows at her, picked up the suit, went into the bedroom.

Take the money, Claire thought.

Chapter 31

By 2:30, Vinny Delario had eaten three egg rolls, an order of shrimp fried rice, and a plate of lo mein. He'd thought about ordering the mu shu, but didn't want to get plum sauce on the envelopes. His problem now, he'd drunk two large glasses of Pepsi and half the pot of tea that the waiter kept pouring into his cup every time he brought a new order.

"Listen, I gotta pee," Vinny whispered into his collar. Across the restaurant, he saw one of the two black women at the table by the window look up at him, shake her head. He looked over at the door, saw it swing open, a cop coming in. He walked toward the back of the restaurant, paused at the takeout counter, then turned to lean on it, glancing around the place. Near the window, the two women were laughing, one of them holding a hand up, coughing. The place was empty, except for them.

The cop glanced over at Vinny, nodded. He walked over to the booth, sat down.

"How ya doing?"

Vinny shrugged. "Okay. You?"

"Not bad." The cop stared at him. "I know you from someplace?"

"We meet at Marty's?"

The cop nodded, leaned forward, one hand under the table. Vinny reached into the manila envelope on the bench next to him, slid out an envelope, passed it under the table. The cop folded it in half, slipped it into his pocket. He slid out of the booth, stood there looking down at Vinny.

"Take it easy."

"Yeah, I'll see you 'round."

Then he turned, went back to the takeout counter, paid for a couple egg rolls in a waxed-paper bag. Then he walked out, turned left up the street, past the windows. The two women kept talking, one of them swishing her shoulders like she was imitating somebody. They both laughed, not looking at him.

Vinny glanced up at the security camera, wondered if Richter was watching. He was back in the office behind the kitchen, where they'd set up the taping equipment. They had guys in a van out on the street, getting shots of the cops walking into the restaurant. The whole place was wired for sound, just in case the microphones they taped to his chest went out.

Now, Vinny crossed his legs, wincing. He looked straight into the camera, mouthed the words slowly —

I have to pee.

An autopsy was performed on Angel Cardoza at 10:30 on the morning following his death. Fielding sat in, giving Nicolaides a chance to finish the paperwork. When he'd left the squad room, Lou was seated before the ancient IBM Selectric, picking his way among the keys.

"Not too late to switch," Ray told him, smiling. "If you want to watch the cut."

Nicolaides reached for the Wite-Out. "I'm cool."

And so Fielding sat with his notebook open on his knees, one knuckle pressed to his nose, watching Wickert adjust the microphone that hung on a boom just above his head, slip on his latex gloves, and choose a scalpel from a metal tray beside the autopsy table.

"Sure you need that?" Fielding indicated the gash in Cardoza's throat. "Looks like somebody did your work for you."

"Anybody can open a book," Wickert said. "It takes an educated man to read it." He paused, probed the edges of the neck wound with the tip of his scalpel. "Actually, it's a nice cut. Very smooth."

"That tell you anything?"

Wickert shrugged. "No struggle. Looks like a vertical pull at each end of the cut, which suggests the killer was reaching around from behind, pulling the knife toward the base of the skull."

He moved to the head of the table, demonstrated.

"We found him in a recliner," Fielding told him. "Laid back like in a barber's chair."

Wickert nodded. "I see this kind of cut with gang killings. They suspect some guy's an informer, cut his throat, pull his tongue out through the wound. They call it 'the necktie.' Same clean cut, same angle. A couple guys hold the victim down, the killer puts his knees on either side of his head to hold him still. We get denim fibers out of the hair sometimes."

Fielding scribbled some notes. Wickert moved around to the side of the table, started giving an external description of the body into the microphone. He paused, turned to look at Fielding.

"You got some kind of gang war going on uptown?"

"Not that I know," Fielding told him. "Why?"

Wickert shrugged, turned back to the body. "Last one you guys brought in had some gang traits. The eyes."

"Yeah, I was just thinking about that when you mentioned the informer thing. You thought it was a witness killing. Like she saw something."

"Well, that was speculative, of course. We see 'em all here. Sometimes a pattern seems to appear. And, other times . . ." He shrugged. "Enough sand piles up, you get a mountain."

"Yeah. Dave's handling that one, but it looks like the gang angle wasn't productive."

Wickert made his incision, started narrating his findings into the microphone. Fielding scribbled *Necktie?* in his notebook, drew a box around it. It *felt* like a gang hit — three victims killed the same day, all slashed to death. You couldn't write it off as a jealousy killing, not when you looked at the victims. You catch a guy screwing your woman, you kill him on the spot, not six blocks away. Or say the killer just found out, he kills the woman, tracks the boyfriend down at his apartment, cuts *his* throat? Fielding shook his head. It didn't make sense.

Fielding glanced up at Wickert; he had Cardoza's heart in his hand, examining it. He carried it over to a scale on the counter behind him, weighed it. "Six hundred twenty grams," he said into the microphone.

He looked over at Fielding.

"This guy wasn't gonna be around long anyway."

"Yeah? How come?"

Wickert laid the heart in a metal dish, started to section it with his scalpel.

"He had a heavy heart."

Chapter 32

Sitting in his living room in a pale blue dressing gown, sipping from a tiny cup of espresso, Adalberto Cruz looked every inch the wealthy man. Like a diplomat, Moser thought, maybe a rancher down in Argentina.

What he didn't look like, Moser decided, was a man whose little girl had been dragged from the river three days ago.

His face was calm, his eyes like quicksand. You glanced away, felt his eyes moving across your face, taking it in. Like a specimen to add to his collection. All without the slightest hint of motion, just a brief flicker in his eyes.

"You must be quite a businessman, Mr. Cruz."

"I am." He gave a slight smile. "But why do you say?"

Moser waved a hand at the apartment. "You've reaped the rewards."

"Ah. You're impressed by my surroundings." He leaned forward, poured coffee from a silver service. "Many people inherit wealth, Detective."

Moser shrugged. "Maybe."

"Is there something I can help you with?"

Moser reached into his coat pocket, drew out the security camera print from the flower shop, passed it across to him.

"You ever seen this guy?"

Cruz took the photograph, glanced at it. "No."

He slid the photograph back across the table. Moser left it there, took a second print from his pocket — the guy from the morning deliveries, balding, expensive suit, gym bag in his left hand as he reached out to ring the bell.

"How about this one?"

Cruz took the picture, glanced at it. Then he laid the picture on the table, reached for his espresso cup.

"I think you are asking a different question now."

Moser shook his head. "Just trying to identify anybody who had contact with your daughter on the day she disappeared."

Cruz raised the cup to his mouth, sipped at it carefully, taking his time. "This man is none of your concern,

Detective Moser. I suggest you look elsewhere."

Moser leaned over, slowly, placed the photographs side by side on the table. Then he glanced up at Cruz. "Are you refusing to answer my question?"

"This you ask to protect yourself."

Moser sighed, looked around at the expensive apartment, the careful furnishings. "Mr. Cruz, this is my job. You watch the cops on TV, they always talk about, 'He had the opportunity and the motive.' My experience, that's a load of crap. Most of the guys we see, they've got no motive, except they're pissed off, or it's some guy knocking off a liquor store, he's had too much already, shoots up the place. The way it works on the street, you look for opportunity. Nine times outta ten, that's how you catch 'em. Look at the guys who *could've* done it, you find out one of 'em bought himself a gun couple days before. You get him down to the station, ask him, 'Why'd you kill him?' He says, 'His dog crapped on my shoes.' So much for motive, right?" He paused, tapped up the photograph from the flower shop. "This guy, we think he sent flowers to your daughter the afternoon before she . . . disappeared." He moved to the second photograph. "This guy we know came to your house every morning, early." He sat back, spread his hands. "Best we can tell, they're the only people she had real contact with that day. So, you want suspects, these are the first two guys I got to look at."

Cruz placed his cup on the saucer, carefully, then put both on the table. He stood up, looking down at Moser. "I regret that I cannot help you."

Moser looked up at him, rubbed at his jaw. Then he picked up his photographs, slipped them back into his pocket. "You know, I've seen all kinds of things, working Homicide," he said, getting up off the couch. "But one thing I've never seen is a man handle grief without acting like the world's just stabbed him in the eye."

Cruz stared at him, and Moser saw the muscles in his jaw tighten. "What one feels, Detective, may not be what one shows." He turned, crossed to the window, looked out. "I am giving you the chance to catch this man, because this is how it is done here. I understand this, so I watch. I keep my peace. When this time has passed, I will see what must be done."

"I'm gonna pretend I didn't hear that, Mr. Cruz."

"As you wish."

Moser watched him turn, his eyes empty. "You're angry. That's how it is. But you start trying to handle this on your own, I can't cut you any slack. You see what I mean?"

"You've made yourself quite clear."

Moser watched his face. It looked like somebody had chipped it out of stone. "But you're not gonna listen."

Cruz tipped his head slightly. "I do what I must."

Moser looked away for a moment, shook his head.

"I came up here as a courtesy," he said. "I also figured I'd ask for your help. Maybe you'd thought of something in the last few days — names of Eva's friends, places she liked to go — anything that could help me catch this guy. But it looks like you've got other ideas."

Cruz was silent, his eyes returning to the window.

"This isn't a game, Mr. Cruz. Justice isn't a private matter." Moser paused. "At least, not on Park Avenue."

Cruz smiled. "Come here, Detective."

Moser sighed, walked over to the window. Cruz pointed down at the street.

"Two months ago, a man was killed on that spot. He was out walking his dog, just after midnight. Somebody took his wallet, put a knife between his ribs." He looked over at Moser. "You cannot protect us, even here. If you can't help this man, or my Eva, to stay alive, why should I trust your justice?"

"Because you don't have a choice. We're the only game in town."

Cruz smiled. "Are you?"

Chapter 33

Javier Estora pulled into the parking lot of a diner on Rockaway Boulevard, swung past the entrance toward the back of the lot. He spotted a pair of squad cars parked under a street light. Four cops shared a booth in the window, laughing. One of them twisted around to say something to the waitress as she walked past. She came back to the table, took his nose in her fist, leaning down close to his face to shake her head. Javier could see her mouthing the word *NO* very slowly, turning the cop's head back and forth. The other three cops were busting a gut, one of them slapping the table, choking on a mouthful of his sandwich.

He kept going, around the side of the building to the back, pulled up next to a Dumpster. A floodlight mounted on the corner of the building lit up the whole lot, except where the Dumpster threw a long shadow. The lid was up, and there was garbage strewn across the ground beside it where someone had tried to toss a bag in and caught the edge, spilling meat scraps, plastic wrap, and rotten vegetables across the ground.

Javier smiled. Like old times.

He'd come to this country seven years before, worked as a busboy in a diner out in Borough Park. Noon to midnight, seven days a week. A place so bad, even he wouldn't eat there. He went home every night to an apartment in Washington Heights he shared with five other men. Three months of this before he figured out the deal. The cashier was an ancient Greek, who perched on a stool behind the small counter at the entrance. When customers came in, they'd lean across the counter, whisper, "Reservation for Mr. C." He'd crook a finger at Helos, the waiter, who'd seat them, wipe down the table with a dry rag, then go behind the counter for coffee. For some time, it puzzled Javier why so many customers got up and left, even before placing their orders. The food was bad, but how could they know that? Were they glancing over at the other tables, changing their minds at the sight of fried potatoes drenched in grease, vegetables still frozen along the edge, pork chops the color of burned cardboard? Only when Demetrios, the cashier, exploded at a couple of kids from Bensonhurst as they approached his counter, demanding to know why they didn't stay to eat, what were they *paying* him for, were they just stupid, giving him money for nothing? — only then, as Demetrios reached for the money, muttering under his breath, did Javier experience a revelation, coming to a sudden halt just inside the kitchen door with his tray of dishes. Ah! How could he not see it?

From that moment on, he watched Helos closely, noting how his hand dipped into the pocket of his apron before reaching for the rag he used to wipe the tables, how the rag always swept over the edge of the table, dropping a small packet of cocaine into a customer's lap, how those customers barely touched their food, pausing on their way out the door to hand Demetrios a thick wad of folded bills, not waiting for their change. Javier watched as Demetrios took frequent trips to the walk-in freezer on busy nights, a freezer that had not worked in the three months he'd been there. For another month, he considered what he'd learned, what he now saw as obvious to all but him, an innocent in such things.

For Javier Estora — the only name he answered to now — had spent his adult life as a playwright, founder of a leftist theater group that staged spectacles of resistance before audiences of bewildered peasants in the mountains outside Guatemala City. When the death squads came for him in the summer of 1987, he'd crawled through the bathroom window of his tiny house, hid in the bushes, trembling, as they systematically destroyed his books, his typewriter, the framed photograph of Augusto Boal that hung above his desk. When he emerged from his hiding place, he found that they'd scrawled a slogan across the front door of his house: *Happy is the people who needs no heroes.* Brecht, misquoted. The irony, he concluded, of a cultured fascist. Two days later, from his hiding place in Escuintla, he'd sent a message to his father, a director of the National Bank in Guatemala City and a supporter of the military regime. The note was returned, unopened, but scrawled on the outside of the envelope was a telephone number and the words *Sería padre tomar el fresco.* He dialed the number, told the man who answered that he was interested in getting some fresh air, and the man told him to bring $5,000, American, to the car-rental desk of a tourist hotel in downtown Guatemala City.

"I don't have the money," he told the man.

"Who does?"

He gave the man his father's name, and the phone went dead. Twenty minutes later, his stomach twisted with anxiety, he called back.

"Pack your bags," the man told him.

The next day, clutching his false papers, he boarded a flight for New York. *Javier,* he whispered to himself. *Your name is Javier Estora. Do not forget.*

And so, he became Javier Estora, leaving his former life behind like a snake shedding its skin. *Or a butterfly,* he thought, *emerging on brittle wings.* He had been, in this new life, a busboy, a thief, an arsonist, and now, an elegant dealer in antiques in a gray Cadillac Seville. For, once his eye had been drawn to the walk-in freezer, he'd found himself dreaming each night of butterflies, golden wings spread, soaring over fields of flowers. During the day, as he cleared the grease-coated dishes from tables near the window, his mind brooded on a simple idea, a gift from his enemy — *Happy is the people who needs no heroes.*

One night, as Demetrios locked up the cash register and Helos lingered in the kitchen, Javier hauled six bags of garbage out to the Dumpster in the alley behind the diner. On his way back into the kitchen, he slipped a thin strip of cardboard from his pocket, tucked it into the door latch. As Demetrios locked the front door, he walked down to the corner, boarded a bus that had just pulled up. He waved to Helos, who scowled back at him, getting into his car as the bus pulled away. Javier rode the bus three blocks, got off, and walked back. He circled the block once to make sure the parking lot was empty, then slipped into the alley behind the diner.

The freezer was padlocked, but Javier found a hammer in the storeroom, snapped the lock off its hasp. Inside, he found a few sacks of potatoes, some broken tables, and an old metal cash box on a shelf by the door. He'd seen boxes like it in bodegas in Escuintla, figured that he could pry the lid off with a screwdriver or smash it open with a rock. But when he tried to lift it off the shelf, he couldn't budge it. He peered under the shelf, saw that it was bolted on. There was no exposed screwhead, no way to get at the bolt to cut it. He leaned his head against the cool metal wall, closed his eyes. His legs ached from twelve hours of busing tables. In his mind, he could hear the clatter of dishes, smell the grease that he couldn't wash from his hands at night. For a moment, he thought he might cry.

His eyes opened. He looked over at the box on its long shelf. He could see food crumbs scattered along the length of the shelf, a dull stain on the wall where a spill had never been cleaned. The shelf was mounted on a standard, which rose up the wall like a tiny railroad track. *Or a ladder,* he thought, *climbing to heaven.* His eyes closed, then opened again, following the standard up the wall, then coming back down to the shelf. His hand came up; he ran one finger along the edge of the shelf, feeling its smoothness. Then his hand slipped under it, he took a slow breath, let it out, and gently lifted the shelf off its bracket.

Now, sitting in his car in the dark, eyes closed, one hand resting on the steering wheel, he could feel the elation that shook him at that moment. He'd lifted the shelf down, laughing aloud at the thought of Helos carefully bolting the box to the shelf, Demetrios peering over his shoulder, nodding as the drill screwed the bolt home. He carried the shelf into the alley, leaned it against the back wall of the diner. It was six feet long, the box attached near one end. He went back into the diner, through the kitchen to the dining room. At the far end of the room, away from the front window, he found a candle on a table, left over from a noisy party of Greeks, guests of Demetrios, who'd stayed from six to midnight, eating olives and feta from a bowl in the middle of the table. He lit the candle, put it back on the table. Then he went back into the kitchen, raised the stovetop, blew out the pilot light that flickered at a small notch in the pipe between the burners, turned the gas to high, and lowered the lid. On his way out, he hung the broken padlock back on the freezer door, wondering exactly how hot a fire has to get before it melts steel.

Many times, in recent years, he'd tried to imagine how he must have looked, carrying that six-foot kitchen shelf across Brooklyn in the middle of the night. He stopped in a vacant lot a few blocks away, found a spot behind a pile of rusted metal awnings, and broke the cash box open with a concrete block. Inside, he found a thick wad of cash and twenty-three small packets of cocaine. He stuffed the money in his jacket, unzipped his pants, and hid the cocaine in his underwear. In the distance, he could hear the wail of sirens.

He walked four blocks to the subway, caught the train into Manhattan. At 4th Street, he transferred to the A train, rode it to the Port Authority. He checked the bus schedule, found a 6:00 A.M. departure for Miami. As the bus pulled out, the sun was rising over the East River.

Five years later, he was back. He owned a small shop in Park Slope, lived comfortably on two floors above the store. He dealt in Chinese jade, lacquer boxes, decorative screens. From time to time, the phone would ring, and a voice he knew would request a special item — a carved box chosen from his collection, with an intricate system of locking drawers.

Such a box lay on the seat beside him now, the delicate carvings on its lid tempting him to unwrap the layers of tissue paper, run his finger over them. He loved the feel of polished wood, the scrolling lines of the design.

A car turned into the lot, circled the diner, pulled up in the shadows beside the Dumpster. Javier could see it was an Acura, gray, with two men in it. The driver got out, came over to his car, tapped on the passenger window. Javier touched a switch on his armrest, popped the lock. The man got in, ran a hand over the leather upholstery, whistled between his teeth.

"Nice ride."

"Thank you." In the glow of the streetlight, Javier could see the man's pale skin, his dark hair. For a moment, he thought of Bela Lugosi, hands raised in terror against the rising sun. He pushed the thought aside. "You have something for me?"

The man jerked a thumb at his car. "My partner. Should I call him over?"

Javier tipped his head slightly. The pale man turned, raised a hand to the man in the other car. Javier let one hand slip down between his legs, his fingers closing on the grip of a .38 he kept tucked beneath the seat. He slid it up his leg, let it rest in his lap, the barrel pointed at the man in the seat beside him. He twisted slightly in his seat as the partner got out of the Acura, came around the back of the car, opened the door, and got into the backseat.

Javier nodded, but the man ignored him. He shook a cigarette from a crumpled pack, dug in his pocket, came out with a book of matches. Javier watched as he folded one down, struck it with the tip of his thumb, and held the matchbook up to his face, the glare making his eyes look strangely yellow. He crushed the flame out between his thumb and forefinger, folded the burned match back into the book, tucked it into his pocket. Then he turned his gaze to the window, smoking.

Javier frowned. "You have the money?" he said to the silent man. The man ignored him. Javier looked over at the pale man beside him.

The pale man smiled. "No money, tonight."

Javier felt his stomach tighten. His fingers closed around the gun in his lap.

The pale man glanced at the man in the backseat, then down at the gun in Javier's lap. He raised both hands, palms outward, smiled. "My partner has a message for you. From Cruz."

Javier swallowed, hard. "I don't know what you mean."

The pale man looked amused. "No?"

Something flashed before Javier's eyes, and he felt a sharp burning across his throat. He gasped for breath, but none came. His hand came up, the fingers scrabbling at the wire that dug into his throat.

Miiko reached across, jerked the gun out of the man's hand, tossed it into the backseat. The man's eyes were bulging, both hands now scratching at the skin on his neck, blood on his fingertips. He made a clicking noise in his throat, blinked. His tongue came out. For a moment, nothing happened. Then his head slumped forward. Eduardo leaned across the front seat, lowering him until his head rested against the steering wheel. He kept the wire taut as the man gave a jerk, then lay still. His eyes were open, staring at Miiko.

"Man, that's fuckin' gross."

Miiko got out of the car. For a moment, he thought he might throw up again, but he swallowed it back. He leaned against the car hood, laughed. Imagine the cops, they got a serial killer with a delicate stomach. Little puddle of vomit at every killing, like a trademark. *Catch me before I puke again!*

Eduardo reached across the front seat, picked up the box on the seat, tore the paper off. He examined it, turning it in his broad fingers, trying to get it open. Then he leaned forward, smashed it against the dashboard, twice. He slid two fingers into a hole where the wood had splintered, came out with a plastic bag. He tore it open, scattered the white powder across the front seat, tossed the bag onto the floor on the passenger side. Then he got out of the car, came around the back, got into the Acura. He took a piece of paper from his pocket, unfolded it, and made a check beside a name with the stub of a pencil.

Miiko grinned, shook his head. "Man, seems like a fuckin' waste." He climbed in behind the wheel, started the car, got the air-conditioning on. He put his face up next to the vent, feeling the burst of cold air on his neck, his eyelids.

"Ah, that's nice."

He sat back, started to put the car in gear, but Eduardo's hand closed on his like a clamp, held it still. He glanced over, saw Eduardo was staring out the window, his cigarette held down between his knees. Miiko followed his gaze, saw a police cruiser at the edge of the parking lot, waiting to turn into traffic. It pulled out, and another behind it. A moment passed, then Eduardo released his hand. Miiko backed out, swung around the back of the diner to the street.

"You hungry? I know a great Jamaican place, up by 145th."

Eduardo kept his gaze on the traffic, silent.

"They got all that jerked stuff. Jerked

chicken, jerked pork. You like things jerked?"

Eduardo looked over at him, smiled. *Stupid question.*

Chapter 34

Richter tapped on the door of DeStefano's office, waited as he got off the phone. When he hung up, Richter laid a surveillance transcript in front of him, said —

"We've got a problem."

DeStefano looked up at him. "One time, I'd like somebody to come in here, say we *solved* a problem." He sighed, picked up the transcript, glanced at it. At the top of the page, it said — SUBJECT: STOLL, MARTIN. The transcript itself was brief, a telephone conversation recorded at 11:40 P.M. from an unknown male caller. It read:

STOLL:
  Hello?
CALLER:
  This Marty Stoll?
STOLL:
  Yeah. Who's this?
CALLER:
  You got a rat in the house.

STOLL:

What?

CALLER:

Just thought you'd want to know.

CALL TERMINATED

DeStefano tossed the transcript back across the desk. "You trace the number?"

"Pay phone, out on Flatbush Avenue, near Atlantic."

DeStefano folded his hands, stared at the papers piled on his desk. "Who knows about Delario?"

"Just the surveillance team. But it's possible someone made us during the payoffs." Richter shrugged. "You always take that risk, working an informant."

"Can we protect him?"

"We've got surveillance on his house. When he's out, we're with him."

"Has Stoll tried to contact him?"

"Not since the call."

DeStefano leaned his head on his hands, thinking about it. "Any way to divert attention from him?"

"Like how?"

"Get him thinking it's somebody else."

Richter thought about it for a moment, then smiled. "Yeah, I think we could do that."

DeStefano put on his reading glasses, reached for a file in his in-box. "All right. I don't want to know the details. You have my authorization. Do what you think necessary."

Richter nodded, picked up the surveillance transcript. "I'll take care of it."

Chapter 35

The way Tony Giardella always pictured it, he was sitting in a barber chair, hot towel wrapped around his face, like Albert Anastasia. Sheet draped over him, the barber suddenly going quiet as he looks up, sees the guy come in. Tony, under the towel, hearing the *snick, snick* of his scissors give way to silence. Some nights, he dreamed it, like slow motion: reaching up, pulling the towel away, seeing the guy there in the entrance, shotgun in his hands. The guy smirking at him, saying —

"Hey, Tony! I got something for ya!"

That's where he woke up. He'd find the sheet tangled around him, like he'd tried to throw it off at the last moment.

Like that would help.

A couple years back, he'd seen an old Clint Eastwood movie, three guys come into the barber shop, one of 'em spins the chair around with his foot. Clint, shaving cream all over his face, doesn't even blink. He's got his gun drawn under the sheet, blows one of 'em right through the front window. Spins the chair, shoots the other two. All three of 'em caught by surprise, their guns still in their holsters.

Tony thinking — *Hey, is that fair?*

But Clint, he just gets up out of the chair, real slow, pulls the sheet off, wipes the shaving cream from his face. Tony couldn't remember if he'd paid the barber.

"My luck," Tony told Bobby Amondano, later, "the guy shows up when I'm at the *dentist.* I'm sittin' there, I got Rothberg's fingers in my mouth. I mean, where's the dignity in that?"

The two of them sitting in the Azores, the booth back by the kitchen, Bobby stirring his coffee.

"You're lucky the guy didn't shoot you right there."

Tony sighed. *Lucky.* He'd cracked a molar on a breadstick at Il Pescatore, then put off making the call, his mind on other stuff, until he felt another piece break off, this morning, all he was eating was scrambled eggs.

So there he was, he told Bobby, stretched out, Rothberg staring down into his mouth, the guy wearing some kind of plastic eye shield, surgeon's mask over his mouth, made him look like he was getting ready to head over to Newark, fish around in the sewers. Wearing those rubber gloves, the drill in one hand, tiny mirror in the other, you feel like he's getting ready to carve up a brisket. And the nurse, cute little Japanese girl, she's reaching across with a long tube, sucking hunks of tooth from his mouth so Rothberg can get in there with the drill. He closed his eyes, tried hard to imagine he was lying on a deck chair, next to a pool, cool drink in his hand.

And then, just like in his dream, it got quiet. He felt Rothberg draw back, slowly. The nurse still had the tube in his mouth, but he could tell she was looking at something else now, the thing sucking away at the side of his tongue. He was just getting ready to reach up, pull the tube out — *Hey, what the . . . ?* — when he felt the gun brush gently against his ear.

He knew what it was, right away, not moving a muscle as the guy leaned down, whispered into his ear —

"Hey, Tony. I got a message for you, from Frankie in Miami."

And Tony winced, recognizing the voice, that New Orleans mumble, like he was chewing gum while he talked. He raised both hands, said quickly —

"Hey, this about Joey? 'Cause I got it taken care of."

The guy laughed. "I'm glad to hear it, Tony. But that's not why I'm here." And Tony felt him lean in close, whisper in his ear, "We still got the little problem of the money, right?"

Tony felt him draw back, the gun coming back to nudge his ear. He swallowed, wondered if he'd have time to hear the shot before it blew his head apart, then felt the guy reach over, stuff a twenty-dollar bill into his open mouth.

"Wait," Bobby said, looking up at him. "You could tell that?"

"What?"

"It was a twenty."

Tony shook his head. "I found out later. Rothberg took it out, wiped it off. I still got it, in my wallet."

"And that's all he said?"

"That's it."

"Cesare, right?"

"Only guy I know sounds like that."

Bobby sipped at his coffee. "He's tellin' you to clean this thing up, or you're gonna have to eat the money."

Tony winced. "How'm I gonna do that? Four million?"

"Hey, it could be worse."

"Yeah?"

"You got your tooth fixed, huh?"

Yeah, right.

Like he had four million . . . no, four million *five*, for Christ's sake, he could just write it off.

"Hey," he told Bobby, "It ain't so simple. I got expenses."

Knowing, even as he said it, what he sounded like. One of those guys, he bets the fuckin' New Orleans *Saints* every week, maybe 'cause that's where he lost his virginity, goes to a Shylock, two months later, he's begging the guy not to break his arm. *C'mon, I got expenses . . .*

He'd wondered, lying there while Rothberg reaching in with a pair of tweezers to pull out the twenty, if there was any way he could get this guy over to the York tomorrow morning, solve the whole problem. He'd told the guys from Miami they were bringing Joey out

354

through the garage, like the deputy'd told him. Maybe ask this guy, Cesare, to help 'em out, keep him busy for a while.

Rothberg staring at him, his face pale behind the Plexiglas eye shield. "Are you all right, Mr. Giardella?"

"Yeah, I'm fine." He sat up, swung his feet off the chair. "We gotta do this today?"

Rothberg looked at the twenty-dollar bill in his hand, passed it across to the nurse, who wiped it on a paper towel. He pushed up the eye shield, ran a handkerchief across his forehead, glancing over his shoulder at the door.

"Uh, I've got the tooth opened up. We should get you fitted with a temporary crown, at least."

Giardella reached in, ran a finger over the top of the tooth. There was a large hole along one side, the edge jagged.

"Do you need a few minutes?" Rothberg asked.

"Nah. Let's just get it done." He settled back into the chair, closed his eyes. "You think maybe we could close the door this time?"

Chapter 36

Moser hung around the squad room, catching up on paperwork, until almost nine. He'd just gotten up to take some forms over to the copier when the phone rang. He picked it up, said —

"Moser."

"Hey, Dave," Marty Stoll said. "You need a ride?"

Moser could hear laughter in the background, music.

"I figured you weren't coming in today."

"Yeah, I was a little late, but I made it."

He heard Stoll put his hand over the phone, say something he couldn't make out. Then he came back on the line.

"So what's the story? Should I come by?"

Moser glanced at his watch, thought about spending two hours on the train, said —

"If you're heading out, yeah."

"Okay, I get off duty in a few minutes,

but I gotta hang around up here for a while, see a guy. You in a hurry?"

Moser looked down at the papers piled on his desk. "I got things I can do."

"I'll call you when I leave. You can meet me on the corner."

"Like the song."

"Huh?"

"See ya, Marty."

He hung up the phone, thought about walking down to the New China for mu shu, but came to his senses. He got some coffee from the machine in the hall, carried it back to his desk. When he got back to the squad room, he found a sheet of paper on his chair. He pushed some files aside to clear a spot for his coffee, picked up the paper. It was a memo from Ray Anundaz, the desk sergeant working the day shift, cc'd to the Cruz file: Malcom Davis, owner of Flowers by George, on Lexington, had stopped by as requested by Detective Moser, but after three hours viewing the Category 1 Offender books, he'd failed to identify the man who purchased flowers from him on the morning of . . .

Moser tossed the paper onto the pile on his desk, settled into his chair. He put his feet up on the edge of the desk, peeled the lid off his coffee, and closed his eyes.

Malcom?

When the coffee had lifted the weight from his eyelids, he leaned over, pulled one of the cardboard file boxes marked *CRUZ* from beside his desk, dug through it until he found the manila envelope that contained his case photos. With one arm, he shoved a pile of papers aside, opened the envelope, shook the photographs out onto his desk.

Eva Cruz in ski clothes, smiling. Eva posing for her student ID, shoulders bare in a pale sundress. Then, too quickly, Eva floating just under the river's gleaming surface, naked on the autopsy table, a series of shots as the autopsy was carried out, in which she ceased to be Eva Cruz, became something unrecognizable, painful to contemplate.

Moser forced himself to look at each photograph, carefully. Then he slipped the autopsy shots back into the envelope, folded it closed. He reached around to where his jacket hung on the back of his chair, dug out the surveillance photos. For a moment, he sat looking down at the shots of Eva lined up before him. Then, carefully, he laid the two surveillance photographs at the end of the row — the bald guy first, arriving in the morning, then the shot of the man at the florist's counter, a digital clock in the upper right corner of the picture showing the time: *16:22:49.*

Moser sat back, let his eyes move along the row of photographs. Slowly, as if he were reading the story . . .

At the shot of Eva in the river, he paused. Something wasn't right. He glanced at the last two pictures, came back to the girl in the water, her face veiled by her drifting hair. Gently, he reached out, slid the picture from its place, moved it down past the surveillance photos, to the end of the row.

His eyes settled on the photograph from the florist's shop, the pale man passing money across the counter.

Buying her flowers.

Moser crossed the street, walked up the block to stand at the corner, next to the Social Security office. Standing there, he caught himself glancing over at the precinct, a squat brick building with a row of dirty apartments rising behind it. Like somebody had dropped it there, he thought, by mistake. Maybe that wasn't so wrong. There were black windows along the second floor, a wheelchair ramp running down the front wall. To Moser, it looked like a tank, all set to rumble down Broadway, seize the high ground.

He'd heard a story that after they'd put it up, somebody'd realized there was nothing on the building to show it was a police station. So they'd hung a large *34* next to the entrance, black letters. Moser could picture it, the divisional brass standing around on the sidewalk, making sure the maintenance guys hung the numbers straight, saying —

That'll do it, huh?

Like you couldn't tell from the lot full of squad cars next to it, the row of unmarked Fords parked out front. Take a cop out of uniform, Moser thought, smiling, what's he look like? Crown Victoria, neutral color, black-wall tires.

Two young patrol officers came out, wearing sweats and carrying a basketball. They headed up the street to the schoolyard at P.S. 48, where they could shoot baskets under a sign dedicating the building to one of their own, Officer Michael Buczik, the last officer from the precinct to be killed, L.O.D. Nobody'd had the heart to tell the school they'd spelled his name wrong.

Watching them, Moser remembered the first time he'd walked into a precinct house, raw meat. What surprised him was how familiar it all seemed, like any construction site, or auto body shop, a place where guys hang out, tell stories, scratch their balls, lean on the squad room wall, one hand rubbing at the knot over their eyes, to take calls from their wives. Only, next to the phone was a list of officers killed since 1934, and every man felt the silence that drifted at the edges of the place, the way a man's whole body changed when he strapped on the gunbelt.

At times, Moser wondered how it looked to outsiders, people who wander in off the street to file a complaint, guys they dragged in for questioning. Just a row of black metal desks, a floor that needed sweeping, milk crates on a shelf stuffed full of files, like a guy who fixes cars, keeps his receipts in a shoebox next to the phone. Radio playing softly, light R&B. The desk sergeant, a guy you could tell had played ball in high school, twenty years ago now, filling out a form in ballpoint pen, his hand pausing over the page as he squints through his glasses. A sign over his head, saying CORRUPTION CAN BE REPORTED TO INTERNAL AFFAIRS DIVISION. Somebody had scratched out *can,* replaced it with *must.* Across the way, two women read newspapers in the clerical office, drinking coffee from mugs that said *World's Greatest Mom!*

Picturing it, Moser wondered how he'd gotten there. Like a guy driving home at night, not thinking about it, he pulls into the driveway, looks up, realizes he's at a house he lived in years ago, his ex-wife's car parked in the garage, a curtain moving in an upstairs room. Too late to back out, no way to go in. Just shake your head, try to figure out how so much could have changed.

Moser saw a man get out of a car up the block, reach up with his hands behind his neck, stretching. He came up onto the sidewalk, walked over.

"Hey, Dave." Tom Richter glanced back at the station house, smiled. "Looks simple from out here, huh?"

Moser shrugged. "Bring 'em in, write 'em up."

"Yeah, that's what they tell you."

Moser looked over at him. "You got something on your mind?"

Richter smiled, reached into his pocket, came out with a photograph. He passed it to Moser, who held it under the streetlight, glanced at it. It showed him getting out of Stoll's car in front of the station house. He was looking up at the building, his face tired. Stoll, behind the wheel, was watching him get out, thoughtful.

"Little tip, Dave? Find another way to get to work."

A gold Cadillac Seville pulled up in the bus zone, and the passenger window eased down. Marty Stoll leaned across the front seat, called out —

"You comin', Dave?"

Moser walked over, got in. He glanced up at Richter. "You know Marty Stoll? He's down at the Three-Oh."

Richter came over, leaned down against the passenger window. "Nice car."

Stoll stared at him for a moment, then smiled slightly. He reached out, ran a hand across the dashboard.

"Fine Corinthian leather."

Moser got home after ten. His head was throbbing from riding the whole way in silence, Stoll glaring out at the traffic, like he wasn't even there. He flicked the television on as background noise, opened a can of tuna and a bottle of Sam Adams. He caught the last inning of a Mets game, watched Ryan Thompson go down on strikes to end it while he mixed some mayo into the tuna, ate it right out of the bowl, standing there at the kitchen counter. Then he drank some more of the beer, glanced out the window at Marty Stoll's house as he waited for the station to cut away to the local news. A television flickered behind an upstairs window, another downstairs in the den. Marty watching the ball game, Rita in bed with a doctor show.

Jesus.

Moser walked down the hall to the bathroom. When he came back, the news was on. The anchor was doing an on-camera interview with the Assistant Commissioner of Police on the steps in front of One Police Plaza. Moser reached over, turned the sound up in time to hear him say the magic words — *per-vasive pattern of corruption* — before they cut back to the anchor.

"Shit."

The anchor launched into another story, so Moser flipped the channel, got a clip of the Assistant U.S. Attorney, Merrill Conte, refusing comment as he got into a car outside the federal build-ing. *Yeah, right.* Send your assistant to get the car out of the garage, pull it up right in front of the building, so the news crew can get a nice shot of you ignoring them. Drop a few hints to your favorite reporter, get twenty seconds on the late news declining to say what you know. Then call a news conference, attacking the local media for reporting unauthorized leaks. A few days later, indict a couple dozen cops. Make sure your wife keeps the VCR tuned up, get it all on tape. *Power.*

The anchor was replaced by a grainy photograph of a fat guy coming out of a restaurant. He was wearing an expen-sive gray suit, carrying what looked like a gym bag. He'd been caught glancing up at the camera, curious. A reporter talked away in the background, identi-fying him as Joseph Tangliero, a member of the Luccario crime family, rumored to be cooperating with federal authorities in their investigation. Moser dug a toothpick out of a drawer, slid it into the corner of his mouth. He stared at the man's face; his frozen smile looked almost innocent, the grin of a man trapped by the camera. The face looked familiar, like a lot of guys Moser had seen. Only, by the time he saw them, they were lying on an autopsy table, Wickert using a power saw to open their skulls. If he'd paid off cops, Moser might have seen him around the precinct. But no envelopes landed on Moser's desk; if one had, he would have carried it down to the desk sergeant, told him —

"There's been a mistake."

And that would have ended it. It was easy to stay clean in Homicide: corpses don't ask favors.

Now, watching Tangliero's picture give way to an aerial shot of a six-car pileup on the Merritt, Moser imagined he could almost feel the earth tremble as several hundred cops lurched out of their La-Z-Boys, heading for the liquor cabinet. He glanced over at Stoll's house. The upstairs television was off, the room dark. Downstairs, he thought he saw a shadow move across the window, and then it was gone.

He drained the beer, left the bottle in the sink. He flicked off the kitchen light, went into the living room, stretched out on the couch. Forty minutes later, he glanced at his watch. He got up, went into the kitchen, unplugged the television and carried it back into the living room. He set it on a chair against the far wall, plugged it in, settled back on the couch. It was a movie he recognized from about ten years back, Kathleen Turner and William Hurt rolling around on a bed, sweat shining on their bodies. She gets him to kill her husband, then sets him up to take the fall.

He watched it for a while, his memory starting to fill in the parts he'd missed. Realizing, Jesus, that's Ted Danson as the guy's buddy, in a black wig, made him look like Monty Hall. And Mickey Rourke, playing a punk, rubbing a finger across his lower lip every few seconds, so you'll know he's *acting*. Everybody wearing those seventies clothes. More than ten years. Fifteen, maybe?

He liked the guy playing the cop. Black guy, he's the only cop in some little Florida town. The whole movie, he never takes his hat off — one of those snap-brimmed Uncle Lou hats, like the old guys wear out at Yonkers Raceway. Sitting there in his office, feet up on the desk, he's got that hat on. A real character. They give him the worst lines in the movie, nothing but how the guy's screwin' up, he's gonna get himself in trouble, this guy has fun with it, turns it into music. Sits down at the table in a coffee shop, tips that hat back, orders himself a "Co-co-la."

Moser smiled. A whole movie full of stupid guys, only the cop sees what's going on. William Hurt, you can't believe he doesn't see it coming. She's smiling, saying things like, *Baby, I love you, don't you know that?* and *Oh God, it's never been like this,* he doesn't notice she's about to lay one upside his head. Blind.

And then, without warning, Moser felt himself stiffen. The realization catching him up short, like the *tsing!* of a tripwire in the second before the lights go out — *Yeah? What'd you see?* Glancing around at the empty room, now. He'd missed it. No way around that. For weeks, he'd come home from work, find Janine sitting in the dark, she'd tell him —

"I'm just resting my eyes."

And he'd shrug, write it off as a tough day, get a beer from the refrigerator. Two weeks later, he came home, found the house stripped bare. Like waking up in a movie theater, finding the lights on, everybody gone. It scared him, made him wonder what else his eyes were missing.

Some detective.

He lay there, watching William Hurt play it out, seeing it all clear when it was too late. He felt like someone had drained the strength from his body, even the little it took to turn his head a few inches, glance away from the screen.

And if he did?

An empty room, the darkness surrounding him.

Chapter 37

Joey Tangliero prepared for his initial day of testimony before the federal grand jury by consuming a three-egg Denver omelet ("In honor of my forthcoming relocation"), a double side of bacon, rye toast with butter and grape jelly, hashed brown potatoes, orange juice, and a pitcher of coffee. He spent the next hour in the bathroom, talking quietly to himself. Toward the end, Claire heard him vomit loudly, twice. When he emerged, a faint sheen of sweat glistened on his forehead.

"You okay?"

He nodded, crossed to the fruit bowl on the coffee table, pulled a banana off the bunch. He peeled it, ate the whole thing without speaking. When he finished, he dropped the peel back into the bowl, pressed a hand against his stomach carefully.

"I always heard that's good luck. Puking before a show." He burped quietly behind his hand, shook his head. "I think they just tell you that, you won't feel so bad you got your head in the toilet."

Claire checked her watch. "You think you're done?"

"Yeah, I'm done."

"Then it's time."

She took a cellular phone from the pocket of her jacket, dialed. When McCann answered, she said, "We're ready." Then she hung up.

Joey paused at the mirror in the entryway, checked his tie. He was wearing the gray double-breasted, dark blue shirt, a pale rose tie. "I look all right?"

"You look like you know what you're talking about."

Claire reached under her jacket, unsnapped the safety strap on her holster. With her hand on the .38, she stepped to the door, unfastened the latch, opened it a crack.

"We clear?"

Evans, one of the two second-shift deputies, glanced down the hall in both directions. "Clear."

His partner, Coley, raised a hand to him from the elevator. When it arrived, he stepped halfway in, blocking the door open with his body. He waved to

Evans, *come on.*

Claire took Tangliero by the elbow. "Okay, let's go."

She stepped out into the hall, drawing him after her. Evans stepped back to let them pass, his jacket swinging open a few inches, so she could see the MAC-10 machine pistol on its strap beneath his arm, his hand reaching in to flick off the safety. Then she was past him, moving fast up the hall, a half step ahead of Tangliero, pulling him along. For a moment, she wondered if she felt nervous, then thought —

Not yet.

She swallowed, hard. Her skin itched like mad under the flak jacket. Up ahead, Coley was leaning out of the elevator, checking the two side corridors that met at the elevators. Claire watched his face, envying his calm. Thinking, she must be crazy, law school wasn't *so* bad, really, and, hell, they weren't paying her enough for this shit . . .

But here was the elevator, and she was shoving Tangliero in, hand on his chest, backing him into a corner where she could shield him with her body. Or, Jesus, *part* of him, at least. A good shot, she thought, could probably blow a few nice chunks off his hips, leave her without a scratch. Weight loss, the U.S. Marshal's way. Like trimming a slab of beef.

She turned, saw Evans step into the elevator, the doors closing. Watched him lift his cellular phone, hit the speed dial with his thumb, say, "We're comin' down."

She drew the .38, got both hands on the grip, pressed back against Joey until she felt his stomach against her lower back, felt him try to suck it in, then a moment later, his hand coming up, settling on her ass. She drove an elbow into his gut, heard him give a cough, and the hand went away.

Evans stood watching the numbers light up. As it passed three, his hand came up, hesitated, then pressed the emergency stop button as they passed two. The elevator sighed to a halt, Joey whispering —

"What's wrong?"

His voice nervous, suddenly. Evans turned, raised a finger to his lips. For a moment, they all stood there in silence, listening. Claire could hear the other elevators moving in the shaft, a clicking sound as they passed each floor. Then, faintly, shouting. No shots, just the voices of men who expected to be taken seriously, making it all very clear.

Then, just as quickly, it was over. The shouting died away. Evans's phone chirped. He answered it, listened for a moment, said, "Okay." He tucked the phone into his pocket, pressed the Start button on the elevator panel. He glanced over at her as they started down, nodded.

"All done."

Behind her, Claire heard Joey let out his breath slowly. His stomach sagged against her, spreading out across her back. She moved away from him, slid the .38 back into the holster.

Joey took out a handkerchief, wiped his face.

"I hate to tell you this," he said, "but I just farted."

Later, as they waited in the tiny office down the hall from the grand jury room, Joey started to shake. He was sitting behind the desk, fiddling with a rubber band between his fingers, when suddenly he looked up, said —

"Fuck this."

And Claire, looking over, saw his hands were trembling. His forehead glistened with sweat. For a moment, she thought he might burst into tears. He stood up, hands flat on the desk.

"You hear what I'm saying? Fuck this shit."

Then, just as she started to get up, he swallowed, took a deep breath, and raised a hand to stop her. He stood there for a moment, not saying anything, then sat down, heavily.

"Okay," he said, his voice quiet again. "I'm all right now." He took out his handkerchief, wiped it across his face, avoiding her eyes.

Like it just hit him, Claire thought.

When they'd reached the garage, McCann and two other men had been waiting for them, all of them carrying the short, pistol-grip Mossberg shotguns they used for close work. Two black vans stood with doors open nearby, their paths blocked by several unmarked cars. Otherwise, the garage was empty, silent.

Claire, hustling Joey into a waiting car, had watched him glance over at the vans, thoughtful. He was quiet during the ride downtown, looking past her at the people on the sidewalk. McCann, turning to look back from the front seat, told him —

"Be you, pretty soon. Couple days with the grand jury, we can start working on a new identity. Before you know it, you'll be on the street. Get yourself a burger, you want."

Claire, watching Joey frown, wondered why McCann had chosen that moment to let the red clay hills of Georgia back into his voice. She tried to picture Joey on a street in Valdosta, saw him glance over at McCann, thinking the same thing.

Pair of overalls, straw hat. Maybe get himself a pickup truck, she thought. Hang a Mossberg on the gun rack, use it for hunting squirrels.

But Joey didn't say anything, quiet now. He just shrugged, went back to watching the street. They caught a long light in midtown, and Claire saw him lean forward, craning his neck to get a look west down the avenue. When the light changed, he sat back, told Claire —

"That's my part of town. The Azores,

it's down there a couple blocks." He sighed, folded his hands in his lap, like a kid waiting outside the principal's office. "They make a good carbonara, you're ever in the neighborhood."

Now, sitting there in that tiny office, she saw him start to shift and squirm in his chair.

"I gotta take a leak."

Claire glanced at her watch. "I'm not supposed to let you move around until Conte's ready for you. They'll take you to the men's room before you go in to the grand jury."

He got a look on his face, like he couldn't breathe. "Look't, my bladder's not so good. Somebody just tried to kill me, okay?"

Claire sighed, wondering what he'd do if he actually *saw* the guys, up the hall now, three of 'em, each handcuffed to a different piece of office furniture in the U.S. Attorney's offices, the guys from the Organized Crime Strike Force letting 'em sit there for a while, get to feeling lonely, before they went in, started firing questions at them. Not so dangerous-looking, now. Might take some pressure off Joey's bladder.

But then she remembered the smell when they'd opened the trunk of Tony Giardella's Lincoln, found Joey curled up inside. She snuck another look at her watch, said —

"Okay, we got a few minutes, I guess."

Joey stood up, looking relieved. "Hey, thanks. I owe you one."

She took him down the empty hall, her hand resting on the .38 at her waist. At the doors to the bathrooms, she hesitated, then pushed open the men's room door, calling out —

"Zip 'em up, gentlemen. I'm seizing this bathroom for the U.S. Marshal's Service. Everybody vacate the premises, now!"

An attorney from the tax enforcement division poked his head out of one of the stalls, his face startled.

"What's going on?"

"Finish your business, sir. This facility is closed."

The face disappeared for a moment, then the toilet flushed, and the attorney hurried out. Claire, stepping back to let him pass, felt a wave of disgust, watching him go past, rubbing his hands on his pants. *Takes, what? A minute to wash 'em?*

She took Joey's arm, pulled him into the men's room, left him by the urinals as she went along the row of stalls, pushing the doors open. Empty. Two of the toilets had been left unflushed. No big surprise. She'd grown up with two brothers.

Beyond the stalls, there was another row of sinks, a pair of hand dryers, and a second door. She pushed it open, glanced through. It led into the next hallway.

She came back along the row of stalls, nodded at Joey. "Okay, go ahead."

He looked at her. "What? Like this?"

"You want to go, now's the time."

He glanced over at the urinals, then back at her. "I can't do it with you standing there."

"Use a stall."

He bit his lip. "I got what's known as a nervous bladder. Means I can't do it unless I'm alone. It's enough of a problem, there's other men in the room. I know you're standing out here, it's not gonna happen."

Claire rubbed at her face. "There's two doors, Joey. I can't guard both of them."

He looked at the doors, thinking about it. "Maybe we can lock one?"

Claire stood against the wall next to the men's room, trying to look official. *More like a hooker,* she thought. *Found herself a good spot.*

She didn't like it, letting Joey out of her sight. If McCann came by . . . or, Jesus, Conte? They'd have her ass for it. But what choice did she have, Joey whining at her that he had to go, too embarrassed to do it with a woman there? She wondered, the guys who guarded Valachi, Sammy the Bull, or that guy in the movie, what's his name? Henry Hill. You think they had to deal with this kind of crap?

The room was as secure as she could make it. She'd pulled a metal toilet roll from one of the stalls, used it to wedge the door mechanism, up on her toes, straining to jam it into the angle where the two bars folded together. Then gave the door a yank, making sure it worked before turning to glare at Joey —

"You satisfied?"

He shrugged. "You gonna wait outside?"

Like she *wanted* to stand there, listening to him take a leak. Something she could tell him when he came out,

380

maybe. How moments like this, she wanted him to know, gave her a *special* thrill, made it worth spending all her time in hotel rooms, listening to a bunch of sociopaths, one step from Rikers, complain about how fucked-up their lives were. All that, plus a GS-4 salary.

She glanced at her watch. He'd been in there almost five minutes. How long could it take?

She tapped on the door, waited, then pushed it open an inch or two, said —

"Hurry it up, okay? They come for you and we're not there, I'm gonna catch hell." She waited, but Joey didn't say anything, so she let the door swing shut, thinking — *Great. Probably take twice as long now.*

She waited a few more minutes, until she felt herself start to get angry . . . remembering, as she banged on the door, the look her father used to get, standing there outside the ladies' room at the mall with the other husbands, every one of 'em looking like somebody had taken a riot stick upside their heads, waiting as their wives "freshened up."

His face the closest thing to rage she'd

ever seen. All of it boiling to the surface, right there — fury, contempt, that twitch at the corner of his eyes that told you he was asking himself why, *why,* any man *ever* got married.

She opened the door a crack, stuck her head in, said —

"All right, time's up, Joey. You got more, we can come back later."

She waited a few seconds, didn't hear anything, thought, *fuck it,* and pushed through the door. Smiling to see he'd chosen the last stall, trying to get as far away as he could, so she wouldn't hear him. She walked past the row of stalls, stopped in front of the one closed door, said —

"Don't make me come in there."

But knowing, even as she said it, that the stall was empty. She bent over, looked under the door. No legs. Straightening, not wanting to glance over at the far door, but doing it anyway, knowing what she'd see . . .

The metal toilet roll, lying there on the floor, next to the door.

"Ah, fuck. *Joey.*"

Chapter 38

Merrill Conte leaned back in his leather chair, slowly. He folded his hands in front of his chin.

"Let me get this straight," he said, taking his time. "You're telling me that Mr. Tangliero simply *walked* out of the building?"

Not taking it so badly, Claire thought. Considering.

Then she glanced over at McCann, saw him clear his throat, say —

"Uh, that is our information, yes."

Well, maybe not. She looked back at Conte, saw him smile, thinly.

"I take it this wasn't in the plan?"

"No sir, it wasn't."

Conte nodded slowly. "Then the question must be, do we consider this negligence or . . . something else?"

Claire swallowed, glanced over at McCann, saw him nod, like he was thinking the same thing. Both men looking over at her now, frowning.

Shit.

"Deputy Locke's handling of the situation will be subject to an internal review by the Marshal's Service," McCann said. He turned back to Conte. "However, I might be able to clarify some aspects of Deputy Locke's role in this matter."

"By all means."

McCann leaned forward, pressed a button on a tape recorder on the edge of the desk. "This is a recording made by Deputy Locke three days ago."

They heard traffic noise, then the sound of a car door closing, and the street sounds were suddenly muffled.

"How ya doing?" A man's voice, with a thick Queens accent. "You don't mind, I gotta ask Pauli here to check you out, okay?"

"Sure."

Conte glanced over at Claire, saw her lips tighten as a series of rustling sounds came from the speaker. Another man, very close to the microphone, said, "You mind opening your jacket, please?"

More rustling sounds. Conte smiled. "They do a thorough job."

She smiled. "They missed a few spots."

Conte took a moment to imagine the scene, his eyes moving over her slim body. Then the second man said, "She's clean."

"Okay, leave us." A brief burst of street noises, then a car door closed. The first man gave a laugh. "Sorry 'bout that. Pauli, he gets a little carried away sometimes. But we gotta be sure, you know?"

"I understand."

"Like being a kid again, huh? Backseat and all?"

There was a moment of silence. Conte saw Claire smile slightly, shake her head. Then her voice on the tape said —

"You have something for me, Mr. Giardella?"

"Yeah, sure." The sound of an envelope being torn open. "That key opens a safe-deposit box. When it's done, you get another one, just like it."

"I don't see any money."

"Open the box, you will." Giardella laughed. "I keep tellin' you, it ain't like the movies out here."

A pause, then Claire said, "Okay, now what?"

"Now we talk 'bout how it's gonna happen." Conte heard a lighter being flicked open, struck. Locke coughed.

"Sorry. Crack the window, you want." Giardella puffed. "I smoke these things, so I can't smell 'em. My wife, she hates 'em. Won't let me smoke in the house."

"Joey Tangliero smokes the same kind."

"The fuck. I gave him his first cigar. He was sixteen, maybe. Scrawny kid, used to run errands. Now, he weighs, what? Two sixty, on a good day? You seen him eat?"

"I'm afraid so."

"All of a sudden, he's gotta be a comedian. Tells me it's a dream, since he was a kid. I told him, 'Hey, I *knew* you when you was a kid, and the only dreams you had left a stain on your Jockeys.' I mean, I've heard this guy tell jokes now, fifteen years. He's a funny guy, you're sittin' around, having drinks. But I'm here to tell ya, this is no comedian."

"I gotta get back, Mr. Giardella."

"Yeah, okay. Listen, here's the thing. We know where he is. We know when he's gonna testify. We know all that stuff. All we need from you is the setup. How many guys, how they're bringin' him out, like that. You tell me that, I'll tell you what to do when it goes down.

Then you just get outta the way, we'll take care of it. Okay?"

"It's gotta look good. Like I'm doing my job."

Giardella laughed. "Oh, it'll look good. Don't worry, it's gonna be a work of art."

McCann leaned forward, switched off the recorder. Conte looked over at Locke. She met his gaze.

McCann cleared his throat. "Two days ago, Deputy Marshal Locke had a subsequent conversation with Mr. Giardella by telephone. She was instructed to call a number in Staten Island if the plans for moving Tangliero were altered in any way. Otherwise, she was told to expect the hit to take place in the hotel garage, as Tangliero was moved from the service elevator to the car. She was told where to take cover. Based on this information, we were able to stake out a position within the parking garage from which we could observe the killers' arrival. The idea was to take them while they're preparing the hit, see if they'd turn on Giardella."

For a moment, nobody spoke. Conte glanced over at the others, frowned. "I gather Ms. Locke had authorization for this contact?"

McCann nodded. "Deputy Marshal Locke approached me after her first contact with Mr. Giardella, and I gave my authorization to proceed with the operation."

"But you felt it unnecessary to notify my office of this development?"

McCann nodded. "I understand your concern. But we felt that the operation was subject to compromise, the more people we notified."

Conte stared at him. "In other words, you wanted to cover your ass. They kill my witness, I won't know you could have shut them down."

McCann shrugged. "We turned the gunmen over to your office."

"And they've given us squat." Conte leaned forward, tapped his desk with one long finger. "Meanwhile, I'm up there in front of the grand jury, I get a note saying my witness went for a walk."

"We'll get him back."

Conte turned to Claire. "You know where he's going?"

"No."

"Back to his buddies. He thinks if he tells 'em a few jokes, they'll have a good laugh about the whole thing, it'll all be like before." He folded his hands, looked at her. "You want to see the body, they get finished with him?"

Claire said nothing. The muscles in the back of her neck ached.

"We've got a surveillance crew on the Azores," McCann said. "Some detectives from Internal Affairs are watching his apartment out in Queens until our people get there. He shows up at any of the usual places, we'll pick him up."

Conte settled back in his chair, sighed. "He'll go to a friend, ask him to make it right with Giardella. This friend, he'll say, 'Sure, no problem.' He'll call up the Azores, cut a deal. Couple days, we'll find Joey in a ditch."

McCann got up, unplugged the tape recorder, starting winding the cord around his hand. Claire waited until he was done, then got up, seeing him pick up the machine, glance over at Conte, say —

"Let's hope he's smarter than that."

Chapter 39

Tony Giardella pulled into the parking garage, stalled the Toyota on the ramp up to the second floor.

"Son of a bitch!"

He felt himself start to roll backward, heard a horn blare behind him. "Shit!" He yanked the emergency brake, pushed the clutch in, hit the ignition. The engine caught, and he shoved the gear shift into first, let the clutch out fast. The car jerked, died. He slammed the steering wheel with his fist.

"Ah, you're fuckin' dead! I'll kill you, car!"

He rolled his window down, tried to wave the car behind him past. The driver shouted something he couldn't hear. Giardella stuck his head out the window, glared back at him.

"You got a problem? Come say that to my face!"

The guy threw his hands up, put his car into reverse, backed down the ramp. Giardella watched him disappear onto the floor below.

He looked down at the gear shift, then at the emergency brake. He took hold of the brake lever, let it down slowly, letting the car roll back down the ramp, out onto the parking floor. A man walking toward the stairs stopped to look at him. Giardella glared at him.

"What're you looking at, ya fuck?"

The man turned, walked quickly into the stairs. Giardella got the car started, backed up a few more feet, and revved the engine. He shifted into first, let the clutch out easy. By the time the car hit the ramp, he was in second, the digital speedometer showing thirty. He kept it there, his foot hard on the gas, as the car climbed the circular ramp six floors to the roof.

Giardella felt slightly nauseous as he pulled up next to the Lincoln. When he got out, he had to lean on the hood for a moment to keep from puking. He waited until he was sure, then walked slowly around the front of the Lincoln, got into the passenger side. Bobby Amondano looked at him, shook his head.

"What'd you, push it up here?"

"I'm startin' to hate that fuckin' car."

He leaned his head back against the leather seat, closed his eyes. "I talked to my lawyer, he said even if Joey dies, this whole kidnapping thing gets dropped, the feds can still keep my Lincoln. You believe that?"

"*If* he dies?"

"When." Tony glanced over at him. "We just got unlucky, okay?"

"Frankie's startin' to get impatient. Look, I wasn't gonna tell ya this, get you all nervous, but I flew down to Miami Tuesday. Frankie, he says, 'C'mon, let's take a walk on the beach.' I'm like, you wanna take a *walk?* He doesn't want to talk in the hotel now. Afraid they've got him bugged. Makes everybody walk around in a bathing suit, he can see you're not wired." He looked at Giardella. "You ever see Frankie in a bathing suit?"

Tony shook his head.

"It's not a pretty sight." Bobby rested both hands on the wheel, sighed. "This thing, it's got him crazy. We get out there on the beach, I start explaining about this thing with Joey, he tells me, 'No names!' How do we talk business, we don't use names? All he does is say, 'Is the money safe? Is it safe?'

Sounds like the guy in the movie, the dentist. I told him, 'How the fuck do *I* know if it's safe? Ask Tony.' "

"Me?" Tony swallowed, hard. "Hey, I told those guys not to do it in the garage. I mean, we got the information, you can do it any way you want, right? Tell the broad we're doin' it in the garage, then hit 'em both up in the hallway. They told me they're gonna use their 'professional discretion.' So now it's *my* fault they screwed it up?"

Bobby turned to face him. "Joey's your boy. This thing with the cops, it was your idea. They take you down, those cops go with you. Then you know what's gonna happen? Six months, every cop in the city's gonna be trying to prove what an honest guy he is, making arrests, gettin' in our faces. And that's *if* " — he raised one finger — "*if* your boy Joey don't get us all put away. That happens?" He shrugged. "Hey, Frankie ain't gonna like Lewisburg. They got no beach there."

Tony Giardella felt his stomach begin to churn. "I'm takin' care of it. Couple days, this whole thing'll be over."

"Yeah, it will." Bobby looked over at him. " 'Cause Frankie, he ain't gonna wait much longer, you know?"

Great, thought Tony. He looked over at the Toyota. *Probably bury me in the fuckin' car.*

Adalberto Cruz frowned, folded the newspaper so that he could prop it against the silver coffee urn as he spread Mazola on his toast. He laid the knife against the edge of his plate, took a small bite of the toast, leaned forward to get a better look at the photograph that accompanied the story.

The man lay across the front seat of a car, a sheet draped over him. His hand had slipped off the seat, lay curled on the floor like a dead crab. There was a gun next to it, a small revolver, but at the wrong angle, as if the hand were preparing to grasp it by the barrel. Cruz noticed that the man wore a gold watch, the band half covered by his sleeve. A Rolex, perhaps. His knees, twisted under the steering wheel, were turned in at an awkward angle. *Like a young girl,* Cruz thought, smiling.

He turned his attention back to the headline, PARK SLOPE MAN FOUND DEAD, with a second headline, in smaller type, just below — *Drug Link Suspected.*

Cruz nodded, raised his toast to his mouth.

Exactly.

Chapter 40

The guy at Rent A Wreck told Moser he could give him an '84 Chevette, blue, for $12.50 per day.

"Does it run?"

"Oh, you want one that *runs*?"

Moser stared at him for a moment, the kid moving papers around on the counter. Then he sighed, reached for his credit card.

It ran, but there were splits in the upholstery on both front seats, and the radio faded out whenever he hit a bump. Still, it was better than riding the train.

He drove it into the city, parked it on the street in front of the station house. Walked up the steps, nodded at the desk sergeant, went through the metal fire door to the locker room. A couple of beat cops were standing around a bench, laughing. They looked up as Moser walked in, going quiet. They watched him walk down the row of lockers, stop in front of his own, staring at it in silence.

Taped to the door, just below the handle, was a dead rat.

Behind him, Moser heard the cops get up, walk out. In the hall, they burst out laughing.

On his desk, Moser found a message slip. It said: *Call Tom Richter, IAD.*

Moser felt the anger swell inside him. He picked up the phone, dialed the number on the message. When Richter answered, he said —

"You're setting me up. Why?"

He heard Richter lean back in his chair, slowly. "What makes you say that?"

"I come out of work last night, you grab me on the sidewalk. This morning, I find a rat taped to my locker. I come up to my desk, there's a message lying here says 'Call IAD.' So you tell me. What the fuck should I think?"

Richter was silent for a moment. In the background, Moser heard somebody shouting, then laughter. Then Richter, his voice quiet, said, "We need to talk. That's why I came to see you."

"I got nothing to say to you. Don't call me, don't leave messages. Just keep away from me. You got that?"

"Dave, it's about Eva Cruz."

Moser found Richter sitting against the wall in a booth at the back of the coffee shop, his legs stretched out across the bench seat. He walked over, slid into the seat opposite him. Richter took a moment to set his cup down on the saucer.

"Thanks for coming, Dave."

Moser nodded, lifted his cup to get the waiter's attention. They both waited, silent, until he filled it, walked away. Then Richter took a paper from the inside pocket of his jacket, unfolded it slowly, smoothed it on the edge of the table. "You're working Eva Cruz?"

"Yeah. Why?"

"Stoll ever ask you about it?"

"Why would he?"

Richter sat back, smiled. "Cop talk. We'll just sit here, throw questions at each other." He laid the paper on the table, slid it across the table to Moser. "You recognize that?"

Moser turned the paper so he could see it. It was a copy of a records request, dated April 12, 1995, for an immigration record. In the blank for SUBJECT OF INVESTIGATION, the requesting officer had typed in carefully: *Eva Cruz.* Moser frowned, turned the page over, glanced at the signature at the bottom of the form.

Martin Stoll.

Moser stared at it for a moment, then looked up at Richter. "What's this about?"

Richter leaned back against the wall, rubbed at his knees as if they were stiff. "You remember I told you we got an informant, identified Stoll as a dirty cop?"

Moser nodded, kept silent.

"As part of his testimony, he says he made a regular series of payoffs to a number of cops at precincts across Manhattan. It was a mob deal. They washed the money through corporate accounts, then took out a percentage to grease the cops. But the guy at the center of this deal, who moved all the money? Big mystery. The informant, he won't say. So we get the feds to start tracking money the other way, looking for clean money paid to our OCFs as investment income. It took almost a week, but we got a name. InterAmerican Development Corporation. You want to guess who's the signatory on all the corporate transactions?"

Moser glanced down at the paper. "Cruz."

"That's your victim's father, right?"

He nodded. "We knew he was into something. But I ran him through the computer, nothing. He checked out."

"Same with the feds. They've got an immigration sheet, says he was admitted as a political refugee back in the eighties, but that's it."

Moser thought about it, shook his head. "What's this got to do with my case?"

Richter smiled. "A couple days ago, the money dried up. The feds got a tip that this guy, our informant, was about to get whacked, which is how we got our hands on him. The way he tells it, his people got all tense when the well ran dry, decided he'd been skimming on 'em."

"Was he?"

Richter shrugged. "Probably. He's a wiseguy, right? Anyway, the guy needed help, we were waiting for him. We got enough to shut down the whole operation."

"So why don't you?"

"We need confirmation. This guy's tossing around a lot of accusations. Some cops are gonna get dirty. We want to be sure."

Moser picked up his coffee cup, looked down at the sediment floating in the bottom. "Thoughtful of you."

Richter sighed. He felt the side of the cup with his palm. "I'm gonna get this warmed up. You want some fresh?"

Moser shook his head, watched him raise his cup to the waiter. He came over with a pot, topped it off. When he walked away, Richter said —

"Some guys down at Hudson Street have a theory. They think you're in with Stoll."

Moser watched him pick up his napkin, wipe his hands, carefully. "Why?"

Richter shrugged. "Makes sense, right? You're his friend."

"Should I get a lawyer?"

"Depends."

"On what?" Moser felt his throat start to tighten. He took a deep breath, got his voice under control. "You want to cut a deal with me? I got nothing to tell you."

Richter smiled. "I hear that a lot."

Moser stared at him for a moment, then crumpled up his napkin, tossed it on the table. "Fuck this."

Richter watched him stand up, take out his wallet, toss a dollar on the table. "Sit down, Dave."

Something in his voice made Moser pause, look at him. He looked tired, his face creased with exhaustion. There was a red spot at the base of his throat, where he'd scraped himself shaving. Moser slid back into the booth, slowly.

Richter sat forward, said, "I'm takin' a chance tellin' you this. You're dirty, it'll come back on me."

Moser picked up the scraps from a sugar packet, started tearing little strips of paper off one end. "You think I'm dirty?"

"I'm talking to you, aren't I?"

Moser thought about that for a moment, then nodded. "Tell me about Cruz."

Richter shrugged. "Figure it out. The money dries up, his daughter takes a midnight swim in the East River." He took a sip from his coffee, his eyes squinting against the heat rising off the cup.

"And you think a cop?"

"Not a pretty picture, huh."

Moser watched him set the cup back in the saucer. Careful, like he was trying not to spill it.

Chapter 41

From his room on the seventh floor of the Days Inn on Atlantic Avenue, Joey could pull the curtain back, look east two blocks to the big casinos along the boardwalk, a glance of the moonlit ocean beyond.

Atlantic Ocean, he thought, right there. People get sick of gambling, they walk out the door, find an ocean waiting for 'em. You can kick back, lie on the beach. Take a quick swim.

Maybe drown yourself, you been losing. Free.

Man, hard to believe New York was on the same ocean. You had to drive, like, two hours out through Brooklyn, wade through all the people on Jones Beach, just to get a look at it. But what he couldn't figure out about Atlantic City was, there's the ocean, right? Boardwalk, next to it. So how come you had to cross *Pacific* Avenue to get to his hotel, right there on Atlantic Avenue? Who thought that up? Stick a different ocean in there, like nobody's gonna notice?

Like sister cities, maybe. He let the curtain fall back. *One'a those advertisements they stick in hotel rooms, get you to try the rest of the chain.*

Joey took a scrap of paper from his pocket, sat on the bed, scribbled —

See our other ocean, now!

He tucked the paper away, glanced over at the television. He had the sound on low. Some weather guy was talking about a tropical depression way down in the Caribbean, off Puerto Rico. He kept waving his hands over a map, these big sweeping gestures like he was pushing it up the coast, trying to bring it ashore right here, Atlantic City. Like the guy wanted it, some big hurricane blowing in off the ocean. Good for business, probably.

He glanced at his watch. Twenty-four hours, still, before he could walk over to the Taj. He'd paid cash for the room, registered as Moe Howard. Stuck in his room now, nothing on TV but weather. Not ready to show his face on the street. Not yet.

Walking out of that bathroom in the federal courthouse, down the hall to the stairs, he'd kept thinking every guy in a cheap suit he passed was about to reach out, tap him on the shoulders, say, "All right, that's far enough," or whatever it is that U.S. marshals say, some cowboy thing, like in the movies. Thinking about it as he reached the stairs, how they'd say it, making himself take it easy, not too fast. Just a guy who's done with his business, on his way home.

He couldn't believe it when he reached the street, taking a breath like it was his first one in days. He made a quick left, then a right, not paying attention to where he was going, really, just getting away. Then, when he'd put a few blocks behind him, he went into a bank, got in line, watched the door. An old woman came in, pulling her groceries in a metal basket. Then a black guy in a UPS jacket, heading back toward the loan desks. After that, nobody. When he got up to the teller, he dug in his pocket, like he was looking for his checkbook, made a face like, *Ah, shit,* then shrugged, walked away.

Street smarts.

From there, he caught the subway uptown, got off at 53rd, and walked up

Madison two blocks. He turned west on 55th, walked up the block, slowly, stopped in front of a carved wooden door, three steps up from the street. There was no sign on the building, just a number on the side of the awning to say you'd arrived: *57 East 55th.* Some nights, he saw the building in his dreams, imagined himself climbing the steps, running his hand along the gold rail, to push through the doors, greet the man behind the desk with a smile, then climb the winding stairs to . . .

He sighed, walked up the block to the bank on the corner. Standing there, alone, in the tiny room where the vault attendant had left him — green walls, table, two chairs, like the room for attorney conferences up at Rikers — emptying the stacks of bills from his safe-deposit box into a pair of canvas gym bags, he remembered a few years back, when his sister gave him Milton Berle's book for Christmas. That night, he'd stayed up late, reading about how they sat around in the afternoons, window table at the Friars Club, six extra chairs pulled up, shooting jokes at each other, the old guys making 'em all wait while they told showbiz stories, argued over the ten weirdest acts in vaudeville, the ten ugliest women, the ten guys with the most toes. He got to the part where Red Skelton tells Berle how one day it dawned on him why all the comedians he ever met were *angry* — "We all grew up in some ghetto over in Brooklyn. Comedy, it's our way of getting *even!*" — and Joey had laid the book down on the edge of his bed, feeling something loosen in his chest, like a knot coming untied.

He got up, walked into the bathroom, looked in the mirror. Yeah, he was angry. That's why he'd become a wiseguy, right? He had antisocial tendencies, on account of his growing up in Queens.

Well, that and the fact he hated working.

Staring into the mirror, his face somber, unshaven, he'd thought, *Okay. Be angry.* He'd give it three years. If he landed on his ass, hey, what's lost?

Starting to get excited now, his eyes coming to life. He'd work the open mikes, get some new jokes. Jokes with *edge* to 'em, the kind that leave a scar, they get too close. Then, one day, a few years down the line, he'd walk up those steps on 55th, just before noon, nod at the doorman, climb the stairs to take a seat by the window. The old guys glancing over at him, smiling, waiting to take a shot at him . . .

Only every time he asked for a night off, Tony'd stick that cigar in his mouth, stare at him, say —

"I'm not paying you enough?"

"Nah, Tony. It's not like that. You don't get paid for open mike. Everybody starts that way."

And Tony'd sigh, shake his head. "You wanna work for nothing, I got stuff you can do."

And that's how it went. For six months, he'd hang out at the Azores every night, waiting for Tony to give him something to do. Most nights, he'd come downstairs about ten, look over at Joey, say, "You still here?"

After a while, Joey stopped talking about going to the clubs. A few weeks passed, then Tony had to run down to Miami, see Frankie about a dispute with a guy who ran a sports wire out of a travel agency near Rockefeller Center. Joey drove him out to the airport, carried his bag in to the gate, waiting for him to say, "Listen, I got some stuff I need you to do the next couple nights . . ."

But what he said, looking out the window at the airplane, was "Jesus, I got a headache. You got any Advil?"

Sweat on his forehead, looking at that plane like he could see every bolt in the wing.

"Maybe they sell it at the gift shop. You want me to check?"

Tony shook his head. "Nah, fuck it. Stuff puts me to sleep anyway. Frankie's guy is pickin' me up at the airport, taking me over to the hotel. Frankie, he's gonna want to eat, get some girls in." He glanced over at Joey. "Maybe you should come, do some'a those jokes he likes."

"My mom's sick," Joey told him. "I told her I'd come over."

Tony sighed. People were starting to get on the plane, a woman tearing their tickets at the door.

"All right, gimme the bag."

Joey watched until the plane pulled out, then drove back into the city, slowly. He stopped at the Azores, picked up the week's worth of cash to deliver to Cruz, tossed the pair of gym bags into the trunk of his car. Then he drove home, picked out his blue Collezioni double-breasted, a gray silk tie. He laid the clothes out on the bed, took a long shower, then stood before the fogged mirror with a towel around his waist, both hands resting on the edge of the sink. He watched as the fog on the glass cleared, his face coming into view as a smear of pale flesh. His stomach felt queasy, his legs weak, like if he let go of the sink, he might go right over on his ass. He closed his eyes, forced himself to breathe slowly. When he felt steadier, he opened his eyes, shook his head.

"Jesus."

He combed his hair, shaved, then shook a few drops of Drakkar Noir into his palm, rubbed it into the raw skin. He examined his face in the mirror, checked his teeth for food specks. Then he took a deep breath, smiled broadly, said to the mirror —

"Ladies and Gentlemen, the *real* wiseguy . . . Mr. Joey Tangliero!"

Now, stuck in this hotel room, three hours on the bus coming down here, he winced at the memory. For six months, that was as far as he got.

Staring at himself in the mirror, his face, like the audience would see it. Too fat, too old. Like your uncle Mort, lives up in the Bronx. *Anyway,* he thought, *you got all this money lying around, you're gonna just leave it, go out to a club?* After a while, he'd hang the suit back in the closet, go sit in front of the TV until it was too late to go out. The next morning, he'd ride into the city, drop the gym bags with Cruz, pick up the money at the Azores to do his route. Thinking about it. Getting quieter with every week that passed. Then one day, Tony called Joey into his office, shut the door behind him. "What's your fuckin' problem? You got PMS, or what?"

Joey'd shrugged. "Just, you know . . . I'm gettin' older."

Tony sat behind his desk, lit up a cigar, looked at him. "So, what? You hit fifty, you're takin' a vow of silence?"

"You ever think about doing something else, Tony?"

"Like what?" Tony flicked his ashes into a paper cup. "Work in a fuckin' office? Have a store, you gotta worry 'bout some punk's gonna come in, try to rob the place?" He shook his head.

"Look't me, Joey. I got thirty guys answer to me. I got all the money I need. I want some ass, I pick up the phone. Some guy pisses me off, same thing. You tell me, what's to want?"

Joey nodded. "Yeah, I know." He was silent for a moment, then looked up at Tony. "It's just . . . You ever had something you gotta do?"

Tony took the cigar out of his mouth. "Sure. This morning I had'a take a crap. Happens all the time."

Joey watched the red tip of his cigar jump as he flicked the ashes into the cup. "Me, I gotta make people laugh."

Tony stared at him. "That's it? Joey, you make people laugh all day long. Only reason we haven't had you whacked, you make us laugh."

"It's not like that, Tony. You guys are my friends." He turned toward the window, jabbed a finger at the office building across the street. "It's *them*, see? What I want is to *hurt* 'em. Put 'em on the floor, so they're begging me to stop. Only I know they want it, right? They *paid* for it."

Tony frowned, puffed at his cigar. "That's how you feel?"

"Yeah."

He stared out the window for a while, watching some guys cleaning the windows on the building across the street, then he shrugged. "Okay, get us some tickets. We'll come back you up."

Just like that. Leaving the office, Joey paused at the top of the stairs, put one hand against the wall to steady himself, thought, *Okay, now you got no choice.* He took a deep breath, walked down the stairs, straight out through the coffee shop to the street, where he hailed a cab, told the driver to take him to 55th and Madison. He had him pull up in a loading zone across the street from the Friars Club, rolled the window down, and looked up at the second-floor windows. The cab driver watched him in the rearview mirror, expressionless.

Joey, gazing up at the sun reflected off the glass, thought about the story of the old-time comedian who goes to court on a morals charge. The prosecutor asks him, "And what is your profession?" The comedian looks up at the judge, says, "I'm the greatest comedian in the world!" Later, his lawyer asks him, "Why'd you say that? You ruined my case!" The comedian says, "Hey, I was under oath, wasn't I?"

That's comedy, Joey thought. *The guy's sitting there in court, the judge is about to send him upstate, he still can't pass up a punch line.*

The Friars threw him a party when he went away. "Come back when you get out," they told him. "You can visit your jokes."

Joey sat back, rolled up the window, told the driver, "Okay, take me back."

So he was in a hurry that night, that's all. He picked up the money back at the Azores — two gym bags, heavier than usual — and put 'em in the trunk of his Chrysler to drive home, when he thought, *Ah shit.* The money. He couldn't leave it at his apartment; some punk breaks in to grab his TV, finds two gym bags full of cash. He'd have to stick it in his safe-deposit box, pick it up in the morning. It makes sense, right?

So now he's gotta drive *back* up to 55th, leave the car in a bus zone while he runs in with the gym bags. Ten minutes later, he comes out, some guy's strapping his car up to a tow truck. He slips the guy a fifty, gets him to unhook the car. Gets home, just time to grab a couple pieces of salami out of the refrigerator, get shaved, showered, and dressed — pausing to tell his best jokes to the rows of suits in the closet — before heading out to the club.

Scared? Jesus, yeah! But not enough, it turned out. Driving out there, no idea what was coming — that he'd spend the next week in a hotel room with an Assistant U.S. Attorney, a pair of deputy marshals, cops. Wondering, the whole time, if they'd found the money. Tony going crazy, probably.

The thought made him smile.

Joey flicked through the channels on the TV remote. Nothing. He wished he could get out, maybe head over to Harrah's, check out the action. What he needed was a disguise. Get a pair of Bermuda shorts, T-shirt with *Atlantic City!* on the front, some flip-flops, top it off with a baseball cap, pair of sunglasses. Just another plumber in for a three-day-weekend special — bus ride, hotel, gambling, show.

Only he didn't want to play it that way, like some guy works in a grocery store in Manhasset, left the deli counter for a couple days on the town. He was gonna be patient, one time in his life, wait for his moment. What he had in mind, a man needs to be dressed right. Show you got respect for quality, the finer things. Not some guy, he's there tryin' to win a couple bucks to pay his car note. This kind of thing, a man needs a clear head, a quick smile. Confidence.

What a man needs, no question, is a new suit.

Twenty-four hours, the tailor told him, looking up at him, those little glasses perched on his nose.

That's cash, right?

Yeah. Joey Tangliero, he always paid cash. Restaurants, tailors, hookers, cops. You pay your way, you can stay all day. Or was it *play?* He always forgot.

Joey, feet up on the bed, stretched out, hands behind his head, brought the TV back to the weather channel, watched the weather guy bring that storm down on the Jersey coast for the third time.

Come on, baby. Bring it home to papa.

Joey starting to enjoy the idea, imagining how it would look, howling in off the water, right at all those expensive casinos. Blow the windows out maybe, money flying through the streets. Kids from the projects six blocks from the fancy hotels running through the streets with butterfly nets. Guys in Bermuda shorts laying side bets on 'em.

He glanced over at the window. Shit, it could happen. And him sitting around with just over a million five, in a pair of gym bags under the bed. He shut his eyes, tried hard not to picture it, but there it was: the window shattering, curtains flapping in the wind, the bed thrown back against the wall, his bags ripped open and spilling money across the floor, the wind catching it, swirling it around the room, then sucking it out the window, gone.

Fuck that.

He reached over, hit the remote on the bedside table, switched the channel, got a monster truck rally on ESPN, from Texas. Big pickups, bouncing over a whole row of Toyotas, those huge tires crumpling 'em like beer cans. Some guy in a cowboy hat comin' out to wave a flag, they reach the end.

"Texas," Joey said, aloud. It made him think of the cowboy, McCann, calling the witness protection program *the heartland express.* "Get you out there with the real folks, see how they live."

On the television, some guy with a guitar, big feather sticking out of his cowboy hat, was singing to his pickup. Behind him, the crowd swayed, singing along.

Yeah, right.

He wasn't going nowhere, at least for twenty-four hours. Then he'd pick up his new suit from the tailor's shop a few blocks over on Pacific, get down to the Taj in time to catch Benny Leonard, the nine o'clock show. After that, slip a few bucks to the guy working the stage door, try to get backstage.

He'd imagined it, the bus carrying him down the Jersey Turnpike, past the chemical plants, oil tanks, scrap metal yards. Benny, sitting in his dressing room in a silk bathrobe, feet up, expensive Scotch, maybe a good Cuban cigar. Enjoying that moment, 'cause he's earned it. Closing his eyes, he's back on stage, the circle of light. Heat rising off the crowd, their teeth shining up at him.

Laughter.

Joey shivered. The *man!* Get in there, talk to him while he's still easing down from it. Make your pitch, as a fellow comic. Maybe toss in a few jokes, your best stuff. Couldn't hurt, right?

And then, you got him smiling?

Joey hit the remote to kill the TV, leaned back, hands behind his head.

Bring out the money.

Chapter 42

Ray Fielding walked past the file room, stopped, went back to look. Moser stood in front of the copy machine, a thick file spread out on the table next to him. He was taking each page from the file clips, laying it on the glass. Then he'd close the lid, look up at the clock on the wall above him while the light moved across the glass. Fielding watched him do three pages, then said —

"What's the matter with the feeder?"

Moser looked back at him. "It's broken."

"You call it in?"

"Lou did, yesterday. They haven't come out yet."

Fielding nodded, peeled the lid back on his coffee to take a sip. "You got a lot to do?"

Moser nodded at the file on the table. "What you see."

"Cruz file?"

"Uh huh."

Fielding leaned against the edge of the door, watched him do two more pages. "What's going on, Dave?"

Moser reached over, took the stack of copies out of the machine, laid them on the table next to the file. "Just making a copy. No big deal."

"Yeah?" Fielding walked over to the table, looked down at the stack of papers. "You do this for all your cases?"

Moser turned back to the machine. "Stay out of this, Ray. It's not your problem."

"Hey, I see you start covering your ass, I get worried."

Moser didn't say anything, reached past him to pull another page off the file clips, laid it on the glass. He closed the lid, hit the button. Fielding watched a strip of light turn the palm of his hand yellow for a moment, then it was gone.

"I know you, Dave. You got something, makes you nervous."

Moser glanced over at him. Fielding leaned back against the table, folded his arms. Moser reached behind him, took another sheet, laid it on the glass. He took a moment, getting it straight, said —

"Guy from IAD called me. Cruz is tied

up in some kind of money transfers, paying off cops. A few days ago, the money dried up. They think maybe Eva was retaliation."

Fielding looked down at the file on the table beside him. "Shit."

Moser closed the lid, hit the button. The light passed across his hand, the front of his shirt. He opened the lid, slid the page off the glass, laid it on the stack beside the file. "The guy let me know they're watching. I don't close the case, they'll think I shoved it in a drawer, let some cop walk."

"And if you close it?"

Moser smiled. "Then I'm a rat."

"So what are you gonna do?"

"Work the file." Moser smiled. "Maybe I'll get lucky, find out O.J. was in town."

Fielding looked down at the file. An envelope lay open next to the autopsy reports. He could see a stack of photographs, the envelope folded around them. He picked it up, slid the pictures out. Crime scene shots, autopsy photos, two of the girl — Eva Cruz — smiling, then a pair of security camera photos of a bald guy, waiting in Cruz's entry hall, and a guy standing at a store counter, both shot from above.

"Who're these guys?"

Moser glanced over. "My suspects."

"Yeah?" Fielding looked at the pictures again. "So you're making progress."

Moser lifted the lid, slid the paper off the glass and laid a new one down, working two-handed now. Fielding watched him hit the button, look up at the clock again, waiting.

Fielding picked up the envelope to put the pictures away, then paused, staring down at the guy standing at a store counter.

"Dave, you get an ID on this one yet?"

Moser looked at it, shook his head. "I got a pretty good idea, the other guy. That one, I got it from a florist down the block. He sent her flowers the night she died."

Fielding reached over, laid the picture on the copier. "You had a good look at this guy?"

"Ray, I've been staring at that picture for three days. You got a point to make here?"

"Notice anything about him?"

Moser looked down at the picture. Black and white, bad angle. What was he supposed to see?

"I don't know, Ray. You sayin' we know this guy?"

"No," Fielding picked up his coffee off the table, smiling. "But I can tell you one thing. It ain't O.J."

Fielding put the coffee on his desk, walked over to where Nicolaides was hunched over an Investigative Summary with a bottle of Wite-Out, using a black ballpoint pen to correct his typos.

"Lou, you got the Cardoza file?"

Nicolaides glanced up, nodded to a stack of folders on the corner of his desk. "Take 'em all, you want."

Fielding picked up the top file, opened it, saw the autopsy photos of Angel Cardoza he'd brought back from downtown. Under it, he saw the computer run on their suspect — *Miiko Reyes.* A kid who sold drugs up by Fort Tryon Park, went by the street name Blanquito, because of his pale skin.

"Hey, Lou?" He waited until Nicolaides finished blowing on the Wite-Out, looked up. "This kid the neighbor ID'd, Miiko Reyes. You get anything new on him?"

Nicolaides shrugged. "What? Since yesterday?"

"You check out his place in Bay Ridge?"

"I talked to the landlady. He skipped out, like six months ago. Still owes her two months rent."

"She say anything else?"

"Yeah. She said, 'You find him, shoot him for me.' "

Fielding looked down at the kid's sheet. "You talk to his parole officer?"

Nicolaides spread his hands. "Ray, look at my desk. I got four open cases, not one of 'em would I give a shit about if I wasn't holding the paper. I got a drive-by, the victim was in here three times last year as a suspect, I got that kid got thrown off the roof over on 178th, had six crack vials in his pocket, a homeless guy, got knifed by one of his buddies in the IRT tunnel, and this piece of shit. You want the file, take it."

Fielding closed the file. "It's your case, Lou."

"Am I cryin' about it?"

"I want Dave to take a look at this guy. I'll bring it back when I'm done."

426

Nicolaides reached for his Wite-Out. "Whatever."

Fielding walked back to the file room, laid it on the table next to the Cruz file. Moser looked over.

"I got something here you should look at." Fielding opened the file, pulled the computer sheet off the clips. "I ran this guy for Lou a couple days back. An old lady identified him on a killing up by Fort Tryon Park. Miiko Reyes, used to sell rock up there. This kid's street name was Blanquito. The old lady remembered him because he's got real light skin."

Moser took the sheet, read it over. "You get a picture?"

"Lou put in a request to Records. Looks like it hasn't come yet."

Moser nodded, passed the sheet back to Fielding. "Okay, so?"

"Your guy in the picture, he's got the same look. Hispanic, but very pale. How often you see that?"

Moser shrugged. "This neighborhood? You see all kinds."

"Looks like the right age, too."

Moser laid a page on the glass, closed the lid, looked up at the clock. "You're saying, what? This guy sends flowers to

427

Eva Cruz down on Park Avenue, then comes back uptown, kills somebody else?"

Fielding dug through the file, pulled another page off the clips. "Could be more. We got a pair of stabbings, three victims. Same day, couple blocks apart. The first place was a stash house, for laundering cash. Lou says they found counting machines, rubber bands, that kind of stuff."

Moser was looking at him now.

"No cash?"

"Nothing. Lou thinks a robbery."

"But you don't."

Fielding smiled. "That's where it gets interesting. We got a second killing, linked by the woman's address book. A guy with his throat cut up on Nagle. Toss that in, it starts to look like a gang hit."

Moser glanced down at the papers he was copying, shook his head. "Won't work, Ray."

"Tell me why."

"Gang hits, drug money. We're a long way from Park Avenue, here."

"Couple miles."

"You know what I mean."

Fielding reached over, picked up the

envelope of photos, slid out the shots of Eva Cruz in the river. Then he leaned over, laid them on the copier lid in front of Moser.

"Way I remember it, Dave, we found your girl up here."

Chapter 43

What Benny Leonard needed was a
drink. End of a long weekend, he's
just come offstage from a set, a crowd
he'd swear they wheeled 'em in from
the cardiac care unit, for Christ's
sake, one idiot laughing his head off
in the back, got one of those real
whiny laughs, *heh, heh, heh,* makes
you want to reach down his throat,
yank the rat out of his chest. This guy,
he's actually slappin' the table, so the
whole crowd's turnin' to get a look,
right? Like playing the Hair Club for
Men. He gets, what? Maybe three
laughs, the whole night, not counting
the village idiot? Gets off the stage
with all his major internal organs, all
he wants is a drink and twenty minutes with the cocktail waitress workin'
stage left, the blonde. That's the
kind'a night he's had, so now he's
gotta sit down, talk to some guy wants
to be a comedian?

Marv, his personal manager,

shrugged. "He says he knows Frankie Luccario."

"That *momzer?*" Benny stripped off his dinner jacket, flung it on a chair. "With his poo-poo jokes. He should choke on his own phlegm."

"Benny, these people own like half the comedy clubs on the East Coast. Frankie Luccario, he owns ten, clear. The man asks you to tell some jokes, you tell him the jokes, okay?"

"I'm serious here, Marv. I don't play Italian wakes. You know what an Italian wake is?"

Marv sighed, picked up Benny's jacket, hung it on the back of the door. "What?"

"You go to an Italian wake, it's like a surprise party. Nobody knows who the guest of honor is, till it's too late. They bring out the food, tell ya what a swell guy he is, *then* they kill him."

"Keep it down, okay Benny? We're not in the Poconos, here."

Benny took a cigar from the pocket of his coat, lit it. "Yeah right, Atlantic City. You see what I'm sayin'? The Italians, they want to get out of town, they go to *Jersey.* I mean, look't this place. Newark by the Sea. A Jew, he's gonna want to see a cow, at least, maybe some shrubbery."

"There's lots'a Jews here, Benny."

"Sure, now." He settled into a worn recliner, puffed at his cigar. "I mean, take Vegas. Fifty-two hotels, middle of the desert. Whose idea was *that?*"

"Ben Siegel."

Benny glared at him. "So, this guy, he's gonna break my legs, I don't tell him he's funny?"

"Don't fuck with him, okay Benny? You piss these people off, you don't work. It's that simple."

Benny slipped his shoes off, heel to toe, then eased the chair back. "So bring him in. I'll wipe his ass with my new tie."

Marv opened the door, stuck his head out into the hall, then stepped back. Benny waited until Marv waved him into the room — a fat guy, bald across the top, stuffed into an expensive suit, so tight he looked like an ad for condoms — then grabbed the handle on the recliner, pulled it upright. The guy, smiling at him, raised both hands.

"No, please. Don't get up. You been working."

That's all it took for Benny to recognize the voice. *The laugher.* He shot a look at Marv, laid the chair back, waved the guy over to the couch.

"So, Mr. . . ."

"Joey, call me Joey." The guy sat on the edge of the couch, leaning forward, like he didn't want to get too comfortable.

"That's your name? Mr. Joey?" Benny puffed at the cigar. "We're in a Quentin Tarantino movie, here."

The guy laughed, *heh, heh, heh.*

"That's some laugh you got there. Really, I know a urologist up in the city could take care'a that for you."

Heh, heh, heh!

Benny glanced at Marv, chewing at the cigar, thinking, *Jesus.*

Joey felt nervous, not wanting to let it show. He sat back, smoothed his tie, the smile plastered on his face. Like Frankie, telling his poo-poo jokes, five or six in a row, to soften you up. You gotta pretend they're funny.

"Listen, Mr. Leonard . . ."

"That's Mr. Benny to you."

Heh, heh, heh.

"Don't laugh. Name like that, I might'a had a career."

Joey, laughing, dug in his pocket for

a handkerchief, swiped it across his forehead. "You kill me," he said. "Really."

"Yeah? This is Atlantic City. That can be arranged."

Heh, heh, heh.

"Where'd that come from, anyway. 'You kill me.' This is a compliment?" Benny gestured with his cigar. "For that, I should get paid more."

The guy was nodding, one hand raised, like he was telling him okay, he could stop. *Like those animals,* Benny thought, *they meet in the woods, they gotta roll on their backs, show each other their throat.*

Benny waited until he caught his breath, glanced at his watch. "So Marv tells me you're a comedian."

The guy dabbed at his forehead with the handkerchief, shook his head. "I'm an amateur. Not like you."

Benny took the cigar from his mouth, pointed it at him. "Hey, I'm glad. There's six guys out there doing my act already. I caught one of 'em in Reno last year. After the show, I went backstage, I told him, 'Kid, you got a great act. Mine!' " He stuck the cigar back in his mouth, waited to see if the guy would laugh.

But Joey just smiled. "You heard that one, huh?"

"It's in Berle's book."

"Yeah, but did anybody ask him where he got it?" Benny shook his head. "Don't talk to me about Berle's book. He asked me to read it, before it came out. I said, 'Milton, how come I'm not in it?' He says, 'You want to be in it?' He takes the book, snaps it shut on my nose. 'There, you're in it!' Some friend." He glanced over at Marv. "Anyway, I thought I told you to kill him."

"Who?"

"Berle."

"I did. Nobody noticed."

Benny sighed, looked back at Joey. "Everybody's got a bit. Am I right?"

Joey smiled. "Not like you."

"We did that part already. You work clubs?"

"A couple."

"How'd you do?"

Joey looked down at his shoes, noticed where the shoeshine guy in the men's room off the main lobby had left a clump of polish under the edge of one lace. *Shit,* he thought. *And I tipped the guy a buck, he did such a nice job.*

He looked up at Benny. "I bombed."

"Happens." Benny puffed at the cigar for a while. "You come here for advice?"

"Not exactly."

"So what do I can you for?"

Joey smiled. "Huh?"

"It's an old line. We did it in a sketch on Sid Caesar's show. I play the boss, Sid comes in to ask for a raise, he's all nervous. I'm at the desk, punching buttons on an adding machine. I don't even look up, right? A real son of a bitch. He sits down, I say, 'So, Sid, what do I can you for?' Sid, he does six minutes, silent, trying to get out of the room. Brought the house down."

"I guess I missed that one."

"Tell me about it. I did guest shots on all the big shows, always on the holidays. They'd tell me, 'Benny, we need you for the holiday show.' Of course, I'm honored. I figure it's a big deal, right? The whole family's together, they turn on the tube, watch Sid dress up like an elf. Every year, I fell for it. Spend the holiday week in New York, rehearsing. Christmas Eve, we go on the air. We do a great show. The studio audience, they're in *pain,* we're so hot. After the show, I go backstage, the crew's got a TV set up in the green room. You know what they're watching? Fucking Perry *Como*. Turns out, all of America's tuned in to 'Perry Como's Hawaiian Family Christmas.' My own mother, I ask her how she liked the show, she says, 'Oh dear. Was that tonight?' It upset me, I admit. Then I realized, Hey, wait a minute! I can still use all those jokes in my act."

"You ever wish you'd been bigger?"

"Nah, I leave that to my girlfriends."

Marv leaned forward, caught Joey's eye. "Don't ever ask a comic that. Trust me, there's not one of 'em wouldn't trade their children for a shot on the networks."

Benny took his cigar out of his mouth, smiled. "Marv's the genius booked me as a judge on *Star Search*. 'It's good exposure,' he says. I taped it. You know how long they show me? Fourteen seconds. Once with me waving to the audience when they introduce the judges, then twice I'm laughing at some idiot who juggled those little chocolate Easter bunnies, bit their ears off in midair." He shook his head. "This he calls a career."

Joey leaned forward. "I wonder if you'd be interested in a proposition."

Benny looked over at Marv, sighed. "Marv, I asked you to bring me a broad. That nice little waitress over in D section, with the ponytail. So what do I get? You show up with this guy, now he's gonna proposition me."

Marv shrugged. "I thought you could use a change."

Benny turned back to Joey. "He figures he hasn't screwed me enough." He glanced at the tip of his cigar, saw it was dead. He dug a lighter from his pocket, lit it up. "So, you gonna tell me about this proposition?"

Joey rubbed both hands on his knees, like he was getting ready to pick up something heavy. He took a deep breath, said —

"I want to open a club. Strictly comedy. I'd like to use your name. We go partners. I put up the money, all you gotta do is come in a couple times a year, make a guest appearance. Maybe get some of your friends in the business to stop in, give the place some shine."

Benny glanced over at Marv, then back at Joey. "There's a lotta clubs around. You know how long most of 'em last? About six months."

"Tops," Marv said.

Joey raised one hand to stop them, nodding. "I know. But, see, I got a concept. I figure we call the place 'Benny Leonard's Laugh Track!' With an exclamation point, up on the sign. We put one'a those laugh meters up on the stage, like they used to have on talent shows? People come to the club, they can lay bets on which guy gets the most laughs."

Benny was silent for a moment, the cigar sticking out from between his teeth, his mouth open. "Did Burns put you up to this?"

Joey shook his head. "Think about it a minute. What do people want, they're going out? They want a couple laughs, drinks, maybe a chance to win some money." He waved an arm at the room. "You ever see a casino without a comic?"

"He's got a point," Marv said.

Joey grinned at him. "See? It's a great idea, right? Like going to the track, only you get to hear some comedy, too."

Benny closed his mouth around the cigar, puffed at it. "You put up the money?"

"It's all fixed. All I need is a big name, somebody can pull the crowds."

"So why me?"

Joey spread his hands. " 'Cause you're the best."

Benny took the cigar out of his mouth, grinned at Marv. "You hear this guy?"

"I heard him."

"How come you never say things like that?"

" 'Cause I know you."

Benny sighed, looked back at Joey. "See how he talks to me?"

He reached down to pull the handle on the recliner, tip it forward. He got up, walked over to Joey, extended his hand.

"It's been a pleasure, Mr. Joey."

Joey looked at his outstretched hand, then up at his face. "That's it? You're not even gonna think about it?"

"Did I say that?" Benny shook his head. "I'm tired. I just finished a show. What I need right now is a drink and a decent piece of Atlantic City ass. You go on home, leave your number with Marv, here. I'll sleep on it, okay?"

Joey hesitated, then stood up, slowly. "You're gonna sleep on it?"

Benny frowned, glanced over at Marv. "I just said that, right?"

"That's what I heard."

Benny turned back to Joey, shrugged. "That's what I said. I'll sleep on it."

Joey closed his eyes, let out a long breath. Then he opened his eyes, just a crack. "So can I have the piece of ass?"

Benny stared at him for a long moment, squinting through the smoke from his cigar. "Marv, get this guy outta here, before he steals my whole act."

After Marv swung the door closed behind him, Benny gave a sigh, eased himself back into the recliner.

"Tell me something, Marv. I'm curious. Where do you *find* these guys? You go out in the street, I'm up on stage, look for crazies?"

Marv went over to the makeup table, started to straighten up. "Just want you to meet your public, Benny." He glanced in the mirror, saw Benny close his eyes, puffing at the cigar. "You want me to go find the waitress?"

Benny opened his eyes, stared at the ceiling for a moment. "I don't suppose she does rope tricks."

Marv smiled, shook his head.

"Then we better skip it."

"Don't worry, Benny. Something'll come up."

"Yeah, like my cholesterol."

Marv finished at the makeup table, went over to the door. "You want that drink?"

Benny sighed, rubbed at his forehead. "Sure."

Marv started to open the door, glanced back when he heard Benny say, "And Marv?"

"Yeah?"

"Get on the phone with Miami. Check this guy out."

Chapter 44

Eden Howe lay on her belly, her arms folded under her chin. Her eyes were closed, and Moser wondered if she was asleep. He ran the tip of his finger lightly down her back, and she smiled, murmured something. Her skin glistened, like honey in the yellow light.

He leaned down, kissed the sole of her right foot softly. Then the inside of her knee. He ran the tip of his tongue up her thigh, and she stirred, stretched until the muscles in her legs trembled. She turned over, her arm draped across her eyes. He touched her knee, and her legs parted.

"Hmmm," she said. "Who says you can't find a cop when you need one?"

He'd spent the last few days trying to think up a decent reason to call her, but couldn't bring himself to pick up the phone. But his eye kept coming back to it, whenever he sat at his desk, trying to make his way through the Cruz file. Finally, he'd picked it up, dialed her number. A machine answered, played the first few bars of "There's No Business Like Show Business," and then a woman's voice told him that if he was Martin Scorsese, Christian Slater, or the Creative Arts Agency, he could leave a message for Tonya, Sue-Ellen, or Eden at the tone. He'd left his name and the number at the squad room, asked Eden to call him back when she had a minute, as he had just a few more questions he'd like to ask her. Twenty minutes later, he was getting coffee from the machine in the hall, when Lou Nicolaides stuck his head out the door to tell him he had a call.

"Hi, it's Eden Howe," she said when he picked up the phone. "Sorry about the message on the machine. My roommate's trying for Miss Congeniality."

"I've heard worse. A guy I know has a tape of two lions eating a wildebeest. You can hear it screaming. He comes on at the end, tells you he's out getting a bite."

"Tasteful."

He smiled, let the silence shame her. He could hear traffic in the background.

"You at home?"

"I'm over in the East Village. I just called in for messages."

"Oh. Well, I wondered if we could meet. I have a few things I'd like to —"

"Where do you live?"

"Out on the island. Hempstead."

"Too far. Is there someplace else we could meet?"

"Can you hang on a minute?" Moser put her on hold. He closed his eyes, pressed his hands to his temples, racking his memory. *C'mon, c'mon.* Then he picked up the phone, dialed an internal extension.

"Vice. Jerry Brent."

"Hey, Jerry. Dave Moser. You still got that place up on Eighty-fifth?"

"Just till January. Then it goes co-op, and I gotta decide whether to buy."

"You working tonight?"

Brent laughed. "This is the vice squad, Dave. I work every night. These people sleep during the day, like bats."

"I got a favor to ask. I need to borrow your place."

"Yeah? You got a date, Dave?"

Moser could hear the phone go muffled, as Brent covered the mouthpiece with his hand. He called out to some-

445

one, and Moser heard laughter, whistling.

"C'mon, Jerry. Yes or no?"

Brent got back on the line. "The place
is a mess, but I guess you won't care,
huh?" He laughed.

"Thanks, Jerry. I'll stop by for the key
in a few minutes."

Moser hung up, punched the flashing
button.

"You there?"

"I almost gave up on you."

He gave her the address, signed himself out on the duty board, flagged down
a cab. By the time he got down to 85th
Street, she was sitting on the steps
outside the building, reading a beat-up
copy of *To the Lighthouse*. She was
wearing a black dress, her Doc Martens, white socks. As he came up the
steps, she stood up, tucked the book
into her backpack. She put her hand
on his chest as he dug out the key, ran
her finger slowly down the line of buttons on his shirt. She followed him up
the stairs without a word, waited as he
unlocked the apartment door. She
glanced around the small apartment,
smiled.

"Cops."

He closed the door behind them, reached for her.

Now, she lay with her head on his chest as the light faded beyond the filthy windows. He wrapped his arms around her small waist, pressed her against him. Their breath slowed. She raised her head, looked up at him, and let his lips touch hers, lightly. The streetlights came on. Down the block, someone shouted. He could smell cooking.

"I'm hungry," she murmured.

"Don't move a muscle."

She laughed. "You sound like a cop." She pushed up off his chest, leaned back on her arms, stretched. He reached up, touched her small breasts. She caught his hands, held them there.

"Nice fit."

"Victoria's Secret." She laughed, squeezed his hands. "Sorry. I bought a sweater from them last year. Now I get a catalog every two weeks."

"I get 'em at Christmas. Before Valentine's Day. The husband editions."

"You look at them?"

"They sit in the bathroom for a few weeks."

She smiled. "Perfect girls in a perfect

world." She eased herself off him with a little sigh, settled beside him. He raised up on an elbow, looked at her. Her skin glistened from the heat.

"It's not so perfect."

"No?"

"This is better." He rolled over, sat on the edge of the bed. "But I gotta go to the bathroom." He heaved himself up, but she clambered off the end of the bed, beat him to the door. She put a hand on his chest, pushed him back, smiling.

"Ladies first."

He caught her around the waist, lifted her up, and pressed her against the wall, kissing the base of her throat. She wrapped her arms around his neck, rested her chin on the top of his head.

"Tell me the truth," she said. "Did you really have questions?"

Sometime after midnight, Eden got up, started gathering up her clothes. He lay on the bed, watching her move about the apartment in the darkness. She leaned on the dresser, pulled on her white socks. He felt something grip at his heart.

"Stay."

She stood very still for a moment, a boot in each hand. "I've got an early class."

"I could drive you by your apartment in the morning, pick up some clothes."

She sat on the edge of the bed, set the boots on the floor carefully. She looked over at him, put a hand on his chest. "I'm meeting my boyfriend, for breakfast."

Moser looked up at her, steadily. "Your boyfriend."

She smiled. "Ah, look at you. You're shocked."

"No." He was silent for a moment, watching the half-moon vanish behind a cloud in a window across the street. "Disappointed, I guess."

She leaned down, kissed his chest. "That's sweet." His hand came up, rested on her bare shoulder.

"Don't be angry, Dave."

"I'm not."

She looked at him for a moment, then nodded. She bent, picked her dress up off the floor. She stood up, slipped it over her head. Moser watched the dress slide down over her shoulders, her breasts, her narrow waist.

Without warning, he felt exhaustion

creep over him. He closed his eyes. Distantly, he heard her moving around the apartment, then something brushed against his cheek.

The door clicked, and the room was silent. Moser felt himself slipping back into a dream, where Eva Cruz knelt on a bed in a darkened room, smiling, her black hair tossed by a wind across her pale shoulders.

She reached out for him.

Chapter 45

Marty Stoll stood at his living room window, lights off, watching the street. In the next block, two men were sitting in a car, their heads outlined against the glare of a streetlight behind them. Stoll let the curtain fall back. He held a glass of Scotch in one hand, hung on to the bottle by the neck with the other.

They were closing in. Surveillance, phone taps, a rat. The whole pile of shit. They let you swim around in it for a couple days. When you stink bad enough, they bust you. He'd spotted two guys in an unmarked car following him on the job, started holding back at red lights, then jumping the light at the last minute, leaving 'em sitting there.

He shook his head. *Like that was gonna help.*

By the time they got this close, they had you. All you could do was ditch 'em for an hour, use that time to clean up the mess. He pushed the curtain back, looked out at Vinny's house across the street. He'd spent the evening working on Moser's car, Stoll watching it from his window, silent. What'd he know 'bout this kid, really?

Likes to do favors for cops.

He remembered when he was a kid, he spent a summer at camp upstate. Hated every minute. One day, it was raining, he sat in the boat shed, watching a dozen red ants kill a spider. A real battle. The spider crouched in the middle of his web, grabbing 'em when they got too close, using his jaws to snap their heads off. No contest, one on one. But gradually the ants closed in on him, climbing onto his web at different places. Watching it, he'd thought they'd get stuck, but they didn't. Instead, the spider got frantic, rushing around, trying to push 'em off his web. Before long, he had ants hanging off him, tearing at him with their jaws. He tried to shake them off, but they hung on. He crawled slowly across his web, until Stoll couldn't see the spider anymore. Just a ball of ants, still moving. Then it stopped, and the only motion was the ants, crawling over each other to get at it. Stoll watched it for a while, saw the ants carrying off legs, chunks of the spider's body. Then the rain stopped, and a counselor yelled for him to come play softball.

Looking out at Vinny's house, Stoll thought, *That's the trick. Don't let 'em get on your web.*

And if they were, already?

Tear it up. Break the threads.

Stoll raised his glass, felt the Scotch burn its way through him. He turned away from the window, glanced around the dark room. The furniture threw faint shadows on the wall. He could walk through the room, feel his way by habit. But looking at it now, the room seemed unfamiliar, the shapes distorted. Nothing was the way it was.

It made him want to toss the bottle at the dark mass of Rita's breakfront, hear the glass shatter. Or, even better, turn and sling it through the window, try to crack that smooth surface, not the glass, but what lay beyond.

Instead, he raised the bottle, poured more Scotch into his glass. He went into the kitchen, set the bottle on the counter, dialed a number that Miiko Reyes had given him, let it ring twice, then hung up. He hit the redial button, let it ring once, hung up. No connection, no tape. IAD wiretaps were voice-activated; he'd told Reyes not to answer his phone right away, listen for the signal. It meant, meet me at the corner of Amsterdam and 132nd the next morning, eleven o'clock.

Time to start feeding the ants.

Chapter 46

"You coming in?"

Moser glanced up, saw Fielding was out of the car, standing on the sidewalk, watching him. Moser looked at the notepad, open on his lap. During the ride over to Brooklyn, he'd dug out his pen, trying to focus his thoughts on Miiko Reyes. But his mind kept working around to Eden, raising her arms to slip her dress over her head. The page was empty.

He closed the notepad, tucked it into his pocket. Fielding watched him roll the window up, get out. He locked the door, glanced up at the Kings County Courthouse up the block.

"You okay, Dave?"

Moser nodded. "You called this guy, right?"

"Did I *call* him?" Fielding raised his eyebrows, looked out at the traffic going past. "Dave, I don't know what's in your head, but I don't need this."

Moser glanced over at him. "What?"

455

"You *know* what."

"No," Moser said, slowly. Staring at him. "What?"

Fielding gave a thin smile, shook his head. "Jesus. This how you were with your wife?"

And he walked up the block toward the courthouse. Moser stood there, watching him.

Yeah, he thought. *It was.*

Alan Kuntz, the probation officer who'd handled Miiko Reyes, told Fielding he'd been a science teacher over at Catholic High for six years, then went into social work before ending up in Corrections.

"I'm moving down the food chain."

He dug through his file cabinet, came out with a thin manila folder. He sat down, tossed the file on the desk. "It's my name. I get all the good jobs."

Fielding smiled, leaned forward to pick up the file. "Must save you time on the introductions."

"Just what I need, these guys. Save time."

While Fielding looked at the file, Moser glanced around the office — black metal desk, two plastic chairs, a window with bars on it. Guy gets out of prison, comes to visit his PO, he'd feel right at home. Kuntz had hung a few pictures on the wall: guys on boats, holding up fish.

Fielding looked up. "You got a current address for this guy, Reyes?"

"What's current? The kid finished his probation back in the spring."

Fielding paged through the file. "What's Liquid Assets?"

"Liquor distributor over in Queens. Reyes drove a truck for them."

"Any chance he still works there?"

Kuntz shrugged. "Sure, if they haven't caught him stealing yet."

An hour later, Moser watched Fielding come out of the warehouse, pausing under the sign that said LIQUID ASSETS to look up at the sky, wipe his neck with a handkerchief. He walked across the parking lot to where Moser waited in the car. He'd moved it into the shade of a TEC-SOUND billboard, the guy in the picture grinning, eyes manic, while a pair of speakers on both sides of his head blasted so loud his hair was standing straight up. The slogan said, *You won't believe your ears!*

Moser, staring at it, thought, *No shit.*

Fielding got into the car, let one hand rest on the wheel while he ran the handkerchief across the back of his neck, tucked it into his pocket. "Man, it's hot."

"Any luck?"

Ray reached down, started the car.

"He quit six weeks ago."

"They have an address for him?"

Fielding shook his head, reached down to start the car. "No such luck."

Chapter 47

Miiko pulled into the parking lot of Mad Mike's Stereo on Hempstead Avenue in Levittown, let the car idle for a minute while he checked out the lot. A couple cars up near the door, where the customers park, a few more around back. He saw the yellow Charger, backed into a spot off by itself, a few spaces away from all the other cars. Miiko smiled. He knew this guy, went to school with guys just like him. He likes his car, wants to keep it nice. So he parks it way off by itself, making sure nobody scratches it, pulling out.

Miiko parked the Acura next to the entrance, went inside. He could feel the .38 that Stoll had given him pressing into his back, where he had it shoved into his waistband. The place had an open sales floor, with little sound rooms off the sides, two display rooms at the back. He stood in front of a clearance stack of Samsung receivers near the entrance, glanced around for cops. A couple young guys were checking out the stereos on the main floor, some older men in one of the back rooms looking at big-screen TVs. They had banners hanging from the roof that said NO PAYMENTS TILL JANUARY! And RED SALE! signs on everything.

He cut across the sales floor, walked past the glass listening rooms until he saw a kid with stringy blond hair dangling in his face unloading speakers from boxes. He stuck his head in the door.

"Vinny around?"

The kid looked up. He was wearing a clip-on tie with a picture of Jerry Garcia. He grabbed the end, flipped it back over his shoulder to keep it out of the way. "He's a couple doors down. With the CD players."

Miiko let the door swing closed, walked on toward the back of the store. In the last room, Vinny Delario was hooking up the wiring on a display of CD players, plugging them all into a single control board so customers could switch from one to the other by turning a knob. Miiko went in, shut the door behind him. He walked over to a Sony CD unit, squatted down to examine the controls.

"Can I help you with something?"

"Maybe." Miiko kept fiddling with the controls on the stereo, trying different settings. "You Vinny?"

From the corner of his eye, he saw the guy straighten. He was missing two fingers from his left hand. A plastic badge pinned to his shirt said *Vinny.*

"Yeah. I know you?"

"We got a mutual friend. Marty Stoll."

Vinny stared at him for a moment, then glanced over at the soundproof glass; across the sales floor, at the credit desk, an IAD man sat reading a newspaper. Miiko stood up, ran his hand across a row of CD players until he came to one he liked. Nice big volume dial that felt good to the hand, digital reads, sharp design.

"Who makes this?"

"Don't even think about it," Vinny said. "It's a piece of crap."

"Yeah?" Miiko looked at it, shook his head. "You just can't tell, huh."

Vinny shrugged. "You gotta listen. That's why we have these rooms."

Miiko looked over at him, grinned. "For guys like me, huh? Need somebody to show us how it works?"

"Sure." Vinny edged toward the door, hooked a thumb at the showroom floor beyond. "Listen, I'll get Richie for you. He's the guy really knows these systems."

Miiko shook his head. "Nah, that's okay. I'm not buyin' a CD player."

"That's fine," Vinny said, smiling. He got the door behind him, his hand feeling around for the handle. "We get a lot of people, just come in to look."

"Like that guy at the desk?"

Vinny paused. "What?"

Miiko smiled, glanced over at the credit desk. "The cop. Over there, reading the *Post.*"

Vinny followed his gaze, swallowed hard. "That's Jimmy, our credit manager."

"Bullshit." Miiko turned back to the CD players, ran a hand over cool metal. "Marty's real disappointed in you, Vinny. He thought you were smarter than that. Once these guys get a hook in you, that's it. They'll pimp you 'round, rat jobs. Maybe get you set up on smack, keep you easy to handle. Then one day, you'll do something they don't like, and they'll toss you. Just like that. Some judge'll ship you upstate, and your first day on the yard, one'a the guys you ratted out will walk up behind you, stick a knife in right here." He reached around, touched his lower back, just below the ribs. "That's it for Vinny."

Vinny looked pale. "Listen . . ."

Miiko held up both his hands. "Hey, you don't need to tell me nothing. I'm just doin' a job, here."

Vinny jerked the door open, backed out. Miiko watched him turn, walk quickly across the sale floor, calling out to the guy at the credit desk. He pushed through the glass door, followed. He saw the cop glance up from his newspaper. He had one of those cop mustaches, hair combed over a bald spot, the only guy in the store wearing a jacket and tie. Some fuckin' disguise. Vinny reached the desk, turned to point at him. The cop looked over at him, slid off his chair to come around the desk, get between them.

Miiko spread his hands, said, "Excuse me, could I get some help here?"

The cop glanced back at Vinny, like, *What, this guy?* Miiko reached under his jacket, jerked the .38 from his waistband, shot him in the chest. The cop staggered back against the credit desk, went over it. Vinny screamed, twisting away. Miiko swung the gun around, put it about six inches from the side of his head, shot him. Vinny dropped to his knees, one hand coming up to grab the edge of the desk. Miiko shot him again, behind his right ear, and he collapsed to the floor.

Miiko took a step to his right, glanced at the cop. He was lying on his back, not moving. Miiko turned, glanced around the display floor. Several customers stood frozen, staring at him.

Miiko grinned. "No credit, my ass."

Then he shoved the gun in his pants, walked out.

Ray was pulling up to the tollbooth on the Triborough when Moser's pager went off. Fielding looked over at him, watched him pull it off his belt, check the display.

"It's alive," Fielding said.

"New batteries."

Fielding rolled his window down, stuck his arm out, waited until he caught a break in the traffic to swing across two lanes to the Bridge Authority office. He pulled into the lot, waited while Moser went in to make the call. He watched the tolltaker in the nearest booth, a young Hispanic woman, lean out to take the money from each driver's hand, her lips moving slightly to the radio she had playing in her booth. Pretty girl. He wondered if guys hit on her when they stopped to pay the toll — *C'mon, baby. Let's take a ride.* Six hours in a hot booth, with just a radio, taking money from people's hands every few seconds, they think she's looking for a date? You get married, after a couple years you realize that most women you meet, what they're thinking about is getting home, taking off their shoes. He smiled. Meet a nice girl, you're giving it your best shot, she's thinking how she's gotta stop at the drugstore, buy more Band-Aids for her ankles.

The door opened, and Moser got in. Fielding glanced over.

"What's up?"

"My neighbor, Vinny Delario. Somebody just put two bullets in his head."

By the time they got to Hempstead Avenue, the parking lot was packed with cop cars, EMS ambulances, and a pair of news vans with satellite dishes mounted on their roofs. The store's entrance was taped off. Moser brushed past a reporter doing his lead-in for the camera, ducked under the yellow tape, flashed his badge at the uniformed cop at the door, and walked back toward the cluster of cops near the rear of the display floor. The place looked pretty much the same as when Moser had last been there, picking up a few weekends of repossession work back when he was still in uniform. Same stacks of equipment, same SALE! tags everywhere. They'd put in a couple new sound rooms, added a showroom for TV gear at the back, but that was it. Moser saw Mike Delario, the owner, arguing with Richter and some local detectives near his office in the back of the store. He walked over.

Delario glanced over at him as he came up. "Jesus, Dave. Don't tell me you're with these assholes, now."

Moser looked at Richter. "No," he said. "I'm not."

"This fuckin' guy come in a couple days ago," Delario said, glaring at Richter. "He wants to put an officer in my store. He says they heard on the street

466

some punks were planning to rob me. 'No big deal,' he tells me. 'You won't even know the guy's there.' So what's he do? Sits at my credit desk the whole time, reading the fuckin' newspaper. My customers want to talk about credit, I gotta ask him to move. This is my protection? Now I got two reporters outside, telling the whole tri-state area how a cop got shot in my store. I *need* this kind of publicity?"

"Sorry about Vinny," Moser said.

"Fuck him. He had it comin', bringing this kind'a shit into my store!"

Richter said, "You got a minute, Dave?"

Moser glanced over at Fielding, watching him. He nodded to Richter, and they walked down the hallway that led past the business offices to the warehouse at the back of the store. Richter stopped at the water fountain, ran some cold water over his hand, then rubbed at his eyes.

"So you were using Vinny," Moser said. "To get at Stoll."

It wasn't a question; he just wanted to hear Richter admit it. Instead, Richter bent over the water fountain, took a long drink. Then he straightened, wiped his mouth on the back of his hand, looked back down the hall. The EMS guys were wheeling out a stretcher, a body bag strapped to it.

"You ever think about getting out?"

Moser shook his head. "Not much. It's what I do."

"I been thinking about it a lot lately. I got a cousin down in Atlanta, owns a Toyota dealership. He wants to expand, get into boats. Needs somebody to manage it."

"You know anything about boats?"

He shrugged. "They float." Then he smiled. "That's more than I'm doing, at the moment."

"Why'd you call me?"

"I need your help."

"Bullshit."

Richter turned to look at him. "Dave, your buddy Stoll just crossed the line. One of his people shot a cop."

"You know that for a fact?"

"You want to see the security tape?"

Moser followed Richter into the office. A table against one wall held security equipment. A detective was standing next to a video monitor, the screen divided to show four different overhead angles on the store. The screen was frozen, a few customers visible near the front of the store, standing in front of the stacks of audio gear.

"Watch the top left," Richter said. The detective pressed a button on the video recorder, and the screen came to life, the customers moving slightly. After a moment, the door to one of the sound rooms opened, and Vinny walked out quickly. He crossed out of the camera range, appeared in the upper right segment of the screen, which showed the credit desk, the IAD man glancing up from his newspaper.

"Okay, now watch the upper left," Richter said.

Moser watched the door to the sound room open, and — Jesus! — recognized the guy the moment he came out. Dark hair, very pale skin. The same guy as in the florist's tape. Miiko Reyes. Moser watched him cross into the next part of the screen, pull a gun from under his jacket, shoot the IAD man as he came around the desk. Then he shot Vinny, twice, walked out.

Moser glanced over, saw Richter watching him.

"Run it back," Richter told the detective.

They watched it twice more. Then Richter nodded to the detective, walked out. Moser followed him into the hall. He watched Richter reach up to rub at the muscles in his neck.

"Mike Golding," he said. "He had fourteen years on the job. That son of a bitch never gave him a chance."

Moser nodded.

"They'll give him the dress funeral," Richter said. "Cops in uniform, bagpipes, the whole ceremony. But you know what pisses me off? There'll be guys there who'd rather spit on his coffin than salute it. Couple days later, we'll start hearing about all the cops who went out for beers after, raised their glass to the man who shot him. Like he wasn't a cop, just 'cause he worked Internal Affairs." He shook his head. "It's a fucked-up world, Dave."

Moser kept silent.

Richter leaned against the wall, looked at him. "You recognized the shooter. I saw it in your face."

Moser looked down at the floor for a moment, then rubbed at his eyes. "This a test, Lieutenant? That why you got me out here?"

"No, but you got me curious. You know him?"

"Maybe. I got a print from a security camera, looks like this guy."

Richter smiled. "Eva Cruz?"

Moser said nothing for a moment, staring at him. "You gonna tell me what's going on, here?"

Richter pursed his lips, glanced back down the hall, watched as the ambulance crew wheeled out the second stretcher. Then he looked back at Moser, as if he'd come to a decision.

"I busted this kid a few years back," he said. "Miiko Reyes. We had information that he was fronting for some cops up at the Three-Oh, selling 'em around to the local street dealers. They'd take payoffs for a few weeks, then bust the guys, turn 'em over to the INS for deportation, and keep most of the stuff they seized. One of the dealers got pissed, tipped us off. We followed this kid around for a week, got some nice shots of him talking to Marty Stoll in a chicken place over on Amsterdam. We knew he was doing a little dealing on the side, so we decided to run him in, see if we could lean on him to testify against Stoll. I spent

471

about six hours in an interrogation room with this kid, he never once broke a sweat. Told me he didn't know any cops, always walked the other way when he saw one coming. After a couple days of this, we figured, fuck it. We handed the possession-with-intent charge over to a prosecutor, told him not to make any deals unless the kid wanted to talk to us." Richter shook his head. "He never said a word. Did his time up at Rikers, got out, and we lost track of him." Richter looked at Moser, hard. "But I still got those pictures of him talking to Marty Stoll."

Moser let his eyes wander across the tiled floor. He remembered leaning against the same wall, staring at the tiles, while he waited for Mike Delario to count out the cash to pay him, moonlighting Saturday afternoons a few years back. The floor had yellowed, and there were scars in the wall where the warehouse guys had scraped against it, wheeling out the new stock. Nothing had changed, he thought. And everything.

"Dave, I think we'd better have a serious talk about the Eva Cruz case," Richter said.

"That an order?"

Richter tipped his head, looked at him. "No. It's a request for cooperation."

"You know what it means, I cooperate with you?"

"I can guess."

Moser nodded. "Then you see where I'm at. I like my job. I'd like to keep it. But if I get a reputation as a rat, I spend the next twelve years out on the salt. Nobody talks to me, my partners can't trust me. That's it, end of story."

"So you'd let Marty Stoll get away with killing a cop."

"That's your case. If he did it, I hope you get him. I got my own case to close."

"And if they're the same case?"

Moser shrugged. "Imagine my surprise."

Chapter 48

Moser got into the car with Fielding, stared out the window. Ray looked over at him, but didn't say anything until they were on the expressway, heading into the city.

"You okay?"

Moser was silent for a moment, then shrugged. "He wants me to help him."

Fielding glanced over at him. "You going to?"

"No." Moser watched the traffic for a while. "He showed me the security tape."

"Yeah?"

"It was our guy."

"Who?"

"Miiko Reyes."

Fielding glanced in the mirror to check the traffic, pulled the car over to the side of the road, brought it to a stop. He turned to stare at Moser.

"You want to tell me what's going on, Dave?"

Moser kept his eyes on the windshield, the cars whipping past them. "Richter told me the kid's tight with Marty Stoll. They busted him a few years back, tried to get him to rat the cops out. He took the fall, kept his mouth shut."

They sat there in silence for a few moments, then Fielding put the car in gear, waited for a break in the traffic, and pulled out. "I hope you know what you're doing, Dave."

Moser smiled. "Yeah, me too."

Miiko swung onto Amsterdam, pulled to the corner at 132nd. Marty Stoll stepped out of a doorway, walked across the sidewalk, got in. Miiko swung out into traffic, turned west at the next corner.

"So?" He glanced over at Stoll. "You hear?"

"It was on the radio," Stoll said.

"Yeah?" Miiko grinned. "No shit, they were really talking about it on the radio?"

"You shot a cop. What did you expect?" Stoll leaned forward, pointed to the intersection coming up. "Take a left on Riverside."

Miiko waited for a break in traffic,

made the turn. "Man, I never been on the radio before."

"Well, you're on it now."

They crossed 125th Street, entered the park, the southbound lane swinging west of Grant's Tomb. Cars were parked along the edge of the street. Stoll waited until they got a long stretch, said —

"Pull up here."

Miiko pulled over, shut off the engine. "Jesus, you imagine leaving your car here? Might as well put a sign on it, 'Steal me.' "

Stoll didn't answer. He was looking at the river spread out below them. A few yards ahead, a set of concrete steps led down into the park.

"So what'd they say about it on the radio?"

"I just heard a bulletin," Stoll said. "NYPD officer dead in Levittown shooting."

"That's all they said?"

"Yeah."

"When was this?"

Stoll shrugged. "About half an hour ago."

"Maybe they got more now." Miiko turned the key, flicked on the radio. He flipped through the dial, looking for news. He found an all-news station, but they were doing sports, some guy talking about the Yankees' wild-card hopes. Stoll reached over, shut the radio off.

"Hey, what the fuck?"

"You still got the gun?"

"Sure." Miiko reached under the seat, pulled out the .38.

"Give it to me. I'll get rid of it."

Miiko handed him the .38. Stoll took a handkerchief out of his pocket, used it to take the gun.

"You don't take any chances, huh?"

Stoll looked over at him. "I called a guy I know downtown after I heard it on the radio. He said they got a tape of you, from the security camera. They're putting it out to all the TV news shows tonight. Get the public's help to ID the cop killer."

Miiko was silent for a moment. "I didn't see any security camera."

"They're in the light fixtures. The owner put 'em in last year."

Miiko looked at him. "You knew that?"

Stoll nodded. "He asked my advice, which system to buy."

"How come you didn't tell me?"

"Good question." Stoll raised the .38, shot him in the side of the head. The gun was loud in the closed space. Miiko slumped against the window next to him, then slid forward, his head coming to rest against the steering wheel. Blood dripped down the window, and Stoll could see bits of bone stuck to the glass. He leaned over, dropped the gun on the floor of the car, next to Miiko's hand. Then he used the handkerchief to wipe down the dashboard, the seat next to him, and the armrest on the passenger door. He reached over with the hand-kerchief to switch on the radio. Then he got out, wiped down the door handle, and shoved the handkerchief in his pocket. He walked over to the steps, took them down — past the scattered beer cans, burger wrappers, crack vials, and condoms — into the shadows be-low.

Chapter 49

Joey came out of the bathroom, holding his pants up with one hand, had to go around the end of the bed to turn the sound off on the TV, caught the phone on the third ring.

"Yeah?"

"Mr. Joey?"

Joey felt his throat tighten. He buttoned his pants, zipped them up, the belt still loose. "Who's this?"

"Marv Kalb. Mr. Leonard's manager."

Joey took a deep breath, let it out. "Sure. Good to hear from you."

On the TV, some guy was spraying a can of black paint on his bald spot, showing the audience how it looked just like hair. The camera cut to the crowd, applauding.

"Mr. Leonard wants to know if you could have dinner with him this evening."

Joey felt the excitement start to rise in his belly. He hit the remote, shutting off the TV, made himself take a few seconds to buckle the belt. "Uh, this evening. Yeah, I could do that. Should I come over to the hotel?"

"Actually, I'm calling from New York. Mr. Leonard had an appointment in the city this afternoon. He'll be free around seven. He wondered if you could come up, join him at his club."

Oh, Jesus! Joey climbed across the bed, grabbed the bus schedule off the dresser. "Uh, hang on. Let me check."

It took him a minute, looking at the card, to figure out that there was a 3:40 departure, would put him in the Port Authority at 6:32. He glanced at his watch. Twenty minutes to catch the bus.

"Marv? Seven o'clock is fine. I may be a few minutes late if traffic's heavy."

"Fine. You got a pad, for the address?"

"Go ahead."

"Okay, it's 57 East 55th Street. That's between Park —"

"I know where it is," Joey told him.

Marv hung up the phone, looked over at Benny. "Okay, he'll be there."

"Terrific."

Benny stood at the window, his back to the room. Mort Reinert, his agent, sat behind his desk with his hands folded, not saying a word. Over on the leather couch, the guy from Miami, Cesare, had his feet up on the coffee table, his ankle-high Italian boots resting on a copy of *Premiere*, Jack Nicholson's face under his heels. He had his hands behind his head, gazing up at the ceiling, toothpick in his mouth.

"This club," he said. "They got a service entrance?"

Benny turned, looked at him. "What?"

"Some way I could sneak in there?"

Benny glanced over at Mort, his mouth open. "You hear him?"

Mort spread his hands, shrugged.

Benny turned back to the guy, pointed his cigar at him. "Leave the club out of it. Nothing happens in there, understood?"

Cesare closed his eyes slowly, then opened them. He looked over at Benny, like a snake coiled up in the sun, lazy.

"What?"

Marv winced. He gave Benny a plaintive look, like *Jesus, Benny. Please don't piss this guy off.* What was he asking, really? Little help, getting the guy in a car. Said they wanted to have a talk with him, simple as that. And if the guys in Miami had a stake in half the clubs on the East Coast, hey, could that hurt? But, oh man, *please,* this is *not* the kind'a guy you want to get pissed off at you!

The guy lifted his feet down off the coffee table, coming forward to rest his hands on his knees, staring at Benny.

"That's *my* place, okay?" Benny glared at him, his hand coming up to point at him, trembling. "You wanna have a talk with this guy, fine. That's none'a my business. But not in the club. That's like a church. It's sanctuary."

Marv braced himself, waiting for the guy to get up, throw 'em all out the window, six floors to the sidewalk below, but he just looked at Benny for a moment, then shrugged.

"Okay. They got a parking garage?"

Benny raised the cigar to his mouth, looking at him. After a moment, he said —

"Circle Parking, on 54th by Madison."

"You park it, or they do?"

"They do."

Cesare looked down at his knees, picked some lint off his pants. "Okay, so we'll do it there. You got a car?"

Marv looked up. "I do."

"Park it in the garage, get a ticket." He stood up, looked over at Benny. "You bring the guy over, I'll take it from there."

Benny didn't say anything, watched the toothpick moving around in his mouth. Cesare shrugged. He turned, opened the door and walked out of the office. Benny saw Mort's secretary, a young blond girl, look up, watch him walk out.

After a moment, Mort called out, "Ellen?" The secretary glanced over. "Would you mind closing the door?"

Benny walked around the desk, eased himself slowly into a chair. He heard the door shut quietly behind him, looked up at Mort, shook his head.

"You believe that guy?"

Chapter 50

"Looks like you got mail." Fielding nodded at a manila envelope on Moser's chair.

Moser set his coffee down, picked up the envelope, tore it open. Inside, he found a sheaf of photocopies, no cover memo. Moser settled into his chair, glanced through them — a series of police reports, in Spanish.

"Ray, how's your Spanish?"

Fielding glanced up, the telephone pressed to his ear. "Better than yours. Why?"

Moser got up, brought the papers over to Fielding's desk, laid them in front of him. "What's this word?"

Fielding squinted down at the page, then dug in the inner pocket of his jacket, took out a pair of reading glasses, slipped them on. "Exhumation." He shifted the phone to his other ear, took the papers from Moser's hand, looked them over. "It's a pathologist's report. Female juvenile, in an advanced state of decomposition. Body exhumed in a mass grave, in June 1995. Evidence of trauma, multiple gunshot wounds." He glanced up at Moser. "What is this?"

Moser took the papers from him, flipped the stapled packet back to the first page, pointed to the heading on the form — *Policía Nacional, República de Guatemala* — then ran his finger down the page until he came to a name.

Eva Cruz.

Moser walked downstairs to the front desk, told the sergeant on duty, "I need to borrow Maria for a couple hours."

The sergeant looked up at him, raised his eyebrows. "What am I, her pimp?"

"Just thought you should know."

Moser walked over to the small office where a woman was entering traffic citations onto a computer. Maria Portera was a small, compact woman in her forties, black hair pulled up in a bun. Every day she walked down the hill from Nagle Avenue to work at the precinct, her purse tucked under her elbow. In seven years, she'd been mugged once. A junkie tried to grab her purse at knifepoint at the corner of

485

Broadway and 189th. She'd handed it over, and as he turned to run, pulled a can of Mace from her coat pocket, sprayed the whole can into his eyes. Then she used the empty can to break his nose. Twenty minutes later, when she'd dragged him into the station house, the junkie begged the cops on duty to lock him up, get him away from her.

"Hey, Maria." Moser tapped at the door to the office. "You busy?"

She looked up at him, then down at the stack of citations next to her computer. "What's it look like to you?"

"Sorry. I need a favor."

"No."

Moser shrugged, turned away. "Okay, I thought maybe you could help me with an investigation."

She hesitated, looked over at him. "What kind of help?"

"I need you to make a phone call."

"Yeah? To who?"

"Guy in Guatemala."

An hour later, Maria put her hand over the receiver, said, "Okay, he's faxing it."

Moser walked over to the fax machine,

waited as it began to hum, then watched it churn out five pages. He picked them up, walked back to his desk, settled into his chair.

"Okay, we got 'em. Tell him the pictures came out fine."

Maria nodded, said something in Spanish into the phone, laughed, then hung up. She got up, slid the phone back across the desk to Moser. "He said you should let him know how it turns out, he'll update his files."

"Thanks, Maria."

He spread the papers out on his desk, looked at them. The first page was on letterhead, summarizing in labored English what Maria had found out over the phone. At the top of the letterhead, was the organization's name — *CONAVIGUA* — which Maria had explained stood for "National Coordinator for Guatemalan Widows," a human rights group. The next two pages were photocopies from the confidential personnel record of an officer in the Guardia de Hacienda, the Treasury Police. After that was a list of names. On the last page was a series of photographs, copied onto a single sheet for faxing. At the top were two family photographs, each showing a wealthy couple posing with their young daughter. Under one photograph, someone had written *Cruz,* and under the other, *Andrade.* Two families from Zone 12, the letter explained, a wealthy district in Guatemala City: one liberal, a family of lawyers, the other conservative, an old family with connections to the army. Still, the photographs seemed mirrors of each other.

So much in common, Moser thought, studying the photos.

At the bottom of the page was a photograph of a military unit, twelve men posed in front of a truck. Moser slid his drawer open, took out a magnifying glass. He looked at the picture for a long time, examining each man's face.

At last, he sat back, smiled. Look close enough, it all makes sense. He tossed the magnifier aside, picked up the list of names, walked over to the computer terminal. The first name on the list was *Benitez, Joaquin Yano.* He skipped that one, typed in *Cardoza, Angel Ramon.* The computer screen went blank for a moment, then brought up a case number, Homicide, 34th Precinct, dated two days before. Moser stared at it for a moment, thought, *Ah, Christ.*

He glanced at the list, skipped over the next three names — *Cruz, Adalberto, Cruz, Eva,* and *Cruz, Lara Estebel,* which he guessed was the woman in the family photograph, the mother. He typed in *de Guzman, Valeria.* A moment later, the computer brought up a second case number, same date. He typed in *Estora, Javier.* Another case number, this one way out in Queens.

He sat back, looked at the list. There were fourteen names left.

Fielding hung up the phone.

"Jesus. I just spent an hour and twenty minutes, talking to the municipal tax board. You believe that?"

The phone rang at Nicolaides's desk. Moser got up, walked over to answer it.

"Homicide. Moser."

Fielding watched him open a drawer, dig out a message pad. "Where?" He scribbled a note. "Yeah, thanks."

"New case?"

Moser tore the top sheet off the message pad. He stood looking at it for a moment. "Uh, not exactly."

"Good." Fielding smiled. "So aren't you

gonna ask me if I got anything from the tax board?"

"You get anything?"

Fielding folded his hands behind his neck, stretched his shoulders. "Guess who's owner of record for Liquid Assets, Inc."

"Who?"

Fielding grinned. "Adalberto Cruz." And he sat back, spread his hands, triumphant.

Moser hated to ruin it for him. "That's great, Ray."

"You see the connection, right? We got Miiko Reyes tellin' his parole officer almost a year ago how he works for Liquid Assets. I check with the tax board, they tell me Cruz owns the company. So maybe he met the daughter while he worked there."

"Uh huh."

The grin faded from Fielding's face. "You okay, Dave?"

Moser glanced down at the sheet of paper in his hand. "Guy just called for Lou from the Three-Oh. They found Miiko Reyes in a car over on Riverside Drive. He took a bullet in the head."

Fielding sat back in his chair, slowly. "Shit."

"They checked his sheet, saw Lou's request for notification."

Ray was silent for a moment, then he said, "So that's it."

"Maybe." Moser walked over to his desk, picked up the sheet of photographs, brought it over to Fielding. He laid it on the desk in front of him, pointed to the picture of the family at the top left of the page. "You recognize the guy in this picture?"

Fielding picked up the paper, looked at it.

"No."

"You know who that is?"

Fielding tossed the paper on the desk, shook his head. "Who?"

"That's Adalberto Cruz."

Chapter 51

Claire, standing in the lobby of her apartment building, the letter open in her hands, let her eyes skim the first three paragraphs, until she came to the punch line — *three weeks suspension, unpaid, pending the outcome of an internal investigation.* She closed the mailbox, twisted the key to lock it, thinking, *Jesus, that was fast.* Two days, from the moment she'd stood in the men's room, the metal toilet roll in her hand, wishing, oh man, that she could take it all back, do it over, stand there watching while Joey strained over the urinal, trying to squeeze out a few drops to salvage his pride.

Two days. She'd spent it sitting in a conference room on the seventh floor of the federal building, telling her story to three men from Conte's office, answering the same questions five, six times: *No, she hadn't seen any prior signs of his intention to flee. Yes, she'd considered it a reasonable request when he told her he needed the men's room. No, she'd had no unauthorized contacts with Giardella, or any of his associates.* Claire, sitting there at the long conference table, looking at the serious men in their suits, had to fight back a smile, thinking of Joey, that first day in the hotel, taking the cigar from his mouth, slowly, as the door had closed behind them, saying — *So, what do you call a guy, he's the assistant to the Assistant U.S. Attorney?*

After that, more sessions with her supervisor, the local cops, a review officer from the Marshal's Service, whose job would be to conduct the inquiry, present his findings to a hearing board convened to look into the matter. They were more sympathetic than the lawyers, letting her know by the way they held the door for her as she came into the conference room, shook her hand, that they'd been there, knew how easy it was to lose a witness, once they get close to testifying, catch a case of nerves. But, if anything, their questions were tougher, picking away at her procedures, her assumptions, her perceptions of Tangliero's state of mind. By the time they were finished, she felt wrung out. She walked out expecting a dismissal for cause, wondering how she'd look in a security guard's uniform.

"Take the rest of the day," McCann had told her at the door. "Get some rest."

She glanced at the letter in her hand. Mailed two days ago. So they'd known, the whole time.

She folded the letter once, stuffed it into her purse.

She hit the button for the elevator, thinking that if the review went against her, she could expect a transfer. A year of working courthouse security in Minneapolis, or Boise. Okay, she could live with that. Get a decent apartment, maybe buy some clothes. Then hang in there, work her way up to the fugitive team. She liked the idea of that, busting into houses wearing a Kevlar vest, throw the guy up against the wall, dig out the cuffs.

Better than sitting around hotel rooms, anyway. Some guy with hair on his back watching Ricki Lake interview transvestites, telling her about the good old days, when they used to go down to the Village, beat up queers.

The elevator came, and she got on. With Joey, at least all she'd had to live with was the bad jokes. That, she thought, and watching him eat. She couldn't bring herself to feel angry at him. He saw his chance, took it. Who could blame him?

Next time, though? He could hold it.

She unlocked the door of her apartment, tossed the mail on the kitchen table. Three weeks. Maybe she could work on the place, paint the living room. She went into the bedroom, stripped off her work clothes, tossed them on the bed. She dropped her .38 into the drawer of her bedside table, then pulled a pair of sweatpants out of the bottom of the closet, a *CRIMSON TIDE!* T-shirt that she wore to work out, kept hanging on a hook. She got down on the floor, did thirty push-ups, then turned over, did the same number of sit-ups, legs raised, the muscles in her belly trembling with the strain. She lay on the floor for a few moments, catching her breath, then did the whole thing again. Afterward, she dug her Nikes out of the tangle of shoes in the bottom of her closet, sat on the bed to lace them up. Sweat dripped from her face. She pulled the bottom of the T-shirt up, wiped her face on it, went over to the window, waited while the old air conditioner shuddered to life. A run, then a shower. By the time she was done, the room would be cool.

She was on her way out the door, pausing to grab her can of pepper spray off the entryway table, when the phone rang. She stood there for a moment, looking at it, in no mood to talk to anyone, but curious. She waited until the machine picked up, heard a man's voice, hesitant, saying —

"Uh . . . yeah. This is Joey Tangliero. I just wanted to call, say I was sorry for what happened, and . . ."

Claire shoved the door shut with her foot, grabbed for the phone.

"Joey?"

He sounded embarrassed, now. The relief when he'd got the machine going out of his voice, as he said —

"Oh, you're there."

Claire reached down to shut off the machine, then paused, her finger on the button, letting it record:

"Joey, where are you?"

"I'm okay. I got some things to take care of in the city, then I'm gonna take off for a while."

She could hear people talking in the background, crowd noises. She glanced at her watch: 6:49. Commuter crowd.

Joey said, "I've just, you know, been thinking 'bout what this must'a done to you. It's been on my mind. Something I gotta clear up, before I get on to new things, you know?"

"So tell me where you are, I'll come pick you up."

He laughed. "Nah, I don't think so. Listen, I gotta go. I got some important business, tonight. I just wanted to get straight with you, okay? So my head's clear."

"They're gonna kill you, Joey."

"Who? You mean Tony, those guys? Fuck 'em. They gotta find me first."

And then she heard it, faintly, in the background — like tin cans falling into a piano. A large Plexiglas case, near the top of an escalator. Inside, a pair of silver balls ran along a track — bouncing over bells, rolling down the sides of a steel drum, dropping through a hole onto a pair of cymbals with a crash. When the balls got to the bottom, they dropped into a cup on a chain, which carried them back to the top. Like the escalator a few feet away, she thought. She could picture kids leaning against the case, watching it. In the background, people carrying suitcases. The whole building like that Rube Goldberg machine, people running on their little tracks. Maybe they stop to watch it for a minute, not getting the joke.

Port Authority.

"Listen," Joey said, "I gotta go."

"Stay right there," she told him. "I'll come get you."

Chapter 52

What she did, after Joey slammed the phone down, was flip open the phone book to the blue pages at the front, run her finger down the page until she found the number for *Transit Police, Port Authority Substation.* She dialed the number quickly, and when an officer answered — "Transit Police, Port —" she cut him off, identified herself as Deputy U.S. Marshal Claire Locke, told him that she'd just received a call from a suspect, she believed from the pay phone bank near the kinetic sculpture in the terminal. Could they get an officer up there to have a look, *fast?*

"What's he look like?"

"About five eight, two-fifty, mid-forties, with black hair, going bald."

"Okay, hang on."

She carried the phone into the bedroom, started getting dressed. She had to put the phone down to get the T-shirt over her head, took a second to reach over, grab the .38 out of the bedside table. When she picked up the phone, she heard a tiny voice saying —

"Deputy?"

Like a movie she saw when she was a kid, some scientist gets hit with a compression ray, shrunk down to an inch tall; he hides out from the bad guys in his girlfriend's apartment, falls into an empty cat food can in the kitchen garbage, has to get her attention before the cat sees him. She's cooking dinner, keeps hearing this weird squeaking sound — *Help me!* The cat, a big tabby, going over to the garbage can, curious. You see this huge paw, from inside the can, coming at you.

She picked up the phone, said, "I'm here."

"We missed him," the officer told her. "He ran out the front, jumped in a cab."

"Shit."

"Wait. We keep an officer out front, handles the taxis. He got the cab number. I got a guy on the phone to the company right now, see if they can get hold of the driver, find out where he took the guy."

Claire pulled her pants on, clipped the holster to her belt. She reached for her shirt, saw it was wrinkled from lying under the pants, then thought, *fuck it.* She pulled it on, had it buttoned up, unzipping her pants to stuff the bottom in, when she heard the guy on the phone say, hand over the receiver —

"Yeah? What's the address?"

Then he got back on, said, "Got it. The driver made a pickup at Port Authority, dropped the fare at Park and Fifty-fifth."

"Great. Thanks a lot."

"Hey, no problem."

The desk sergeant at the Transit Police Port Authority Substation hung up, glanced over at the officer leaning against the door. He looked up from the sheet of paper in his hands, reached over, laid it on the desk. It was a photocopy of a mug shot, a picture of a man in his mid-forties, balding, grinning at the camera. He held up an ID board saying — *Tangliero, J.*

"That the guy?"

"Yeah, that's him."

The desk sergeant nodded, picked up the phone. He dialed the phone number typed below the photograph, heard —

"Twenty-fifth Precinct. Lucas."

"Tell Marty we found him."

501

* * *

Claire hung up, then lifted the receiver again, dailed McCann's office extension. After four rings, it put her through to voice mail, "Hi, this is Jim McCann. I'm not at my desk . . ."

"Shit!" Claire broke the connection, dialed the message desk in the front office. When the receptionist answered, she said —

"Margie, this is Claire. Has McCann left for the day?"

"I think he stepped out for a few minutes."

Claire hearing it in her tone — *he stepped out* — like she was talking to someone off the street.

"Margie, listen, I need you to page him for me. I just got a call from Joey Tangliero. He's headed for some kind of meeting at Park and Fifty-fifth. Can you get that message to McCann?"

"I'll try."

"Tell him I'm heading over there now."

The receptionist saying, "Claire?" as she hung up the phone. Getting ready to ask her if she knew what she was doing, the word out about her suspension by now. *Yeah, right,* Claire thought, grabbing her jacket off the bed. *She probably knew before you did.*

She locked the apartment door, ran down the hall to ring for the elevator. Waiting for it, she thought, *Okay, say you find him. Then what?*

Suspended, she had no authority to take him into protective custody. If he wanted to walk, that was his business.

The elevator came, the doors creaking open. She got on, hit the button for the lobby, thinking —

Yeah, but does Joey know that?

Chapter 53

Joey couldn't believe it. It was like the guy was *waiting* for him. He gets out of the cab, takes a moment to look up at the windows rising six floors above him — the Milton Berle Room, the Frank Sinatra Room, the George Burns Card Room — thinking, *Oh man, this is it!* And what happens? The door opens, Benny Leonard comes out, doesn't even see him, he's too busy yelling at Marv.

"What'ya mean you didn't call?"

Marv, catching the door behind him, was holding a plastic garbage bag, folded around something, twice, the way guys used to carry shotguns. "Since when did we need to call?"

"Since now!" Benny turned, saw him standing there on the sidewalk. His eyes widened, surprised. Playing it, Joey thought. Like those old skits they used to do. Guy's talking to a blonde, turns around, his wife is standing there, arms folded. Double take.

"Jesus, here he is." Benny came down

the steps, shook his hand. He turned back to Marv, said, "The man's my *guest*. Can we not insult him, here?"

Marv looked at Joey, spread his hands. "What can I say? I'm sorry."

Benny sighed, shook his head. "I said to him, 'Marv, call.' But he knows better."

"What's wrong?"

Benny waved a hand at the building behind him. "They got a wedding. Whole place is shut down. I mean, it's Thursday night. Who the fuck gets married on Thursday night?"

Joey looked up at the building, felt something drain away in his chest. Benny put an arm around his shoulders, said —

"Schmucks, that's who! They should be home, watching television, where they belong. Let 'em watch . . ." He turned to Marv. "What's his name, he's married to the shiksa, they fight."

"Reiser."

"God bless you." He turned back to Joey. "They should stay home, watch a half hour of that, they won't *want* to get married, we can have dinner in peace!" He paused, reached up to take the fabric of Joey's jacket between his fingers. "Nice suit. You get this local?"

Joey, feeling numb, told him, "Atlantic City."

"Yeah?" Benny put his arm around Joey's shoulders again, turned him toward Park, moving him past the office tower next door, rows of trees in little brick planters, like they wanted you to think you were home in Westchester, out walking the property. "This guy got a name, Mr. Joey?"

Twenty minutes to walk one block, Benny stopping every few steps to argue with Marv about the restaurant. *Lutèce*? Nah, it's gone. *Four Seasons*? Please, their prices? Ask me, they charge by the fork. *Sign of the Dove*? That's what? A place, sells candles down in the Village? I'm gonna *eat* there?

Marv sighing, shaking his head. He turned to Joey, asked — "You have any favorite restaurants?"

Joey thought about it, almost told him, *Well, I know a good coffee shop . . .*

"I don't get out much, lately."

Benny stared at him. "You're a comedian, you don't get *out?*" He shook his head. "I was starting out, I went fourteen years, never once ate a home-cooked meal. That's how we lived." He shrugged. "Now? Ask me when's the last time I went to a restaurant, it's not eggs or Chinese. I'm working, they feed me. It's crap, but you got a nine o'clock show, who's got time to go out? I'm in town, I go to the club." He grinned at Marv. "You know what's funny? As we speak, there's comedians all over town having dinner with their *wives.* Can you picture it?"

Marv winced. "Nah, you think so?"

"First time in twenty years, some'a these guys." Benny dug a cigar out of his coat pocket, unwrapped the plastic. "Tomorrow morning, all those wives'll pick up the phone, call their lawyers."

They were on 54th, coming up to a parking garage, taking their time. Benny distracted, looking in shop windows, like he had something on his mind. Joey watched him stop to light up the cigar, take a few puffs, blow the smoke out easy, just like on stage. The guy different in person, but the same too. Like some part of him never stopped doing the act.

"Comics work," he said, staring at a shop window. "They don't sit home.

You'd play the men's room at Grand Central, just to be *working*."

"What's the worst place you ever worked," Joey asked him.

Benny looked at him. "You gotta be careful, a question like that. Back at the club, you'd have thirty guys fightin' each other. 'Hey, you think *that's* bad?' " But he paused, thinking about it, standing there in the street with his cigar, all the commuters, heading for their trains, having to stop, fight the crowd to get around them. Benny ignored them, looking up at the smoke rising off his cigar, remembering.

"The worst place." He rolled the cigar between his fingers. "Tell you the truth, it's the place I'm working now."

Joey looked at him, surprised. "The Taj?"

"Nah, I mean *any* place I'm working. They're *all* bad. The lights are too bright, or maybe it's too cold. You don't get the laughs, or you get 'em in the wrong place, throws your timing off. After? You look back, it wasn't so bad. But you want the truth? It's a crappy way to make a living. The only thing worse is anything else."

He looked over. Joey nodded, his face serious.

"But, I'll tell you, there was a club," Benny said. "You ever been to the Gag Factory, down on Forty-fourth?"

"I don't think so."

"They went under, what?" He looked over at Marv. "Twelve years ago?"

"Whatever. Not soon enough."

Benny nodded, held his cigar up toward the sky. "They should rot in hell, those bastards. They'd bring in name talent, big guys. Everybody worked there. But they were too fuckin' cheap to give you a dressing room. They put you in a toilet, back off the kitchen, to change. And I'm talking *in* the toilet. This place, it *stunk.* I played there, what? Three nights?"

Marv shrugged. "You go find a booking Labor Day weekend."

Benny spread his hands, innocent. "Did I say? I'm answering the man's question, is all." He turned to Joey. "Three nights I worked there, the toilet overflowed every night. Ruined my shoes. And the crowd? You know who came to this place? Taxi drivers. You ever try to get a laugh from taxi drivers? Half of 'em don't speak English. A room full'a turbans, I'm lookin' at."

"Now he's lying," Marv said.

Benny sighed. "Okay, so that part I made up. But the place? I'm here to tell you, that was the worst." He puffed at his cigar. "To get to the stage, you had to go through the kitchen, up this set of metal stairs, then along this hallway. Cinder block, like a prison. They kept boxes of food stacked back there. The weather got hot, it used to rot. You'd be holding your breath, waiting to go on. A couple years ago, some guy was waiting to go on, he took out his pen, wrote on the wall — *Fuck me, if I ever play this place again.* Every guy who played there used to sign his name, before he went on. It got to be a thing, for luck. You'd write your best line, how crappy the place was. Every week, the owners would drag one of the busboys back there, give him a bucket of cheap paint, tell him to do the hall. Same paint, every week. Cheap blue stuff, they got it at Sears out on the Island. They kept the cans in the bathroom, under the sink. All the comics, we used to piss in the cans. After a while, the paint got so thin, you could see like six layers of writing under it, all the guys who played there before you. The whole place smelled like piss. So you'd stand there, some guy's onstage warming up the taxi drivers for you, you're thinking, 'Man, this is the worst place I've *ever* been.' You want to go back to the bathroom, slit your wrists. But then the guy says your name, everybody starts clapping, you walk out onstage, and it's lights, a mike, a crowd. That's all it takes. Forty minutes later, you've done your set, now you got to walk back down that hallway. You're back in the shit. You don't believe it? Hey, there's the writing on the wall, to remind you. See, that's the thing about this business, kills some guys. You get up in the lights, people laugh, it feels good. But you can't escape what you are, my friend. You still got to walk back to the toilet, see the writing on the wall."

"What'd you write?"

Benny looked at Joey, thoughtful. "Christ, I don't remember." He shook his head. "I'm gettin' old."

"You *are* old," Marv told him. "Your age, Benny, the only thing left to *get* is dead."

Benny sighed. "This is what I gotta listen to."

He stuck the cigar back in his mouth, a sorrowful look on his face. Joey frowned.

"C'mon," he said to Marv. "He's not that old." He looked at Benny. "You're, what? Sixty-five? Seventy?"

Benny glanced over at Marv. "Where's that garage?"

Claire, standing on the northeast corner of 55th and Park, where the cab let her out, looked up at the buildings, thinking, *Okay, now what?* She could see the Bank of Montreal building, a Mercedes dealership, Chase Manhattan on one corner, and across the street, Sulka & Co., a men's store, the window filled with expensive suits. . . .

She crossed Park to the median strip, waited for a break in the traffic, ran the rest of the way. In the store, a sales clerk stood behind the counter, folding pants over wooden hangers. He looked at her blankly as she described Joey, shook his head.

"Sorry."

She came out onto the street, walked to the corner, stood looking up 55th Street, toward Madison. What was he doing up here? A cab pulled up to the curb a few doors down, and she saw a man lean across the front seat, pay the driver, then get out. He paused, looking up at the building, to adjust his tie. *Jesus,* she thought. *Isn't that Sid Caesar?* She watched him cross the sidewalk, under a round awning with the numbers *57* on the side, climb the steps, and go inside. She walked over to where he'd stood.

A few weeks back she'd glanced up at the woman sitting across from her on the subway, realized — Jesus! — it's *Jodie Foster!* But why would Jodie Foster be riding the Broadway local? Everybody she knew here played spot the celebrity, tossing names around, trying to top each other at parties: Madonna, reading a copy of *Self* in the waiting room of a Park Avenue gynecologist. Okay, that one she could believe. But Barbara Walters, pausing in the doorway of a shoe store on West 72nd to blow her nose? Uh-huh, sure. Probably some woman from Scarsdale, came in to do her shopping. Once, she'd seen a man who looked exactly like Dustin Hoffman coming out of a restaurant on upper Madison. As she stood there on the sidewalk, watching him get into a

cab, a woman came up to her, asked —
"Excuse me, but aren't you Holly Hunter?"

There was a guard behind a small desk just inside the door, reading a newspaper. Next to him was a building directory. She could read a few lines through the narrow pane of glass in the door. It said:

3rd Floor   Frank Sinatra Room
             Celebrity Room
             Ed Sullivan Billiard Room
             Noon to 11:30 P.M.
2nd Floor   Milton Berle Room
             Joe E. Lewis Room
             Noon to 11:00 P.M.
Main Floor   Main Dining Room
             William B. Williams Room
             Reception and Check Room
             Noon to 11:00 P.M.

Claire walked up the steps, went inside.

Circle Parking had an entrance on 54th Street, a small office next to the ramp. Cesare stood just inside the door of the office, watching them walk up the ramp. He wore a blue jumpsuit, a size too small for him, with the words *Red Dot Parking* and *Luis* stitched over the breast pocket. Inside the office, the garage attendant — a little Cuban guy — lay on the floor behind the counter in his underwear. Cesare had run a strip of duct tape around his hands and feet, another over his mouth. The guy had a thick mustache; it was gonna hurt like hell, Cesare thought, getting that tape off.

He stepped out of the office, pulled the door closed behind him. The old guy, the comedian, stopped, halfway up the ramp, staring at him. Cesare recognized the one in the middle: Joey Tangliero. He'd seen him a couple of times in Miami, the guy always telling jokes. Big fuckin' mouth, even then.

"You got your ticket?"

"What?" The old guy looking at him, like he couldn't believe it.

"Your *ticket.*"

Benny turned to Marv, who dug in his pocket, passed him the ticket. Cesare glanced at it, nodded.

"You wait here, okay?"

Joey, watching the guy walk off, thought, *He looks like somebody.* Not placing the face. A guy on TV, maybe.

515

But Benny, looking at him, said, "Hey, Marv. Show him the stick."

Marv glanced down at the bag in his hand, silent. He unwrapped the plastic, took out a long narrow paddle, the wood dark along the handle from sweat. Joey saw that the wood was split from the handle up to the end, like a tuning fork. Benny reached over, took it in both hands, swung it easily like a bat.

"You know what this is?"

Joey shrugged. "No, what?"

Benny smiled. "This, my young friend, is a slapstick. They used 'em in vaudeville, for the knockabout stuff. Guy hits you with this, it don't hurt, but it makes a hell of a sound." He slapped it against the palm of one hand, *THWAP!* "You'd get screams, the audience. Nothing like watching a guy get the shit beat out of him, make 'em laugh."

Joey stared at it, fascinated. "Really, that's a slapstick?"

"Would I kid you?"

He reached out, ran a finger along the edge, gently. "Could I hold it?"

Benny hesitated. Then he shrugged. "Thirty years, guys getting hit over the head with it every night, what could you do?" He handed it to him. "But be careful, okay? This thing's an antique. I got a guy, works down in the theater district, he knows I collect stuff like this. He goes into the prop rooms, some of the old theaters, finds all kinds of old junk. He found this in the Belasco, down in the basement. Whole box of stuff, he thinks, from the Majestic Theater in Baltimore, got torn down back in the sixties, make way for a housing project."

He watched Joey take a few easy swings, holding it southpaw. The guy swinging it like he'd played stickball, no weight at the end so the tip got out ahead of his hands, *swish!* It reminded Benny he had to get onto Mort to line up his Miami dates for spring training. He loved to watch batting practice, see the guys take a few days to find their rhythm, that thing inside made you know to hold back one more second, let the ball come to you. Like working a hot crowd, effortless.

"Work of art, huh?"

"It's beautiful."

"Those old guys, they knew what they were doing." He took it, passed it back to Marv, who put it in the bag, folded it closed. "They went onstage, they didn't fool around. No mercy. They'd throw everything they had at you; that didn't work, they'd make up something. They were serious about it, those guys. Killers."

Behind him, in the back of the garage, Joey heard tires squeal on cement. He saw Benny turn to see a car coming down the ramp, slowing to a stop in front of them, the garage attendant looking at them from behind the wheel. Joey glanced over at Benny, expecting him to walk over to the car, but he didn't. He stood there, silent, watching the garage attendant open the door, slowly, get out.

Joey followed his gaze, saw the attendant looking at him, smiling. He had a toothpick in his mouth, chewing on the end of it so the tip jumped. Joey, watching it, thought, *Miami.* Seeing the guy, Cesare, getting up from a table at the coffee shop downstairs in the hotel, going over to the counter, taking a pile of toothpicks from the little cup next to the cash register, slipping them into his pocket. One of Frankie's punks, the kind he'd send to slam some guy's fingers in a car door, he doesn't pay. Cesare, watching him as he moved away from the car, gave a slight smile, catching the recognition on his face.

He reached into the driver's door, popped the trunk. Then he slipped a hand into his jumpsuit, pulled out a .45. He pointed it at Joey, smiled.

"Hey, Joey. Time to go for a ride."

The guy behind the desk was taking his time, looking at her identification, glancing up at her face, then back at the photograph on her card. He laid it on the desk, slid it across to her.

"You understand," he said, "we don't give out information about members."

"This guy isn't a member. He's a guest, maybe. His name's Joey Tangliero. About five eight, two-fifty. Balding. Dresses sharp."

The man smiled. "That could describe any number of our guests." He reached over to where the guard sat, took a guest book from the blotter, glanced at it, then turned it to face Claire. "We ask our guests to sign in. I'm afraid I don't see anyone by that name on the list."

Claire nodded, looking at the scrawled signatures. "He could be using another name."

The man slid the book back over to

the guard. "This is a theatrical fraternity. We have members in other fields, but most of our members are actors, comics, a few directors." He smiled. "Do you know how many of our members use stage names? Some of them, even *they* don't remember who they are anymore."

Claire glanced out at the street, the light fading. It was slipping away, she could feel it. The excitement when she'd picked up the phone, heard Joey's voice, seemed a long time ago. What had made her think she could catch up with him, or that he'd listen to her if she did?

She looked at the guard. "Have you seen *anyone* who fits the description?"

The guard glanced up at the man from the reception desk, who nodded. He looked back at Claire, shook his head. "Sorry." She saw him hesitate for a moment, then he said, "But if it's any help, I think Mr. Leonard and his manager were meeting someone. They stood here in the entrance for about ten minutes. I think they said something about picking up their car."

Claire stared at him. "Who?"

"Benny Leonard. The comedian?"

For the first time, the guard saw her smile. She had a nice smile, like a breeze on a hot day. He smiled back.

"That's interesting." She slipped her identification card back into her wallet. "You know where I might catch up with them?"

Chapter 54

Joey didn't move.

Cesare sighed. "Joey, we can do this the easy way or the hard way, but you're getting in the car."

Benny took Joey by the arm, shoved him forward. "Do what he says, okay? He's got a gun."

Joey looked at him. "Benny, he's gonna kill me."

"I go to the movies. You think I don't know what it means, the guy says you're gonna take a ride?" Benny thought about it, turned to Cesare. "You guys still *say* that?"

Cesare stared at him, brought the toothpick around to point right at him. Benny took a step back, raised both hands.

"Okay. Whatever."

Cesare walked over to Joey, grabbed him by the arm, dug his thumb into the soft flesh at the inside of the elbow, found the nerve. A flare of pain shot through Joey's arm. He cried out, tried to pull away. Cesare tightened his grip, watched him double over in pain. He bent over, asked him —

"You gonna be good?"

Joey nodded, gasping for breath. Cesare waited for him to straighten, jerked him toward the back of the car. At the trunk, he put his hand on the back of Joey's head, started shoving him in.

"Wait!" Cesare looked up, saw Benny come over. "Let me get my suitcase out."

He reached in, dragged out a large blue Samsonite, set it next to the car.

"Okay. Go ahead."

Cesare gave Joey a shove, bent him over the edge of the trunk. He reached down, grabbed the back of his belt, lifted him off his feet, started to toss him in. Then, suddenly, Joey felt him pause. Cesare let him down against the car's bumper, took a step back.

Joey heard footsteps coming up the ramp from the street. He raised his head, saw a man in a sport coat walking toward them, hands in his pockets like he was digging for his keys. Cesare reached over, shoved his head down.

"We're closed," Cesare said. He held the gun low against the back of his thigh, out of sight. "Come back later."

Joey heard the guy say, "What do you mean, you're *closed?* The sign says open twenty-four hours."

"The sign's wrong."

"But I need my car."

"Yeah? Too bad. Come back later."

Marty Stoll shook his head in amazement. "That's all you got to say? Come back *later?*"

He pulled his hand out of the pocket of his jacket, raised a nine-millimeter semiautomatic, and shot Cesare twice in the chest.

Joey heard the shots, felt the hand on his head jerked away. He looked back. Cesare wasn't there. He put his hands on the edge of the trunk, straightened.

Marty Stoll said, "You're not too smart, are you, Joey?"

Joey looked down at Cesare, sprawled on the floor. Stoll walked over, kicked the gun away from his hand.

Benny was staring at them. "Who the fuck is *this* guy?"

"He's a cop," Joey said.

"No shit?" Benny shook his head. "Hey, that even I knew. Look't him. Wears an Izod shirt under a sport jacket? Got a gun in his pocket? I'm guessing he's not a tennis pro, right?"

Stoll glanced over at him. "How 'bout you shut your fuckin' mouth. How'd that be?"

Benny raised both hands, shrugged. "Okay, this ain't my deal."

"Yeah? Well, it's gonna be your *deal,* you don't shut up."

"Okay, okay . . ."

Marv said, "Benny, shut up."

"What? Am I talkin' here?"

Stoll raised his gun, pointed it at Benny's head. "You say one more word, I'll blow your fuckin' head off."

Benny looked at Joey. "This is a *cop?*"

Joey winced. He watched Stoll's face go red, his knuckle get white on the trigger. Then he took a deep breath, lowered the gun slowly, shook his head. "Unbelievable."

He shifted the gun to his left hand, took a quick step, and drove his fist into Benny's mouth.

Benny stumbled back, grabbed at Marv's arm, and went down. He brought a hand up to his mouth, groaned. Joey could see blood on his teeth. His other hand came up, gripped the leg of Marv's pants.

Stoll looked at Marv. "You?"

Marv shook his head.

Claire, cutting across the street against the traffic, saw the sign out on the curb — ALL DAY PARKING $14.00 — and thought, *No way! Fourteen dollars?* Remembering her mother, the last time she was home, pulling up in front of the Ben Franklin, putting a nickel in the meter, one hour.

Then she heard the shots.

She drew her .38 from the holster on her hip, ducked back against the outside wall of the garage. She hesitated, then swung the gun wide, following it up the ramp.

At the top of the ramp, a car idled, the driver's door and trunk standing open. A pair of old men stood next to it, motionless. Just beyond, a man lowered a gun to rest against his thigh. It looked to Claire like some kind of semiauto, a Glock maybe. Seventeen rounds in the chamber, to her six. *If it comes to a fight,* she thought, *I'm fucked.*

As she watched, the gunman walked over to where a body lay on the floor, kicked a gun away from its hand. Somebody moved beyond the raised trunk, and now she saw Joey take a step back, stand with his hands hanging by his sides. She could hear their voices, the words faint, unclear.

She edged along the wall to a concrete pillar, got it between her and the gunman. She got both hands on the .38, put it on him. Too far for a good shot. All he had to do was take two quick steps to his right, duck behind the car. Then he'd have the firepower, the mobility. And her? Six shots, eighteen inches of concrete. Fuck that.

But as she watched, the gunman switched hands, came around the car, punched one of the old men in the mouth. The guy went down, hard. The gunman walked back to the trunk of the car, told Joey —

"Get in."

Joey stared at him. "What?"

"You heard me. Get in the car."

Joey looked down at the trunk, shook his head.

"No way," he said. "Not again."

Stoll pointed the gun at him. "What're you, crazy? Get in the fuckin' car!"

Joey took a step back. "No."

Stoll reached over, grabbed him by the back of the neck, slammed his head against the trunk. Joey cried out, staggered back. Stoll held on to him, reached over with his gun hand, pushed the trunk open again, and shoved his head down inside. He got the gun hand on the trunk, brought it down to rest against the back of Joey's neck. He bent down, said —

"You gonna listen to me?"

Claire, watching it over the barrel of the .38, thought, *Now.*

"Federal marshal!" she yelled at him. "Put your weapon down and step away from the car."

She saw the guy straighten, look over at her, his gun hand still resting on the trunk.

"I'm NYPD," he said. "Stay outta this."

Claire held the gun steady, combat grip, aimed at his body mass. "I don't care who you are. Put your weapon *down!*"

For a moment, nobody moved. The guy looked at her, then down at the gun in his hand. She could see him thinking about it. Then, slowly, he let go of Joey's neck, took a few steps back, and laid the gun on the ground. He straightened, looked at her.

"You satisfied?"

"Step over to the car, put your hands

on the hood."

He laughed, shook his head. "C'mon, lady. I'm a cop." His hand moved toward his pocket. "You wanna see my ID?"

She took a step closer, her finger tightening on the trigger. "Don't you fuckin' move!"

He paused, then raised his hands. "Okay, take it easy. I'm on your side." He moved over to the car, put his hands on the hood, his feet spread. "This what you want?"

"That's fine." Claire glanced over at Joey. He was leaning against the trunk, blood trickling from his nose. "You okay?"

Joey shook his head. He reached around, dug a handkerchief out of his pocket, pressed it against his face. "I think he broke my fuckin' nose."

Marv helped Benny get to his feet, slowly. He leaned on Marv's shoulder, coughing. Then he caught his breath, rubbed the back of his hand across his mouth, glanced down at the smear of blood.

Claire stepped clear of the pillar, moved in close to Stoll, put the gun against the back of his neck. She took one hand off the grip, ran it under his arms, down along his back. Stoll glanced back at her.

"You're makin' a big mistake."

"You let me worry about that, okay?"

She edged the gun down his spine, crouched down to run her hand along his waist, then down the inside of his legs. He had a gun strapped to his ankle. She reached under his pants leg, yanked it out of the holster. A tiny .25 revolver. She stood up, tucked it into the waistband of her pants.

"Okay, let's see that ID."

Stoll brought one hand down, took his ID holder out of the back pocket of his pants, handed it to her. She flipped it open, glanced at it. *Patrolman Martin Stoll, 30th Precinct.*

She stepped back, kept her gun raised. "Turn around."

He turned to look at her, rubbing at the back of his neck. She checked the picture on his ID, glanced up at his face. Then she passed it back to him. "You're off your beat."

He tucked the ID case back into his pocket. "I'm off duty. I had to come down to pick up a present for my wife after work. So I park my car in the garage, come back an hour later, some guy's holding these men at gunpoint. I ordered him to put the gun down, but he pointed it at me." He shrugged. "I used my judgment."

"Yeah?" Claire jerked her head at Joey. "That include putting him in the trunk of the car?"

Stoll brought his hand up, rubbed at his lower lip. Then he grinned. "Nah, I'd call that inspiration."

Joey felt numb. He leaned against the car, the handkerchief pressed to his face. The pain in his nose was like a fire, but he felt nothing inside. Knowing, now, that the whole thing was a setup. Benny, the club, all of it. He felt like somebody'd stuck a pin in him, let the air out.

He looked over at Stoll, leaning against the car now, arms folded, grinning at the tiny revolver Claire pointed at him.

"You ever use that thing on a real person?"

"Not yet."

Stoll laughed. "You just waitin' your chance, huh?" He nodded at Joey. "You know how much you could make, you used it on him?"

Claire considered him. "How much?"

Stoll put his palms on the edge of the car's hood, hitched himself up. "Well, I'd say that depends. You just cap him, I'm thinkin' you could ask ten percent of what he stole."

"What's that come to?"

Stoll shrugged. "I heard one fifty. But let's say you know how to ask questions, get answers the hard way? Way I hear it, this boy's got a million five stashed away somewhere."

Benny started to cough, violently. "Jesus, Joey! Is that true?"

Stoll grinned at Claire. "Go on, ask him where he hid it."

"I'm not interested."

"No?" Stoll pursed his lips, whistled softly. "What's the matter? Nobody bust your cherry yet?"

Claire's eyes darkened. She took a quick step, raked the gunsight across his left cheekbone. He gave a howl, twisted away in pain. Then, before she could step back, he swung his arm around, caught her with a huge fist against the side of her head. She saw a flash of red, stumbled, felt his hand close on her wrist, wrench the gun out of her hand.

He twisted her arm up behind her back, drove a knee into her belly. Then he slammed her against the side of the car, let her go. She staggered back, collapsed to the floor.

Stoll shifted the gun to his left hand, rubbed at the angry cut on his face with two fingers. He looked down at Claire. She was curled up on her side, her breath whistling. Her eyes were open, but not focused. Like she was looking at something way off in the distance. She had blood on her forehead, where she'd hit the car. He nudged her leg with his foot.

"How much they pay you?"

She looked at him, confused. Her hand coming up to touch the place on her forehead, gently.

"They pay you good?"

She didn't answer, staring at him.

" 'Cause, I'm just sayin', it ain't enough." And he brought the gun up, pointed it at her.

Joey turned away, not wanting to see it. He heard Benny say, "Oh, fuck this!" He glanced back, saw him reach over, grab the plastic bag from Marv, pull out the stick.

Stoll looked up. He saw the old guy take a step toward him, swinging a stick back over his shoulder like fuckin' Wade Boggs. He brought the gun up, seeing the old man plant his feet, elbows out, taking his swing, *THWACK!*, slashing him across the face. Light burst in his eyes, blinding. A wave of nausea seized him, bent him over. A second later, he felt the stick crack down on his wrist, *SMACK!* He cried out, the gun spinning out of his hand. He stumbled back against the car, fell to his knees.

Benny stood over him for a moment, the stick raised. Then, slowly, he lowered it, reached up with one hand to rub at his shoulders. "Jesus, I'm outta shape. The old days, that would'a been a double, at least."

Claire got to her feet, leaned against the car for a moment, unsteady. She looked down at Stoll on his hands and knees, gasping for breath. Then she walked over, picked up his gun, stuck it in the waistband of her pants. She came back to squat next to Stoll, reached under his jacket, took a pair of cuffs off his belt. She grabbed him by the hair, and kicked his hands out from under him. He cried out, crumpled to the pavement. She jerked his hands behind his back, cuffed him.

Then she looked up at Marv. "You think you could go in that office over there, call 911?"

"Sure thing."

"Tell 'em it's a ten-thirteen. Officer down."

Marv nodded, went into the office. She looked over at Joey.

"You're bleeding."

He nodded. "You too."

Behind her, Benny said, "Ah *fuck!*"

They looked at him. He held the slap-stick in both hands, looking at it mournfully. Joey saw that it was cracked near one end, a piece hanging at a jagged angle. Benny looked up at him, shook his head.

"You believe it? I broke my fuckin' stick."

Chapter 55

Moser and Fielding rode the elevator to Cruz's floor, glanced up at the security camera as they got off.

"Smile," Fielding said, and rang the bell.

Eduardo opened the door, stared at them for a moment, then turned his back, walked away down the hall, leaving the door standing open.

Moser shrugged. "I guess we've been invited in."

"That's how I read it."

Moser swung the door closed behind them. Eduardo appeared at the far end of the hall, hooked one finger at them. They followed him into the dining room, where Cruz sat at one end of a long mahogany table, eating broiled fish on rice. He looked up at them, smiled.

"Come in, gentlemen. Do you have good news for me?"

"We're homicide detectives," Fielding said. "The news only gets so good."

"Have you found the man who killed

my daughter?"

Moser opened a file folder in his hand, took out a photograph. It showed Miiko Reyes, slumped in a car, blood streaked down the side of his face.

"You know this man?"

Cruz took the picture, glanced at it. Then he looked up at Eduardo, passed it to him. Eduardo looked at it, impassive, handed it back to Moser.

Cruz sat back, smiled at Moser. "You ask me this question before, I think."

"Has the answer changed?"

Cruz shook his head, slowly. Moser took another photograph from the file, Javier Estora, strangled in his car, passed it to Cruz.

"How 'bout this guy?"

Cruz glanced at it, frowned. "No."

He passed it back to Moser. Moser took out a pair of photographs — Angel Cardoza and Valeria de Guzman, their throats slashed. He handed them to Cruz.

"These people?"

Cruz, with growing impatience, glanced at them, shook his head. He tossed the photographs on the table. "Do you have many of these, Detective?"

"Just one more." Moser took the photograph of Eva Cruz from the folder, laid it on the table in front of him. "Can you tell me who this is?"

Cruz glanced down at the photograph, then up at Moser's face. "Is this a joke?"

"Not to me." Moser took a photocopy of the pathologist's report from the Guatemalan National Police, laid it before him. "See, I've got a problem. It turns out your daughter's been dead for almost nine years."

Cruz stared down at the page. Moser watched his eyes move over the words, pausing when he came to the words *Barrita Vieja*. At last, he looked up at Moser, shook his head, sadly.

"There has been a mistake."

"Has there?" Moser smiled. "See, that's what I thought. Then I talked to the pathologist down there who identified the body. He's got a full set of Eva Cruz's dental records."

Cruz laid his fork against the edge of his plate, silent.

"Anyway," Moser said, picking up the papers, returning them to the file, "he's sending me a copy of her charts by express mail. We should have this cleared up by tomorrow."

Cruz leaned back in his chair, folded

his hands in front of him. "Detective, do you know much about my country?"

"I'm starting to get a picture."

"Then you know we have been through a difficult time in recent years." He spread his hands, sadly. "It was a time of violence. In my work, I made many enemies. When it became time to leave, it seemed wise to allow my enemies to think that I was dead. A friend had contacts in the National Police. I paid them to change the records, to make it appear that we had been killed." He looked at Moser. "Do you have children?"

Moser shook his head.

"Then you cannot know what a father feels when his child is threatened. I did what was necessary to protect my Eva, to get her out of the country safely."

Moser glanced down at his file, frowned. "You had the records changed?"

Cruz nodded. "The dental record that they are sending you, it belongs to a young girl who was killed in the war."

"But they didn't find her body until last month."

Cruz glanced over at Eduardo, smiled.

"Detective, in those times, it was not necessary to have a body. Those who died simply disappeared. For a man to die, his name only had to appear on certain lists."

"So why change the records?"

Cruz shrugged. "I am a careful man."

Moser opened the file, drew out the page of photographs faxed from Guatemala City. He laid the page in front of Cruz, put his finger on the bottom photograph — a military unit, posing in front of a truck. "You recognize the man on the left, here?"

Cruz glanced at the photograph. "Yes, of course. That's me."

Moser moved his finger to the center of the group, let it rest on the tallest man in the group, his face carved from stone. "And this man?"

"Eduardo."

Moser glanced over at Eduardo, nodded. "This creates a small problem for me. According to my information, Adalberto Cruz never served in the Guatemalan Treasury Police. He was a lawyer, who worked on land reform. From what I hear, some of the wealthy landowners down there accused him of being a communist."

Cruz smiled. "As I told you, I have enemies."

Moser took a moment to look at him, then flipped to the next page of his notes. "As it happens, they have no record of any Eduardo Sosa, either. But they do have a file on a man named Eduardo Garon, who belonged to a unit of the Treasury Police commanded by a Colonel Jorge Samayo." He glanced up at Cruz. "Both men are suspected of involvement in a group called *Ojo por Ojo* — 'an eye for an eye' — which carried out political murders during the early eighties. A death squad."

"I have heard the name," Cruz said, with a shrug. "A sad time for my country."

Moser glanced over at Fielding, who was leaning against the door a few feet behind Eduardo. *A sad time.*

Moser took two pages from the file, stapled together. "It seems this Jorge Samayo made a lot of people angry back in Guatemala. They got quite a record on him down there. Even his old buddies in the National Police hate him, which makes my job easier, because they faxed me his personnel record."

He laid the pages on the table,

541

watched Cruz glance at them, then look away.

"That's a disciplinary record, Mr. Cruz. Turns out Samayo, he had himself a neat little business on the side. Some guy in an office makes a list, people he wants killed. Samayo's squad does the wet work, makes 'em disappear. Then Samayo goes to the next people on the list, says, 'See, here's your name. By next week, you'll be dead.' They're terrified. But Samayo, he offers them a chance. He shows them the identity papers he's taken from the people he's killed. They're off the list now, because they're dead. For enough money, he'll sell them the papers, they can use them to get out of the country. Later, he got ambitious, started selling the papers to street punks, ex-cons, anybody who wanted to get into the States as a political refugee. Only his bosses caught wind of it, and they didn't like it. People who were supposed to be dead are suddenly walking around, taking off for the U.S., applying for political asylum. Very messy. The cops trace it back to Samayo, and his name goes on the next list. So now it's time to disappear. He keeps a set of papers for himself, a set for his daughter." Moser glanced over at Eduardo. "Maybe an extra set for the guy who helped him run the whole deal."

Cruz leaned back in his chair, sighed. "Detective, may I tell you a story?"

Moser spread his hands.

"In my country," Cruz said, "the Maya have a story about a great flood, like your story of Noah. The world had become evil, so the waters rose, flooding even the *Altiplano,* the highlands. Only one house remained, at the top of the highest mountain. All the animals came there, to hide from the storm. After a time, the waters began to drain away. When the water had receded from around the house, the animals sent Usmiq, the buzzard, to scout the land. He left the house, circling through the air. After a while, he flew to one of the hilltops that the water had revealed. He found many dead animals there, the bodies rotting in the sun. Seeing them, he felt a great hunger. He forgot his mission, began to tear at the meat with his beak, feeding on the dead." Cruz paused, smiled. "When he had satisfied his hunger, Usmiq returned to the house to tell the animals what he had seen. But they would not let him in. The smell of death that he carried with him was unbearable. To punish him for his disobedience, the animals condemned Usmiq to eat only the dead, and to clean the world of the stench of rotting flesh."

Cruz reached out, laid a hand on the page before him. "This man, I think he was sent to do a job by wealthy men who feared a rising flood. And when he became hungry, they condemned him." Then he sat back, smiled at Moser. "Is it really so different for you, Detective?"

Moser stared at him for a moment, then leaned across the table, said softly, "I talked to some of the human rights groups down there," Moser said, laying the file on the table. "They kept talking about this little town out on the coast, Barrita Vieja. It seems they dug up some bodies out there, all shot to pieces. Not much left of the bodies, so they had to use dental records. But they got some of them identified." He took the list of names out of the file, laid it before Cruz. "They faxed me this list. Now we get to the strange part. Turns out, a bunch of these people are in our computer. We got recent homicide cases on maybe half this list. I could run this list past some of the other departments in the area, maybe pick up a few more." He smiled. "These people, they've got a bad habit of dying in nasty ways."

Cruz steepled his fingers, rested his chin on the tips.

"Still, you know what I couldn't figure out?"

"What's that, Detective."

Moser pointed to a box on the form, where a clerk had typed the word *soltero.* "Jorge Samayo was single. No daughter."

Cruz stared at him. Then he glanced away, his eyes going to the window. It had begun to rain, the window bright with the streetlights.

"It's a beautiful city," he said. "And terrible."

Moser waited a moment, expecting him to go on, then said, "Who was she?"

Cruz shrugged. "An orphan. A victim of wartime, who needed a home."

Moser reached down, flipped the page over. "You remember a man named Luis Andrade?"

He glanced up at Cruz, waited a moment. But Cruz said nothing, his eyes on the window. Moser straightened, said —

"In 1985, Jorge Samayo was accused of attempted rape of a nine-year-old girl. Her name was Elisa Andrade, the daughter of a conservative family with ties to the military. The charges were dropped for lack of evidence." Moser took out the sheet of photographs, laid it on the table. "According to a report by the government's human rights commission, six weeks later, a group of leftist rebels in ski masks came to the home of Luis Andrade, her father. They loaded the family into a half-ton truck, drove away." Moser smiled. "This time it was a wealthy family, so the government paid attention. The bodies of Luis Andrade and his wife, Marta, were found by a road in Escuintla Province a few days later. But their daughter's body was never found." He paused, looked at Cruz. "I'm having her dental records sent, also."

Cruz sighed, glanced at Eduardo. Moser saw Eduardo reach over, stub out his cigarette, stand up. Behind him, Fielding stepped away from the doorjamb, reached under his coat, drew his service revolver. He raised it, brought it to rest against the base of Eduardo's skull.

"Don't do it," he said, quietly.

Chapter 56

Fielding slid the gun down his neck to rest on the knob at the top of his spine. He reached around, slid a large semi-automatic out of the holster under his arm. He glanced at it, smiled. "Beretta Nine. Nasty gun." He stuck it in the waistband of his pants.

Moser looked at Eduardo's face. It was empty, like looking at a gravestone. He stood there, silent. Moser turned back to Cruz.

"You got anything to say?"

Cruz shrugged. "Why should I? It's a remarkable story, but you have no proof."

"We'll get prints from the National Police in Guatamala City in a couple days. Meantime, we can put Eduardo in front of a witness, see if she makes him as the guy who came to see a man named Angel Cardoza the day he died. We'll piece it together, enough to get an arrest warrant." Moser smiled. "Then it won't matter. The guys whose money you've been washing, they'll figure it's time to splatter you across a sidewalk, so you can't cut a deal."

Cruz's face went very still.

"That's what it's about, isn't it?" Moser gathered up the papers on the table, put them back into the file. "You can't move the money until you clean up that mess down in Barrita Vieja. Only now you got people that were supposed to be dead walking around up here in New York. A few weeks ago, a man named Jano Benitez filed immigration papers. The INS sent a routine inquiry down to Guatemala." Moser smiled. "I'm guessing that's what stirred up the pot, right?"

Cruz didn't respond, his eyes on the window again.

"And it won't end. Maybe one of these people sends money home to his family, the check goes through the bank. 'Wait a minute,' they say. 'This guy's *dead.*' Now you got a big problem, 'cause if the human rights commission down there gets an idea these people are alive, they're not gonna release the money when they finish digging up the bodies. It's just gonna sit there, while they conduct their investigations, try to figure out what's going on. So you figured the simplest thing was to take these people out of the picture, make sure they couldn't be traced. But now you've got another problem. How do you kill that many people, without anybody noticing?" Moser drew the picture of Miiko Reyes out of the file, laid it on the table. "What you needed was someone to pin it on. So you found yourself a kid with a conviction for dealing coke, made a point of scattering drugs around whenever Eduardo finished with someone. You figured you'd leave enough evidence so we'd write it off as drug killings, then kill Reyes, dump his body where we could find it. End of story. We close the file, and you wait for the money to be released down in Guatemala."

Cruz said nothing, his eyes calm.

"Only Reyes was a plant. He had some buddies on the cops." Moser watched Cruz glance over at Eduardo, smiled. "You ever heard of a cop named Marty Stoll?"

Cruz sighed. "Detective, do you intend to arrest me?"

"You mean do I have the evidence to convince a prosecutor to take it to trial?" Moser shook his head. "I'll tell you the truth, I don't. But maybe I don't need it. I could get on the phone with the human rights commission down in Guatemala City, urge them to delay releasing the money you've got down there. That ought to make things interesting. We could see how long it takes until your friends down at the Azores decide to clean up your mess." He smiled, gestured around him. "This place, it'll look like a slaughterhouse when they get done. Bloodstains on your pretty white couch."

Cruz smiled. "Are you trying to frighten me, Detective?"

"Could I? You look like a hard man to scare." Moser spread his hands. "Let's just say I'm curious. Maybe they'll turn it over to their friends on the cops. That's what happened to Eva, isn't it?" He put his hands on the table, leaned in close. "You want to know what I think? You know who killed her. You're just waiting to see if we figure it out."

Cruz tapped one finger on the edge of the table, lightly.

"It was Marty Stoll, wasn't it?" Moser watched Cruz's face. It showed no response, emotionless. "But you knew that, didn't you? Maybe not at first, but you figured it out. You got your own connections downtown, you proved that to us the first day. So you put him and Miiko together, figured, 'Hey, this is perfect.' When you killed Miiko, you'd set it up so it looked like Stoll was behind the whole thing." Moser smiled. "Only he beat you to it. Nothing has worked out much like you planned, huh?"

Cruz stared at him, coldly. "I would like you to leave, now."

Moser glanced over at Fielding, raised his eyebrows. "Just like that."

Fielding shrugged. He nodded at Eduardo. "Have to take this boy with us."

"He has a permit for the gun," Cruz said. "To protect me."

Fielding shook his head. "Still got to take him. He's a suspect in a homicide. Got an appointment with a witness."

Cruz raised an eyebrow, looked at Eduardo. *"Está negligente."*

Eduardo swallowed, nodded. Moser, watching it, thought, *Jesus, he's afraid!* He glanced back at Cruz, saw him push his plate aside, wipe his hands on his napkin. He looked up at Moser, smiled.

"I have no knowledge of any actions that Eduardo may have taken on his own time." He dabbed at his mouth with the napkin. "If he has committed any criminal acts, he must answer for them."

Moser stared at him in disbelief. "You're gonna sit there and *tell* me he's taking the fall?"

Cruz shrugged. "We each have our role in life. Eduardo knows his."

He glanced over at Eduardo, gave a quick nod. Moser, turning, saw Eduardo reach up, grab the barrel of Fielding's gun, twist it away from his head. He dropped his shoulder, drove an elbow into Fielding's jaw, wrenched the gun out of his grip, tossed it across the room. As Fielding staggered back against the wall, he reached down, yanked the Beretta out of his belt.

Moser, his hand on the .38 holstered on his hip, froze as Eduardo swung the gun around, put it on him.

"Put the gun down," Moser said, his voice quiet. "You don't want to do this."

Eduardo smiled. His eyes were like brittle glass. He looked over at Cruz, held his gaze, unwavering, as he raised the gun to his mouth, stuck the barrel between his teeth, and blew the back of his head off.

Chapter 57

"Jesus!" Moser stared down at Eduardo's body, sprawled in the doorway.

Cruz stood up, dropped his napkin on the table. "It seems, Detective, that your investigation has reached a dead end."

And he walked out of the room. Moser felt his jaw tighten. Ray, leaning against the wall, two fingers touching the base of his throat, caught his look. He straightened, swallowed to clear his throat, said —

"Let it go, Dave."

Moser looked down at Eduardo's body, then up at the door Cruz had walked through. "He killed those people, Ray. Clearing the field. No more bodies to bury."

Ray raised a hand to slow him down. "Dave, he's right. We don't have enough to prosecute."

Moser's hands twitched at his side. He walked across the room, picked up Fielding's .38, brought it back. He handed it to Ray, watched as he slid it back into its holster.

"Couple days, he'll be gone."

Fielding nodded. "Not our problem, then."

"You thought about what it was like for the girl?"

Fielding looked down at Eduardo, sighed. "We got a body here, Dave. Let's call it in."

"She was *nine* years old, Ray. The man had her family killed, made her his daughter. Only at night, he'd come into her bedroom."

"You don't know that."

"He was back home, in Guatemala, you know what they'd do? Take him out in a field some place, put a bullet in his head."

"That's him, Dave. That ain't us."

"So he walks?"

Fielding shrugged. "Got to play it as it lays."

Moser stared down at Eduardo's body for a moment, then shook his head. "Can't do it, Ray."

And he turned, brushed past him into the kitchen. Fielding grabbed his arm, shoved him against the wall.

"Don't do nothing stupid, Dave."

Moser stared at him. His eyes were like two black stones. Fielding released his arms, said —

"Listen to me. We walk out of here, it's over."

Moser shook his head. He pushed off the wall, but Fielding put a hand on his chest, shoved him back.

"Give me your gun, Dave."

"What?" Moser laughed. "You want it, take it."

Fielding slipped his hand inside Moser's jacket, unsnapped the holster strap, pulled the gun out. He opened the cylinder, shook the bullets into his palm, dropped them into his pocket. Then he tucked the gun in his belt, stepped back.

Moser shook his head. "You satisfied?"

"I'm sorry, Dave. I can't let you do it."

Moser gave a short laugh. He brushed past Fielding, walked over to the counter, where a phone hung on the wall. He picked up the receiver, dialed. Then he leaned on the wall, the phone pressed to his ear, said —

"Janine? It's Dave." He listened for a moment, ran a hand across his eyes. "Listen to me for a second, okay? I'm not calling for you. Put Jimmy on." He looked over at Fielding, winked. "Hey, Jimmy. Dave Moser. How's business?"

Twenty minutes later, Moser led a handcuffed Adalberto Cruz out through the building's garage to the street, where Fielding waited in the car. He opened the rear door, put his hand on the top of Cruz's head, shoved him in. Then he got into the front seat, turned to see Cruz smiling at him.

"You've seen too many movies, Detective. My attorney will have me out of custody in an hour."

Moser turned to face forward in his seat, reached for his seat belt. "Let's go," he told Fielding.

Moser watched the traffic as Ray drove slowly up Park, cut over to the East River Drive at 96th. He followed it up to the Harlem River Drive, got off on Dyckman, took it west to the north-bound on-ramp of the Henry Hudson Parkway.

From the backseat, Cruz said —

"Where are we going?"

Moser glanced over at Fielding. They remained silent, heading north to the bridge. As they approached the toll,

Moser dug a dollar out of his pocket, passed it to Fielding. He rolled the window down, handed it to the woman in the booth. He stayed in the right lane, taking it easy across the bridge. Moser looked down at the moonlight shimmering on the water.

Fielding got off at the first exit in Riverdale, wound his way back through the curving streets above the river until he could see the bridge rising above them. He found the street that led down toward the water, turned into the empty lot behind the Metroliner station.

"I see," Cruz said. "You are trying to frighten me."

Moser got out, opened the rear door. "Get out."

Cruz sighed, slid his legs out of the car, eased out. Moser took his arm, swung the door shut. Fielding leaned across the front seat, looked at him.

"You sure about this, Dave?"

"Just keep it running."

Moser led Cruz over to the stairs, kept a hand on his back as he climbed them, then shoved him along the walkway that crossed the tracks to the platform, near the water's edge. Cruz smiled to himself, looked up at the headlights moving across the bridge, the cars' tires whining on the steel mesh.

"Beautiful night," he said.

Moser shoved him along the empty platform, over to the edge of the tracks. "Jump down."

Cruz looked at him. "You've made your point, Detective. Do we have to go all the way out there? The rocks are slippery."

Moser put a hand on his back, gave him a shove. Cruz dropped to the tracks, stumbled, fell to his knees. Moser jumped down beside him, grabbed his elbow and yanked him to his feet. They stepped over the outer rails, climbed out onto the rocks along the water.

Their feet skidded on a thick layer of slime, and twice Cruz almost fell. But Moser kept one hand tight on his forearm, moving him west, toward the railroad bridge where the Harlem River joined the Hudson. There was a path along the railroad bed, emerging where the two rivers met. A maintenance building was tucked back in the bushes, beside a gravel drive.

Moser pointed to a sloping bed of rocks near the bridge. "That's where we figure she went in the water. We had a squad of cops up here the day she floated, looking for evidence. They didn't find any bloodstains, so we figure she was killed somewhere else." He looked back along the rocks. "Tough work, carrying her out here over those rocks. But Eduardo looked like a strong guy."

Cruz smiled. "Was there something you expected me to say?"

"Nope." Moser glanced back at the parking lot beyond the station. A car came down the narrow road, headlights flaring between the trees, turned in. Moser took Cruz's arm, led him over to the railroad bridge. "Turn around."

"What?"

"I'm gonna take off your cuffs."

Cruz's eyes narrowed. "You're letting me go?"

"Yeah." Moser shrugged. "You were right. We got no evidence. It was a stupid idea, trying to spook a guy like you."

He turned Cruz away from him, unlocked the handcuffs, slipped them into his jacket pocket. "Take it easy."

Cruz stood there, watched him walk

away. His face was curious in the pale moonlight.

Walking back over the rocks, Moser saw four men jump down from the station platform, come toward him. He recognized one of the men from news photographs. Tony Giardella. Two of the men carried baseball bats, a third swung a tire iron at the weeds along the shore, like he was searching for a golf ball. Silently, Moser moved to one side, let them pass.

None of them said a word.

Chapter 58

A few days later, surveillance transcripts from the office above the Azores Coffee Shop arrived on Merrill Conte's desk with the following conversation marked in red:

GIARDELLA
So how ya doin'?
TANGLIERO
Got some pain in my nose, but I'm okay.
GIARDELLA
Hey, better than Fat Frankie, huh?
TANGLIERO
You do that, Tony?
GIARDELLA
Me? Nah. I heard it was natural causes. You know how he was terrified of bugs, right? Thinks all his phones are tapped, his car? Anyway, Tuesday, he goes out to Lucchina's on the Beach for lunch, he looks down at his meatball hero, sees half a cockroach sticking out, chokes to death right there in the res-

taurant trying to cough up the other half. Guy at the next table tried to give him the Heimlich maneuver, couldn't get his arms around him. Some luck, huh?

TANGLIERO

It's how he would'a wanted it, Tony.

GIARDELLA

You think? I always pictured him on the toilet. Havin' himself a good one. Boom, heart attack. He's dead.

TANGLIERO

(laughter) Yeah, that's Frankie all right.

GIARDELLA

So, listen, Joey. We clear, here?

TANGLIERO

Yeah, no problem.

GIARDELLA

Thanks for helpin' me out on this thing.

TANGLIERO

Hey, don't mention it. What's a friend for, huh?

GIARDELLA

No, really. Frankie, he was ready to fry my ass on this deal. I mean, what was I gonna tell him, the money's tied up down there in some bank in Guatemala? Here, just gimme the shovel, I'll

dig the grave first. But you start talkin'
to the U.S. Attorney, what can I do? He
tells me, leave the money where it is,
until we solve this other thing.
TANGLIERO
So he bought it?
GIARDELLA
Bought it? I'm tellin' ya, he paid *cash*.
TANGLIERO
That's great, Tony. Really, I'm glad.
GIARDELLA
Yeah. Sorry 'bout that thing with the
hit. It was under control the whole time,
I want you to know that. I gave the
whole setup to that deputy, the woman?
Even let her come in wearing a wire.
Mike, he had to pretend he didn't feel
it. We were takin' care of you. You know
that, right?
TANGLIERO
Sure.
GIARDELLA
So, you ready to get back to work?
TANGLIERO
What'ya mean work? When did I ever
work, huh?
GIARDELLA
(laughter) That's right, I forgot. But
this club? That's noon to midnight. And
I'm expecting a solid cash flow, okay?

Register receipts, vendor invoices, the whole deal.

TANGLIERO

Cruz came through, huh?

GIARDELLA

Yeah, you might say. We had a talk. He signed a paper. Anyway, we got a need for a ledger now, write some of this cash down. (pause) Listen, Joey . . . You didn't tell 'em anything, huh? I mean, talkin' to 'em all that time?

TANGLIERO

Hey, Tony, you ever hear the one about the alligator, comes into a bar carryin' a handbag? Bartender looks at him, says . . .

Conte sighed, tossed the transcript aside.

That afternoon, Dave Moser rode over to Rikers Island, checked his gun with the guard at the gate, parked his car in front of the prison hospital. He rode the elevator to the third floor, showed his badge at a guard's station, then walked down the hall to where an Internal Affairs detective in a blue sport coat sat on a plastic chair, reading a copy of *Racing News*. He showed his badge, said —

"He's expecting me."

The detective laid his paper aside, stood up, and ran his hands under Moser's arms, down to his waist, then along the inside of his legs to the ankle. He opened the door a few inches, spoke to someone inside. Then he stepped back, nodded.

Marty Stoll was sitting up in bed, eating rice pudding from a tray. A strip of gauze was taped over the bridge of his nose, across both cheeks. His right hand was in a cast from forearm to fingertips. In the corner, a television flickered without sound: a news show, playing the tape that would be repeated many times in the next few days — the Police Commissioner walking into a Harlem police precinct, seizing the badges from two patrolmen, who were then arrested on corruption charges. Moser looked away. The windows beyond Stoll's bed were covered with wire mesh, which let in a few pale streaks of light. Tom Richter sat on a plastic chair beside the bed, scratching at his ankle.

"Hey, Dave." Stoll pointed his spoon at a plastic chair at the foot of the bed.

"Pull up a chair."

"You look like shit, Marty."

"Hey, you're looking at my good side."

Moser glanced over at Richter, saw him raise a hand, nod. "You switching sides, Marty?"

Stoll hooked a thumb at the windows. "Like my view? First thing I saw when I woke up." He grinned at Richter. "This guy, he comes in, says, 'How'd you like to look at that for the next fifteen years?' "

"So you traded in your buddies."

Stoll shrugged. "You got to play it as it lays, Dave."

Moser looked up at the mesh on the windows, smiled.

"What's so funny?"

"Somebody else just said that to me, a couple days ago."

"Smart guy. You listen?"

"Yeah."

Stoll spooned some pudding in his mouth, hit the channel button on the TV, changed it to Jenny Jones, interviewing a woman in a tiny black dress, a guy beside her grinning at the camera. "Look't this shit. 'Sex Stars Meet Their Former Loves.' This guy just found out his high school sweetheart makes porno movies. But she's still the same sweet girl, inside."

Richter looked at Moser. "I heard you guys found Cruz in the river."

"Yeah. They pulled him out in Sherman's Creek, down by Harlem River Drive."

"Who's got the case?"

"Ray Fielding."

Richter smiled. "Of course."

"We figure the cases are linked."

"Any chance you'll close 'em?"

Moser rubbed at his jaw. "Hard to say. Pretty weak evidence chain."

Richter spread his hands. "Any way we can help, let me know."

Moser looked at him for a moment, nodded. He glanced over at Stoll. "Rita asked me to stop by, see if you need anything."

"Do I *need* anything? Like, what? She's gonna send my bedroom slippers?" Stoll gave a harsh laugh, then winced, touched a finger to his face. "Oh man, that fuckin' hurts. I'll tell ya, Dave, I ever meet that old guy, you know what I'm gonna do?"

"I can guess."

"Nah, I'm gonna shake his hand. That was some swing he put on me. He should sign with the Mets."

Richter smiled. "Let's hope you don't run into him anytime soon."

Stoll looked at Moser, grinned. "They're putting me in the witness protection program, soon as I testify. Can you picture it? Send me out to Omaha, put me to work in a hardware store."

Moser shrugged. "It's a life."

"That's what they say. I got my doubts. Meantime, I'm gonna be a TV star. Officer Friendly, the face of police corruption."

"At least you got the face for it."

Stoll glanced at Richter. "You hear him? And this guy's my friend." He shook his head. "It's all over, Dave. I'll spend the next few weeks living with the federal marshals, until I finish testifying, then it's the heartland express. Chicken-fried steak and bowling on Saturday night." He looked at Richter. "Try to get that cute little deputy, okay? The one who busted me. I liked her. Got that southern accent, like Holly Hunter."

"They suspended her. Acting without authorization. I heard she got reassigned."

"Yeah? Where?"

"Boise. Someplace like that."

"Terrific." Stoll shook his head, sadly. "I'll look her up."

Moser reached for the door. "I'll tell Rita you're all right."

"Yeah, thanks. I'll call her, soon as I can." Stoll watched him pull the door open. "Hey, Dave."

Moser turned. "Yeah?"

"Stay blue, man."

Moser let the door swing closed behind him.

LARGE PRINT
Abel, Kenneth.
  The blue wall

	DATE DUE		

JAMES PRENDERGAST
LIBRARY ASSOCIATION

JAMESTOWN, NEW YORK

Member Of

Chautauqua-Cattaraugus Library System